The Angels

The Angels

Alex Kane

hera

First published in the United Kingdom in 2020 by Hera Books

This edition published in the United Kingdom in 2021 by

Hera Books
28b Cricketfield Road
London, E5 8NS
United Kingdom

A CIP catalogue record for this book is available from the British Library.

Print ISBN 978 1 80032 281 3
Ebook ISBN 978 1 912973 35 4

Look for more great books at www.herabooks.com

Printed and bound in Great Britain by Clays Ltd, Elcograf S.p.A.

For my mum

Prologue

There's no one else around, especially at this time of night. She's been sure to check. She doesn't want anyone to see her or what she is doing.

Staring down at what she's carrying in her hands, she lets go and sets it down on the ground under a shelter so it won't get wet. Someone will be along to collect it quickly, she knows that.

The darkness swallows her as the rain cascades down and drips off the end of her nose. Her task is done. She can move on now from this life and start afresh. But can she? Will what she's done always follow her, no matter where she goes?

Backing away, she wonders if she should buy a plane ticket to get as far the fuck away as possible. She's only known one life. Her family's wealth was driven by glamourous girls, dangerous gangsters, drugs and seedy men. The beautiful architectural buildings that surround the streets of Glasgow where she lived and worked bear no resemblance to the truth of her life. The job she did and the businesses she was involved with were all she knew, she was born into that world. She knew society didn't approve, but in some respects she was proud of who she was. But not now, not after this.

Turning, she sets off down the darkened street towards the edge of the town and forces herself to keep facing forward. She can't turn back. Instead, she imagines her future and what it will be like now.

The feeling of disgust with herself and the crime she's committing fills her with dread. If anyone ever finds out about it, she'll never be looked at the same way and neither will her family. Shame would be brought upon them and everything they've built would unravel. This is her only choice, the only way to right a wrong, she's sure of it. Pushing the thoughts to the back of her head, she tries to focus on the future and the good that will come if she can keep the act a secret. If no one knows, then there will be no comeback.

Rushing deeper into the shelter of the dark night, she doesn't look back.

But she hasn't gone unnoticed. Someone has had their eyes on her the whole time. Her secret is not safe the way she thinks it is. Her past will not be locked away.

One day, it will come back for her. She will have to face the past and take her punishment.

Just what kind of punishment is fitting for the crime she has committed?

1

MARCUS

Marcus stands by the grand window of his Glasgow apartment, looking over the city with a glass of whisky in one hand, a cigarette in the other. Autumn was beginning to set in and the reddish-orange sky highlighted the tops of the corporate buildings he looked out at. His six-foot-six-inch stature takes up most of the window space as he looks out, his hand swallowing the glass as his fingers wrap around it.

He's made it. After all the years of working behind the scenes, doing the dirty jobs and getting in among the streets and learning about the clientele, he's finally climbed to the top.

Sharing the spot for a while isn't a problem. He's always known that was going to be the case. Who better to share that top spot with other than his dad while he learns what it's like to run things? His auld man was a force to be reckoned with. One of Glasgow's most feared gang land criminals, Marcus knows he's learned from the best. He has to admit, being delegated the dirty jobs over the years was actually something he'd enjoyed. His auld man had always said from when Marcus was a young lad that he would have to earn his way into the business. Just because he was the first born son didn't mean that he would immediately be entitled. The dirty jobs had been his in. He'll miss that part of it, getting right in the midst of things. The power he felt during his climb was like no other. He deserves his promotion.

The people on the streets of Glasgow respect the family, respect their power. Of course there have been the odd chancers over the years who attempted to worm their way out of having to pay their debt to the family but Marcus has always taken great pleasure in righting that wrong. It's what he does best. Break a leg here, snap a wrist there and soon they'd pay up and with interest too. Being the son of a top gangster is a magnificent feeling; when people realised who he was, he loved watching how their expressions changed. He's heard through the grapevine that people are commenting that Marcus is harder than his auld man and that how, when the time comes for him to take over, everything would change. Things would become darker. They aren't wrong. They'll all do well to remember that.

The hardest job of all was the one that put him at the top. Marcus had been put in charge of a very specific operation and it wasn't just for financial gain. It was personal to all of them.

'Kill two birds with one stone son, and you've got your pick of the worms.' That phrase has stuck with him from day one.

Now, he's succeeded. The plans are in motion and the reins of the business are just within reach. A brand new venture, with the heart of the business run from the most luxurious premises. It's going to make him a fortune. And he's the top man now that his auld man is retiring; all the business ventures over the years, the hard work to get them to where they were now was all his. This was the thing he'd been waiting on as far back as he could remember. Although Marcus knew that his dad would never fully sit back and enjoy his later years. He would always want a hand in some of what was going on and Marcus was fine with that because he would be the boss from now on. It was all his.

'You gonna pour one for me?' Tommy, Marcus's brother asks. Marcus turns and smiles.

'Already waiting for ye, mate,' Marcus replies, motioning towards the drinks cabinet.

Marcus couldn't be happier to have his younger brother as his second in command. He won't trust anyone else. Their bond has grown in strength over the years and now that Marcus is at the top of his game, he couldn't ask for a better team by his side.

'So, where is she?' Tommy asks. 'Yer new bit of meat?'

Marcus laughs and swallows the last of the whisky. He walks across the white tiled floor to the cabinet that houses his favourite whisky, places the glass down on it and runs his fingers across his trim black beard. 'She's out shopping. Buying herself something nice.'

'Where'd ye find this one?' Tommy asks, drinking greedily from his glass.

Looking out at the city of Glasgow at dusk, Marcus is stunned by just how stunning it all is. From up here, no one would know what goes on underneath. Marcus knows differently and he's proud that his family are responsible for most of it.

'Does it really matter? The point is, I have her and it was so fucking easy.'

'Nah,' Tommy says with a grin, staring out at the city alongside Marcus. 'I don't suppose it does.'

Marcus pours himself another whisky and turns to the window on the opposite side of the apartment. From this side of the room, his home has a view of the Southside of Glasgow. Most of the old council buildings, flats and old factory units were derelict now, or inhabited by rats and junkies. Marcus often wondered what the difference was in that. The place looked rough, almost like there was a permanent black cloud hanging over that specific part of the city. Not so easy on the eye, but still from up in the penthouse suites of the Harbour apartments, not too bad. Strolling back to the other side, Marcus stands next to the balcony door and pulls it open. The air is still warm even though the nights are becoming shorter and easing into autumn. It was one of his favourite times of year, knowing that the streets would soon be covered by a blanket of darkness. Perfect for some of his business dealings.

The low hum of traffic from below, along with the gentle breeze, eases the anger that always sits heavy on Marcus's chest. It burns like a constant fire within him. No amount of whisky can erase what he knows. What had happened in the past did still affect him and often left him reeling because how could someone do what they did to him? Growing up with a gangland criminal as a dad was good for Marcus. It showed him the man he needed to be to overcome his demons. If it wasn't for his auld man, Marcus often wondered where he would have ended up.

The sound of a mobile phone ringing brings Marcus back from his thoughts and he glances over as Tommy pulls his phone out to answer it.

Smaller in size than his brother, Tommy stands at six feet exactly. His well-styled hair and sharp sense of dress mean he draws female attention to himself and that's exactly the kind of skill Marcus would need for a successful takeover.

'Aye?' There's a long pause as Tommy answers the call. Marcus can hear the distant voice on the other line. 'Right. I'll let him know. Cheers.'

'What?' Marcus asks, turning back to face the city. The sky resembles a painting, pink and purple with a bright burning orange which highlights the tops of the buildings. This is his place of peace, even though the burn in his chest remains.

'It's done.' Tommy replies. 'The problem's been dealt with.'

Without showing it, Marcus breathes a sigh of relief. There's no room for error. He won't make the same mistake twice.

'Good.'

Tommy is by his side now, holding his glass up. 'Cheers, mate. Here's to new beginnings.'

Marcus takes a drink and smiles. All those years of dirty jobs, the violence and the slog on the streets had led him to this point. Times had been tough back then. But now that he was standing in his penthouse suite with his brother on one side and an entire family empire on the other, he realised that the slog back then had all been worth it.

2

LUDERSTON BAY, SCOTLAND

(Three weeks later)

He threw the stick further this time, but the wind caught it and it landed in the water. Of course, the dog ran straight for it, barking and splashing around as she always did.

The man watched as the dog began circling something. He was too far back to see what it was, a clump of seaweed perhaps. The barking began, short and in quick succession. He shook his head.

'I cannae throw seaweed fur ye, ya stupid dug,' he muttered under his breath as he approached the dog.

'Morning Ray, it's fair cold this morning, eh?' His neighbour, Wilma called from the pavement on the roadside. Ray looked up and smiled, gave a wave but continued on. He'd barely heard her over the howling wind. Pulling his zip up to his chin, he shoved his hands inside the pockets of his coat and kept moving towards Lilly.

Running towards him and barking excitedly, she met his eye before she spun around and ran off again. No stick.

'What is it, girl?' Lilly continued running back and forth. She was trying to show him something. Ray watched as Lilly barked furiously.

As he got closer, Ray saw that his dog was going crazy at a faded purple leopard-print suitcase. It was drenched, with pieces of seaweed tangled in the handle and draped over the top.

Ray was a curious man. A nosey neighbour as most he knew would describe him. And his nose got the better of him. He knew better than to open it but his curiosity wouldn't allow the case to remain closed. Bending down, Ray gripped the zipper between his thumb and index finger and began tugging at it. Opening the case around halfway, he pulled slowly at the top and peered in. Then the smell hit him.

'Jesus!' he said as he fell back onto the sand, the water soaking through the material of his trousers.

Lilly barked, louder and faster as Ray got to his feet and turned away. Taking a deep breath, he counted to three and pulled his phone out his pocket. With shaking hands, he attempted to dial. So much was happening at once. The howling wind, his barking dog. The water lapping up around his feet, the dog circling the case. Circling the body *within* the case.

A body. Bloody hell, this kind of thing just doesn't happen in these parts.

'Hello, I need help,' he managed into the speaker. 'I don't know who I need. The police.'

Swallowing hard, he listened as the operator on the other side of the line asked him what his emergency was.

'I've found a body in a washed-up suitcase on Luderston Bay. *Jesus Christ.*' His voice trembled as he described the scene. 'Female. I think,' he replied to the operator as he glanced back at the case for a split-second. One second too long in his mind. 'I think female, I can see long hair, but it's hard to tell. The body is, well stuffed inside a suitcase.' Saying those words out loud made him feel sick. He wanted to turn back the clock and un-see the dead girl.

It looked like she had been dead for a while, he thought to himself. The skin he could see was greenish black in colour and bloated. Very bloated. It had to be at least three weeks gone. He remembered learning about the decomposition process from an online article. He'd stumbled across it accidentally and found it

9

interesting. Ray never for one moment thought he would have to recall this in a real-life scenario.

Ray didn't hear what the operator said after that. He was too busy trying to contain his stomach. He couldn't help but turn and inspect the body again. This was a family picnic spot, a dog walker's dream, there would be children and families arriving here soon. Hopefully the police would get here in time to erect their forensics tent soon. As dead as they were and as covered as they could be by the lid of the suitcase, the soul who once belonged to the body deserved more dignity than that.

Ray wondered what had happened to the girl. He was certain the body was female. The hair was wet and matted, but he could tell it had once been blonde, perhaps auburn. She was someone's daughter. Possibly some poor wee person's mother. Who would do something like that to another human? What possible reason could there be in the world to warrant that kind of brutality?

Whatever the reason, it would be lost on him. Poor girl, he thought.

As dead as she was, he didn't feel it was the right thing to do to leave her on her own. Emotion caught in Ray's throat then as Lilly appeared at his feet and sat obediently and in silence as they waited for the police to arrive.

3

MARCUS

Marcus stands outside the door of Angel Silk, the most popular gentlemen's club in Glasgow. Packed to the point where men have had to be turned away, the girls are the most sought-after lap dancers in the area. Tonight is no exception and with his main man at his side, Marcus and Tommy are ready to make sure the club runs smoothly. Their security staff are ready to start the night and Tommy leans into one of their men and says, 'Here, keep an eye on this group.'

Marcus glances in the direction in which Tommy is eyeing the group of men. They're in their mid-to-late twenties – and by the looks of it out to cause trouble.

There are four of them, two of whom have clearly had more than their fair share of alcohol for the evening. Marcus glances down at his watch. It's just gone eleven.

Gesturing for Tommy to follow, he heads inside the club to their office and allows the staff to do their jobs.

'A'right boys,' Marcus hears one of the men say. 'Here fur a bit eh the stuff.'

The rest of the group start to laugh and Marcus raises a brow at Tommy.

'If they're allowed entry, we'll keep an eye on them from the CCTV in the office.'

Marcus feels a stir of excitement at the idea of dishing out a few punches, a few kicks here and there with the troublemakers. As he reaches the office door he goes inside. Sitting down at his desk, Marcus puts his feet up and switches on the computer to watch the goings on out at the bar.

'Do you ever miss being on the door?' Tommy asks. Marcus nods in response.

'Aye, it was always a laugh. Seeing some of the poor bastards who actually thought they would find the love of their lives in here getting a knock back.'

Tommy laughs and Marcus keeps his eyes on the screen. The men from outside have indeed been allowed to enter the bar and Marcus knows they're going to be trouble. He's seen men like this many times before.

The office in which Marcus and Tommy are sitting is of high-end spec. Designer furniture, lights, fixtures and fittings make for a glamourous office. Why not? They have the money and it's where they spend most of their time. Marcus had particular taste for the chesterfield range, but instead of going for the usual mahogany and darker colour schemes, he had chosen to go with whites, creams and greys, in line with the name of the club. Chrome chandeliers, mirrored ceilings and bar fronts made the place sparkle and feel a lot bigger than it was. The mixture of old style and up and coming décor had landed the club with a top reputation, with some of the girls calling it a 'classy' place to work.

'Here we go,' Marcus says, placing his feet on the floor and leaning in towards the screen. 'They're only just in and already they've started harassing some of the girls.'

Tommy sighs. 'Shame. Fancy a drink at the bar?'

Marcus smiles and sees the sarcastic expression on his brother's face. This is his favourite part of the job, although he would never actually say that out loud.

The brothers step out of the office and walk across the floor. Already all twelve girls are on their podiums, twirling themselves, hanging upside down as their thighs grip the poles and enticing the customers.

They reach the bar and Tommy orders two beers. Marcus scans the room and revels at how full the booths have become already. White and black leather seats are strategically placed around private tables, which have a pole in the centre, and the red and blue lighting shines down on the girls, accentuating their movements. Then his eyes fall on the group of lads. They've congregated around the centre podium and Marcus can feel a rage begin to burn in the pit of his stomach. He watches as the men distract the girl from her work, pulling at her calves so she has no choice but to move closer to them. One of the men is running his hand up her leg, dangerously high on the inside and she kicks out, catching the man on the shoulder.

There is a lot of noise and laughter from the group and Marcus notices how the girl turns to him, a look of despair on her face.

Marcus makes his way across to the podium, bottle still in hand and brother by his back.

'Are you alright, Amber?' Marcus asks.

She glances down at Marcus and shakes her head. 'No, they're being a bunch of fucking arseholes, Marcus.'

'Ah, come on, it's just a laugh. What else d'ya expect working in a place like this?' one of the drunker men comments.

'No' the night lads, eh. Time you moved on,' Tommy says, standing shoulder to shoulder with Marcus.

Tommy isn't as tall as Marcus, but his broad shoulders and solid stature is still more than the four punters they stand in front of now.

'What d'ye mean, no' the night?' another of the group asks, stepping out in a manner seemingly more confident than he knows what's good for him. 'You own the place or something?'

Tommy glances at Marcus again and Marcus steps forward. 'Actually yes, we do own this place. And exactly what he said. Not tonight. Now, *move* on.'

The group remain, and one of the ones at the back is swaying on his feet. Marcus helps Amber down from her podium and tells her to go back to the dressing room. She does as instructed but not before thanking him and giving his hand a squeeze.

'Look, if it's coz I was touching her, then I'm sorry. I'll pay. I was gonna pay anyway, just thought I'd try before I buy.' The young lad starts to laugh and pulls a small bag of white powder out from his pocket.

'Your money and your drugs aren't welcome here, so like we said...' Marcus steps forward and pulls the small bag from his hand. 'Out.'

'Oi, who the fuck d'ya think you're touching?' The young lad, along with the rest of them, changes his stance and Marcus has to stifle a laugh as they puff out their chests and straighten their shoulders.

Marcus follows their gaze as it turns to the entrance of the club. Four of their security staff have appeared to lend a hand.

Tommy moves behind the group and places a hand on one lad's shoulders, who turns and takes a swing but misses.

The security team are on top of all the lads now and have them pinned to the floor. Marcus basks at the sight.

'Oi, nae need fur that,' one of them shouts as they're pulled to their feet and escorted out of the club to the street. Marcus and Tommy follow.

The excitement continues to build at the idea of how audacious these lads have become. Who did they think they were? Did they even know who the hell they were talking to? Clearly not.

Once at the bottom of the stairs and on the street, the security let go of the lads and push them away from the entrance, where there are more punters awaiting entry.

The four lads glare and smile at Marcus and Tommy before backing away on to the street.

'Yer club's shite anyway. Lassies have probably got a disease,' one shouts and the rest laugh.

'Is that right?' Tommy says under his breath. 'These wee bastards need to know who they're fucking dealing with.'

Marcus agrees and steps out of the doorway, Tommy close behind. They're followed by two of the security lads and the rest stay at the club entrance.

The four lads are too drunk to notice they're being followed as they round the corner and head in the direction of the next club or pub that might allow them entry. They take a short cut through the narrow alley between the back of Angel Silk and a derelict building. Marcus, Tommy and two of their men follow.

'Hawd on, I need a pish.' The drunkest lad stops. The rest turn and realise what's about to happen.

'Hold on lads, we don't want any trouble,' one lad says. It's too late, Marcus has already landed a right hook on his jaw.

Tommy is on another, knocking him to the ground and laying into him. Marcus hears painful cries, pleading for them to stop, but this only spurs him on more.

He lifts the lad up and pins him against the wall. It's dark but Marcus can see the blood pouring from his nose. Already, both eyes are swollen shut, as Marcus begins again. Left and right hooks to the abdomen, and the lad slumps down to the ground and is silent. He turns to see two of his men dealing with the others. Tommy is stamping on the third.

'I'll just leave you lot to it,' Marcus says as he straightens his jacket. Stepping over the crumpled heap at his feet, Marcus rounds the corner and heads back to man the door at Angel Silk.

The men he'd left in his place nod and turn to the side, allowing Marcus to climb the stairs back inside to the office.

He sits down at the desk and switches the screen on the computer to multiple view. The street in front of the club is bustling with a mixture of groups. Some pass by and some join the growing queue of people who want to join the fun inside.

Flexing his fingers, he turns to see Tommy arriving at the office to join him.

'Sorted?' Marcus asks, raising his head as Tommy comes through the door.

'Aye. Sean and Ricky have got this. No need to worry,' Tommy replies quietly.

'I wasn't.'

Marcus notices Tommy glancing down at his hands. 'Mate, how hard did you hit him? Your knuckles are fucked.'

Marcus looks down and notices the blood smeared into his knuckles. He doesn't know if it's his own or belongs to the lad he's certain he'd punched to death.

Getting to his feet, he goes to the sink in the corner of the room and washes his hands. The water in the sink turns a light brown as the soap washes the evidence away. Looking up at his reflection in the mirror, Marcus smiles. The power and the adrenaline inside feel euphoric. Nothing can ever come close to this feeling, there's no drug that can match it.

Marcus leaves the office and heads across the floor. The music vibrates in his chest and he takes a breath, watching the girls as they dance for the punters. The club is packed and that's thanks to the reputation.

'Everything good down there, Marcus?' Lizzy, the house mother, shouts loudly over the top of the music as she passes him. She is heading for the office with a pile of papers in her hands.

'Oh aye, Lizzy. All good.'

She smiles and continues past him.

Marcus turns to see a sea of punters walk through the door into Angel Silk and smiles. Lots of punters meant lots of revenue.

He notices that Amber has emerged from the dressing room looking a lot more relaxed. She can clearly see that the group of lads that were harassing her have been removed from the club.

'Hey,' she approaches him. 'Thanks for that.'

'It's not a bother, Amber. They were being out of order. Are you okay now?'

Amber smiles up at him. 'Yeah, I'm good. Going back on now. When we get home later, can we talk?'

Marcus nods. 'Aye, whatever you want.' Marcus watches as she climbs on to her regular spot.

It's going to be a busy night and Amber is going to be a busy girl.

4

AMBER

We sit down on the sofa and Marcus pulls my feet up onto his lap. He used to do this every night, give me a foot rub after a shift. Now that his businesses are expanding, he's been so busy I've barely seen him. Tonight, I'm excited to have him all to myself after work. It feels like how we were in the beginning, all loved up and all over each other. I miss that.

When I first met him, neither my parents nor my sister approved of him. They didn't think he was good enough for me, based on where he's from or his choice of business. It really got to me because they didn't get to see all the good stuff. How sweet he is, how caring and kind he is. He spoils me, takes me to fancy restaurants, stylish clubs and on holidays. I wear the best of clothes, shoes and fragrances.

Of course my family never actually told me or Marcus straight out that they didn't like him, but the way they behaved around him said enough. 'Do you really see your future with a man who owns a strip club? It's exploitation, Amber.'

At that point, I hadn't told them I was actually working there. They were wrong, it wasn't exploitation. I choose to do what I do. Yes, most people think that working in a strip club is seedy, but with Marcus as my boyfriend and my boss, he wouldn't ever let anything happen to me that I didn't choose. Tonight is a prime example of that. However, as our relationship has progressed, I have been thinking about my future. I suppose my family's words may have stuck around in my mind on some level and as much as I love Marcus and he loves me and I am proud of his achievements, I don't see myself doing this forever. I want to go to university and study arts. I want to work a normal nine to five job and be able to come home and make us a meal at a normal time. I don't want men ogling over me when my boyfriend is watching, even though I know he sees it as a job, the same as if I were serving behind the bar. He isn't the jealous type. If he was, he wouldn't have offered me a job there in the first place.

'How's that?' Marcus says as he massages his thumb into the sole of my foot. I lean back and allow my eyes to close for a moment.

'It's good. Those heels are killers.'

Marcus laughs. 'Good on the old bank balance though.'

I fall silent for a moment and realise that if I'm going to say this, then now is the time. My stomach flips because I don't know how else to put it without sounding ungrateful. But I have to say it.

'Actually, about that, I wanted to talk to you about something. It's to do with the club.'

Marcus raises a brow and readjusts his position on the sofa so he is sitting a little more upright. The nerves kick in but I hold the confidence I have inside and push on with what I've got to say.

So, I tell Marcus my plan. I am honest and he allows me to speak until I have gotten all my words out.

'So, this is you giving me your notice?' Marcus asks once I've finished speaking. 'You don't want to work for me anymore?'

I hear the sadness in his voice and already I feel guilty for making him think I'm ungrateful for what he's provided me with. A home when my family were being difficult, a safe and comfortable place with him as my rock when arguments would break out between me and my sister, or my parents in the early stages of my relationship with Marcus. He always listened and never judged even though what they were saying about him was unfair and unjust. He always stuck up for them, saying that I would always be their daughter and that they only had my best interests at heart.

I shake my head. 'Oh god, please don't say it like that, Marcus. I am so grateful for the opportunities you've given me, but I don't think this lifestyle is for me anymore. The podium and private topless dances are one thing, I can handle that. I'm used to it now.' I think about the topless dancing and how I spend most of my shift wearing provocative underwear. That I can just about manage. It's what often comes after that I have a problem with. The fact that I'm expected to allow strange men to grope me, ask me to do them sexual favours because they've paid extra cash. 'I don't like being paid to go into a back room or a private booth with some stranger and do whatever he wants. It makes me sick and I feel like I'm cheating on you.' I take a breath. I can almost feel invisible hands on me as I remember the last private session I was booked in for. 'It's not just that, though. I want to try to make amends with my family. I miss my sister. She had a baby just a few months ago and I've only met my nephew once. They'll think I don't give a shit.'

I remember how they would treat me when things with Marcus stared to get serious. They made it clear from the start that they didn't like him, that they thought he wasn't good enough for me. I get that they were just looking out for me but I'm a big girl. Thing is now, if they knew what kind of job I was doing for a living and who I was actually working for, it would just make things worse. All I'd told them was I was working in a club behind the bar. I left out the part that I was mostly dancing on it.

'I mean, I haven't really spoken to them in a while and I want to change that.'

'Sounds like you're blaming me for that, Amber,' Marcus says, pushing my feet off his knees. I let them fall to the floor and sit up straight.

'Don't make it like that. I'm not blaming you at all. I think there were just a lot of misunderstandings and miscommunications in the beginning. And you always said yourself that they only ever wanted what was best for me. This has absolutely nothing to do with you, Marcus. I just see myself being more than a stripper in a gentlemen's club.'

'Yeah, I know. You want to go to university to do your art degree. I've heard that so many times, Amber, but have you ever actually done anything about it?'

I don't like his tone, how he's said the words but I ignore them.

'I can't do it for the rest of my life.'

He doesn't reply, only stares out at the TV. I wish I could tell what he was thinking. I don't want him to think I'm building up to leaving him. That is the last thing I want. I watch as his knees begin to rock back and forth gently. It's what he does when he's trying to think of a solution. It's what he did just before he asked me to come and live with him for a while, just until things blew over between my family and me. Now that I think of it, perhaps I could have talked to them more. If Marcus and I had gone to them as a couple and allowed them to see we were happy, then maybe things could have been different. Now is the time to fix things before it's too late.

'Marcus?'

He takes a deep breath, smiles and leans in. Kissing me gently, he pulls away and says, 'Amber, you know I love having you close by. Working at the club is the perfect way to have you near me. The little things on the side, they bring in the extra cash. I'm only trying to help you to get your life sorted again. It's not ideal not seeing your family as much, I get that. But they hate me, Amber. And there will be nothing you can do to change that. If you stop working at the club and start to sort things out with your family, you know what will happen. They will try to turn you against me like they did in the beginning.'

When I think about my family – my mum, dad and sister – it kills me that we're not on good terms. I spend so much time with him and not a lot with them, and I think it bothers them.

But that's what you do when you fall in love, isn't it? You want to be with that person all the time because that's what the heart wants. When my sister got engaged, she told me that Marcus wasn't allowed to come to the engagement party or the wedding because he'd been rude to her and told her that she and my parents were trying to control what I did because they didn't like him. I was livid and asked Marcus about it. He said my sister had overreacted but if she didn't want him at her wedding he would stay away for my sake.

How could my family expect me to ask him to do that? I was in love and they just didn't seem to get that. I told them that if they couldn't be happy for me then I would have to move out and that their behaviour was only pushing me closer to Marcus. Things were strained with us once I moved in with him and it hurt that our relationship was broken.

Marcus's voice is soft, pleasant. But there is something else in it that I don't recognise. Fear that I'm going to leave? I've had boyfriends in the past, some nice, and some not so nice. I know the difference. The not so nice ones punched me when I said it was over. One even tried to lock me in when I tried to leave. With Marcus, it's different. He loves me, he would never do anything to hurt me. He gave me a job and a roof over my head when times were tough. That's why telling him this was so difficult. Guilt rippled through me at the mere idea of telling him I no longer want to work at the club. But it was the right thing to do. To be honest with him is to be true to myself.

'Please don't think for one minute that I want to hurt you. I don't. I just don't want to be...' I try to think of a better description than sex worker. 'An escort.'

'You're not an escort.' Marcus laughs and takes my hand in his. 'You're one of my best girls. The most popular. You keep that place running all on your own, Amber. How could I possibly let you go?' He tucks a lock of my hair behind my ear and kisses me on the cheek.

'You see, that's the problem Marcus. I know I'm the most popular and it's wearing me out. I don't ever get the chance to stop. If I'm not dancing then I'm...'

'Hey,' Marcus says and I hear the irritation in his tone. 'It's a job. It's money and good money at that.'

I eye him and realise that he isn't taking me seriously. How do I tell him it's not his choice without coming on too strong or hurting his feelings?

'So, let's just forget that this happened and get on with things as normal. Okay?' He leans in and kisses me on the cheek again before getting to his feet and moving to the kitchen. The irritation is gone from his voice now. 'What's the alternative? Go back to your controlling family, who would rather see you miserable and drive a wedge between us than see you happy with me?'

'No. This isn't just about my family,' I reply. I stand up but don't move towards him. 'Marcus, you're not listening to me. I *am* giving you my notice. I don't want to do this anymore. And if you love me then you'll respect my decision. This was only ever meant to be a temporary thing until I could get my shit together. It doesn't matter what job I go on to do next, we'll still be together. Okay?'

My heart is pounding in my chest now as he stops, his back to me. Turning, he smiles and moves closer, slides an arm around me and pulls me in.

'If that's how you feel, Amber, then there's nothing I can say to make you change your mind. Is there?'

'If this was any other job you know I would stick it out for you. But this isn't something I'm able to do anymore, I'm sorry. And if you really love me, which I know you do, then you won't push me further on this.'

Marcus strokes the back of my head and buries my face into his chest, rocking me back and forth like a baby. I smile and sigh in relief that he has finally understood where I'm coming from. Being an exotic dancer who provides extras isn't something I'd ever planned. Basically I'm a prostitute but instead of walking the streets I have a permanent residence at the club.

'You don't have to do what I ask,' Marcus finally says as he pulls away. Cupping my face in his hands, he smiles down at me.

I lean up and kiss him. As I pull away, I notice his expression has changed, to a look I haven't seen in him before.

'But you *will* do what I tell you.'

Before I can respond, I'm knocked back by a force that is too quick for me to comprehend. I land on my back and my head feels like it has exploded. I cry out in pain as I stare up at Marcus. He takes a step forward. This is not the Marcus I'm in love with, but a stranger.

'Get up,' he growls. My face is wet and I'm scared to touch it because I know it's blood. A man his size headbutting a girl like me, it was bound to happen. 'I said get up!'

I'm frozen in fear as I stare up at Marcus, in disbelief at what he's just done to me and how he's speaking to me now.

He lurches forward and grabs my wrist before pulling me to my feet. I attempt to tell him to stop but it comes out as a whimper as he drags me towards the hallway. I resist, pulling back but I am no match for his size or strength.

'Don't fuck with me, Amber. I've done nothing but support you up until this point. You're making me good money and you're not about to stop. Do I have to go to your family and sort them out in order to make you respect me and what I've done for you? Do I have to tell them all about their daughter, and how she strips in front of strange men for money?'

His words are like a knife in my gut as he wraps his fingers in my hair and pulls me towards the bathroom. I can't fight back as he forces me inside. 'Sit down,' he says, pointing at the toilet. He's breathing quickly, full of rage, and I am confused. What happened to my Marcus? Where did he go and who is this thug standing in front to me?

'Marcus, please. I thought you loved me?' I say, tears streaming down my face. Where has this come from? Now that

23

I want to make my own decisions, he's becoming violent. How am I supposed to get myself out of this?

'Amber, you could have had this so much easier, and in a way you did for a while. All you had to do was follow the rules. But you chose to be difficult. You're one of my *employees*. One of many. Most of them are compliant. Some of them are not.' He closes the bathroom door and is towering over me as my brain runs through a million different thoughts so quickly I don't have time to process them. He grabs a handful of tissues and begins wiping my face. He isn't gentle and my head is throbbing.

'I'm sorry,' I say, the word making me feel sick. Why was I saying sorry? I was the one bleeding.

'Are you going to walk out of here and disobey me?' he asks, throwing the tissue in the bin.

I shake my head vigorously in an attempt to keep him calm. 'No. I promise I won't. I'll stay and keep doing what you tell me.'

His eyes are wide as he regards my promise. Then they soften and he steps back and into the hallway. I get to my feet, the pain still intense from the blow. He moves to the side and allows me to pass. I am headed for the lounge but as I am about to pass the front door, I lunge at it, pull the handle and make a bid for my freedom.

I'm in the communal hall, taking the stairs two at a time and ignoring the pain in my head and the blood still trickling down my face. I want to scream but I'm too focused on getting to the front door of the building. He's behind me, his steps inching closer. I reach for the handle and just as my fingers brush against the metal, he has me in a headlock. His arm is around my neck, squeezing tightly as he pulls me back from the door and up the stairs. I kick, punch and struggle as much as I can but it's no use. I'm back in the flat and he throws me down on the floor as he locks the door. I turn and try to crawl away from him but before I can create any space between us, he's on top of me, twisting me round so he's looking down at me. The fear that gripped me turns to terror when I see what is in his hand. A gun. He presses it to my forehead and I close my eyes, hold still.

'I've had enough of girls like you, thinking you get to decide what's happening around here. I've already had to deal with one, and I don't give a shit if I have to deal with another. Trust me, Amber—' the words come through gritted teeth '—I will not hesitate if you insist on pulling this kind of shit with me.'

Make it quick, I think to myself. *Just kill me quickly so I don't have to endure this terror anymore.*

–

My eyes flicker open and I see Marcus sitting back, arms crossed as he watches me. Smiling. I forget for a second what happened. Then I remember and the fear comes gushing back. I try to sit up but he forces me back down. It doesn't take much. His hand on my chest, the other pointing the gun in my face. I don't resist. Instead I lay my head back and allow him to control me because it's either that or immediate death. I don't for one second doubt that he would do it. *He's controlling you, Amber. He doesn't like that you're close with your family.* My sister's words echo in my ears and tears prick the corners of my eyes. Jesus Christ, am I that naïve and stupid that I didn't see this coming?

I'm in the bath but water doesn't surround me. He's above me now, his hand gripping my arm. Tugging. My arm feels tight, like it's going to pop.

'What are you doing?' I say, my head fuzzy and painful. 'Marcus, please,' I start but it's too late. I see what is in his hand now. Feel the prick on my skin. I want to fight but the fear grips me and holds me in the bath. I want to cry. How can he do this to me? I thought he loved me.

'You're my girl, Amber,' he whispers as the needle plunges into my skin. 'Always have been and always will be. And you will stay here with me until I decide what you'll do next. Now, you sit back and enjoy this hit. It's going to be like nothing you've ever experienced before, so I'm told.'

I'm warm, comfortable. I feel more relaxed than I've ever felt. Euphoric even. The warmth spreads through me and I succumb to it, hoping that whatever he has given me is enough that I won't wake up to this nightmare. The words I hear before finally giving in will stay with me forever.

'And if you so much as think of leaving again, I'll make sure you don't have a family to go back to.'

5

JADE

Clutching at my chest as it constricts, I push my way through the crowd in the supermarket and hope that I don't die in the middle of the dairy aisle. I can't breathe, yet I can feel the air in my lungs. It's hot and dry like when you open the oven on Christmas day and the turkey has been in for three hours.

'Hey, watch where you're going, you ignorant...' I don't hear the rest as I reach the exit. I burst through the doors and into the street. Next to the trolley park is a bin and I lean over it as I retch, my body rejecting the panic and anxiety inside.

Embarrassed, I stand up and take the tissue from my pocket and wipe my mouth before heading across the car park. Keeping my head down, I walk in the direction of the bus stop but I won't stop there and wait for it. I'll keep walking because I can't be in a crowded place today. As much as being outside in an open space can trigger an attack, being around others can often be worse.

Crossing the canal bridge at the Fish and Chip boat, the traffic sounds become distant as I approach the bandstand. That's where it happened, twelve weeks previously. My attack. It's strange that I can walk past it, but I won't look directly at the spot in which I thought I was going to die. That night changed my life. It was my own fault for walking home from work that night. I never normally go round the back of the centre but it was the quickest way out.

I enter the shopping centre and head down towards Chalmers Street. It's already busy for ten in the morning but it's pay weekend so people will be out spending their money. Again, I keep my head down and move forward, past various charity shops and pawn shops. When I exit the centre, I turn right and head towards Kilbowie Road. A bus puts on the air brakes. A loud whooshing sound escapes from somewhere under the bus and my heart almost leaps out of my chest. I turn to the driver and want to give him a stern look but decide against it.

The air is cold this morning as the sun sits low over Clyde-bank. I hate this place, even more so after what happened. It's all a little greyer after seeing the place for what it is. The people who inhabit this place after nightfall are unpleasant, unkind. I never knew my attackers but I think they were female based on their cackles as they laid into me. Junkies no doubt, looking for money to get their next fix. Scum. I hate what they've done to me, what they've turned me into. It was completely unprovoked and in the end they didn't take any of my belongings. Instead, they took pleasure in hurting me and when I called out for them to stop, pleaded with them to leave me alone, that seemed to spur them on even more.

I see the Breathing Space centre where it sits just off the road and contemplate going in. It's not the first time. Every day I walk past I think of going in. Of course, I choose to keep walking because going in there means talking to someone about what I had to go through and what I've lost. That makes it more real than it already is and I can't deal with that right now.

Before I know it, I've reached my flat. The flat that will no longer be mine in the next few weeks if I don't try to get some rent money together. Losing my job at the bank was the unneeded blow that came after I'd got out of hospital. Redundancy by all accounts, but deep down I wondered if it was because I'd been off for so long and they were looking for any excuse to lay people off. I'd managed to work my way up in the bank and was doing well, earning a decent salary and getting ready to start thinking about buying my own place.

They say they pay off some of the higher earners first, don't they? Not that the thought helped. My confidence had already been knocked after the attack, but to lose my job on top of that was what inevitably stripped me of who I was before.

As much as I try to push through the fear, it's getting worse by the day. I'm inside, locking the doors and checking the windows are secure. The building anxiety makes me twitch and I feel a dull throb in the injured areas. Ribs, stomach, arms. Almost kicked to death and laughed at, spat on; how can people be so cruel? The bruises are gone now but the memories will never fade and I know that the pain I feel is all in my head. Physically I am healed, only left with some scarring that can easily be hidden by a shirt or top. But mentally, I don't think I will ever be healed. I hate what they've turned me into. I'm not normally a bitter person, but I hope that whoever did this to me gets a bit of the same, if not worse.

I'd happily watch them suffer.

Just as I sit down on the sofa, there is a knock at the door and I jump. Irrational fears that they will come back for me have gripped at my soul ever since. No matter how many times I say out loud that I am being stupid, it doesn't make a difference.

Just as I get to my feet, my phone vibrates and when I pull it from my pocket, I see it's from him. I smile when I read it.

Marcus 13:53
It's only me. X

I get up and unlock the door before pulling it open. He's leaning against the railing and smiling gently at me. 'Can I come in?'

I let him in and he pulls me into his arms. He just knows how I'm feeling and his presence alone makes me feel better. We haven't been seeing each other for long. It started not long before I got out of hospital. I met him in the newsagent's on the hospital grounds. I was reaching for a bottle of water and it fell out of my hands. He picked it up for me and we started chatting. I'd never imagined meeting a potential boyfriend in a hospital. I suppose stranger things happen.

'You were out today?' he asks.

'Yeah, just went to get some bits from the shops. Nearly had a bloody panic attack in there. So bloody embarrassing.'

'Hey, no need to be embarrassed. You're home now and I'm here.' He smooths my hair with his fingers and hugs me tighter.

We move into the lounge and sit down on the sofa. He smiles and rubs at my shoulder and I think how lucky I am to have found him.

'Any luck on the job front?'

'No,' I sigh, shaking my head. 'Trying to get a job these days is hard enough without worrying if I'll have a full-on panic attack in the middle of the interview.' That worry alone makes me not want to leave the house or even apply for jobs.

Marcus doesn't say anything, he just lets me speak. I feel safe to talk about how I'm feeling around him. He's the only person I have who cares about me.

'How's the phone? It's what you wanted, wasn't it?' he asks, picking it up and tapping away on it.

'Yeah, it's great. Although to be fair, I don't have anyone else really to call on it. Just you.' I smile, my heart swelling in my chest.

Marcus puts the phone down on the coffee table and places a hand on my knee. 'Hey, what have I said? If they cared enough, they'd be here. But they're not. I am. I'll always be here for you.'

My smile widens as he leans in to kiss me. I fall back on the sofa and welcome his weight on top of me. I feel like he's my security blanket, my defence wall.

'When's the rent due?' he asks.

'Two days ago,' I say, biting my lip as the worry floods back in.

'Have you considered my offer? It's really no trouble at all.'

I have considered it, I've thought about it every day for the last week.

'You really want me to move in with you for a while until I get back on my feet? I mean, we haven't even made us official yet.'

'I didn't think we had to. If I was interested in anyone else then I wouldn't have spent the last six weeks with you, Jade. And I wouldn't have offered for you to come and live with me if I didn't mean it,' he says, pushing a lock of hair behind my ear. My skin prickles with excitement as his fingers brush against my face. Of course I want to move in with him until I can get my shit together.

Maybe I'll never want to come back home. He may not want me to leave once I'm there.

I'm unable to hide the happiness at hearing that he already regards me as his girlfriend. I didn't think things would get better after the attack. It seems the universe is looking after me now.

31

6

LIZZY

The girls are working and dancing their hearts out during their warm-up for tonight and as I stand back and watch them, I feel like a protective mother as well as a businesswoman. As much as I need them to work hard and do what they do best, I also want to make sure that they're happy and feel safe here.

Some girls are quieter than others, some take a while to come out of themselves and really show us what they've got. And there are others where it's clear that dancing comes naturally to them. Amber is one of those. She is so elegant on the poles and extremely fit. The punters love her, a little too much sometimes. It's not just my job to know the girls like they're my own, it's also my job to know the punters. I never forget a face and if I see anyone giving the girls hassle, then I'm straight on to Marcus and Tommy, who inform their security team about who not to allow back into the club. In this kind of business, you need security who will be ruthless with their tactics. I don't normally see how they work with my own eyes, but I know how it can go. The place feels safe with them around.

The girls will often come to me with their problems and I am more than happy to listen because once they've cleared some headspace, they perform a lot better and that means the club brings in more revenue. Often the topics will consist of; *My boyfriend doesn't know I do this job, my parents have thrown me out, my boyfriend cheated on me…* Sometimes all the girls need is an ear and for most of them, I am the only mother figure they have in their lives.

'Good job, girls,' I call over. They smile in thanks, some of them clinging to the poles by their thighs, upside down. I remember when there was a time I could do that. I wouldn't dare try now. No one wants to see a middle-aged woman hanging from a pole in her underwear. Well, the men in this club certainly don't. They come here for the young meat, as some of them have openly stated.

I head into the dressing room and see the remainder of the girls applying their makeup and picking out their outfits for their shift ahead.

'All good in here, girls?' I ask. They glance at me from the mirror and the dress rack and nod. 'Club opens in thirty minutes, move your backsides.'

They laugh because as much as I sound harsh, they know as well as I do that they can take it. And if I thought any of them weren't up to the job of an evening, then I would send them home. There have been many occasions when I have tried to, but they've refused. Sometimes a chat can work wonders.

I head to my office and smile at Marcus and Tommy who have just arrived. Business partner and head of my security, I don't know how I would run this place without them.

'How's things, boys?' I ask.

'No bad, Lizzy. How you doing?' Tommy replies.

'Can't complain.'

'Give us a bell when the next booze delivery arrives and we'll give you a hand with it,' Marcus says.

I thank them and go into my office and close the door, before sitting down behind the desk and glancing at the accounts sheets in front of me. I push them to the side and lean back. Going into business with Marcus and Tommy made a lot of financial sense. I had once owned Angel Silk by myself, but I'd come into a little financial difficulty and had started to seek an investor so I didn't lose my livelihood. Then I'd found Marcus and Tommy's security firm and they made me an offer I couldn't turn down. This place is still mine and I am proud of it and proud of the girls for helping it to get to the successful stage it's at. Not only was I responsible for my own livelihood, I was responsible for theirs too and I couldn't let them down.

Now that things have settled back down financially and I've relaxed back into things, I've allowed myself to believe that I'm successful again. And wealthy too because of the work I have put into the club, and I'm not ashamed to say I'm proud of myself for that. I could have given up when things got tough, but I didn't. I wonder if my dad would be proud of me for what I've achieved. If he was still here, he might be able to see past the trouble I caused back then and accept that I am a changed woman now.

7

JADE

I admire the new necklace and the man standing behind me as he secures it at the back of my neck. His fingers brush against my skin and a flicker of excitement washes over me, like a small electrical shock. Every nerve in my body is buzzing as our eyes meet in the mirror.

'You like it?' he asks. I can't help responding with a smile.

I've been living at Marcus's flat now for a few weeks and already it feels like home. He is showing no signs that he wants me to move back to my own place and if I'm honest with myself, I'm happy with that. I don't want to leave.

'I love it, it's perfect.'

As he pulls his hand away, I notice a scar about an inch long. 'What happened to your hand?'

He looks down at it and shakes his head. 'Cooking accident. Knife slipped when I was peeling potatoes a few months back.'

'Shit, must've been a sore one,' I say, taking his hand in mine and raising it to my lips. I kiss the scar and he laughs softly.

Happiness in this form isn't something I expected to happen when I met Marcus. After the attack, all I wanted to do was curl up into a ball and never venture outside ever again. The fear of it happening again is overwhelming, even with him by my side.

'It suits you,' he says, spinning me around and kissing me. His arms envelope me and it's all I can do to stop my legs from giving way.

'You spoil me too much,' I say even though my lips are still pressed against his.

'That's because you're worth spoiling. After what you've been through, why wouldn't I want to make you feel good about yourself?'

He pulls away and sits down on the bed to put his shoes on. I hate it when he has to go out to work and I'm stuck here on my own. The night shift allows too many hours for my mind to conjure up memories from the darkest corners. I let out a long breath and sit down next to Marcus.

'Don't do that, Jade. You know I'd love to stay here with you all night but if I did that I wouldn't have a roof over my head let alone yours.' I know he doesn't mean the words to sound as harshly as I hear them. It's not his fault I don't feel safe in the flat by myself. I don't feel safe at all these days, but certainly safer when he's around. I can't expect him to stay glued to my hip purely so the panic in my chest doesn't develop in to a full-on attack.

'It's fine,' I reply, getting up from the bed and moving towards the window. 'I'll be okay.'

The familiar niggle and reminder of the pain from my ribcage makes me shudder with fear.

'Why don't you come out with me tonight? You could sit in, watch what's going on. Might spur you on to get a job yourself?' Marcus suggests. But the thought makes me feel sick to my stomach.

As much as I love Marcus, going with him to his job as a security manager doesn't scream any sort of fun or relaxation.

'I can't. Not now. It's too soon.'

'Jade, it's been four months since the attack. I think you're clinging to the safety of indoors and it's going to make things worse in the long run.'

Marcus finishes tying his shoelaces and gets to his feet. I turn and look out of the window at the outside world. I struggle to be outside for much longer than a couple of hours. Being out of the confines of the flat is much more bearable when I'm with him. However I feel so much better when I'm indoors. Sometimes I think I should stay inside forever, so I don't have to think about what might happen when I go out. Even the thought of that scares the hell out of me.

The late hour has cast a dusky pink sky over the city. My heart is telling me to get outside and forget my past because what I am becoming isn't healthy. But the uncertainty of it all screams from the pit of my stomach and it's all I can do not to let that scream climb up inside me, clawing its way to the tip of my tongue. But I don't want Marcus to think that I'm weak. Because if he thinks that of me then I might never get better and he might get sick of me. Then what would I be left with?

'I'm not clinging to anything. I can deal with this on my own. I don't need help.' The tone that carries my words doesn't have enough conviction in it even to convince myself.

Marcus crosses the small bedroom and I'm in his arms again. He hugs me, tighter this time and I have to fight back the tears.

'Then I'll have to stay,' he says. 'I can't leave you here like this.'

'No, you won't. You have work to do and I don't want to be the cause of you losing a night's wage. Go, I'll be fine.'

Pulling away, he gives me a smile. It's forced but it'll do for now. I won't be fine on my own. I lied then and there is no doubt he knew I was lying.

I don't think I'll ever be fine again, not completely. Although, having Marcus by my side means that some of my past pain will begin to fall into the background. Surely.

8

MARCUS

The news of the body washed up at Luderston Bay is a shock to the system. He'd been promised the situation had been taken care of but clearly that's not the case. Marcus calls an emergency meeting with his team and by the looks on their faces, they're just as shocked as he was upon hearing the news. Luckily for them, the bay is a good thirty or so miles down the coast. That and the fact that the girl wasn't recorded as missing mean that they can stay out of the spotlight if the police come sniffing around.

'Careless, just utter carelessness. How is it that after it was claimed she was dealt with, she surfaces at a family fucking hotspot, eh?' Marcus shouts, banging his fist against the desk.

'The case was weighted, Marcus. Unless the bricks somehow managed to get out, we don't know how this has happened. Tide maybe?' Tommy replies.

Marcus begins pacing the floor as he tries to remain calm. The girl caused him enough problems when she was alive, he doesn't need this from her as a corpse.

'What do you want us to do boss?' Rory asks. Marcus stops and looks across at the young and relatively new lad on his team. Marcus has taken on more staff in recent months to bear the weight of the job because he doesn't want to be working on the front line anymore. Rory was just one of them. Recruiting girls and role playing as the perfect boyfriend is taking its toll on Marcus now that the business is growing. He doesn't have time to be playing house.

'Just keep your ears to the ground, all of you,' he says, standing behind the desk. 'Lizzy knows fuck all and I want it to remain that way for now. As far as she's concerned, things are normal.'

'Boss.' The word rings out in unison and the boys disperse. Marcus sits down behind the desk and Tommy leans against the wall by the door as the last of the boys leave the office.

'Look, things will be fine. Any possible evidence of her involvement here will have been washed away in the Clyde. Try not to worry,' Tommy says, lighting a cigarette.

Marcus isn't worried, this isn't the first time they've had to deal with a troublemaker. He's more annoyed that things aren't going his way. That body resurfacing is a headache he doesn't need right now. Marcus's auld man had handed the reins of the business over to him and trusted him to keep building the family empire; if the body at the bay became an issue, the reins could quite easily be taken away again. Marcus can't have that. He is on the cusp of integrating another girl into the business, his last ever girl. He wants it to go smoothly and the resurfacing of a body is a distraction no one needs.

'Is she ready?' Tommy asks.

'Almost, couple more weeks and we should be good to go. She's a pain in the arse this one, a bit too clingy so I've still got some work to do. But she'll be worth it. The punters will love her.'

Marcus has to admit that Jade is beautiful. With her long, dead-of-night black hair, hazel eyes and paler complexion, she's the kind of girl the club is missing.

Tommy smiles and a blue plume of smoke filters through his nose. Marcus is happy to have his brother working by his side. His right-hand man who can sort things out in a second to keep the business running. Being head of recruitment, Tommy keeps the girls coming via the new lads on the team. They keep their ears to the ground, scout new girls for the punters. As well as recruiting new girls, Tommy works alongside Marcus to make sure the security side of the business is in the best shape it can be, by hiring security guards to man the doors at the club. They have exterior and interior security. The interior security make sure that the girls have extra eyes on them. Not only that, but they report back if punters become too familiar without paying. Paid dancing and paid sex are two very different entities at the club and Marcus and Tommy make sure the punters know that.

The punters are taken to private rooms and booths for paid extras, but it's all done on the quiet. It isn't exactly laid out like table menus but the punters know they can get it if the price is right.

'You'll be glad to know that young Rory has two girls on the go. Like putty in his hand by all accounts.'

Marcus glances up at Tommy, smiles and says, 'He'd better not be the type to get carried away on his own lies. I've seen it happen, lads falling for the girls and letting that get in the way. It's not good for business.'

'Nah, that'll no' happen. Rory reminds me of you when you were his age. Money is his drive and there's no girl that comes close to the amount he's being paid to work for us. He's sorted, don't worry about that.'

'Do you think I just sit back here and worry myself to death?' Marcus shakes his head as Tommy laughs.

When Marcus thinks about Rory, he is reminded of a young version of himself. He's driven, determined to get the job done. He'll go far indeed, most likely break away and start up his own business. But for now, he works for Marcus McAdam, and Marcus will make sure that Rory does the job he is paid to do, and do it well.

'How's Amber doing after her little tantrum?' Tommy asks.

'She's complying. Doesn't have much choice now that she's an addict and I'm the only one who can supply her,' Marcus replies.

'Bit strong though, is it not? Forcing a needle into her arm.'

Marcus shoots Tommy a look and his eyes narrow. 'You suddenly a saint now?'

'Nah, just meant there might have been another way.'

'Aye, well, I was out of suitcases.'

Tommy lets out a guttural laugh and Marcus smiles. Tommy, always trying to be the voice of reason. It never works though, Marcus will always do things his way. It's his business in the end, and what he says is the way things go.

Marcus is relieved thinking about Rory working with Tommy in recruitment. It's exhausting that Amber's outburst and his manipulation of Jade are coinciding, but business is business. He's had very little sleep since but once Jade is embedded at the club, he'll be able to sit back and relax a little and focus more on the business as a whole.

'Right, well I'd better get cracking. New girls arriving tonight and I want to make sure that the rooms are ready. I want to keep up our five-star rating in case there is ever a TripAdvisor version for strip clubs-come-brothels.' Tommy laughs, standing up straight and moves towards the desk to stub his cigarette out in the ashtray.

'Oi,' Marcus raises a brow. 'Gentlemen's club.'

Smiling and shaking his head, Tommy leaves the room and Marcus sits back on his chair. It rocks back and forth slowly as Marcus wonders about Luderston Bay. Will the police come knocking? Now that a body has washed up, they'll surely be on the lookout for where she came from. But it isn't the police he is concerned about, it's the other girls. If any of them have an ounce of bravery in them, they might talk. Marcus has to make sure that doesn't happen. A warning will have to be issued. A clear and *stark* warning that anyone who so much as blinks in the direction of the pigs if they come knocking, they will receive the same treatment.

There are other ways to get rid of a body.

9

AMBER

I hate this place. This building. After being forced to move here just a couple days ago, I haven't had a conversation with any of the others who live here.

The girls here are cliquey. Anytime I pass them on the landing they'll stop talking and I feel their eyes on me. It makes me feel strange, like there is something they know about me that I don't know about myself.

If only they knew my story, if only they knew how much crap I've had to endure in the past few weeks, then maybe they'd be a bit kinder. Although as a human, it's hard not to pass judgement on someone new. It's natural to be curious, to wonder about a person. I suppose that's what they're doing. I wish they would just ask me and make things less awkward.

As I approach the building with my shopping bags, I struggle with the door. It's locked, so I place one bag down to retrieve my keys from my pocket when it opens from the inside.

I look up to see a girl around my age. 'Oh, thanks,' I say, offering a smile. There is a flash of recognition on her face and she's familiar to me. She's a dancer at the club too.

'No bother,' she says as she tries to push past me to exit the building.

'Oh hi,' I say. 'I think I know you. You work at Angel Silk?'

She turns to face me. 'Yeah, I do. Yasmin.'

Whenever I've seen her dance, she seems to do it with such elegance and certainly with a smile on her face. Like she enjoys it. Maybe she does. In truth, that's likely what people think of me when they see me up there on that pole. It's an act, I suppose, we are to pretend we are happy to have the job we do.

I nod at her, smile. 'Amber. Well, see you at work then.' I head for the first set of stairs when she begins to speak.

'You're Marcus's girl, aren't you?'

I freeze. Marcus's girl? No, I think to myself. I *used* to be. Before he turned into Satan in a Range Rover.

'How do you know that?' I turn back to face her. I don't want to go into detail with her, hence my response. Her eyes lock with mine and I realise she could be my enemy. Perhaps she doesn't like that I'm here. Perhaps she thinks that because I'm Marcus's girl, I'll make more money than she does. That is definitely not the case. I choose not to say much else in case what I do say gets back to him. He has eyes and ears everywhere. He made sure to tell me himself.

'So, are you?' she presses.

I shake my head, try to keep my expression as neutral as possible.

'But you were?'

'What's it to you? You been spying on me or something?' I eye her suspiciously.

'I've seen you with him at the club. He brings you there in his car, picks you up after. You're with him all the time. Like his pet.'

I feel my jaw drop at how audacious she is with her words. 'Excuse me?'

'Sorry, I didn't mean it the way it came out. It's just.' She stops. Hesitates. 'No, in fact never mind. I shouldn't have said anything.'

Before I can stop her, she steps out of the building and disappears from sight. I stand there, on the first step, for a few moments, staring at the door and wondering what it is that she wanted to say to me. It's clear she has something on her mind.

My shoulders twinge under the weight of my shopping bags. I readjust my grip and climb the stairs to my front door. I let

43

myself in and begin to unpack the various essentials. Bread, milk, eggs, baby wipes and lube. As I put the items away in their proper places, I can't get the girl out of my head. Her questions hang in front of me like a thick mist that won't clear.

She asked me more than once about being Marcus's girl. It wasn't fleeting curiosity that made her question me. So what was it? What was it she wanted to say before she thought better of it?

–

The pole in my hand vibrates under the music as I dance. I wouldn't call it dancing tonight. It's more of a sway, a movement that shows I'm here in body but certainly not in spirit. Was I ever here in spirit? In the beginning, perhaps. Back then, I was naive. Stupid and blind to this world. This was the kind of place you saw in Hollywood movies, not Glasgow. Now, Angel Silk is my only source of income and it's not even that much of an income. Being an exotic dancer doesn't pay as well as some would think and I don't even get to keep it. Marcus takes all of my money for rent and for my new drug addiction.

On the podium, I try to conjure up as much enthusiasm as I can. I grip the pole and pull myself up. I used to be better at this. Much better. I was in good shape in the beginning, good upper and lower body strength. But since I've been introduced to heroin and become dependent on that poison, I've spent less time practising and warming up during the day. I've not bothered to keep myself physically strong. Or is that the way it happens when you become a junkie? Nothing else matters other than where the next fix is coming from.

Although, having said that, this place is my only source of income. I need to be on some level of decent otherwise I won't get paid. Only private dances pay the wages. It's lucky I'm a good actress.

The club is quiet tonight. Monday nights are normally slow, but this night in particular is worse than normal. I concentrate on making my body move in a way that will attract attention. I need to sort myself out and the only way to do that is to earn money.

I'm still one of the best dancers here despite my problems, along with one or two others. I would do well to remember that. So, I continue on the pole on the podium. For the clients, the podium is like window shopping. If you don't have money, it's the done thing. If you have plenty of cash and there's something on the mannequin you think would look good on you, you buy it.

As I spin around the pole, using my arms to pull myself up, I see her. She catches my eye and for a moment, we're locked in each other's stare. She turns away and something in her stance tells me she wants me to stay away. I can see the regret in her face, her body language. She wishes she hadn't opened her mouth.

I don't like being questioned without an explanation, especially if that person can't even finish what it is that's on their mind. Seeing as it's quiet, I take the opportunity to step down from the podium and make my way over to Yasmin.

She is standing by a table of men dressed in crisp black and navy suits. Businessmen. It wasn't until I started working here that I realised it was another word for sleaze balls. They come here every week for a meeting while most likely their good little wives are at home washing their laundry and cooking their food. All the while their dirty husbands are at Angel Silk, leering over girls young enough to be their daughter in their underwear, paying for private topless dances and more. The dance part I can deal with. No touching involved. It is the more that really sticks in my gut.

I reach her and tap her on the shoulder.

'Can we chat?' I ask.

'Erm…' She hesitates. 'Yeah. Okay.' She finishes taking a drinks order from the men at the table and I ignore the one to my left. His eyes are in perfect line with my breasts and I feel his breath on my skin. I step back and follow her to the bar. She hands the drinks list over to the barmaid but doesn't turn to face me. I follow her gaze and realise Marcus is standing by the main entrance door. He is watching her. He is watching both of us.

I reach over and lift a small pad and pen from the bar top to show that I am ready to do the rounds and take drinks orders. There are two other men sitting in the far corner of the club and I eye them, making sure that Marcus can see me doing so.

I drop my gaze as he passes us. I feel a gush of air against my skin and I hold in the urge to shiver. Marcus goes into Lizzy's office and closes the door.

'Not here,' she says. 'Back at the flat. Ye know, later, when our clients have left.'

I flash a look at her and she sees this. 'What?'

'Clients? You're one too?'

'Aye, what else did you think I was doing there? It's not exactly the Hilton, is it?'

The barmaid sits the drinks order on Yasmin's tray and she carries it to the table where the suits were sitting. They cheer and smile at her and she dances for them, teases them with her body as it ripples at the waist.

I thought I was the only one who could lie like that. Seems I was wrong.

–

After a shift at the club, I am usually taken home and dropped off at the door. Marcus would watch me go up, sometimes he would escort me to the front door. It would depend on what kind of mood he was in. Tonight, he drops me at the main entrance and speeds off without saying a word. He doesn't have to. All he needs to do is give me that warning look and I understand. Fuck up and I'm in trouble. Refuse a client, and I will suffer.

46

Thankfully, tonight is slow in terms of my other work. Being a prostitute isn't pleasant, especially when I have no other choice. Tonight is easier than most. Only two clients have booked in for me. One with a foot fetish, and one who has a thing for school uniforms.

Once the latter has left, I scrub myself in the shower and when I am finished, I get into a fresh pair of pyjamas and light a joint. The closest thing I can get to a hit. Marcus is being an arsehole and choosing when I get a fix. A proper fix. The weed is no comparison but it will do for now.

A gentle knock on the front door alerts me that someone is present. A client I haven't been told about? No, Marcus wouldn't do that. He likes me to be prepared for each one and pyjamas, wet hair and the place stinking of weed isn't prepared.

Another gentle but firmer knock this time reminds me that I was going to be talking to Yasmin at some stage and this must be who is at the door. I peer through the spy hole and then I open the door.

'Hi,' she says. 'Can I come in?'

'Of course.' I step back and allow her to cross the threshold into my flat, not knowing how this conversation will go.

10

AMBER

'You've worked at the club a long time?' I ask as I hand her a bottle of beer from the fridge. She smiles in thanks and I sit down on the opposite end of the couch to her.

'Yeah, too long,' she replies, taking a drink from the bottle. 'You're good at what you do, you seem confident yet you never really speak to the rest of us. You came in not long after me.'

Her comment and blatant openness surprise me. We've just met, this is the first time we've properly had the chance to speak about things and she doesn't seem too bothered by the fact that she doesn't know me or my true relationship with Marcus. I could tell him everything she says, how is she to know that I won't?

She's right though. I have been there a while. Too long. Eight months to be precise. And no, I haven't spoken to many of the other girls, if any at all. I'm not there to make friends. I am there to do a job. To make money.

'I'm just shy,' I say and Yasmin laughs loudly. 'It's true. It's not like we have a lot of time is it? It's a case of get in, get ready, warm up and then tend to the punters.'

Yasmin takes a drink. 'Oh fuck off. *Shy?* No one in this business is shy, sweetheart. You're coming across as stuck up, Amber. Not that I'm saying that's what you are. But let's face it, you're the best dancer in the place, the one who earns the most and you were or still are going out with the head of security. You kind of get why they think you're up yourself?' She laughs, a little sarcastically.

48

I hold her gaze for a moment, too stunned to be able to respond. Then I laugh too. Shy, I was not. Never had been. Damaged would be the more appropriate word, yet I wasn't going to say that to her. Not right now anyway. And no, definitely not stuck up. You need to be able to love yourself to possess that kind of trait.

'Jesus, you don't sugar coat things, do you? Okay, maybe not *shy*. Reserved. How's that? And definitely was going out with. Not now.'

'Aye, reserved. I suppose you could say that's a substitute word for the phrase scared shitless.'

She catches my eye but I look away. There is something about her expression, a knowing glint in her stare. We're not too dissimilar and I want to know more about why she said that, scared shitless. Is she the same as me? In a predicament she has been forced into?

'What were you going to ask me yesterday?' I say.

She takes another drink from the bottle and places it down on the table before lighting a cigarette. The other half of my joint lies in the ashtray but I don't pick it up. What's the point? It won't hit the spot, not really.

Yasmin takes a deep breath, inhaling a lungful of smoke. It comes rushing out of her nose and she picks up the bottle again. She's nervous about what she has to say.

'So, you *were* Marcus's girl then?' she asks.

'Yes, I was for a while. I'm not now.'

'And how did it end between you?'

'Not good,' I say, the word catching in my throat.

'Nah, didn't think so. Did he…?' She falters.

I don't push her. Instead I take a sip of beer myself and wait for her to be ready. We seem to be suffering from the same fear. Marcus is dangerous. He's like a life-threatening disease that no amount of drugs can eliminate.

'Did he ever talk about Crystal?'

I am surprised by her question, expecting something along the lines of *did he ever hit you? Rape you? Stick a needle in your arm and have you hooked on drugs?* Perhaps that was to come later. Instead, I search through the memories stashed away in the back of my head. Many pathways lead to the earliest of days in our relationship, when things were sweet between us. He was the type of man who would spoil me, kiss me and hold my hand in public. He'd buy me presents, endless gifts of jewellery and clothes. A brand new phone, designer handbags and countless other items.

In all my conversations with him, he never once spoke of his past. Never spoke of family or friends other than Tommy. Crystal was never a name that came up.

I shake my head.

'Bastard,' Yasmin says through gritted teeth.

'Who is she?'

'She was you.'

'Excuse me?' I reply in confusion.

'Crystal was Marcus's girl long before you. When she arrived at the club for the first time, she was the type of girl you would have seen in high school and avoided. She was gorgeous and she knew it. Shame she didn't know much else.'

'What do you mean?' I ask, intrigued by this.

Yasmin takes another drink, and puffs on the cigarette again. 'What happened between you both? How did you end up here?'

I admire her ability to turn the question back around to me. I smile a little and shake my head. I could ask her the same thing. And I wonder if she's genuine, because why would she trust me when we've only started speaking? She could be working for Marcus, being paid extra to keep an eye on me.

'Yasmin, I don't have time for this. I haven't slept in around twenty-four hours. Marcus is due here soon.' *To bring me my fix*, I think to myself. 'So if there is something you want to tell me, just say it or go.'

Yasmin raises a brow and smirks. 'Look, all I will tell you is that Crystal was Marcus's girl. Like you, she was one of the top dancers. She and I became close and she told me that she was going to leave him and that she didn't like the way he was treating her. That his line of business wasn't something she wanted to be involved in. Like I said, she reminded me of the girls from school you would have avoided. Loud, mouthy and would make their opinion heard. I think that was her downfall.'

I don't like the sound of that. Maybe she is genuine after all?

'She used to live in this flat, right here where you are now. He put her here, told her to shut her mouth. She changed after that, went downhill rapidly. No longer was she gorgeous, but a shadow of herself. Greasy skin, flat and lifeless hair. I'm sure she was on something most of the time before she went missing.'

I sit forward on the sofa and run my hands through my hair. The closer Yasmin gets to the climax of this tale, the closer I am to having a panic attack.

'I came to see her one day and she had packed her stuff. She was a mess but she was determined she was leaving, even asked me to go with her.'

'Why didn't you?' I ask.

'Why are *you* still here?'

I nod, a mutual understanding between us. A mutual, unspoken trust.

'Marcus started off as Crystal's boyfriend before he became her boss. It was the same with me and Tommy. I was heartbroken when I realised what was going on. Tommy charmed me into a corner and now I can't get out.'

Tommy, Marcus's brother and business partner. A silence weighs heavy in the air between us and I realise that Yasmin and I are the exact same. We fell for men who tricked us into thinking they were good people. I can see in her expression the anger and hurt that Tommy has caused her.

'Anyway, that was the last time I saw her. I went to work at the club that night and she didn't show up for her shift. When I got back here, she was gone. So was her stuff.'

I watch Yasmin for a while as she smokes the rest of the cigarette in silence.

'So, she left?'

'I thought so, until this…' Yasmin digs into the pocket of her jogging trousers and pulls out a folded-up newspaper piece. She hands it over to me and I open it.

Once I'm finished reading it, I look up at her in horror.

'Yeah. I know.'

'Are you sure this is her?'

'Dead sure. The boss man doesn't like to be told no. And this here is proof of that.'

I notice tears building in the corners of Yasmin's eyes and a lump forms in my throat. We sit in silence for a few more minutes before Yasmin rises from the sofa and heads to the front door.

She doesn't say anything. No goodbye or see you later. She merely turns, offers a thin smile and leaves the flat. I hear her go into her own living space on the floor below and close the door.

Then I sit back, close my eyes and cry quietly.

11

AMBER

I stare at my reflection in the mirror, at the girl I am now and wonder if I'll ever get back to my old self. It would be an incredible achievement after all I've been through. I check my makeup and add a little more eyeliner, mascara. My lashes are fake but a little more to flutter at the men helps bring the cash in, according to him. Anything more is better than none. It has been a few weeks now since Marcus plunged that first needle into my arm. It has taken a lot to adjust to this new way of life. Drug addict, pole dancer and prostitute. That last word still feels like a knife to the chest, which in some respects I think I'd rather have. I've had to endure experiences I didn't think were possible, men I didn't think existed. The day I sold sex for the first time is the day I became someone else. No longer me but a product for clients with very specific needs. I try to shut my mind off, go into a kind of auto pilot where I carry out my job the way a machine would. Automatically and without emotion. It's never once been that easy.

It feels a lot longer than that. As much as I hate this job, I'm glad to be back to some sort of normality, if you can even call it that. Glad to be alive, surrounded by other people, not just Marcus or private clients.

'Amber, can you pass me that bottle of water?' a new girl asks. I don't bother to ask what her name is. I don't care if I'm honest, the new girls come and go so regularly these days it's pointless getting to know them. All I want is to go out there, dance, and take money from the sleazy bastards who inhabit this place for my savings so I can get the hell away from them, as far as possible although I have a strong suspicion that Marcus will soon be taking all of my cash from me to pay for the flat and the drugs. I sigh at the thought. Well and truly trapped. I'll have to think of another way of getting money directly into my pocket if I've any hope of getting away from this place.

I pick up the bottle to my right and hand it to her. She smiles at me but I return my gaze to the mirror and apply more red gloss to my lips.

'Can I ask you something?' she asks and I refrain from rolling my eyes. Before I can answer, she continues. 'Did you ever tell your parents, family and friends that you work here? I mean, I want to but I think they'll give me hell for it.'

I shake my head, attempting as little communication with this girl as possible.

'Me neither. My dad would kill me. I'm only doing this to get me through my degree then I'm out of here,' she says. Ha, I think. Good luck with that one.

A few of the other girls turn when the door of the changing room opens. When I see Lizzy behind me in the reflection of the mirror, I turn too.

She starts banging on about remembering the rules and prices and I lose interest very quickly. I lost interest quickly a long time ago. Before I met Marcus I'd never have placed myself here. I had it all, family, friends, freedom. Now look at me.

The girls get up and move towards the door and I follow. I catch a glimpse of myself in the mirror by the door and I stop, take a last look at myself before the night begins. I've not lost my figure, that's for sure. Lost a few curves here and there perhaps, but I still have it. I'm one of the most requested dancers in this place, despite my new drug addiction. Fact. My long auburn curls flow down my back, settling just at the bottom of my spine. It's my selling point apparently and it seems I'm hiding my flaws well.

'You're the fiery one,' one punter once told me. 'I like that.'

Marcus said that was what attracted him to me in the first place. He lied.

I give the roots of my hair a ruffle before stepping out to the bar area. Marcus will be downstairs, scrutinising the punters before deciding whether to let them in. My stomach rolls at the thought of another shift, but I swallow hard and put on my best Amber smile.

I eye Lizzy, standing by the end of the bar, and approach her. I have an idea. 'Lizzy, you got a minute?'

'Shouldn't you be up there?' She regards me with a raised brow. I know that look. It's the 'don't bother me right now' look. If only she knew what was really going on. Maybe she does and she's in on it? If I truly believed that I wouldn't be asking her the next question.

'I need an advance,' I say. I wait, hoping that she will help me out and keep this between us. That's what house mothers are for. She's here to look after us.

'What's up?'

'Nothing.' I break eye contact. I don't want her to see it in me, the desperate need to disappear. 'Just need an advance.'

'Amber, now isn't the time to be discussing this. Come and see me at the end of the night and we can talk about it then.'

I want to cry, the emotion building in my chest. Tonight is only my second shift back from my two week break from hell all courtesy of Marcus. I try not to allow the memories of that fortnight enter my mind. I don't know how much longer I can do this. My savings are gone since Marcus decided to stop giving me the cash I normally earn from this place and take it directly for my rent, as well as the drugs he got me hooked on. I can't carry on with this lie, so I walk away, take my position at the pole and let the music fill my mind. The deep bass pumps in my chest, alighting every nerve in my body. That along with the coke will keep me going, until I need another fix of the stronger stuff. It won't last long, it never does these days. As time goes on, these substances seem to have less of an effect, meaning I need more of them to get what I need. A higher feeling to take the edge off what is now my life. The coke was just the start of Marcus's plan to get me to this point. I remember the first time we'd taken it together, one of our first dates. I was always a bit of a party animal in my younger days and he must have seen that in me, known that I wouldn't have knocked back a line if offered to me. We'd had such a good night that each and every time after that when he offered me some, I took it. Of course I did. I was in love, infatuated by Marcus. Tall, handsome and charming and I was doing whatever I could at that time to keep the feeling of electricity between us alive. That first night seems like such a long time ago now. All of it does.

I sway to the music, twirl around the pole to warm up my muscles. Already I feel eyes on me. Likely the other girls watching me as I dance. Lizzy made me their coach when they first started. I showed them everything they need to know. Well, not *everything*. There had been no one to show me how to deal with the clients who wanted to buy sex after hours. That was one thing I'd had to figure out on my own and something I wasn't willing to talk about with anyone.

I twirl around again before gripping the pole and lifting myself off the floor. Marcus catches my eye as he stands by the bar next to Lizzy. I pull my eyes away from his gaze and pretend not to notice. He's watching me. He's *always* watched me. Now, after the stunt I pulled a few weeks ago when I'd tried to leave, he'll never stop.

12

LIZZY

I watch the door, expecting that the usuals will appear this evening. They always do, never miss a night especially when their favourite girl is on the pole. The idea that they'll get a private dance for a measly ten quid is heaven to them. Of course, no touching allowed however that rule isn't always followed closely, even by the girls.

Glancing down at my watch, I give a nod at Marcus and he disappears down the stairs to unlock the door. As the music starts up, I make my way from behind the bar towards the dressing room and knock on the door before opening it. Peering round, I see the girls adding the finishing touches to their appearance before they begin their shift.

'All good?' I say, watching their reflections in the long mirror on the back wall. They all nod and smile in reply. 'Amber?'

'Yes ma'am,' she smiles back sarcastically. 'Ready and waiting to take money from the sad bastards who shall cross our threshold tonight.'

'Good girl.' I return the smile and close the door behind me. 'Remember, tenner for a ten-minute dance and if they want more?'

'Aye, we know,' Amber says. 'Tenner for one, twenty-five for three, blah blah.'

I regard her suspiciously. Eyes wide, I think about whether Amber is sober and then immediately realise that most of the girls' senses are likely to be heightened. It's something I turn a blind eye to unless it affects the running of the club. Not that it normally does. I've worked here for around thirty years, started out when I was just eighteen, learning the ropes when my dad ran the club. Took over when he died, not that I had a choice. I know only this way of life, much like most of the girls. I've seen girls come and go, sometimes on a weekly basis. Amber has been part of the Angel Silk team for eight months now. She's my best girl, if a little self-destructive. She helps keep the girls on their best game even though she doesn't do much. The girls look at her, watch her dance. See the punters drooling over her and they want a piece of that to build up their cash. I think they're envious of her talent.

Amber reminds me a little of myself from when I was younger. I was always running my mouth, speaking my opinion or just being a sarcastic little shit. I hold a soft spot for Amber, not just because of that but because of her long service. No girls ever normally last the year even though I run a tight ship. This place is my livelihood, these girls my source of income. I won't allow anyone to fuck that up no matter how much of a soft spot I have for any of them. But I know how to look after my girls too and if allowing the odd line here or there is the way they can get through a shift, then who am I to stop that? They make their money and so do I. Tonight, I place a box of cupcakes down on the centre of the dressing table and I see their eyes light up.

'Just a little treat for you girls. I know you'll dance the calories off later.' I smile and so do they.

I watch the men who hover on a nightly basis and wonder what went wrong in their lives for them to feel the need to hang around here, pretending to be friends with the girls. Bringing them snacks, drinks and general chit chat at the bar in between dances isn't something I'm fooled by even if some of the girls are. These men want to believe they're in control of these girls because they pay for their services. Of course this is not the case, quite the opposite in fact. These men have no control over their own lives and whatever has gone wrong, they cling to the idea that this is the place they can come to so they can claw some of it back. My girls are very good at playing a role, pretending that the punters have them right where they want them.

So much has changed since I first came into this business. I wanted to be one of those dancers but my dad never allowed it. Not when he owned the place. Instead he had me run the club alongside him, learn the trade so that when the time came, I could take over. There were only around six girls. The oldest girl was twenty-five back then. Now, most of my girls are no older than twenty. The men in my day came to the club dressed in suits, made little noise or fuss. They sat back and enjoyed quietly. Nowadays, things are quite different. The way some of the men behave baffles me, like they've never seen the female human form before.

They come in their groups of five, ten, even twenty or so of them for stag parties, birthdays. Any excuse to come to see young girls strip off. And I say young girls because they seem so much younger these days. Breast, bum and face enhancements seem to be an attraction for men, and are much more readily available now than they were twenty years ago. The porn industry has a lot to answer for, and as much as I am happy to accept men into my club, I feel like they have an unhealthy, unrealistic view of women when they work in strip clubs.

'Right, I'm ready,' Amber says, standing up and wiping her nose. I was right.

'Have a good one, girls. You know where to find me if you need anything,' I say, turning my back and heading for the door. They're good girls, but if they stay in this line of work, on the wrong side of the pole, they'll never be rich.

I walk out to the bar and see that Marcus, my business partner, has already allowed a group of men inside. Mixed age it would seem. Stag do or lads' night out, most likely. They're already rowdy, so I decide to keep an eye on them. I've seen groups of them before, more times than I care to remember. I know Marcus and Tommy will keep an eye on them too along with the security inside the club.

I stand at the end of the bar as the girls take their spots on the poles.

'Lizzy, you got a minute?' I hear Amber say. I turn and she is standing behind me. Not at her pole.

'Shouldn't you be dancing?' I reply, raising a brow.

'I need an advance.' She hovers, stares at me intensely as she waits for my reply.

'What's up?'

'Nothing, just need an advance.'

'Amber, this isn't the time to be discussing this. Come and see me at the end of the night and we can talk about it then,' I say before eyeing her usual pole, indicating it was time for her to get to work. She remains in her place, continues to look at me as if silently pleading before dropping her gaze and moving away from me.

Picking my phone from my pocket, I glance down at the screen and a message plagues me.

I know what you did!

'You alright, boss?' I jump when a hand falls upon my shoulder.

'Jesus, Marcus!' I exhale quickly. 'You nearly gave me a bloody heart attack. Yes, I'm fine, why?' I say as I shut the screen off and slide the phone back into my pocket.

'There's a queue of guys outside, couple of stag parties and that. Looks like it's going to be a busy night.'

'Good,' I say. 'Don't let anyone in who's too far gone, don't want any trouble or self-important arseholes thinking they can lure my girls into more than they're entitled to. Oh and Marcus?'

'Aye?'

'Don't call me boss. We're partners, remember?'

'Sixty-forty.' He smiles before disappearing down to the entrance again. Sixty-forty was better than zero and that's what would have happened to me and the club if Marcus and Tommy hadn't come along when they did. The club was the only thing I had left that once belonged to my dad in terms of what he'd built up as a business. I didn't want to lose that, it would feel like him dying all over again. He was a good man, a good dad. But as a boss, there were times where I felt like our father–daughter relationship lines became blurred when it came to business.

My phone beeps again and the same message comes through again. The texts have been coming every few days for the last few weeks. The same words each time. *I know what you did*. A trail of ice-cold horror creeps down my spine and I shiver at the thought, at the memory. Pushing the images from my mind, I focus on the night ahead. I can't think about that. It's too awful. Too disturbing.

The beat of the music thumps in time with my heart. The girls sway around the poles and the men come in floods through the doors.

13

MARCUS

Closing the door, Marcus turns to Tommy and Rory who are sitting on the opposite side of his desk. As he takes a deep breath, he can tell Rory is nervous. And so he should be. Bringing new girls on the scene is a tough job. Marcus knows that better than anyone.

'So, Rory. How are things going with your new recruits?' Marcus asks, moving towards the desk and sitting down. He can see Tommy's expression. Pulling his face as straight as he can so as not to start laughing. They both know Rory is shitting himself and Marcus wants to ramp that up a little. But not so much that he'll scare the lad away. If he pulls this off, he could be a real asset in the recruitment process with Tommy.

'Aye, all good boss. The girls are ready and waiting to start tonight.' Rory sounds more confident than he looks.

'Is that right?' Marcus asks, narrowing his eyes. 'And you have profiles for these girls?'

Rory pulls a file out from under the desk and passes it across the table.

'Tommy, you've checked them out?'

'Aye, they're little crackers. Will fit right in.'

Marcus opens the file and stares down at the pictures of the girls. Young, fresh faced. No more than eighteen years old. Inexperience could be their downfall, but if Rory has done his job properly, then he will have sorted that out.

'And they completely trust you? Think you're legit and they've fallen for the "I'll do anything for you charm" you told us you had?'

Rory smiles. 'Aye, they have that. Have been all over me for weeks. I'll be sad to give up all that free sex. But it's like you said boss, on to the next.'

Marcus raises his head and fixes his gaze on Rory. Tommy was right, Rory was like a younger version of himself. And now, Marcus didn't want to kid on with Rory that he was in trouble. He wanted to pat the boy on the back and hand him a whisky.

'Right, get them up here and tell them to introduce themselves to Lizzy. She'll take it from there.'

Tommy takes a deep breath as Rory gets up and leaves the office. 'And you're sure she's still none the wiser about what's going on?'

Marcus shakes his head. 'Nah, she's not got a clue. She's got shit going on other than this place, Tommy. She'll be glad when more girls arrive asking for a job. The more girls, the more money.'

Nodding, Tommy pulls out his phone and gets up to join Rory outside. Marcus closes the file and slides it into the desk drawer before glancing at the computer screen which presents the club to him. He can see Amber now, dancing on the podium and doing what she does best, earning him money.

He thinks back to the other night when he'd gone back to her flat after dropping her off. He'd pushed her onto the bed and told her to do what he'd instructed. There had been no fight, no refusal from her. She knew better than that by now. Amber was not his girlfriend by any means, but she still belonged to him. However that night she'd stunk of weed, was off her face and it had put him off. Normally she turned him on so much he couldn't control himself, but things had changed. He knows he is the reason for that. If he has to sacrifice getting his end away so he can keep hold of her for business reasons, then he's fine with that. There's always Jade, although she never quite does it for him the way Amber did.

Things in the business are changing, and Marcus knows he has to move with the times. No longer will he pose as the doting, charming hero boyfriend. He had Rory and some other lads take over that side of things for him now. If he wants a woman for sex, he'll have to find one out with the business. Using his own supply of girls could get messy. It certainly did in the beginning.

14

LIZZY

The beat of the music coming from the club vibrates in my chest and the thrum of voices and laughter penetrates the walls of my office. However, my brain doesn't process it properly. I feel like I'm inside my own cloud of darkness as I sit at my desk, staring at my computer screen. As I read those eleven words, over and over again, I try to tell myself that it's spam. Junk mail. Nothing other than some scrawny little keyboard warrior trying to entertain themselves. However the more I read it, the less I am convinced that is the case.

> I'm closer than you think and I know what you did.

Who is this person? How do they know what I did? No one knows, not even the people closest to me, which isn't a lot. All the more reason for me to be sure that they are in the dark, unaware of my crime. Saying it out loud, admitting it to just one person would mean it really happened and that I was capable of doing something so horrific, so wrong. It would mean realising the person I'd become. Things are already so dark in my head and I can't look at myself in the mirror, not properly.

'Lizzy, I'm on a break. You got a minute?' Amber says, peering around the office door. I look up and pull down the laptop quickly, shutting out the past.

'Yes,' I say, glad of the distraction. 'Come in, take a seat. But make it quick, I'm interviewing two girls in about ten minutes.'

Amber sits down opposite me and I regard her expression as though she needs something, needs me to do whatever it is she desperately requires. I've known Amber long enough to know that something is wrong. Her hopeful eyes are heavy on mine and I don't have time to be sympathetic as much as I'd like to be. Without allowing her to speak I get in there first.

'Amber, why do you need an advance? Is it for drugs? Alcohol? Both?'

She sniggers and draws her eyes away from me but I don't fall for her attempts at a bad attitude.

'Well?'

'Lizzy, I take the odd line here and there. We all do, keeps us alive late into the night when we have to dance for the sad bastards who grace us with their presence. But I'm not so desperate that I would need an advance on my wages for a couple grams.'

I can't help but smile in response. Most bosses would sack her on the spot for her shitty attitude alone, let alone if they suspected her of taking drugs on the job. But I like her, I like the way she handles herself and how she handles what I've just thrown at her. What I don't like is how she is dodging my questions, and now my eye line.

'Amber, I don't care what you've got yourself mixed up in. All I care about is if I can help you out or not. I want to help, but I need to know what I'm helping you with.'

Amber sits back in her chair and takes a deep breath. She isn't going to divulge that information, I know her well enough to know that if she wants to tell me then she will. Until then, I won't be able to help.

'I need to get back out there,' she says. Getting to her feet, she doesn't hold my gaze and I wonder if I should stop her from leaving.

'Amber, you know where I am when you are ready to tell me what is going on. Until I know, I can't help you.'

She doesn't respond, doesn't even turn to acknowledge that she has heard me. I want to go after her, shake it out of her.

However, I know only too well, if you have a secret you want to keep hidden, you won't do anything to let it slip.

She leaves and there is a knock at the door. My new girls have arrived.

15

AMBER

I watch him. Marcus. My Marcus. He really is something. Kind, considerate. Generous. Would give you his last penny if it meant you would find yourself in a better place. I shake the memories from my head. Remembering him fondly, the images of the Marcus who fooled me flooding my mind, is something I don't want to do, but it happens all the time. And it's nothing but a let-down, a disappointing thought. It's humiliating in truth.

There are two definitions of 'My Marcus' now. The one who was there for me when my parents were giving me grief about spending too much time with him. He cared for me. Loved me. Because there is some small part of my brain that still stupidly believes that he loves me now, like he did back then when we first met. Strong arms that could wrap around me twice over. Arms that made me feel safe and secure as I trembled, cried myself to sleep. Strong arms that could make me feel like the most important girl in the world. I miss that feeling. I miss that version of Marcus. But he isn't real. Never was. He was only ever that version to wear me down, make me think that he was the only person in the world I could have in my life. I thought my parents were pushing me away because of him. But in fact, it was him pulling me from the life I had with them.

Now, 'My Marcus' is just boss man. Businessman and head of security. He watches me in a different way now. Lizzy has no idea what is going on in her club. No clue whatsoever. She thinks that Marcus and his team are what her girls need. She's wrong on so many levels. I worry for her when it all comes out. I worry for all of us.

As soon as things begin to unravel, we'll all be in danger. You see, he was My Marcus, and I was his girl. But I'm not the only one. We're all his girls, even if some of the others don't realise it yet.

Seeing his face every day, mourning the Marcus I fell for and knowing he never existed alongside knowing that he is one of the darkest and most dangerous men I have every met… why wouldn't I try to leave? If there is no one to save me, I should try to save myself.

16

JADE

One, two, three… Breathe. Just breathe.

The pain in my ribs is unbearable yet I push on, force myself to move. Another sharp intake of breath and the pain intensifies. I stop, holding the air in my lungs.

The sound of distant laughter echoes in my ears as I collapse onto my chest. The cold, wet concrete seeps through my shirt and onto my skin as I try to open my eyes.

One, two, three. Breathe. Just breathe through it. It'll be over soon.

Another pain.

Another blow.

I've always been scared of death, it was a real phobia. I'd looked it up on the internet. Thanataphobia. I don't suffer from the phobia, it doesn't affect my daily life. But I do think about it daily. When will it happen? How will it happen? Will I know about it?

It looks like my time has come. The strange thing is, I'm not scared now. I want it to come quickly, so I don't have to be scared of what they were going to do to me next.

-

I wake with a start. I'm upright. Short, sharp breaths cause a pain in my chest. I slow my breathing as my surroundings become familiar again. It was another nightmare. The same, recurring horror that I was subjected to in sleep. I can't escape that night whether I am conscious or not.

I let out a sigh, a long and deep breath of frustration. I am sick of this. So sick of feeling trapped inside myself. Inside the flat. I can't go out. I can't stay in. I'm hardly sleeping these days either. Losing so much weight is the only good thing to come out of this. I was a size sixteen when it happened. Now, I'm lucky to fit into a size eight. I worried about excess skin but I don't seem to have that problem.

'Morning.' A hand lies gently on my back and I smile, all of the worry and anxiety suddenly dispersing. 'You okay?'

I turn to Marcus and he is smiling sleepily up at me. This is the first time I've woken up and he's been next to me in weeks. He has been so busy at work, staying there for hours on end. Sometimes days. Looking after your own business is tough, he consistently reminds me when I mildly complain about his absence. However, I'm not complaining this morning. Not when he is the only person who can make me forget just by a glance. The light in his eyes makes the darkness go away.

'Yes.' As I lie down next to him, he props himself up on his elbow and stares down at me. 'Don't kiss me, I have morning mouth.'

He laughs as he nuzzles into my neck. His hands hold me close. Skin to skin. I can't help but succumb to him. I'm his. He is mine.

'Let's go out today,' he says. 'We could go for lunch? A drink? Shopping?'

I want so badly to go. I do. My heart wants to say yes, to jump up and shower. To be able to walk out the front door without even thinking about it is something I long for. My mind holds me back.

'Hello? Earth to Jade?' Marcus's hands squeeze at my skin a little and I let out a laugh.

'Yes,' I force the word out. 'I'd like that.'

The look on his face is priceless. He's proud of me for agreeing to leave the house for longer than an hour. Because lunch, a drink and shopping will take a lot longer than that. He pulls me closer, nuzzles into my neck again. I feel the muscles as my hands run over his back. I'm so fortunate to have found him. I feel a lot safer with him around. I love that he makes me feel this way.

I think about Paul then and wonder what he's doing with himself these days. It's a shame things got in the way of us. He was a nice guy but I had to end things between us. It just wasn't going anywhere. He was into the relationship more than I was.

'So, fancy cutting our time in half and sharing that shower?' Marcus says, bringing me back to reality. The cheeky smile across his face makes me laugh.

'You think we can both fit in that shower?' I reply, cocking my head to the side.

'If you wrap yourself around me enough, then yeah I think it's achievable.'

Laughing again, he jumps up and lifts me off the bed before carrying me to the bathroom.

As much as I want this to become the norm for me, to be able to get up and get ready to go out and spend the day with my boyfriend, I know that it's never going to be that easy this quickly.

As soon as I know we are away from the comfort of the flat, my rising panic will return. And Marcus will have to take me home. There is only so long that he will be able to put up with that before he will start to get annoyed by it. Things are going to get better. I will make sure of it. With Marcus's help, I'll get back on my feet and we'll be able to act like a normal couple. That's all I want.

I can't live my life inside these walls. I won't let what they did to me dictate how I live my life.

The sound of the water cascading around us in the shower drowns out the distant memory, the recurring nightmare that is my reality. As Marcus lifts me up, pulls me closer and my back rests against the cold tiles, I push the darkness inside me to the back of my head. As Marcus looks into my eyes, I know he can see past my trauma, can see me for who I am.

17

JADE

As we walk along the canal front below Marcus's apartment, the smells of the water and the city surround me and for the first time in a long time, my head is clear. There is no taunting, no laughter in the back of my head. All I can hear are the seagulls as they circle above. The swish of the river as it laps up against the edge. There's a breeze today, but I can still feel the warmth of the sun as it beats down on my face. This is where I want to be. Free to be able to walk along without the fear that someone will attack me. I feel safe here.

'Hey, you off in your own little dream land?' Marcus says, squeezing my hand.

I smile, close my eyes against the breeze and take a breath. A contented sigh to let him know that yes, I am in a daydream but I am also fully aware he's beside me.

'What you thinking about?'

'Nothing, actually. For the first time in a long time, I'm not thinking about anything at all. It's nice that my head is so empty.'

'Awe,' he says, pulling me in close. I'm against his chest, his muscular arms enveloping me. 'You mean I'm not in there?'

'Of course you are,' I laugh. 'You have your own little space in there.'

Marcus holds me close and for a split-second I think I'm going to start crying. Happy tears for the most part, but there is a part of me that I know is still dealing with the trauma of what happened to me. If it hadn't been for Marcus, goodness knows where I would have ended up.

'You know, it looks like fresh air and sunshine is the best thing for you. We've been out for two hours and you're fine.'

As soon as I hear the words, my skin begins to tingle. He's right, I hadn't noticed. Now that Marcus has pointed it out to me, all I can think about is the fear that has a sudden grip on me. I stare up at him, wondering why he would have pointed that out to me. Why couldn't he have just left it? I may not have noticed.

'Shit, sorry. I shouldn't have said anything,' he says, as if hearing my thoughts. 'But look, you're fine. I'm here. No one is going to hurt you. You are safe.'

'Am I?' I reply, my voice trembling a little more than I'd intended for him to hear. 'Because I don't feel safe. They were never caught, Marcus. The people who attacked me. It's as if they vanished into thin air. What if they're watching me, waiting to get me and finish me off so I can't tell the police what they look like?'

Marcus shakes his head and I wonder if he is getting sick of my anxiety. I wouldn't blame him if he was. I'm annoying myself these days. I never used to be this nervous. Before the attack, I'll admit I was a nervous person with little going on in my life. But never this intense.

'Jade, they won't even remember you. These types of people just move on to the next. As harsh as that sounds, you're nothing to them. So don't worry about them coming back to find you. You think they'd get past me?'

I smile at his enthusiasm to want to help me grow. I know deep down that if that were to happen, it would take a long time.

'Why don't we go back to the apartment, have a drink?' he asks. 'Just the two of us.'

Perched on my toes, I stretch up and kiss him. 'That sounds perfect.'

Marcus's apartment is like heaven compared to most places and I love it just as much as I love him.

74

Marcus opens up another bottle as I down the rest of mine. I've relaxed a lot more now that I'm back in the safety of the flat. The music is pumping and it's drowning out the laughter inside my head. Leaning back, I close my eyes and relax. Marcus's hand slides into mine and I feel his lips on mine.

'Hey, can I ask you something?'

'Hmm,' I respond. 'Anything.'

'How would you feel about doing a couple shifts at the club? Just serving the punters and that?'

I open my eyes and stare at him. 'What club?'

'The one I own forty per cent of,' he replies, as if I'd known this all along.

'Marcus, you told me you worked in security management.'

'I do, that's my job at the club.'

Maybe I misheard him. Perhaps he has told me this and I just didn't hear him because I had my own shit going on, taking up too much space in my head.

I take a deep breath and sigh. Does he think I'm ready for that? Do I believe I'm ready for something *like* that?

'You're doing so well Jade. The punters would love you. You're a good laugh, pretty. You'd fit right in.'

I've never been to this club. I don't even know where it is. But then, maybe earning my own money and being close to Marcus every night wouldn't be such a bad thing. Living with him and working with him, that sounds pretty decent. Maybe we could even save up some money and move to a nicer place.

'You think so? Don't you have to consult your business partner?'

'No, like I said I own forty per cent.' He shoots me a look I didn't expect but it disappears quickly.

'Well, okay. Why don't we go down and you can introduce me to everyone?'

Marcus smiles. 'That's my girl.'

I take a breath, try to steady the terror within. I can do this. I have to do this for Marcus. What better way to thank him for everything he has done for me? I'll be fine. I'll just have to manage my nerves. I can't go through the rest of my life being terrified of normal things.

18

AMBER

It's two in the morning. The last punter has just left the club. One of my loyal regulars for the last year. Lizzy has told me before that he won't pay for a dance from any other girl if it's my night off. Not that I get many nights off these days.

The music dies and the lights come on. I squint at the illuminated floor. The tables are littered with empty beer bottles and glasses. Successful night. I head to the bar where Lizzy is waiting for us to hand out our takings. As always, I've earned the most.

'Ninety for you, Amber.' Lizzy hands me my envelope and smiles. 'Good enough for you?'

That amount equalled to eighteen private dances at ten pounds each, of which the club takes half and I take half. That meant I walked away with a fiver per dance. A fiver. It was disgusting really, minimum wage was much higher than that. Not that I would actually see any of that money as cash. I was being paid by having a roof over my head and drugs in my veins. Not what I'd imagined for myself. I fake a smile back at her, knowing what she means. It doesn't matter what I earn, I think. Marcus will only take it from me when I get home.

I listen as Lizzy hands out envelopes to the rest of the girls. It was particularly busy this evening. I danced non-stop.

'Marnie, forty for you.' I glance up at Marnie, who has been with the club for six months. It's hard to read what she thinks of her takings for the night. Not that I care because I don't know anything about her other than her name. But I envy her because once we all leave here tonight, she gets to go home. I haven't seen her at the flats where me and the other girls stay, so I assume she isn't one of his 'recruits'. He'll be watching her though, seeing if she's vulnerable enough. If she's not, he'll steer clear. I hope for her sake she's a strong girl and this is only a stopgap for her. Unlike me.

'Leoni, twenty for you. What happened tonight?' Lizzy asks. I glance at Leoni who is shaking her head.

'Dunno Lizzy. Guys just weren't up for it th'night.'

'It'll pick up, don't worry,' Lizzy says, moving on to the next girl. I shove my envelope in my bra and head for the changing room. I have another shift to get to. Just as I place my hand on the door, Lizzy says, 'Girls, can I have your attention for just a moment?'

I turn back to face everyone. The girls are all staring at Lizzy and I wait for her to continue speaking.

'I just wanted to let you all know that Yasmin has decided to leave us.'

My stomach churns on hearing the words.

'How come?' one of the girls asks. My mouth has gone dry.

'She sent me a text message, telling me that she was sorry to do this but she was handing in her notice, effective immediately. Apparently there is a problem at home and she's been asked to travel back to help with it.'

'Lizzy, did she say anything else?' I say, almost choking on the words.

'No. We'll be sad to see her go but you know what they say, the show must go on girls. I'm sure she'll be back once things at home are sorted.'

I hear some of the girls begin to chat about Yasmin. *Why didn't she message me? I thought she'd have told us. That's shit, she was a laugh.*

I go into the changing room and close the door behind me. I pull my jeans and T-shirt over lingerie, and all the while my heart is thumping in my chest. Was that text to Lizzy genuine? Maybe she would still be at the flat when I got back? If she is, I'll ask her straight. If she's not there then I know it's a cover-up. He saw us chatting at the bar. Marcus. He'll have known Yasmin was telling me something she shouldn't have. She said it herself, that she shouldn't have said anything.

Pushing Yasmin to one side in my mind, I try to concentrate on the shift ahead of me.

I could say no. Decide that this isn't the life for me anymore and refuse to be part of this sordid situation I find myself in. Of course, I know it's never that easy. The last couple of weeks are testament to that. I've tried to get out of this. Tried to tell Marcus that I was giving him my notice. He laughed at me, told me that it wasn't an option.

'Don't start your shit, Amber. You know the score. How else are you going to pay your rent? How would you be able to afford your habit? Which, by the way, you're getting at a discount. I shouldn't have to remind you of that.'

The words ring in my ears as if he were saying them to me now. Although it wasn't his words that affected me. It was what he did. How he made sure I would never be able to escape his clutches. I'm a smart girl, I knew what I was getting myself into. In the beginning I liked being with Marcus, the boss. I loved that I was his girl and that I was the top dancer at Angel Silk. It was never my long-term plan but Marcus had other ideas. I never knew that I would have my freedom taken away. Marcus fooled me into thinking that he loved me. He fooled me into thinking that I loved him. How wrong I was.

Checking that I have all my belongings, I fling my bag over my shoulder and leave the club. Lizzy gives me a wave from the bar and I wave back. She really has no idea. None at all. I worry for her but I worry more for myself.

As I head for the door, I see Marcus standing outside, chatting to the other doormen. He smiles at me and I pretend to ignore him. The doormen utter goodnight to me as I round the corner and wait by the car. Marcus appears just moments later, unlocking the door. I climb in and pull my seatbelt around me, wishing that I had means of escaping the hell I was in.

'First week back, eh? It went well, I hear.' Marcus says as he closes the door and starts the engine.

'It was alright,' I reply. I grit my teeth at the fact that he knows how much I've earned tonight. He'll take half of it, if not more.

'So, you know the drill. I drop you back at the flat. When the door goes you open it. You're polite. No funny business Amber. Or this time…'

'I'm here, aren't I? I'm doing everything you tell me,' I snap.

He eyes me but I refuse to meet his gaze. He's much more dangerous than I ever gave him credit for. Now that I know what he's capable of, I'll have to be much more careful about how I conduct my plans.

'Don't get lippy, Amber. You're walking a very fine line after the stunt you pulled when you tried to leave me. You're lucky I was in a good mood that day.'

Unlike the day Crystal decided to leave, I think to myself. I've had a glance over the newspapers, watched the regional news since Yasmin told me about Crystal, since I read the report of the body being washed up at Luderston Bay. There's been no more information. No name released. If the police know who Crystal was, they are keeping it quiet. I can't let what happened to her happen to me.

He pulls the car onto the street and we drive out of the city towards the flat. Home and work. I'd prefer to keep them separate but Marcus is in charge of that, so the choice isn't mine to make.

The street is empty as we pull into it. The high flat consists of ten apartments, all of which are either owned or rented by Marcus. All of which are occupied by people like me. From around nine at night, until six in the morning, men come and go. All appointments are made through Marcus. All payments in cash and he takes most of my earnings.

In the beginning, it was small things, such as massages. Sometimes, the men only wanted to talk. About failed marriages, financial troubles. That didn't last long though and it didn't take long to work out that they were only building a foundation, trying to gain my trust. Because at that point, I was still Marcus's girl and he was mine. That's what he used to say to me. 'You're my girl, Amber.' It used to make me giddy with excitement that someone like him could be interested in someone like me.

He stops the car and kills the engine. I look up at my window and want to cry but I won't let him see the weakness in me. I take a silent breath and turn to face him. No longer My Marcus, but Marcus the Boss.

'I've left you a stash in the bedroom. Clean up before the first client arrives, eh? I don't want them thinking they've walked into a shithole,' he says, staring out at the street.

'How many tonight?' I ask, trying to sound as though it's a normal question for me to ask.

'You've got five. Two regulars, three new guys.'

As strange as it sounds, I'm relieved. The new guys will just want a chat. Hopefully.

I get out of the car and climb the short flight of stairs to the main entrance of the building and I think of that Arctic Monkeys song, 'When the Sun Goes Down'. Marcus really is the definition of scum. I hate him with every breath in my body. That's what I will use to push me on to attempt to get away from him again. One more try. If I fail this time, I won't get another chance.

As I climb the stairs, Yasmin's front door comes into my line of sight and I stop outside it. Holding my breath, I listen carefully for movement inside. Nothing. I hear nothing. Feeling brave, I lift my hand and gently tap on the surface. I wait. After a few seconds, I take a deep breath and lift my hand to knock again when I hear the main entrance door open. A rush of adrenaline forces me away from the door and I climb the stairs quickly to my own flat.

Why didn't Yasmin answer? I know why. Because she's gone. Marcus or his men have done something to her because she spoke to me about Crystal. She's gone and I feel like it's my fault. If we hadn't spoken, if I'd just kept myself to myself like I always had, she'd still be here. She would still be alive. I have no proof she's dead, but what else could have happened to her? Perhaps the same thing that happened to Crystal? As horrific an idea as that is, it would make sense. Yasmin told me about Crystal going missing, the suitcase washing up at Luderston Bay and how it was on the news. Now that I think about it, it's so obvious that the same fate has fallen to Yasmin as to Crystal.

I can't worry about that right now. I have to go on pretending that I don't know anything. It's my only hope to survive.

Opening the front door, I step inside and I know Marcus has been in here. Keeping an eye on things. Keeping an eye on me. I can smell the lingering scent of his aftershave. Smell the persistent lies he told me when I first met him, when I was blissfully ignorant to who Marcus really was.

Sighing, I drop my bag to the floor and go into the kitchen. I open the fridge, pull out a beer and drink it down quickly, knowing fine well I'll need more than a beer to get me through the night. I move along the small hallway into the one tiny bedroom and switch on the light. He's laid out what I've to wear for my shift and I shudder at the thought. Should I even bother to shower? These people don't care about what I look like, not really. They're here for a quick fix and that's as far as it needs to go. I decide a quick spray of deodorant will suffice and change into the lingerie and dress Marcus has chosen.

Then, I hear a knock at the door. My heart starts to race.

Again, I think. Here I go again.

19

LIZZY

'All good out here?' I ask the boys as I do a final check of the bar before closing up for the night. The girls have all gone home for the evening. Or should I say morning. It's almost four and I have never felt so drained. My mind has been racing ever since the messages started. Even though I tell myself it's not real, because no one knows what I did, I can't shake off the feeling of being watched. I suppose that's what the person behind the messages wants me to feel. But I still can't work out who is sending them and what it is that they want from me. It seems that the closer it gets to the anniversary of that night, the more and more messages I am receiving. So maybe I've been wrong the whole time. Maybe someone did see me, and they do know what happened. But why now? If someone did know, then why did they wait for so long before beginning to taunt me?

'Aye Lizzy, all good here,' Tommy replies. 'You want me to walk you to the car?'

'Thanks. Just need to grab my bag from the office and I'll be right out,' I smile back at him.

Shutting down the computer in my office, I notice an email notification on my screen and I choose to ignore it. If it's important, it'll still be there tomorrow when I come back in. Then I wonder if it's from my new mystery messenger. *Of course it's bloody not* I tell myself. *It's all just a load of bullshit.*

I grab my bag and coat off the back of the door before switching off the light. I lock the door behind me and when I turn, I notice the lights are off in the bar. It's dark. Black. So black that I can barely see a thing in front of me. A little surge of adrenaline hits me then and the hairs on the back of my neck stand up. Just like that night, I think. When I...

Pushing the thought out of my head, I rush across the floor to the exit and when I pull at the handle, nothing happens.

'Shit,' I whisper. I pull again. And again. Nothing. It's stuck. Or locked. 'Tommy?'

It's odd, to see the club from this perspective. Chilling, in all honesty. Even though I've owned this place since my dad died ten years ago, I don't recall ever seeing it in complete darkness. I don't like it at all.

'Tommy, are you there?' I call, making my voice so loud that the irrational thoughts inside my head worry that I have awakened something evil from the darkness. 'Come on, Tommy. This isn't funny. Open the fucking door.'

Panic rises in my chest and I feel like I can't breathe. No matter how deep a breath I try to take, my lungs don't seem to fill. I haven't had a panic attack since I was nineteen. Since that night.

Feeling along the wall to my left, my fingers fall upon the light switches and I flick them on. As the room is flooded with light, I settle a little before searching my bag for the keys to open the door. Why the fuck would Tommy lock the door, knowing fine well I was just coming out behind him? He was meant to walk me to my fucking car.

I take a breath, allowing the anger to dissipate. There will be a reasonable explanation for this. Tommy wouldn't have locked the door on purpose. Maybe it wasn't him. Maybe it was another of the security boys. My mind races at the same speed as my hands as they search for the keys inside my handbag. I don't feel their cool metal against my hands, so I give the bag a shake, hoping that I will be able to hear them jangling around inside. Nothing. No welcoming sound of keys hidden in a side pocket. They're not here. But they must be. I remember putting them back inside when I opened up twelve hours ago.

Tipping the bag upside down, I scan my belongings on the floor. No keys.

'Where the fuck are they?' I say out loud as I get to my feet. And then I remember. I locked the office door just seconds ago. I must've left them in the lock when I noticed the lights were off. Glancing over at the office door, I see them hanging there and I shake my head in frustration. Crossing the floor again and reaching for the keys, I grip them firmly in my hand and head back to put my belongings back in my bag.

'I'm going mad with these late nights,' I whisper to myself as I scoop up my makeup, tampons and phone. When I look down, at the floor, I see the photo that I have been carrying around with me. It's face-down on the floor and emotion catches in my throat as I pick it up to place it safely back inside my bag. I don't look at it. *Can't* look at it.

I get to my feet again with the keys still in my hand and when I look up, the exit door is open. Confusion washes over me when Tommy appears at the top of the stairs, staring at me with a blank expression.

'Ready boss?' he says.

'I would've been if you hadn't locked the bloody door on me and turned off all the lights.' Tommy's eyes narrow upon hearing my words, as if he is oblivious to what has just happened.

'Sorry, Lizzy. I don't know what you're on about. I've been waiting downstairs so I can walk you to the car.'

'Well, if you didn't lock the door then who did? Marcus? Because it wasn't me. I was in the office shutting down the computer.'

Tommy shrugs, scans the room with his eyes and then says, 'No, he was downstairs with me. Want me to take a look around before we leave?'

'No, it's fine.' I shake my head. 'There's no one else here except us.'

I shut off the lights and pull the door behind me. Lock it. The rest of the security boys are gone, except for Tommy and

Marcus, who is at the bottom of the stairs on the street. He's waiting for us to leave so he can pull down the shutter.

'Marcus, were you upstairs a minute ago? Someone locked me in and the lights were out,' I ask, disregarding Tommy's assurances.

'Eh?' Marcus replies. 'Nah, I was down here with Tommy waiting for you. Are you okay? You look like you've seen a ghost.'

I give a tight-lipped smile and then shake my head. Of course it wasn't either of them. I know that. So who was it? Fear grips at my chest but I don't show it. It runs so much deeper than what is on the surface and I don't want to move into territory where I might have to explain a lot more than I am willing to.

Tommy walks me to the car and when I get inside, I lock the doors, sit back and take a deep breath. What *was* that? I'm so tired. Maybe it didn't happen. Maybe my mind is playing tricks on me because I haven't been sleeping well. It's coming up for the date. Thirty years since it happened. Has it been that long?

Shaking the face from the vision my memory is putting before me, I start the car. As I'm pulling on my seatbelt there's a knock at the passenger window. I almost let out a scream in fright as I turn to face the window.

'Jesus, Marcus.' I roll the window down a little and I note the concern on his face.

'Are you alright?'

'I'm fine,' I lie.

'You sure? You look pretty shaken up. Is there anything I can do?'

Nothing that will change the reason I'm so jumpy, I think to myself. I shake my head, give another tight-lipped smile and put the window back up. I don't allow Marcus to say another word. If I do, if he exerts any sort of kindness, I might just break down and tell him what is on my mind. And I can't do that. I can never tell a living soul. It would destroy me.

20

AMBER

Before I open the door, I take a breath. In the beginning, I used to worry that when I opened that door to let the next stranger in, they would lose themselves in the act of role play, go too far and I'd end up dead. But I remember when clients first started coming to the flat, some were tolerable, some nervous, kind and sometimes friendly. That made the whole process a little easier to bear. It wasn't until I'd been with ten or so clients that I began to realise that my biggest threat was Marcus. If I didn't wear what he told me to or look my best then I was in the shit. Just the threat alone was enough to make me do whatever he said.

Exhaling, I pull the door open to client number one of the evening. It's a newbie. A young guy. Younger than my regulars. I smile at him and he looks so nervous I almost feel sorry for him. He looks up at me as if gaining silent permission before he steps over the threshold. I gesture for him to go through to the bedroom and I follow him. I take the few seconds I have to try to read him just by seeing the back of his head. Why does he want to come to a place like this? To see a girl like me? Is he lonely? Is he secretly a psycho who will stab me as quick as sleep with me? Unlikely, although not impossible.

As he turns and faces me, I can see the fear in his eyes. A bit like how I must have looked the first few times I did this. Doing this kind of job is terrifying in general, but when your boyfriend and the person you're supposed to be able to trust the most in the world sets you up for this kind of life, it's even more disturbing.

'Hi, I'm Amber,' I say softly, putting on my client voice. 'You must be?'

'Kev.' A one-word answer kind of guy. Great. Easy. Quick and over with.

'How long have you paid for?' I ask.

'An hour,' he replies. He says it like he is asking my permission. Although it's not mine to give. I don't even get to handle the cash. Marcus is a lot of things but he isn't stupid, he doesn't trust me and quite rightly so. If I had enough cash, I'd be out of here as quick as I could. But I have nothing and I am stuck here with no other choice.

'Okay. Have you chosen from our list how you would like to spend that hour?' I say, approaching him as he sits down on the bed. My veins are beginning to ache. My nerves and muscles tingling, indicating that I will be needing a top-up very soon. I can't think of that now, so I push the thoughts out of my head. I can handle another hour. I'd give anything now to go back to how I was before Marcus had me hooked on heroin. Back then, I'd feel like I just needed a joint to calm the nerves before a client arrived. Now, I feel like I am constantly on edge, regardless of who is at the door or what time of day it is.

'I've never done this before,' Kev whispers meekly. I regard him for a moment. He's been pushed into this. I can tell. He doesn't want to be here, or at least he doesn't think he does. I've seen this before in men. They're on a stag do at the club. They hear about what the girls can do out with closing hours. Their friends egg them on to pay for extras and when it comes to it, they freeze and the girl has to get it out of them, so to speak.

Kev is a little different though. In this moment, he genuinely looks terrified. I sit down on the bed next to him and he shifts. This is going to become a counselling session. Thankfully, I can handle that tonight. One less man to have to pretend with. I might only have to use my ears for listening tonight.

'Well, there's a first time for everything,' I reply as I place a hand on his forearm. He looks down at it and then into my eyes. That's when he starts to smile which soon becomes a laugh. My stomach lurches.

He gets to his feet, stands in front of me and spins me round so quickly I almost fall off the bed. He pulls at the little clothing Marcus chose for me this evening. I close my eyes and go to another place inside my head. A faraway place deep in my memories where I hope I won't remember this. But it doesn't work. I need something more in order to disappear.

Kev isn't meek or nervous at all. He was just playing a sick game. He'll have done this before with other girls. An hour with him will feel like an eternity.

–

I should have been prepared. Should have recognised the game he was trying to play. Pretending to be scared to lure me in. He was rough, unkind. I hate men like him, the ones who think that girls like me are property to him because he's paid another scumbag for my time. There are no men who are nervous around women like me in the field of work I do. There are no two ways about it. I hate all men.

I wait until I hear Kev leave. I don't see him to the door, but when I hear it close behind him, I get up and lock it. Biting my lower lip so I won't cry, I know I have some time before the next client arrives. I glance at the clock. Four-thirty – it's still dark outside and I'm willing the sun to rise so my shift can be over and I can have some normality before more of the same rolls around again later tonight.

My skin is itching now, my stomach knotting and cramping. My body is crying out for the warmth and relief that only comes from a needle. I go to the kitchen and open the cupboard where I keep my kit. I always say I won't do this. I won't be this person forever. But with every needle, I am a step closer to eternal hell.

As the needle pierces my skin, I barely feel it as the warmth quickly takes over. I'm gone. Far away now, in the place I'd wished for when Kev was here. I go to the bedroom and lay down, allowing the drugs to work their magic. Stomach pain ceases, my skin cools.

This is the part I long for. Where I can disappear and hope never to return. It's never enough though. Marcus makes sure there is only enough to take the edge off for a while. I've often thought about what I would do if I had enough to end it all. Would I have the balls to go through with it? To sink off into the darkness and never wake up? It would be so much easier to die, than to wake up to this reality again. This kind of life is never easy. Some girls don't get out alive. Look at Crystal and Yasmin. Others don't get out full stop.

I won't allow myself to be in either category. I will not become the next Crystal or Yasmin. I will get out alive and I *will* change my life.

21

LIZZY

Moving slowly along the driveway and pulling up outside my house, I kill the engine and lean back on the seat. What happened back at the club was all in my head. I know it was. I've allowed those stupid messages to get into my head when I promised myself I wouldn't let that happen. I know there is no one out there who knows what I did. What happened was absolutely necessary for everyone involved. I would have been stupid to let it go any further than it had. As much as it almost killed me, I know I did the right thing. But then what if I'm wrong about it all? What if these messages had nothing to do with what happened that night? They could be coming from a disgruntled ex-employee of my dad? I knew the kind of work he did back in the day, but I'm sure there will be people out there who would have seen the wrong side of him, lost money perhaps?

I shake my head. No. It wouldn't make sense for any of that to be happening now. It's too much of a coincidence.

Now that I'm home from a long night at Angel Silk, all I want is a hot bath, a glass of wine and to crawl into bed. I get out of the car and as I approach the front door, I can't help but notice that the security light doesn't flicker to life. What is it with me and lights tonight? Sighing in frustration, I pull my phone out of my bag and turn on the torch app. Living in the middle of nowhere on my own isn't something I'd imagined would happen to me at this age. But I'm married to that club and there was no way I was going to give up this house. Not after all the years my dad had put into making it my home. When my dad died, I decided to step back from the life of the Glasgow underworld. As much as Gordon Aitken's reputation lives on in the streets of Glasgow, I didn't want to carry on his legacy.

'No more drugs,' I'd said to him when he found out he was dying. He'd told me he wanted to hand over the club to me, that he wanted me to carry on with the business. 'I'll only do it if I can do it my way, Dad. No more rival gangs, no more enemies. And no more drugs. I won't be part of it. All I want from that club is an income.'

He'd been too weak to fight me on it. So, I got to do things my way and Dad sold off his other businesses to associates and people he had worked with and trusted over the years. Taxi firms, other nightclubs and I'm sure other ventures I'd been kept in the dark about. Dad was the only one who knew what had happened all those years ago. He kept his profits and tried to hand some to me. But all I'd wanted was Angel Silk. I accepted some of the money to do the place up, bought my own house with some and told him I'd donate the rest to charity. He'd laughed it off when I told him that. He didn't believe me. But when he died, that's exactly what I did. I didn't need all that money. All I needed was a roof over my head and a business that would keep the cash coming in. I suppose in some sense if I had kept all of Dad's profits I may not have needed to find an investor.

I shine the torch towards my front door and my heels clunk against the cobbled drive as I walk towards it. I put the key in the lock, turn it and open the door. The house is so big and quiet and stepping into it at this time of the night, when it's dark outside and the silence is deafening, always causes an uneasy feeling. But tonight is different. Worse in a way. Something is wrong. The security light is still in darkness and the house doesn't feel as welcoming as it normally does. I reach into the hall and switch on the light. Nothing happens.

'Oh for fuck's sake,' I whisper into the darkness. I can't be bothered with this tonight of all nights.

The torch from my phone illuminates the floor and I turn to close the door. That's when I hear it. A crack, loud and inside my head, like a white-hot poker has been shoved into my ear. I stumble back, dropping my phone. Keys clatter to the floor and I stumble again as another crack comes. This time I feel it on top of my head. The pain vibrates down the back of my head, into my neck and down my spine. I lose my balance and I fall.

'Long time no see, Lizzy.' A voice comes from somewhere around me but I can't focus on its direction from the pain searing in my skull.

I search the darkness of the house before I fall unconscious. I see nothing. No one.

I fall into a darkness deeper than the night and as I do, I feel hands on my wrists. I try to fight, try to stop what is about to happen to me, whatever that might be.

There is no mistaking that whoever this person is will be the same person who has been taunting me via those messages.

'It's about time we had a chat about what you did,' the voice says. It's closer now. In my ear.

I recognise it now. I know who it is. I know why he's here.

The heat of the pain in my head turns to ice.

He won't allow this to end any other way. I'm going to die here tonight and there is no one around to stop it from happening. Terror grips me as I drift out of consciousness.

22

JADE

Nerves begin to creep in as we approach the street where Marcus's club is situated. I haven't ever been in this part of the city before. It's a side to Glasgow I immediately didn't like the look of. A little more run down than the rest, seedier. It's not a place myself or any of my friends frequented when we were growing up. I say growing up, I mean when we were sixteen and attempting to get into nightclubs with our fake IDs. I look back on that memory with a smile and wonder what happened to them. My friends. I haven't heard from or seen any of them in a long time. We all drifted apart after we left school a few years ago, not for any specific reason other than our lives took different paths. I bet they're all doing really well now. I was doing fine until Dad left when I was sixteen and then my mum got a new boyfriend and buggered off to live in Spain. I was on my own and as much as my friends tried, there was nothing any of them could do to help me.

I got a council flat and went to college for a year to study admin before getting a job – a job I lost after two years of hard work and an unprovoked beating. I didn't think life could get worse after my parents deserted me, but it did. I didn't bother contacting Mum to tell her about what happened. She wouldn't have known what to say or do. She was never the maternal type. I was on my own until I met Marcus.

At least now I can say I am looking at a potential job. Bar work can't be too difficult to learn. Pouring pints and serving double vodkas sounds like something I could pick up easily. It's the fear of being out of the flat for longer than I have managed over the last few months that I am worried about. Marcus mentioned that a shift could be anything from four to eight hours and as much as I smiled and agreed I would manage that, I know deep down it could bring on a panic attack.

'You okay?' Marcus asks as we stop at the red light. He reaches across and rests his hand on my knee. 'You've been really quiet all the way here.'

'Have I?' I play down the rising panic. I don't want Marcus to think I'm a weak little woman. I want to be strong. I want him to see me as more than I am because I will become more than this.

'You know you have. Jade, just try to relax. It's all good, this is what you need. A fresh start.' He squeezes my knee before letting go and releasing the handbrake. He pulls into the right lane and indicates right.

Glancing up, I see the sign for the club. Angel Silk. The silhouette of a woman standing against a pole sticks out above the door. I frown as I turn to Marcus.

'You part-own a lap dancing bar?' I ask, trying to hide the shock from my voice. How could he have failed to tell me that?

'A gentlemen's club.' He keeps his eyes on the road.

'What's the difference?'

'The clientele.'

I take a deep but silent breath so that he doesn't sense my panic, although I know he can probably already tell I'm not comfortable. It's not just the fact that it's a lap dancing club that bothers me. It's the number of people I'll be surrounded by that worries me. Girls can be catty, bitchy. They can be nasty, I have been at the end of just how nasty they can be. Spent several weeks in hospital because of a group of girls. I don't want to put myself in a position in which I may have to deal with that again.

Marcus pulls up outside the door and tells me to get out and wait for him to park the car. Already my heart is beginning to race and the impending sense of doom is upon me. I want to cry, to tell him not to make me get out of the car without him, but I don't want Marcus to think I'm a kid. So, I get out of the car and stand next to the door and wait for him to arrive.

'You alright, hen?' a girl asks as she appears from the entrance to the club, smoking a cigarette. I glance at her and notice how pretty she looks. Tall, slender figure draped in a short, silk dressing gown. Very apt for the place. I can't help but notice the dark circles under her eyes even with all the makeup she has plastered on her face.

'Just waiting on my boyfriend,' I reply, trying not to make eye contact.

'You want one?' I glance at her and she offers out a cigarette.

I shake my head and turn to face the direction in which Marcus has taken the car. Hurry up, I think to myself.

'Your *boyfriend* brought you to a gentlemen's club?' She sniggers. 'Charmer, eh?'

'He *owns* the place,' I say trying not to sound too smug even though I want the ground to open up and swallow me. I don't want to be here. I want the safety of the walls at the flat. Of the locked front door and the ability to shut out the world.

The girl stops then, her eyes narrowing as if she is trying to penetrate my thoughts. She opens her mouth to speak but instead she puts the cigarette she had offered me back in the box and continues smoking her own. The look on her face, clouded by a bluish haze, makes me uneasy and I decide to start walking in the direction of where Marcus drove off to park the car. I've only taken around ten steps when he comes into view and I sigh with relief.

'There you are,' I say.

'Where are you going? I told you to wait on me at the door,' he replies, pulling me in to his chest.

'Sorry, but the girl at the door was acting weird.'

Marcus doesn't reply and when I look up at him, he is staring at the girl. As we draw nearer, she keeps her back to us. Marcus stops beside her and lets go of me.

'Tommy around?' he asks the girl.

'He's just inside.' Turning, she blows smoke out of her mouth and it whips around my face.

I can tell she doesn't like my presence. Jealousy, perhaps, by the look on her face. Maybe she has a thing for Marcus? Another unwanted problem to add to my list.

'Come on inside, Jade. I'll show you around and then introduce you to everyone.'

He takes my hand and leads me up the stairs. I don't look around but I know the girl with the cigarette is behind us, climbing the stairs too. We walk through a door and a wide space opens up. Inside, there is a bar to my left running along the length of the wall. Blue LED lights highlight bottles of spirits on glass shelves. The one thing I notice is the mirrored walls on the opposite side of the room. There are booths along the back wall, each with their own podiums and a pole in the centre which is fixed to the ceiling.

There are girls behind the bar, dressed in very little material. Underwear or bikinis, I can't make out which. All beautiful girls. It crosses my mind that I will likely be asked to dress the same way. I don't know how I feel about that and decide I'll speak to Marcus about it when we leave.

Music fills the room and girls are already dancing around the poles even though the place doesn't have customers yet. I highly doubt that the men who attend this club are gentleman-like but I don't say anything.

'Can I see behind the bar?' I ask, glancing over at the girl standing behind it.

'Sure,' he says and leads me towards it. 'Have you ever pulled a pint before?'

'No,' I shake my head. 'But I'm sure I'll pick it up quickly.'

My attention goes to the girl who was outside as she passes us. Marcus smiles down at me and lets go of my hand.

'Amber? Come here, I want to introduce you to Jade.'

Amber, I think to myself as she turns and begins walking towards me. She has a smile on her face but it's not genuine. She doesn't want to be around me. The feeling is mutual.

'You're starting tonight?'

Her tone is flat, uninterested and I want to ask her what her problem is. Instead I look up at Marcus and then back to Amber but before I can tell her that I'm only in to see the place tonight, Marcus says, 'She's doing a couple hours behind the bar first.'

First? What did he mean by that?

'Right, you'd better come with me and we'll get you sorted,' Amber says, turning her back to me and moving towards the bar.

'Right, I'll be back to pick you up in a couple hours.' Marcus leans down and kisses me on the cheek.

'Wait, I start now?' I panic. I'm not ready for this.

'What else did you think you were going to be doing? I've got stuff to do tonight, Jade. Amber will sort you out. Don't make a big deal of this. I'll see you around midnight, okay.'

It isn't a question. I watch as he disappears out the door and down the stairs. I glance over at Amber who is standing by a door to the right of the bar and tapping her foot on the floor. Impatiently waiting for the new girl. My palms are sweating, heart banging against my chest. I breathe through the rising panic and put one foot in front of the other as I move towards her.

'Sit over there and we'll find something for you to wear,' she says, pointing at a long, mirrored dressing table with several chairs lining the floor.

'Shouldn't you be showing me how to pour pints and stuff?' I ask, my throat dry and scratchy.

Amber turns and smiles sarcastically at me. 'Love, you're not pulling the pints. You're doing table services. Now, what size are you? You look an eight,' she says as she pulls a minimalist outfit from a rail next to the dressing table.

'No, Marcus told me I was working behind the bar,' I say as I shake my head at the outfit. 'And I'm not wearing that. Sorry.'

Amber smiles and hangs the outfit back on the rail. She walks effortlessly towards me in her ridiculously high platform heels and sits down next to me. 'Jade?'

I nod in response.

'I know what job you're here to do. Marcus told me last night. You're here to work the bar like I said. You'll take drinks orders, collect them from the bar, and serve them to the customers. Then…' She trails off and horror grips at my soul.

'And then what?' I almost shout.

'Think about what you saw out there. You're not here to pull pints, love. You're here to dance, make the men in here feel good about themselves.'

I shake my head, get to my feet. 'No. I'm the owner's girlfriend. He wouldn't bring me here to do that job. I'll speak to Marcus, he'll tell you this is all a mistake.'

Amber gets to her feet. She towers over me and when I look up at her, somehow I know she's telling the truth even though I don't want to believe it.

'Love, you can tell Marcus you're not doing this. But I wouldn't advise it. Just keep your head down, do the job and wait for him to pick you up. There are a few outfits and some makeup over there. Doll yourself up. A tip for you, do it all with a smile and it'll make things easier.'

Amber turns and walks out of the room leaving me on my own. I'm panicking. Breathless. Marcus wouldn't expect me to do this kind of job. He wouldn't. I'm his girlfriend. He wouldn't want me to dance around for strange men in my underwear.

I turn towards the door because I am not going to do this. Then I stop. If I walk out of here and refuse to work, it will cause a fight between us. I don't want Marcus to get angry with me. He's done so much for me since we met. Given me a place to stay, showered me with gifts and money when I was at my lowest. He loves me. I love him. I don't want to ruin that, or ruin our future together.

Turning to the rail, I pick an outfit that I think has the most material and put it on.

–

I'm standing at the side of the bar feeling the most exposed I have ever felt in my life. Amber stands next to me and she is smiling at the men as they walk through the door. Some in groups of five or six, others with one accomplice. I even notice there are men here on their own.

'Keep an eye out for that one there,' Amber says into my ear as she keeps her eyes on one man. I follow her gaze and see him take a seat at the other end of the bar, next to a booth in the corner. 'He thinks because he brings the girls snacks that he has more access than the rest of the punters.'

'Snacks? Do you mean drugs?' I ask, bewildered by the idea.

'No, I mean snacks. Multi-packs of chocolate bars, crisps, sweets. He sees himself as a sort of carer. I think it's just the role he likes to play. Creepy as hell if you ask me.'

Bringing sweets was the creepy part? The whole place and everyone in it made me feel that way.

Thinking back to when I first met Marcus, I would never have believed that he would be running a place like this. In the beginning, he told me he was in security management. Then I found out he part-owned a nightclub. Now I am standing here in lingerie, surrounded by other girls dressed the same and ready to dance for strangers for a few quid, I'm beginning to think deeper about Marcus. Why would he tell me only a fraction of the truth? Why would he want me to work as a dancer here?

'You okay?' Amber asks but it's a half-hearted question.

'I just…' I trail off, not sure if the next words to come out will escape my lips without tears following.

'Look. If you want my advice keep your head down, say nothing out of turn and you'll be fine.'

I glance at Amber and wonder how she got here. Before I can ask her, the music is suddenly louder and she is pulling at my hand. 'You ever danced before?'

'Not like this,' I shout over the music.

'Just watch me. You'll get the hang of it.'

She drops my hand and it falls to my side before she climbs up on a podium, surrounded by cheering men I hadn't noticed arrive. Her moves are effortless as her skin shines against the soft lighting above her. I can tell she has done this for a while, given how easy she makes it look. I can't take my eyes off her as she moves, her limbs seemingly free from her body.

How the hell am I going to be able to do that on cue? I turn towards the door in the hope that Marcus will be standing there, watching and laughing at his sick joke. Of course, he isn't and I have to face facts. I either dance, earn and shut up or leave and face the consequences of losing Marcus.

Amber eyes me and gestures to the podium next to hers. She's telling me to get up and start. I move, one foot in front of the other in these stupidly high heels. Wobbling a little as I climb up, I stand there watching her, taking in every move she makes. I feel eyes on me and notice that the men who are watching her are watching me too.

I freeze in fear, self-conscious that my darkest thoughts are exposed as I tower above everyone. Then, Amber's hand is in front of me. An offering. I glance at her and she is telling me to cross the space between our podiums and dance with her. I don't know if that is better or worse than dancing on my own. I take her hand and step across.

The men cheer louder this time as Amber works around me. I don't relax at all as she spins me around. That's when I see him standing by the door, just like I'd hoped. But he isn't laughing. Instead, his expression is blank as he watches me.

So I respond to Amber and begin dancing too. More sway than dance. But I want to prove to Marcus that I am grateful for his support in getting me back on my feet. Even if I am in six-inch heels and my underwear, secretly hating every second of this.

I spin slowly and when I look back, Marcus is gone and I feel sick.

23

AMBER

The rough material of his jeans rubs against the back of my leg as I lower myself over him. The silver lining of this is he could only afford a ten-minute dance so it will be over quickly. The smell coming from him is a mixture of soap, beer and sweat. I learned the act of breathing through my mouth in the very beginning and now I have it down to an art, but this is hard to push past.

'What is this, two for one?' he laughs and I grit my teeth as I eye Jade as she stands in the corner.

'Nah, call it a training course.'

He laughs and my stomach lurches a little. As I keep my back to the man and sway over the top of him, I lock eyes with Jade. She seems distant, worried, and I remember that feeling well. It was at this point in my own situation that I knew things weren't right. I was confused, hurt and scared about what was going on.

I finish the private dance and the man thanks me. He winks at Jade and I can tell by the look on her face that she is repulsed. Maybe even feeling guilty that she is technically cheating on her man. That's how I felt at the time too. It was all part of Marcus's plan, all in his thinking long before it reached mine.

I sit down and adjust the straps on my stockings, put my bra back on as Jade remains in the corner.

'Oi, you alright over there? You look like you're about to throw up.'

'I can't do this,' she says for around the hundredth time.

'Aye, you can. Like I told you, you don't have a choice. Plus, once you get into it, you'll end up enjoying it,' I lie.

Jade raises a brow as if she knows I'm not being truthful. I have to lie though. If I don't, Marcus will know I've told her the truth and I can't risk that.

'How long have you worked here?' she asks.

'Around eight months now.' Eight months of hell, I think. I'm Jade eight months on and I remember what it felt like to think I was in love with the most amazing man on the planet. Someone who supported me in my darkest time and helped me to get back into the world of work, as he called it. I never thought for one second he would end up pimping me out. It was happening before I'd realised it.

'You must really enjoy this line of work to still be here eight months on,' she says. I stifle a snigger.

'Who can truly say they love their job? I think we'd all much rather be at home on the sofa stuffing our faces with chocolate than be at work.'

She laughs a little and it's the first time I have seen her break out a smile in the hour she has been here. I begin to wonder what her story is, where she's come from and how Marcus managed to make her think she is in love with him. Because she won't be, she'll just think she is because of the way he's treating her now. That feeling will subside soon. Just like it did with me.

There is an awkward silence between us and there is a moment when we lock eyes and something inside me wants to scream at her to run away, to get as far away as possible and never come back. I tried and it didn't work. Instead, Marcus put me into what he deemed as isolation. I was refused food and water. I was injected with heroin which I am now highly addicted to. The first hit was like nothing I'd ever experienced. It sent me to a faraway land where I had no idea what was going on around me and I felt like I was away for days. I was kept in Marcus's isolation for two weeks after I told him I was giving up my line of work and now he's forced addiction on me so that I never want to leave. I want to warn Jade but I value my own safety before anyone else's.

'I could tell out there you've never worked a pole before?' I say, breaking the silence.

'No. You make it look so easy.'

'It is if you have good core strength. But don't worry, you can just sway around it and tease them. If you stick with me I'll get you some topless dances. It's the only way you'll make any money. Lizzy will explain all the rules and boring stuff later when she comes in. In fact, she should actually be here by now.'

'Lizzy?'

'The house mother. She owns the place with Marcus and Tommy who manage all of us,' I say.

'Marcus told me he was in security management,' Jade replies, confusion present in her voice. 'And that he owns a share of this place.'

Some truth, I think to myself. The only thing is he's left out the part about being the boss of several prostitutes and a dead body. She follows me out of the private booth as I walk across the bar area towards Lizzy's office. I stop outside and knock on the door. We wait for a few seconds and I knock again. Nothing.

'She's not here?' Jade asks, her voice barely audible above the music.

I don't answer, instead I open the door and I see Marcus sitting behind the desk. He has the phone to his ear and when he looks up, he looks past me at Jade but his expression remains neutral. He waves us in and I reluctantly move inside the office. Jade moves past me and sits down opposite Marcus with a stupid-looking grin on her face.

'Aye, no bother Lizzy. Sorry to hear that. Cheers.' He hangs up the phone and something inside me turns to ice. Lizzy isn't coming into the club tonight. That can't be a good thing.

'What's up?' I ask quickly.

'Lizzy's not well. Some sort of bug. The doctor has told her she needs bed rest for the foreseeable and she's asked me to let you girls know she won't be back for a while.' He turns away from me and smiles at Jade. 'How are you getting on?'

'Erm…' Jade pauses before looking up at me. I pray she has good things to say about me. 'It's all a lot to take in on the first night. Amber's been showing me the ropes.'

Marcus nods in my direction. It's not a sign of appreciation. It's a warning to keep up the front, otherwise I'll have to go into his isolation again, and this time I may not come back out.

24

LIZZY

I wake; my head is fuzzy and aching as I try to open my eyes. I'm surrounded by darkness and the air is cold against my face. Am I outside? I can't tell. I try to move but my arms are bound behind me. The skin on my wrists burns as I try to wriggle them. Trying not to allow the panic overwhelm me, I attempt to move my feet. Those, too, are bound at the ankles and it's then that I realise I am blindfolded. What the fuck is going on?

I hear a knock from somewhere around me and I can't fathom from where. I don't even know where I am. I could still be in my house. I try to think back to when I arrived home after work. It was around five in the morning perhaps. I remember the security light wouldn't come on when I got out of the car. The person who struck me over the head must have seen to that. Taking deep breaths, I try to remember as much as I can but the pain on the back of my head is clouding the images.

Another sound, closer this time. The shuffling of feet against wooden floors. Keys jangling. Whoever hit me and tied me up is still around and I don't know how I am going to get myself out of this. I think of Marcus and Tommy and wonder if I could somehow get a message to them. But I would need my phone for that and I'm not that stupid to think my kidnapper wouldn't think to take that from me.

Shit, shit, *shit*!

The person is getting closer and I hear them above me now, descending stairs. I recognise the creaks in the floorboards. I'm in my own house. I've lived here long enough to recognise those sounds. The door to the basement opens and the person is inside with me. They're breathing steadily as they inch closer to me and it's all I can do not to scream for help. Although, there is no point in doing so because my house is in the middle of nowhere and the nearest village is over two miles away. The words *please let me go* are on the tip of my tongue but I won't give this person the satisfaction of hearing my fear. That's not how I was brought up.

'Hi Lizzy,' the voice says. Male. Familiar. 'I'm sorry it had to come to this.'

I don't say anything in response to hearing him scraping a chair across the floor. It stops in front of me and the sound of my hammering heart is echoing in my ears. I hear him sit down, can almost feel his breath on me.

'You see, you didn't really give me much choice in the matter. Instead, you caused me a lot of anger, a lot of hatred.'

His voice is low and it vibrates in the air around me. I slow my breathing to show I'm not scared. But I am, because I remember recognising the voice before I passed out. It makes sense now, the messages, reminding me of that night. Yet, I could still be wrong. So I play dumb.

'Why are you angry with me?' My voice is trembling a little and I could kick myself for allowing it to show.

'Ha,' he laughs and slaps his knee. I jump and suddenly, he's pulling at my blindfold. He wants me to see him. And there he is, hovering over me. Those eyes so familiar, so unchanged. A few more lines around them.

'Awe, Lizzy, Lizzy, Lizzy. It's nice to see you up close after all these years of watching you. I have to say, I admire you. Deciding not to follow in your father's footsteps is highly impressive. Anyone else I've known in this world just falls deeper into it. But not you. Not Lizzy Aitken.'

'Why are you angry, Barry?' I ask. But I know, deep down, I know what he's going to say. 'Why are you so angry that you've felt the need to smash me over the head and tie me up after all this time?'

'All this time? You know precisely how long it's been, don't you Lizzy?'

My skin is tingling with fear. He knows and he's going to punish me for it. I don't blame him. Question is, how did he find out?

'Yes, I know how long it has been Barry. A long fucking time. Just get to the point.'

He sits back down opposite me and smiles again. The same smile he had when I was going out with him. I was just a young girl. A teenager. That look was the thing I loved about him, how it was able to draw me in. But I had to end it between us for both our sakes. I couldn't have any ties to him because our families wouldn't have put up with it. Now that smile turns my stomach.

'Do you regret it?' he asks.

'Of course I fucking regret it. Every single day of my life,' I say and the emotion becomes too much. The tears begin to flow and I am sobbing now. He doesn't falter, doesn't show sorrow. And why should he?

'You know, I've been thinking about this day for the last thirty odd years. I've fantasised about it. Wondered what you would say, what you would do. Did he know, your dad?'

'Yes,' I say through sobs. 'Yes, he knew I was pregnant but he had no part in what I did. He wouldn't have let me go through with something like that. Sometimes I wish he had known and he would have been able to stop me.'

Barry gets up and begins pacing the floor. He's not just angry, he's livid and looks like he is about to explode with rage.

'You mean you didn't think for one second that what you were doing that night would be damaging to more than just you. It was a good thing I was there Lizzy, to stop our baby from dying.'

I look up in shock. 'You were there?'

'When you abruptly ended things between us for no apparent reason, I decided to keep an eye on you. And it's a good thing I did otherwise our child would be fucking dead.' Barry's hands are on my shoulders now. Shaking me. 'Did you hear me? If I hadn't found our baby lying on the ground...' He trails off and I hear the emotion catch in his throat.

I feel my eyes widen as an icy chill washes over me. I can't breathe as the words echo around inside my head.

'What kind of person does that to their own child, Lizzy?' He sounds defeated now as I hold the tears back. 'You're nothing but scum, you know that? I won't let you get away with this. I'm going to make you suffer.'

I ignore his attempts to try to scare me. He's already succeeded in that. All I can think about now is what I did and how Barry had known all this time.

'Barry, where is our—' I start but before I can finish the question, I feel the back of his hand smash against my cheek before he puts the blindfold back on. I cry out from the sudden pain as a blanket of darkness consumes me. He could be the last thing I see before I die and by the look on his face and the venom in his voice, I don't doubt that he wants to be. I listen as his footsteps become distant. He climbs the stairs and I hear the door click shut. My face throbs.

What if he leaves me down here to die? I'll never be able to make things right or at least try to. I'll never know what happened to my child.

Wriggling my hands and feet, there is no give in what binds them together. In some dark corner of my mind, I thought that this day would come. I'd just never allowed myself to admit it. I'd always been looking over my shoulder, waiting for my past to catch up with me. I am defeated. There will be no escape from this.

25

JADE

I'm back out at the bar area. The club is filling up quickly with men of various ages. Stag parties, a fortieth birthday, a small group of lads around my age. My heart begins to beat faster at the prospect of having to do this. It's not something that comes easy to me, having to flirt. Because that's what Amber has said. Be flirtatious, make them think they can have you, that they own you. I could tell by the look on Amber's face that she didn't like allowing the men in here to believe they had that kind of power over her, but as I watched her, she danced and fluttered her eyes with such conviction that even I believed her.

I can't get my head around how Marcus would think I'd cope in a place like this. He knows about my issues with crowded places. I struggle being around people in a normal situation, and this is certainly not a normal situation. How will I do this without failing in my ability to stay calm?

I walk across the floor and step up on the podium. I size up the pole and remember what Amber told me. Pretend you own it, pretend to be confident and you'll be fine. I couldn't even walk home from work without getting into trouble, and I'm being expected to swing myself around a pole without breaking a bone or having a panic attack about being surrounded by all these people.

Wrapping my hands around the metal, I allow myself to fall back a little and spin around slowly. I watch Amber as she twirls around effortlessly, wrapping her legs around it and spinning herself around. I'm enticed as she does this, as are the men around us. I tear my eyes away from her and a man catches me eye. He beckons me and I glance back at Amber who nods. I've to go.

I step down from the podium and walk towards him, trying not to fall over and break my ankle. When Amber told me to get dolled up and then left me in the changing room on my own, I wanted to throw up. As I stood in front of the mirror, donning some skimpy underwear and heels I could barely stand in let alone dance in, another girl had come in and smiled at me. I saw the look in her eyes. Sympathy. Or was it empathy? Did she know how I felt because she'd done this before too? Or did she feel sorry for me? Neither answer would have made me feel better, but what did was the fact that she helped me to look as though I fit in. She helped do my makeup and sorted my hair into a more presentable style before showing me to one of the podiums. The one I'd just stepped down from.

I reach him and he's sipping on a beer bottle. He's young, around mid-twenties, and appears to be on his own.

'Hi,' he says. 'Can I buy you a drink?'

I don't know how to respond. Is that something I can allow? Neither Marcus nor Amber have said anything about that. Just as I open my mouth to speak, I feel a hand fall upon my shoulder. It's Amber.

'Trying out the new merch, Johnny?' Amber says with a smile. 'You know you can't buy us drinks. Only dances.'

He winks at her and then me. 'So, can I buy a dance?'

Fuck. No. I'm not ready. I'll never be ready for that.

'Why not get two for one?' Amber says. 'Ten minutes, two girls?'

I glance at her in thanks but she doesn't meet my eye – instead she grabs my hand and pulls me towards one of the private booths. I look behind and Johnny is following us with a creepy grin on his face.

'Don't worry,' Amber says. 'He's a regular and harmless. He doesn't even bother if we don't do a topless.'

I sigh with relief as we go inside the booth.

Johnny sits down and takes another sip of his beer and Amber starts to dance around him. She sits on his left leg and invites me to join them. I feel dirty, like a prostitute. Because isn't that what this is? Selling our bodies to earn money?

–

It's been four hours, my feet are on fire and I've done around two hours' worth of topless dances. Some of the men have been perfectly pleasant, some haven't. As the night has gone on I've found my confidence has grown but my panic hasn't dispersed. Amber has been checking in on me every now and then, checking to see if I'm okay. I don't know if it's genuine or not, due to the questions she asked me.

How'd I meet Marcus? How long ago? Did he tell me about this place from the beginning?

There's clearly a history of some kind between them. It could be nothing but I want to know who I'm up against here. Marcus is mine. I won't share him. Maybe I'm being paranoid. Perhaps she's just one of the best in the club and he wants me to learn from the best. That doesn't explain the look on her face though when I first arrived outside the club. She looked at me with an expression I couldn't work out.

'So Jade, how'd you find the first night?' Amber asks as I slip my jeans back on.

'Surprisingly fine. I didn't think I'd say this but it was actually fun,' I lie. I feel sick. All I want to do is go into the bathroom and throw up because my body is trying to reject the disgust and anguish of what I have just done. But I lie because I want to gain her trust so that perhaps she'll open up to me.

'I remember that feeling too,' she replies. 'The novelty wore off once I met the first arsehole who thought because he was paying for a dance he had the right to put his hands on me.'

I look up as Amber speaks and I can't hide the horror from my own expression. 'Oh my god, what did he do?'

Amber stares at me for a second and then purses her lips. 'It didn't take a genius to work out what was on his mind.'

'So what happened?'

'There was a commotion, he screamed. Lizzy appeared in the booth as I was dragging him out by the balls. Marcus threw him out and that was it.' She's filing her nails and not looking me in the eye.

'Marcus threw him out?'

'Yeah. Shame he doesn't do that with all of them.'

Her words make me stop and I shoot her a look. What did she mean by that? Marcus isn't the sort of guy to allow anyone to get hurt.

We both turn when there's a knock on the door and in quick succession, it opens. Marcus peers his head around the door and looks past Amber towards me. 'Time to go.' I finish getting dressed and get to my feet, as does Amber.

'Thanks Amber,' I say. 'See you soon.'

I walk through the now deserted club and Marcus is a few footsteps in front of me. I try to catch up to him, to hold his hand but his paces are wider than mine and I remain behind. Passing by a man on the stairs, Marcus gives him a nod and the man smiles at me. I return the smile and follow Marcus to the car. He is silent the whole way and something inside me unsettles.

He opens the passenger door and I climb in. As Marcus walks around to the driver side, the unsettled feeling in my stomach intensifies. Something has annoyed Marcus. I haven't seen him like this before.

'Are you okay?' I ask.

'Six nights a week,' he replies as he pulls on his seatbelt.

I don't answer, only look at him in silence.

'When Amber said see you soon, she meant you'll be seeing her six nights a week. You'll work nine until two. I'll drop you off and pick you up. You'll earn five of every ten pounds paid for a private dance. So, no dance, no wage. The money goes through the club and then comes direct to me.'

He starts the engine and pulls out of the parking space at the back of the club. As we drive along in silence, I try to choose my words carefully. He's on edge and I know that's not my fault. How could it be? I've done everything he's asked and now he wants more from me. Six nights a week is a lot. I try to play nice. I don't want to argue with him and right now isn't the time to challenge him. I can tell by the look on his face that it would be a stupid thing to do right now.

'Marcus, if I work here six nights a week, I'll never see you.'

'Welcome to the world of full-time work, Jade.'

My heart lurches at how cold his voice has become. I don't feel good about this.

'But don't you feel weird that I'm your girlfriend and I'm dancing for other men?'

'Why would I feel weird? It's just a job, Jade. Business. Get over it, I have.'

I want to cry. Why is he being so distant, so cold about this? I want to refuse to do this but I know it'll make the situation worse.

'So, Amber seems nice,' I say, trying to lighten the atmosphere between us. My voice almost cracks with anguish, giving me away.

'Is that right?' Marcus keeps his eyes on the road as he turns on to the next street.

'Yeah, she showed me how it's all done. Although I could see in her eyes that she was pretending to like me. Tolerate me, even.'

'Amber is there to do a job. End of story.' His voice is low, like he's keeping a lid on some sort of hidden truth.

After around a twenty-minute drive, we're back at Marcus's flat. I sit down on the sofa and he sits next to me. I can't hold it in any longer, I have to ask him.

'Is Amber an ex-girlfriend? When we arrived at the club earlier, she wasn't very forthcoming. Then as soon as you told her to show me the ropes, she obliged immediately. And she was asking me question after question. How long had we been together? Did I know about the club?'

I take a breath and Marcus stares at the small whisky bottle sitting on top of the cabinet. He gets to his feet and walks towards it. Placing his hand on the bottle, he turns to face me. 'I thought this might happen. But she's the best dancer we've got. So I had no choice but to pair you with her.'

'Thought what would happen?' I reply, my heart pounding in my chest.

'Yes, she is an ex-girlfriend. From a while ago. Look...' He opens the bottle, pours a small amount into a glass and swallows it back. 'I'm not going to go into all the details, however when I said that I was ending things between us, she got a bit irate. She said that she wouldn't accept the end of our relationship and she...'

I don't say anything to fill the gap he's left. I just wait for him to continue, dreading what he is going to say.

'Well, she tried to kill herself.'

Shit.

'You see, Amber has a bit of a drug problem. Heroin. She tried to overdose. Of course I found her, got her the help she needed. She has a long road ahead of her but that's why she is still working for the club. If I'd turfed her out on the street she would be dead by now. And so in giving her a role to play with you, I thought that it would mean her being able to focus on something else and she might be able to save herself.'

I shouldn't feel jealous but I can't help how it overwhelms me. He's thinking about Amber in a compassionate way, like he still cares deeply for her. The guilt has got to him and he feels sorry for her.

'Don't you think in doing that you might be leading her on a bit?' I reply. 'Like, making her think that there might still be a chance with you by keeping her around?'

Marcus places the glass down on the side of the counter and faces me. He takes my face in his hands and smiles. 'Like I said,

I'm not going into details about it. So let's just leave it like that, eh?'

He lets go and disappears from the living room, leaving me on my own with my thoughts swirling around in my head. If I wasn't before, I can be sure now that there's still something going on between Amber and Marcus. If I want to find out what, I have to be discreet. I'll have to befriend Amber as well as deal with my anxiety about working at the club. It's the only way to keep Marcus happy. If I refuse, he could kick me out and I'll be back to where I started. Alone.

117

26

LIZZY

My body slams off the side of something cold and hard, metal-like. My head is fuzzy, still sore from when Barry hit me from behind. I try to control my breathing as much as possible but it's hard when the surface beneath me won't stop shaking. I pleaded with him not to put me in the car, but he wouldn't listen and stuffed a rag into my mouth before putting me in the boot.

He wouldn't tell me where he's taking me. Far away so that he can kill me and dispose of my body, no doubt. What I did was unforgiveable, I know that. But do I deserve to die because of it? I don't think so. But there isn't much I can do about it from back here, tied up and in darkness. I'll have to wait until we get to his destination to be able to work out how I am going to get myself out of this. I'll try to contact Marcus and Tommy. They'll be wondering where I am. And my girls, who will be looking after them properly?

Thinking about my dad, I wonder what he would be doing right now if he was still alive. He would have every one of his men out looking for me across the city, knocking down rival doors and threatening anyone he could in order to save me from this situation. But he's not here and that is not an option for me. I am going to have to think of some other way to deal with this. Perhaps play to Barry's heartstrings? Talk about what we meant to each other all those years ago in the hope that I dig deep enough and find his conscience. Even I know it's too late for that after what I did but I have to try. I'll just have to be patient until we get to where he's taking me.

The car veers sharply to the right and I slide across the small space, smashing my ankles against the metal. The car picks up speed and the sound of the engine is a lot louder in here than I'd realised it would be. It almost drowns out the thought that I might not get out of this space alive. We've been moving for what feels like forever now but I know that it's likely been around half an hour, long enough to get me away from civilisation so that if I did manage to make a run for it, there would be no one around to help me.

The car halts suddenly and I hear Barry get out. Footsteps on gravel as he moves around the car to the back where he has me contained. The boot opens and he's standing above me, staring down at me expressionless. He hooks a hand under my arm and pulls me up before throwing me over his shoulder and carrying me away from the car. It's still dark so I can't make out where we are and the fact that I'm upside down is causing a pressure in my head worse than before.

'Where are you taking me, Barry?' My voice is strained.

He doesn't answer and that's when the tears start. He really is so angry with me that he wants to kill me. Why else would he bring me to the middle of nowhere?

'Ah, you made it. She had much to say for herself?' It's a voice I don't recognise.

'Is her room ready?' Barry asks, ignoring the question.

'Aye it's ready. Does he know she's here?'

My stomach lurches at that question.

'Of course he knows,' Barry says as he continues walking with me.

We're in a house, I think. I large house. A dull light glows from somewhere at the end of the hallway and music plays somewhere. Barry puts me down and forcibly sits me on a sofa where he cuts the ties on my ankles.

'What is this place?' I ask, wondering why Barry has decided to untie me.

'That's none of your concern.'

I stare at Barry in disbelief. 'Is this your house?'

He ignores me and starts fiddling with his phone. I look around the room. It still vaguely resembles a lounge. Couches on either side, lamps, curtains. No television.

'Why did you bring me here, Barry? You didn't have to force me. You could have just contacted me like a normal person, I would have spoken to you,' I say, fear now turning to anger.

Barry laughs and begins pacing the room. I look past him to the door. It's closed.

'You know that's not true. Come on Lizzy, you had the same upbringing as me. My dad and yours never saw eye to eye. Rivalry at its best. Never mix with the enemy, they used to say. Did we listen? Did we fuck, now look where it's landed us.'

He's angry but calm all at once. He's right, I was warned by my dad never to mix with the enemy and Barry *was* the enemy back then as was his own dad, Andy. They were what my dad called dirty, got themselves into business that he wouldn't dream of and that was why I was to have nothing to do with Barry in my day. Being the teenage daughter of a top Glasgow gangster meant that I thought I could get away with whatever I wanted, including going against what my dad told me to do. That didn't work out too well for me. When I think about it now, my dad's work probably didn't differ much from Andy's. The thing that angered my dad about Andy and his family was the fact that they existed in the underworld at all. Competition wasn't a bad thing in business, but when it came to the drug and gun trade, among other things, then competition was the last thing the big bosses wanted to deal with.

'Anyway, big Gordy isn't here now, is he? Neither's my old man but hey, we can continue their great work, can't we?' Barry smiles at me. 'Word is you decided not to, instead you're running a legit business over at that Angel Silk. Things going well, are they?'

I turn away from Barry. I should have listened to my dad all those years ago and I wouldn't be in this mess.

'Oi, I asked you a question.'

'Yes, things are fine.' I straighten my back, look him in the eye as I spit the words out like venom. If he wants to kill me then I'm not going to go out looking like some pathetic, terrified little soul. I'll go out with the attitude my dad gave me. 'Look Barry, I don't have anything you'd want so just do me a favour, eh? If you're going to kill me just fucking get on with it otherwise let me go.'

Barry moves towards me, sits down next to me. As his weight falls into the sofa cushion, I feel my body fall towards him involuntarily. I try to shift my position but it's difficult with my hands still bound behind my back.

'Still got some of that Aitken fire in your belly there, Lizzy. I like it, Gordy would be so proud.'

The sound of my dad's name on his lips makes me want to erupt. I let my side down by allowing my teenage self to be carried away by my lust for Barry when I should have known better.

'What exactly is it you want from me, Barry? I mean, you break into my home, tie me up and bring me here. You haven't been clear other than the fact that you know what happened.'

Barry cups my chin with his hand and smiles at me. 'All in good time, Lizzy. You'll find out what is happening all in good time.'

'You know, when people realise I'm missing, they'll contact the police and they'll come looking for me. You won't get away with this.'

Barry laughs and his hand falls from my face. 'Sweetheart, you have absolutely no idea what I'm capable of. They police have zero interest in me. They never have and never will. The sooner you accept that the better.'

27

AMBER

Closing the door behind him, my last punter of the night leaves me alone in the flat and I breathe a sigh of relief. I can't take much more of this, but I have to pretend all is well so that Marcus doesn't isolate me again. Last time he did that, he turned me into a fucking heroin addict. He made sure I had no other choice but to stay put and bow to his commands, make him money by doing anything I'm told by any man who walks through my door.

My skin is beginning to itch again, an unbearable unreachable itch. I hate that I'm happy to know that Marcus will be here soon, to pay me in drugs. How has my life come to this? A lap dancing prostitute with a drug problem. I was doing okay before I met him. My job wasn't the most glamorous, I'll admit. I worked at an insurance company, it was boring and the money was basic. But it was mine. Something I was in control of. My interest in studying art at university was growing and I had saved up some cash so that I had money to live on once I finally got started on my degree. I didn't have much, a grand if that. My parents said they would help me out once I had my offer and I remember them being so excited for me. Then I met Marcus and fell in love, hard and fast. And that grand went on rent as soon as I moved in with him at his flat. Not the one I'm in now but his own flat, the luxurious penthouse that could easily belong to a millionaire. And I'd been happy to pay rent because I loved Marcus and he loved me. I thought he had, I believed him so quickly.

He talked me up to Tommy, said how proud he was of me about wanting to go to university. Said it was a turn-on to have a girlfriend with intelligence as well as good looks. I'd been flattered. What he was doing was building me up, making me feel like he was proud to have me by his side. In reality, he was building me up for a fall and fall I did, from a great height. Soon, I gave up my job in the insurance company. When I found out that Marcus part-owned Angel Silk, he told me that I didn't have to worry about work, that he would take care of us both, how life was too short and that he wanted to spend every second with me. Our relationship was passionate and intense and so I gave up my job. I was addicted to him and he knew it. That was why it was so easy for me to believe that working the bar at the club was right for me. For us. I actually thought being a dancer at Angel Silk would be cool and I'd be good at it because I was physically fit and healthy. I took to dancing as though I'd always been a dancer and I'm ashamed to admit that in the beginning I loved it. It turned quickly once Marcus had near enough broken my relationship with my family and I had no one to turn to. The words 'we told you so' kept ringing in my head when I thought about telling them what was going on.

When I think about what has happened between us since then, it's like I'm thinking of someone else. Like their memories are being projected into my head from a faraway place.

I pour a glass of water for myself and sit down on the sofa just before Marcus appears at the front door. He lets himself in, of course, as if he lives here and throws a small bag at me. I stare down at it in disbelief. That's it?

'I've been thinking about when you told me you were giving me your notice and I've decided that this is the only way I can keep you from going to plan B.' He lights a cigarette.

'I've already told you that there is no plan B, Marcus. You made bloody well sure of that by making sure I got addicted to something only you can get for me.' I spit the words at him and I see the anger in his eyes.

'Yes, I fucking did, Amber. You didn't really leave me much choice, did you?'

I shake my head, knowing fine well that it was always his plan for things to go this way for me. The choice was never mine, always his. I was never his girlfriend, always his employee. I just didn't realise it until it was too late. It's what happens to all the girls he's been involved in. God knows how many that actually is. It's what will happen to Jade, no matter how compliant she is.

'Anyway, I came here to tell you something. You're moving premises.' A thick plume of bluish smoke rises above his head and my stomach drops. 'I don't know when yet, but you're much more valuable to me than just dancing at the club.'

My stomach lurches when I hear that. With Marcus, he can make things as bad as he has to for me in order to earn more money.

'What do you mean? Another club?' As I say it, I pray that it is another club. Just more dancing. But in my heart I know it's something darker.

'Nah,' he says, sucking on a cigarette I hope will choke him to death. 'It's like a gentlemen's club but without so much dancing. You'll be living there soon enough but for the time being you'll stay here.'

Fuck. He's forcing me in deeper than I could have imagined.

'Why can't I just stay here?' I ask, trying to sound as unfazed as possible. I'm not stupid, I know what he's doing. He's sending me to a fucking whorehouse and there is nothing I can do about it. Or is there? Why don't I just leave? Tell him that he can't control me anymore and walk away. If I go home now, tell my family what has been going on, they'll protect me. Won't they? We could tell the police about his threats, about the girls at the club and the plan for the new premises.

'Oi, what would you rather? Organised clients for regular income, or that I chuck you out on the street? You think you'd survive out there, working on your own? I don't.' He says it like he's doing me a favour. 'In the meantime, I want you to continue training Jade so that when the time comes for both of you to make your transition, she'll be as capable of making money as you. You'll go back to the club from time to time but for the most part, you'll work from the new premises.'

I nod, unable to decide whether or not to conjure up enough energy to fight him on this. Whether I want to drag my family into my mess. He would hurt anyone he thought was important to me just to keep me here.

'And keep your mouth shut about this when it comes to Jade. Just do your job and wait for my instructions. Got it?'

I'm silent as he waits for a response. Then I nod. As he is about to leave, I call his name. He turns, glowers at me. 'What?'

'I'm not going there. To that place. Marcus, I want to go home.'

There, I've said it. And with conviction too. I feel my heart begin to race because I know he isn't going to react well.

'You want to go home?' he asks. 'To your parents?'

I nod again, straightening my back. 'Yes. I'm not going to the new premises. I'm not going to become a live-in prostitute for you, Marcus. I'm not your property and you don't get to tell me what to do.'

Marcus opens his mouth and laughs loudly, almost hysterically. I take a breath, ready for the anger to kick in.

'Amber, sweetheart. You're not going anywhere other than where I take you. The only way you will leave me is in a fucking coffin. In fact, I might not even grace you with that. You've got to remember that you're a junkie, Amber. A junkie who relies on me to get your drugs. And if I hear that kind of shit come out of your mouth once more, I'll make sure your next fix is so strong you won't come out of it again, do you understand?'

Marcus has stopped laughing now. His eyes unblinking, and his lips pull into a tight line.

'I said do you under-fucking-stand me?' he bellows, grabbing my face with his right hand and a clump of hair in his left. 'Don't test me Amber or I'll fucking inject you when you're asleep so you never wake up, along with that family of yours. Got it?'

'Yes,' I force the word out.

'Good.' He lets go and shoves me and moves to the door. I jump as he slams it and as I stare down at the bag of powder, my eyes filling with tears. If I had enough willpower to save it, to save enough of those bags for one huge hit, I could put an end to all of this myself. No more pain, no more selling my body to benefit Marcus's pockets. But I can't do that, I don't have the guts for a start. I'm not ready to die because of someone like him. I won't allow him to ground me down that much so soon.

I feel sick at the thought of going to another place. It will be nothing like the club. I'll be stuck in a room for men to come and look at me as if I were a page in a fucking catalogue. As much as I hate the club, the dancing gives me a focus, it's my way of keeping physically fit. And it's better than being sent to a place where the clients would become relentless. One after another.

The faces of my family creep into my head on a dark cloud. Mum, Dad and my sister. My nephew. I miss them so much and I start to cry, long and silent sobs threaten to burst out of my chest. Do they miss me? They were right in their thoughts about Marcus. They saw through him long before I did. I can't believe I didn't listen to them. I allowed my heart to rule my head. They would never have said anything to hurt me, or even Marcus. If they knew what I was going through right now, they would do anything to help me. But of course, Marcus has made sure that I don't have any contact with them. He was clever like that, making me fall for him so hard that I couldn't see past him.

Is it the same for the other girls in my building? They're prostitutes the same as me, but not all of them dancers at Angel Silk. Are they drug addicts like me? Did Marcus do to them what he did to me and plunge a needle into their arms to trap them here?

The thought that men like him exist makes me feel sick. The punters at the club are just as bad. Their attendance and money only keep Marcus's wheel spinning and girls like me in an eternal hell. I think of Yasmin now, wonder what happened to her. Lizzy said she had decided to leave and told her in a text message. Something about that doesn't sit well with me. Maybe Marcus knows Yasmin had been blabbing about Crystal and he got rid of her. If Yasmin is dead, then it means any one of us could be next.

I suppose I might never know the individual stories of each girl at the club and if their story is similar to mine because if I'm too fearful to talk to them about what's going on, then they will likely feel the same. Marcus has me spinning on his wheel of drugs and prostitution so fast, that I am pinned down and may never be able to get off. He won't slow down.

28

MARCUS

Swallowing the last mouthful of whisky, he places the glass down on the counter and glances at the photograph on his phone. A family one: himself, Tommy and his dad. Family was important and going into business with family was the only sure way that he wouldn't get screwed over. Of course there are the younger lads, the new generation but he's been very careful as to who and how he recruited them. They're from his old haunts, where he grew up. They're just like Marcus when he was young, bold and determined. The McAdam name still ranks highly in the East End of the city and Marcus knew that if the opportunity came up, these young lads would jump at the chance to work for him. And that is exactly what happened. No one ever messes with the family, certainly not in Marcus's lifetime anyway. Of course, there are rivals all over the place, but word is that the biggest rivals are no longer a threat and so Marcus knows it's time to make his mark.

'You wanted to see me, boss?' Rory says as he peers round the door.

'Aye, come in,' Marcus replies. Tommy stands by the window and Rory glances at him before setting his eyes back on Marcus.

'What can I do fur ye?' Rory asks, standing up straight as if he's on a job interview. Marcus supposes he is.

'How's things going, Rory? The girls you're recruiting, they're complying with everything you're asking of them?' Marcus asks, offering the young lad a cigarette. Rory shakes his head and clears his throat.

'Well, as you know boss, they're now working fur ye at the club. I'd say they're still pretty pleased with the attention am giving them. Aye, they're complying and without much complaint if I'm honest. Seems they're a couple of good ones. Lonely, major family issues they want to get away from. They've only been too happy to accept my companionship.'

Marcus glances at Tommy and smiles. So far so good. Tommy was right, Rory is just like him.

'And they're at the end of the phone whenever I call. Eager to please, ye know.'

'A phone you provided?'

'Aye, that's right boss.'

Marcus nods, pours another drink. 'And when do you think they'll be ready to move to the new premises?'

'I think another week or two. It's hard juggling two girls, ye know. They want your attention constantly. I need to be careful they don't catch me with the other, otherwise am fucked,' Rory says. Marcus laughs loudly at this, as does Tommy.

'You've got a hard task there, Rory. They work together, you're not worried they'll talk?' Marcus asks.

'Got it covered boss, told them not to talk to the other girls about personal stuff. Told them it's against company policy. They fuckin' lapped that shit up.' Rory laughs and Marcus feels a sense of pride well inside him.

'Right, well you do what you have to do, Rory. Once they're here, you'll be back on the street recruiting again,' Tommy says as Marcus takes a sip.

'Aye boss, whatever ye need.'

Rory is dismissed and as he closes the door, Marcus gets up from his seat and moves towards Tommy, giving him a slap on the shoulder. 'We've got a good yin there. He's a boss pleaser, but not too kiss arse about it.'

With Rory bringing in two girls, and Amber and Jade about to transition from the club to the new premises, Marcus is beginning to get a taste of what it would be like to be making so much money he wouldn't know what to do with it.

'You had another think about going overseas, Marcus? See what the market is like over there and if we can transport any girls over here?' Tommy asks.

Marcus had thought about it long and hard and as much as it would make them a shit ton of cash, he knew that there was so much more risk involved. Recruiting in Eastern Europe would mean having to trust the likes of Rory to travel, to become involved with the Romanian and Polish gang leaders. For a start, Marcus and Tommy didn't speak the language themselves so there was no chance that Rory would be able to get himself understood. And then there was the language barrier with the girls. Eastern European girls were well sought after, Marcus knew there was a market for them here and they were in high demand. But it was dangerous. Too dangerous. With overseas trafficking there was far too much at stake.

'Aye, Tommy I've thought about it. I just don't think it's best for business at the moment. I'm not saying never, just not right now. I want things solid with the club and the new venture first before we start thinking about overseas projects.'

Tommy nodded. Marcus knew he would understand. 'Aye, sounds fair.'

Thinking back to what he has to deal with here, Marcus knows Jade will be an easier task than Amber, even with the latter's addiction. He will need to keep Amber in line. So far, she seems to be doing what he has asked of her, she's started Jade's training, who's also doing what she thinks is best for her relationship with Marcus. He can't wait for that train of thought to come to an end. Pretending to be all loved up disgusts him. Women aren't capable of loving anyone but themselves. He knows that better than anyone.

29

AMBER

How am I going to get out of this situation, away from this life? Marcus made sure I would need to depend on him by sticking a needle in my arm. When he provides me with enough to keep the withdrawal at bay, it doesn't stop the thoughts going through my head. When will the effects wear off? Will he make me wait longer? What if I don't earn enough in dances from the club in order to pay for what I need? Would he lower my dose, meaning the withdrawal would get worse? I've often thought about trying to come off it, tried to stop myself from taking it. But even the thought makes the withdrawal too much to bear. When the bag is sitting there staring at me, there is no other choice but to take it. Marcus got what he wanted, an addict who will do whatever he tells them to.

I've looked into the methadone programmes in the local areas but I know that if Marcus ever found out, he'd kill me. I'll have to do this alone. But I really do want to stop. I know deep down that this isn't going to be easy and I'm likely to fall at the first hurdle, the second and the third if I'm going to try to beat this addiction. It was forced, not something I would have ever chosen for myself. However that doesn't make it easier to try to wean myself off it, because I still have to do my job and pretend I'm okay. It seems impossible but I am determined.

'You're deep in thought,' Jade says as she enters the changing room.

'Just tired,' I say, only half lying. I haven't been sleeping much with everything going around in my head. Jade, Yasmin, the story about Crystal, my family, Marcus, drugs, clients. It was becoming too much.

'Look, I'm just going to come out and ask you this and I want the truth.'

I glance at Jade in the mirror next to me and the expression on her face tells me what I already know. She thinks there is something more between Marcus and me. If the situation wasn't so serious I'd laugh in her face. Instead, I keep a straight face and wait for her to continue.

'I want to know the history between you and Marcus. I know you used to be together, he told me. The question I can't seem to answer myself is why you're still here?'

Aside from protecting my family and stopping myself from becoming the next body in the suitcase headline she means?

I swallow hard, wondering how on earth she can't see him for who and what he really is. Then again, I didn't see him until it was too late. Thinking back, the Amber who was with Marcus is long gone. She no longer exists.

'I don't want to talk about it,' is the only pathetic answer I can come up with. I can't tell her the real reasons. She wouldn't believe me and then she would tell Marcus. Doing that would put us both in danger, me especially.

'No, don't do that. I've seen the way you look at him. You still love him. Is that why you're still here? You think there's still a chance with him? Because if that's the case then let me tell you, it's not going to happen. Marcus is with me now, Amber.' Jade's tone is firm and I pull my gaze from her.

'There is nothing going on between us, Jade. Trust me.'

'Amber, he told me that you tried to kill yourself when he ended it with you. Did he offer for you to keep working here because he felt guilty? Is that it?' Jade says. Her expression is straight, stern.

The shock I feel inside is overwhelming. 'Are you fucking kidding? You fell for that shit?'

Jade seems a bit taken aback by my response. What the hell was she expecting me to say? *Oh yes, I was so desperately in love with Marcus that I just couldn't go on without him.*

'You're thicker than I first thought, Jade.' I shake my head and breathe through the anger. 'The less I have to do with that bastard the better.' The words are out of my mouth before I can stop them. Jade shifts in her seat and I sigh.

'What the hell is that supposed to mean?'

'Look, Jade. Marcus and I were never an item. What we had wasn't real and I didn't try to kill myself. So do us all a favour and just leave it Jade, eh? It's best for all of us if you stop digging now.'

'No, I won't just leave it. I want to know what you meant. If you don't want anything to do with him then why are you still here? And what do you mean it'll be best for everyone if I stop digging.' Jade is leaning in close to me, trying to make me understand that she is intent on finding out the truth. I get it, I do. The problem is, she doesn't understand the severity of her questioning and I need to make it clear to her.

'Okay, fine. Ever had a gun pointed at you, Jade?'

'What are you talking about?'

'If you want to know what it's like to have a gun pressed against your forehead, with someone threatening to kill you if you don't keep your mouth shut, then keep going. Marcus isn't who or what you think he is. He's a monster, truly a monster. I'm not here by choice, believe me. If you had any sense, you'd leave right now and get as far the fuck away from here as possible. It might be too late now that he's got his hook in your back like he did with me.'

Jade watches me, her chest rising and falling rapidly. The colour on her face is beginning to drain and now I know I have her attention. She's worried, panicking that her dream man isn't all he seems. And so she should be. Now that I've told her this, my own life could be in danger if he finds out. But I may have just given Jade an out. I might not be able to save myself, but knowing that I've stopped someone else going through what I've had to might give me some peace before he finally snuffs out my life. Because I am beginning to believe that is exactly what he is going to do.

'You're just jealous,' she says without conviction.

'And you're delusional if you think for one minute he is genuinely interested in you. What man do you know would coerce his girlfriend into becoming an exotic dancer at his club, and that's just to start off?'

'No,' she says, getting to her feet. 'You're just jealous that he left you for me.'

I sigh again, louder this time, and get up. I roll up my sleeves and show her my arms. She stares at them blankly and then up and into my eye. Jade shrugs her shoulders but I know she's playing dumb.

'Look,' I say as I reach out and grab her wrist. 'This isn't a fucking joke, Jade. This is serious. I've been forced to do things I would never in a million years have chosen to do myself. Things that no one should ever have to go through. Your man isn't a man, he's a boss and his only goal is making money. Girls like us are his sales products. I don't know how you can't see it. I'm risking my fucking life saying any of this to you Jade, so believe me when I tell you this isn't a game. This is as real as life can get.'

Jade twists in my grip and I let go but she doesn't react in the way I expect. Instead, she pushes me and I fall back against the wall. Gripping my hair, she pulls my head down and her face is in mine.

'You're one twisted little bitch, Amber. I was suspicious of you from the moment I laid eyes on you.'

I force all my weight up and into her chest, driving her back and she lets go. I get to my feet as does she and we're standing face to face.

'Jade, I couldn't give a shit if you don't believe me. You'll discover the truth soon enough and when you do, I'll probably be dead and you'll realise that it's too late and that you should have listened to me. Marcus McAdam is not a man to be messed with, neither is Tommy or the fucking rest of them. You're living with him now, but soon enough he'll throw you out and you'll end up in the same building as me, you might even end up taking my place, selling yourself to make enough money so he can fund your fucking drug problem.'

'I don't have a drug problem,' Jade says, her brow furrowing.

'Aye, not now you don't. Give it time. When you finally realise I'm telling the truth and you try to leave, that's how he'll get you to stay. It's exactly what happened to me.'

Jade takes a step back and moves closer to the door. 'You're a liar.'

I move towards her and block the door. 'I promise you, I'm not lying. Back when I thought we were a couple, when I thought he loved me and he was a normal guy, I tried to tell him I didn't want to dance at the club anymore. That I didn't want to earn my living like this anymore. His reaction? Injected me with heroin and threatened my family. Told me that I wouldn't have a family if I ever tried to leave him again. That's why I'm still here. I'm addicted to the drugs he put me on and I'm protecting my family.'

She doesn't try to stop me. Instead, she smiles but I can see her eyes beginning to glisten as though tears are threatening.

'Jade, if you don't listen to me and take this seriously, you're going to learn the hard way about Marcus. If you tell him what I've said, then we'll both die.'

Maybe that's not a bad thing. Death. Perhaps it's the only way out of this mess for both of us?

30

JADE

We stand a few feet apart, eyeing one another. The fury inside me remains when Amber's expression doesn't change. Tears of frustration build but I hold them in. How can she possibly be so twisted that she would say these kinds of things about Marcus? I'm not in denial. That's not possible when you're face to face with a liar. I feel a smile creep over me and a laugh escapes my lips.

'You think this is funny?' Amber says, taking a step closer. I move back, not allowing her to close the gap between us. 'The marks on my arms are real, Jade. He forced drugs into me after threatening to fucking shoot me. This isn't a game, its real life. The darkest side of life you could ever imagine and you're part of it, Jade. You think you're just going to dance for him in this shithole and go home at the end of a shift? That's just the start.'

'Shut up, you're a liar.' I say. 'Marcus would never do anything to hurt me.'

Amber does what I say, she stops talking and sits down in front of the mirror. Applying red lipstick, false eyelashes and some highlighter to her cheeks, she doesn't even look at me in the mirror. My heart pounds in my chest as I watch her. She barely blinks.

I think back to the first night I met her and when Marcus told me I'd be working here six nights a week. He had been strange that night, a little distant and insistent. But since, he's been back to his old self, kind, caring and full of affection.

He'd just had a tough night at work, that was all and my nagging about Amber and questioning him on my new job hadn't helped.

Although, something is niggling in the back of my mind. I can't help but think there is some truth to what she's saying but I don't want to admit that to myself. I scold myself for doubting Marcus. He's done nothing but look after me since we met. Why would he want to hurt me if he loves me as much as he says he does?

'You never told me how you met?' Amber says, finally breaking the silence in the room.

'No, I didn't.'

'The thing about Marcus is, he wouldn't have met you just by chance. He'd have had eyes on you for a while before you bumped into him in the bar or the supermarket, wherever it happened. He'd have done his research, figured out your flaws before he made his move.'

Shaking my head, I get up from the seat and move towards the door.

'Then, when you were at your lowest, he'd have made his move. Caught you when you were at your most vulnerable. Made you think that he was the only person in the world who didn't think you were damaged goods. That's what he did with me. It's what he does to all of us.'

My hand is on the door handle, ready to leave and not have to listen to another word she has to say. But something keeps me in my place because her words are seamless, unlike that of a liar making up a story to get their own way.

'Now, god knows how long I've been trapped in this horrible world he's created. But I'll get out. I will. The next time I try to leave will be the last time.'

My stomach flips a little but I don't turn to face her. Instead, I pull on the handle, but just as I open the door, Marcus walks into the dressing room and I'm forced back inside.

'You're not ready yet?' he asks, looking me up and down. 'Come on, Jade. You need to look the part.'

He places a hand on my shoulder and leads me towards the dressing table, sits me down next to Amber.

'Another night of training from one of our best dancers,' he says with a smile. 'Amber, you look after my girl.'

'Marcus,' I say. 'Can we talk?'

I feel Amber's eyes burn into the back of my head as I turn towards Marcus. He looks down at me expectantly but suddenly, the words dry up in the back of my throat.

'I'll have her training the new girls in no time,' Amber says. Marcus's eyes flicker towards her then back to me.

'Good. Make us all some serious cash, eh girls?' He bends down, kisses me on the cheek and heads out the door. He's gone, out of sight and something twists in my gut.

I turn back to the mirror and Amber is holding a makeup bag towards me. I take it from her and don't say anything. Neither does she but it's clear that we're both thinking the same thing. That she's right. Marcus has another agenda. I could see it in his eyes, the way he looked at Amber. I don't want to believe it. I love him and I know he loves me.

'So, you going to tell me how you ended up here?'

I refuse to speak because then I would be admitting that what she is saying is true.

'It's none of your business how I met Marcus.'

Amber shrugs and shakes her head. 'Fine. Don't say I didn't warn you.'

I think about that day I met him. When he picked up the water bottle for me and handed it back. I was in the hospital, certainly vulnerable after my attack. But there is no way he would have known about that. He was there to visit a family friend, from what I can remember.

I shake my head and look at myself in the mirror then look at Amber.

How had she met Marcus?

The end of the night approaches and I put my bra back on for around the tenth time this evening. The men have been relentless, requesting dance after dance. Amber said that ten dances in one night is classed as a quiet shift. I don't feel that way. I feel dirty, cheap. I feel used. I want to tell Marcus that this isn't for me, but I can't get Amber's words out the back of my head. How she wanted to escape and had a gun held to her head.

I leave the private booth after the client and head out towards the main bar area. Amber is on the pole, swinging herself around it and looking as though she is enjoying herself. I suppose that's her job. It's my job now too. I take a deep and steadying breath and catch a glimpse at the clock behind the bar. It's almost one in the morning. Only an hour left until the place shuts and I can go home.

Climbing up on the podium next to Amber, I start dancing in the hope that no other men take any notice of me. The thought of going into a private booth with another one turns my stomach. I grip the pole and start twirling myself around it, trying not to look as provocative as I'm supposed to. I don't make eye contact with anyone in the hope that they'll choose someone else to dance for them. The music beats loudly and vibrates inside my chest as I slide up and down the pole. Then, my eyes are drawn towards a commotion at the door. A group of lads has been let in for the last hour. There are around ten of them and my stomach drops. Why else would they be in here at this time in the morning, other than to pay for a private dance? They're loud, rowdy and make their way over to where Amber and I are dancing. Some of them head for the bar and other podiums to watch some of the other girls. I silently pray that none of them have any money left.

Amber's next to me now, grabbing my hand and leading me towards a booth. 'They've paid for a private dance from each of us. One of the guys is celebrating a birthday or something and they've all chipped in for him to have a dance and they picked both of us. It's ten minutes each. You want to go first?'

I climb down to the floor and glance at the group, who are cheering and laughing as they push their friend into the booth. I want to cry but instead of prolonging the agony, I choose to go in first. I don't make eye contact with Amber or say the words out loud. Instead I pull my hand away and head for the booth. In the last forty-eight hours I've conducted around thirty topless dances and the more I do, the dirtier it feels. I know Marcus will be watching me, or at least have eyes on me from another source, and I don't want to upset him so I plaster on my fakest and most enticing smile and pull back the curtain. As I go inside, I don't look at the man's face. I just go for it and move my body to the beat of the music. Leaning down, my back to him, I roll my hips and dangle my hair across his chest as I lay my head back. It's all I can do not to throw up.

Flicking my hair to the side, I stand up and turn my body around so I'm facing him but again, I don't give him eye contact. Then he says my name.

'Jade, what the fuck?'

I look up and stumble back. It can't be. What the hell is he even doing here?

'Paul!'

'What the fuck are you doing here? Since when were you a fucking stripper?'

I can't breathe. My chest tightens and my skin begins to tingle.

'Jade, why are you here? What are you doing in a place like this?'

I take a few breaths, straighten myself up and look him dead in the eye. 'I suppose I could ask you the same question.'

His mouth gapes as I begin dancing again because I don't know what else to do. He takes hold of my wrist gently and holds me still. 'Seriously, Jade. What is going on? How did you come to work here? Last time I saw you, things were fine.'

'Yeah, and things are even better now,' I lie, pulling away from his grip.

'Not from where I'm standing,' Paul says and that gets my back up. How would he know how things are when he's only been in my company for a moment.

'You bitter about how I ended things or something?'

'No. I'm not a bad guy, I don't hold grudges. I accepted that you didn't want to be with me. But when I heard about what happened to you and tried to reach out, you told me to go away. You said that you didn't need help and that all you wanted was to be on your own.'

'When did you try to reach out? I haven't heard from you since we broke up.'

'Just after your attack. I sent you a message and I got a message back, telling me that you wanted nothing more to do with me and you wanted to be left alone after what happened.' Paul gets to his feet and puts his hands on my shoulders. 'I tried to come round to see you and your neighbour said you'd left.'

My stomach rolls. I didn't send or receive any messages. I shrug away from him, worried that Marcus will appear and lose his shit for a punter putting his hands on me. 'I got a new phone. Lost my old one,' I lie. I choose not to tell Paul that Marcus got me a new phone when we started seeing each other. In fact, I chose not to tell Paul about Marcus at all.

Paul shakes his head and tries to pull me in again but I resist. 'Look, can we meet up and talk about all this? I only want the best for you.'

I take a deep breath, conscious that Amber will be waiting for the private dance to end and for her to take my place.

'Please, Jade. I only want to know you're okay. From what I can see, you're not.'

I fake a smile and say, 'I'm fine, Paul.'

'Doesn't look like it from where I'm standing.'

I turn my back to him and leave the booth without saying a word, praying that he won't follow me and make a scene. Seeing him has reminded me of my past, of what happened and how I've come to be here now. I don't want to meet him or talk about it because it's too painful.

'You okay?' Amber asks as I walk past her towards the podium.

'Fine. He's waiting on you.'

I climb back on to the podium and hope that I can finish up my night up there without any more distractions, all the while I can't help thinking about what Paul said about the messages.

If he received that text, it certainly didn't come from me. Which means it could only have come from the only other person I was spending any time with back then. Marcus.

Amber's words echo inside my mind now. Maybe she was right about him. Had he orchestrated things so that when I got out of hospital, I had no one else but him to turn to?

31

MARCUS

'Amber seems to be playing the game well, I think I can trust her for now. Jade on the other hand, I'm not sure is coping. She's doing everything she's supposed to at the moment, but I think I'll have to take extra precautions to make sure she doesn't do an Amber and try to get out of this. She's asking too many questions and I'm beginning to think she knows something isn't right,' Marcus says to Tommy.

'You think Amber has got into her head?'

'I wouldn't put it past her. She's a fiery one.'

'Isn't that what you liked about her in the first place? You said the punters would like that about her, but maybe she's too much for us. A liability. She proved that already,' Tommy says, placing a drink down in front of Marcus. 'I can take care of her if you like while you focus on Jade. Then Rory can deal with the other two coming in?'

Marcus nods, lifts his glass and takes a drink. 'Aye, that might be best. You get Amber to the new premises and I'll rush Jade through to the next stage. Start her making some real money.'

'Erm, Marcus... I meant take care of her, as in get rid?'

'Nah, no need for that yet. There's still enough time to get some decent cash out of her before we need to rethink the situation.'

'So long as you're sure she's no' a flight risk. If she goes to the police our whole operation is fucked.'

'Am sure,' Marcus says giving Tommy an eye. 'Am no' stupid, Tommy. I know what I'm doing.'

Tommy holds his hands up in defence as Marcus finishes his drink and leaves the office before heading to the dressing room to pick up Jade. He needs to be on his best behaviour, make Jade think everything is going well between them which he thinks she does. She still dotes on him from the way she is behaving and as much as it does his nut in, he needs to keep it that way.

Marcus reaches the dressing room door and stops to listen. He wants to know what's being said behind the door, to find out if Amber is crossing the line. Tommy thinks Marcus is nuts, but Marcus likes to challenge the girls to see if they can be loyal or not. Amber was warned not to mess him around and since then, she's behaved, Marcus made sure of that.

Having many girls on the go is enough to cause a headache, but the money is too good to pass up. It's Marcus's business now and he will not allow anyone to take that away from him, especially not the likes of Amber or Jade. No female will stand in his way. Crystal and Yasmin had to learn the hard way.

32

JADE

As I clip my seatbelt into place, Marcus reaches over and gives my knee a squeeze. I turn to smile at him but he isn't looking at me. He's staring down at his phone and smiling.

'Woman of your dreams messaging you, is she?' I aim for sarcasm but even I'm not convinced of it. I'm becoming more and more suspicious of Marcus after what Amber said and seeing Paul has shaken me, especially after the text message revelation.

'Nah, she's right next to me,' he replies as he slides his phone inside his jacket pocket. 'You and Amber seem to be getting along relatively well.'

Was that a trick question? I don't know how to answer. Be truthful, or lie to his face?

'She's okay,' I say. 'Not your biggest fan right enough.'

'Oh?' Marcus only seems half interested as he starts the car. A top of the range Range Rover. Brand new, black with all the features. Expensive for someone who needs his girlfriend to work in the club to help pay the rent. 'And what did she have to say for herself?'

If Amber is telling the truth about all she has said about Marcus, then what I'm about to say could land her in some serious shit. I don't know if I can handle being the one responsible for that.

'Och, not much to be fair. I think she's just jealous that she's not the centre of your attention anymore. Anytime I spoke about us being a couple, she couldn't even look at me,' I lie.

'I asked her if there was anything going on between you both and she said no.'

Marcus pulls the car out onto the road and heads along the street. He doesn't say anything for a while and my heart flutters in my chest. I'm beginning to wonder more and more who Marcus actually is.

'Do I have anything to worry about, Marcus?' I ask. There is so much more meaning to the question than he thinks. The text message, Amber. What I really want to ask him is who he is, and am I in danger being alone with him?

'Jade, we're not in high school. This is just petty shit. If she still has a thing for me then it's not my fault.'

I beg to differ on that one. I have to keep up appearances. 'Okay. I just don't want anything to come between us.'

'Me either, which is why I have something I want to ask you.'

I look on at him expectantly and something inside me turns to ice. He isn't smiling anymore.

'The group of lads that came into the club near the end of the night, did you know one of them?'

'Why?' I say too quickly. Shit.

'Because you have to remember Jade, I have cameras and eyes on all of the girls in the club. I saw you talking to him in the private booth and you didn't finish your dance. Want to tell me what that was all about?'

My mind races for something to say. 'If you must know, he's an ex.'

'Is he now?'

'Yes, just like Amber is your ex. I was just surprised to see him there, that's all. That's why I stopped dancing because when he said my name, I was taken aback.'

I choose not to say anything about Paul quizzing me on why I was there, that it wasn't the type of place he'd expected to see me working in. If he finds out I think he sent Paul that text as if it was from me, he might get angry. I don't want Marcus to think Paul is a threat or anything to worry about.

'So, what was he talking to you about?'

I lie, tell him that Paul was just asking how I was doing, what I was doing with myself. Again, I don't know why I'm lying but something deep in my gut is telling me to.

'You'd better not be lying to me, Jade. I don't like liars.' Marcus turns onto the motorway and the Range Rover picks up speed. He shifts gears aggressively and I jump.

'Of course I'm not bloody lying. Why the hell would I?' I say.

We're silent for the rest of the journey and my heart thumps inside my chest. When we pull up outside Marcus's flat, he doesn't turn the engine off. The silence weighs heavy on my chest. I reach my hand over and rest it on his but he pulls away and has a sudden grip of my wrist. I almost cry out but my throat closes in shock. His other hand shoots out and grabs me by the face. He squeezes so hard and pinches the skin on my cheeks, yanking my head around so I'm facing him, so close I feel his breath on my face.

'If I find out you're lying about this guy, I won't be responsible for what happens. You got that?' He lets go of my face and throws my hand across to me.

The pain and shock is overwhelming and it's that moment that confirms my suspicions. Of course it was Marcus that sent that text message. His outburst is proof that he is beginning to worry that I am discovering the real Marcus. The picture he has painted of himself is nothing like who he really is. Amber is right. He is a monster. I fight back the tears and do what he says.

He tells me to get out and that he has a lot of things to catch up on at the club, that he might stay at Tommy's place. I attempt to lean over to kiss him because it's what I usually do when we part, but he doesn't respond. Doesn't even look at me. Fear and anxiety twist in my gut as I climb out of the car. I watch as he pulls away at high speed and I wonder if he's telling the truth about work or if he just wants to get away from me so he doesn't hurt me again. I rub at the skin on my wrist and face as it burns from his grip. The atmosphere in the car was odd even before he lashed out. My heart is still pounding as I step inside Marcus's building.

Inside the flat, I dump my bag on the floor and walk along the hall to the spare room. Marcus's office. I'm not allowed in there, never have been and have never disrespected Marcus's request for me not to go snooping around in there. After what has just happened, I need to get in there and find Amber's contact details. I can't wait another sixteen hours or so until I see her again. I need to ask her something. I need to ask her a lot of things.

Opening the office door, I step inside. Framed images of his favourite cars and bands hang on the walls and the desk sits in the centre of the room. I go to the desk and open the drawer on the left and see that there is a diary-like book sitting at the top. With trembling hands, I take it out and flick through it. No contact information for Amber. Sliding my hand deeper into the drawer, I feel a smaller book at the back and bring it out. I open it and there are girls' names, telephone numbers and addresses on every page. Seeing them makes me feel sick but I find Amber's contact details almost immediately.

She has some explaining to do, so I send her a message and hope that she will agree to see me. I just hope that Marcus keeps to his word and doesn't come back to the flat to find me gone. If he does, I'm certain he'll do more damage than just grabbing my face and wrist.

33

AMBER

My seventh client of the night leaves the flat and I go in for my seventh shower of the night. No amount of soap or scalding water can wash away the feeling those men bring to me. I can feel their presence on me days later. What kind of man pays for sex? It disgusts me. Marcus makes sure I'm always booked out so he can earn enough to fund his lifestyle and my new drug habit thanks to him. I've tried to quit, to stop the urge from getting to me, but no matter how much I want to stop taking heroin, the withdrawal is too much to cope with especially when I have various clients to deal with through the night after a shift at the club.

I think about my sister and my nephew. I haven't seen them in such a long time thanks to Marcus. He won't let me leave to go and visit them, to try to make amends. He doesn't want me to have contact with anyone he believes will try to persuade me to leave him. The threats of violence against my family would always be there. The threat alone was enough. Telling me that I wouldn't have a family if I ever left was too terrible to comprehend. I had to have no choice but to stay in the hope that it will keep them safe. I hate him and what he's turned me into.

I picture the lounge at my parents' house, the fireplace covered in framed photographs of my sister and me, from child-hood up until just before I left. I think of one in particular. A school photo. I think I was in primary one and my sister in primary three. I smile out at the camera, a few gaps from where my baby teeth once sat and the adult teeth hadn't quite come through yet. I was their little girl and they had so many hopes and dreams for me. For both of us. I hate what my absence must be doing to them. They'll be getting to share with my sister the joy of my little nephew growing and developing. Hearing his first laugh, seeing him crawl for the first time. I'm missing all of that. The little guy won't even know who I am, that I exist at all. I could have achieved so much in the time I've been stuck here, wasting away. I have to push the thoughts out of my head. It's breaking my heart just picturing all the things I'm missing and the pain I'm causing them.

I remember the first time I met Marcus. I was fascinated by how handsome he was and how much he seemed to like me. The nightclub was busy that night and I was out with a few friends from college. We were nearing the end of our accountancy course and had taken a rare weekend off from studying to go out and let loose. I'd bought a round of shots for us and I caught Marcus's eye from the other end of the bar. His smile dazzled me and before I knew it, we were dancing together. His hands did not wander. He was respectable even though I was hammered and I liked that about him. He seemed to respect me. I suppose that was his way of luring me in to see if he could manipulate me and it worked so quickly. I barely remember the girl I used to be back then, it's as if she never existed.

Stepping out of the shower, I dry off and put on some pyjamas before going into the kitchen. I prep the needle like he showed me and head to the living room. Find a vein and sit back as the poison he has forced on me spreads through me. It's like a relief and a weight all at once. With each hit I'm more addicted and I know it'll be harder to leave, as he intended it. I hate him. I hate myself.

As my eyes begin to feel heavy, the thoughts I'm having intensify. I miss my family so much and the idea of never seeing them again is like a pain I never thought I'd feel. This is all because I fell in love with a thug, a monster. A controlling and manipulative man who traffics women like me for financial gain. We're not human to him. We're products. I want to fight but more often than not it would be so much easier to give up.

Just as I am closing my eyes, my phone sounds an alert. The phone that Marcus gave me when I first got involved with him. The heroin has kicked in now and I can barely lift my arm to reach for the phone, so I lean to the side and lift it from the side table. My eyesight is blurry but I can still see the screen as I fumble with the phone to open the message.

> 05:36
> Can we talk? Jade

I blink as I take in the words. How does she even have my number? I didn't give it to her because Marcus didn't tell me to, and I would never give my number out without checking with him first. My limbs feel heavy as I try to sit back up on the sofa but I manage to find the upright position before typing a reply.

> 05:38
> About what?

I can just about manage those nine letters before the phone drops from my hand and I begin to drift in and out of consciousness. I hear my phone ringing and in my head I'm picking it up, answering it. I'm talking to my sister. She's begging me to come home and start over again with her and the rest of my family. I'm crying, telling her I can't and that it's safer for all of them if I stay away. Somewhere in my mind I know that it's not real because I can still hear the phone ringing. I fight to open my eyes and this time I do find the phone in my hand, lift it to my ear and answer it.

'Hello?'

'Why haven't you texted me back?' It's Jade's voice. She sounds a lot further away in my head.

'I did.'

'I asked you to meet me an hour ago and you didn't reply.' Jade sounds angry. Worried. An hour ago?

'You only texted me a few minutes ago,' I reply as I glance up at the clock. It's almost seven in the morning. How had I lost an hour without even realising it?

'Can I meet you or not? I need to talk to you about what you said about Marcus.'

I sigh and agree. She's coming to me, which I know is dangerous but I'm unable to move at this point.

I try to sit up, get myself together, but this hit is a little heavier than normal. I don't know why. Maybe he gave me more than usual. Not enough to knock me out permanently though. I stare out of the lounge and at the front door, wondering if I'll be able to get up and answer it when Jade arrives. I close my eyes for just a moment to try to gather my thoughts, but it's too late. I'm gone again, dreaming of what life might be like if I was ever to escape Marcus's clutches.

34

JADE

There is a buzzer system on the exterior door, but there is no need to use it as the main door is wide open. Not that I would be happy to press any of the buttons, the thing looks like it has been pissed on.

Climbing the stairs in the communal hallway, I try not to breathe through my nose even though my agoraphobia is at its height and all I want to do is take deep breaths to control the rising panic. The place stinks of god knows what and it's all I can do not to gag. I'm on edge that Marcus will find out I've come to see Amber. Not that I'm doing anything wrong, it's not like I'm cheating on him, but the way he reacted about the Paul situation tells me he wouldn't be happy with me coming to visit Amber at her flat. He was clear before: he doesn't like liars. And going on the look which passed between them, I don't think Marcus would want me asking Amber anything at all.

Finding the flat was easy once I found the address in the diary in the back of Marcus's office desk at the flat.

I reach the front door. Flat 2/1 and it's not what I expected. Amber's the most glamorous dancer at Angel Silk, one of the most sought after, so I thought she would be in one of the more luxurious flats in the city. Seems not. Balling my left fist, I bang on the door twice and wait for Amber to appear. I can hear her moving around inside before a few more seconds pass and she opens it. Without looking at me she turns and walks down a short hallway. I hesitate for a second before stepping inside. The place is relatively clean, untidy but nicely decorated. I move through the hall, past a kitchen towards a living room where Amber is now sitting on a sofa. The curtains are closed and the place smells of sweat. I glance down at the table next to the sofa. A needle. A used needle by the looks of it. I look back at Amber and she is staring at me.

'Got something to say?'

'Are you alright?' I reply without hesitation. Amber now and the Amber I know from the club are like two different people.

I glance around the room again and to my horror, I realise what I'm seeing. My heart picks up speed at the sight of the place, at the state of Amber and I can't stop the high-pitched tone that accompanies my words. 'So you really are a junkie?'

She sits back and gives a guttural laugh. I don't return the humour.

'It's like I told you before, it's not through choice, believe me.'

'Amber...' I start, but I don't know what else to say.

We remain silent for what feels like forever and I can't help but wonder what is going on inside her head. She showed me the marks on her arm back at the club, but I didn't want to believe it. Now that I'm seeing her in this context, I'm beginning to see more and more the truth in what she's been trying to tell me.

'You came round here for a reason. So spit it out. I need a kip if I'm going to make it through my shift at the club tonight.' She runs a hand through her hair and I can't help but feel sorry for her. Then I think about what happened with Marcus, back in that moment in the car, and the reality of my life hits me between the eyes.

I take off my jacket and place it on the arm of the sofa before sitting down. Amber looks at my wrist, red and sore. I hadn't noticed it until she did. Did my face show the same markings?

'Looks sore,' she says.

I run my left hand over it but don't say anything in reply. I'm in half a mind to get up and walk away but where would I go? I have nothing other than Marcus.

'That's just the start of it, love. Wait till the day he punches you in the jaw, or smacks your head off the breakfast table for no reason. You ever tried to cover up those kinds of bruises with makeup? Not easy, I'll tell you,' Amber says as she leans forward and lifts a cigarette from the pack. Lighting it, she sucks loudly on it before a haze of blue smoke is hovering above us. 'So, it's started then?'

'He was upset because he thought I was lying to him,' I say, realising how pathetic I sound.

'You know, Jade I'm not even going to ask you what he was upset about. Because the truth is you don't have to be guilty of anything for him to lash out. You can do all the things he wants you to do and he'll still smash your head off the wall. Or window. Or stamp on you after he's thrown you to the floor.'

Her eyes are on me, heavy but they don't lose focus. Amber is serious, deadly serious, and I'm terrified.

'He'll start pimping you out to other clients soon, Jade. He'll move you to one of his flats, probably in this building. He'll make you work at the club and then when you get home, once you think you've escaped the sleaze bags for the night they'll come knocking on your door. And you'll have to do anything they request because he'll have been paid already.'

I look on at her in horror. 'You're a prostitute?'

'Again, not by fucking choice. And are you really that naive after everything I've already told you? Come on, Jade. I had a life before I met that bastard and fell into his trap. Just like you have.'

'Tell me what he did to you,' I say, feeling defeated.

'I don't have to tell you. You'll work it out for yourself when he does it to you. If you've got even half a brain in that skull of yours, you'll do a runner now. It doesn't matter if you've got nowhere to go. Just run and don't look back. I mean it.'

Amber puts the cigarette on the ashtray on the table and gets to her feet. I watch her as she stumbles to the hall and into the kitchen. I'm frozen in fear. How the hell am I supposed to do this by myself?

I get up and follow her. She's standing by the sink, leaning on it and staring out of the window. I don't want to think about what she's gone through while living in this place because that could be me. She's right. I need to get out.

'Why don't we both go?' I suggest and Amber starts to laugh.

'Jade, did you ever see the news report about the body they found in the suitcase at Luderston Bay?'

I shake my head but I know what she is going to say next.

'That's what will happen to us if Marcus thinks we are trying to outsmart him, Jade. And I can't leave. My family would end up dead and it would be because I did what he's told me not to.'

'Okay, I get the family thing, but how do you even know Marcus had anything to do with the body at the bay? It could be a coincidence.' I'm grasping at any possibility that all of this is a lie, and that Marcus is a good person. The sensation in my stomach is telling me not to be so bloody stupid.

Laughter again, louder. She's become hysterical and falls back and on to the floor, her back against the fridge. She's crying now, her face in her hands and emotion catches in my throat.

'Before me, there was a girl. Crystal. Apparently she was Marcus's bit of stuff. The girls hated her, said she was the favourite. But she was just like us. You and me. Marcus has this sick recruitment process. Picks on the most vulnerable, or the prettiest, or whoever he thinks will make him the most money. Anyway, she disappeared. No one heard from or saw her again. Then all of a sudden, a female washes up inside a suitcase? It was Crystal.'

I shake my head in disbelief. 'No way. That's too far, Amber.'

'How is it too far? He'll stop at nothing to protect himself and his business.' She glances up at me through glazed, drug induced eyes. 'Fine, you don't have to believe me. Go back to him, see what happens. Just keep your fucking mouth shut about me, Jade. I've stuck my neck out for you and if he finds out and I end up dead, it'll be your fault.'

Shortness of breath grips me as I leave the flat and make my way downstairs. I pass a few girls on the stairs as they're coming into the building and they give me a look. The same look Amber gave me when she first met me. They're his girls. His prostitutes. This building is his very own brothel and it won't be long until I'm living here myself. Amber was right. I am her along with whoever else he has used this tactic with. He found me at my lowest point and used it to his gain.

Once outside, I gulp in the fresh air and my mind races. I need to get back to the flat, gather my belongings and get as far away from this situation as quickly as possible. I just hope Marcus was telling the truth when he said he would stay at Tommy's. If he's at the flat when I get back, it'll be too late. There is no way I'll be able to leave. And if I do manage to get away, how will I cope being out there on my own, in a world that I can't control?

35

LIZZY

It has been two days since Barry took me hostage and brought me to this house in the middle of nowhere. I think it has been two days. I can't be sure. I have no phone, obviously he's not going to let me have contact with the outside world. There are no clocks in this room. No TV. No radio. Just silence and it's driving me insane.

I stare at the tray on the table next to me. Toast, a mug of tea and a few biscuits. Hunger strike isn't something I want to resort to, not that I think it would help. I eat the toast and biscuits and drink the tea. It's how I take it. Two sugars and little milk. He's either remembered that from when we were teenagers or he's guessed. Either way, it calms the grumbling inside my stomach for now.

He untied me when I was put in this room, but he made sure the door was locked. And I'm certain that there is someone manning the door on the other side to make sure I don't escape. I've already tried the window. It's locked. I'm thankful the glass hasn't been covered and I spend my time staring out at the field. I think I'm in the middle of nowhere based on the view but I don't truly know where I am. There hasn't been a lot of traffic noise from what I can gather. That coupled with the view makes me think I'm far out from the city.

I get up and begin pacing the room. This is part of my routine now. Up and down the room, back and forth. I've done some exercise, sit-ups, star jumps. Anything to keep me sane. I haven't seen Barry since he locked me in here. He's had others bring my food and water. Each time someone has brought me something, I've attempted to push them to tell me where the house is but I've always been met with silence, as though they've been served a gag order. They're never going to give up the information which would aid my escape. Of course they wouldn't. I've gone over in my mind what it is he wants from me. A slow death? If that was the case then he wouldn't be sending me food.

I think about what it must have been like for him to see me at the hospital, leaving the baby outside for a nurse or doctor to find. I don't blame him for his anger towards me but I had no other choice. There would have been a war between our families. I can't imagine what would have happened on the streets of Glasgow if I'd kept the baby.

Looking out of the window, I begin to think about the club. The girls. Has anyone reported me missing? I don't see a way out of this place unless Barry and whoever is working for him become complacent and there's an opportunity to get out. Highly unlikely.

The door opens behind me and as I turn, a little voice in the back of my head tells me to run at the person standing there. It would catch them off guard, maybe I'd be able to use their weight against them and knock them out of the way and make a run for the front door. I mute the voice as quickly as it begins, because I know that would only get me killed. There will be people manning the exits if I know Barry.

'How you doing?' Barry says, stepping inside the room and closing the door behind him. It locks from the outside. So there is someone keeping an eye on me other than him.

'What the hell do you think?' I say, turning my back to him and glancing out the window again.

'I got your tea right then?'

'Stop pretending you give a shit, Barry. People who hit women over the back of the head aren't kind people, you know?'

Footsteps approach me and I can feel his breath on the back of my neck. I shiver but keep my stance. Never show weakness, that's what my dad would always say. And never turn your back to the enemy. Turning, I am face to face with Barry. He takes a step back and sighs.

'Are you going to tell me why you've brought me here against my will?'

'Aye. You're going to work for me.'

'Work for you?' I say, failing to stop the snigger escaping. 'I don't work for anyone except myself.'

'That's not strictly true,' Barry replies.

I watch him as he pulls an envelope from his pocket and hands it to me. I reluctantly take it from him and open it, my heart thumping in my chest. I scan over the words and my throat constricts. This isn't happening. Can't be happening.

'This is illegal.'

'Nothing I do is illegal, Lizzy,' Barry responds. I glance up at him and then back at the papers.

'I didn't sign these.'

'It looks like your signature to me. You're no longer the owner of Angel Silk, Lizzy.'

Staring down at the papers, I read the words more carefully, hoping that this is all a joke. But it's true. And it does look like my signature. There is nothing about it that looks different to how I would sign a document. Someone has copied it to perfection.

'You won't get away with this, Barry. These are falsified documents. You'll be arrested.'

'Lizzy, let me stop you right there.' Barry leans and I can feel his breath on my face. 'You have to understand something about me. I have various ways of keeping my name clean. You're right, these are falsified documents, but the police are not going to arrest me.'

I raise a brow and keep my eyes locked with his.

'You see, I have friends in high places, Lizzy. And even the police will take a pay off if the price is right. Why do you think I've gotten away with so much over the years?'

It's like a stab to the chest when I hear it. Of course Barry has paid off the police. He would do anything to keep his name out of the mud and himself out of prison. If the police couldn't or wouldn't do anything about this, then the men I'm in business with would when they found out.

'It's not just my club, you know,' I say. 'I'm in business with others and when they find out you did this, they'll come for you.' My attempts at threatening Barry appear to fail as the smile on his face grows wider.

'You done?' He laughs. When I don't answer, he continues. 'So, I want you to meet your new boss.' He walks to the door and taps his knuckles against the wood. The lock turns and as the door opens, I watch the gap grow between the door and the frame. And then I see who has taken my place as manager and owner at the club. 'Lizzy, meet your son.'

He steps inside the room and Barry closes the door. Once again, it's locked from the other side. Nausea builds inside and I can feel the bile rising, but I swallow hard to keep it at bay.

I stare in disbelief, hoping that this is a nightmare I'm going to wake up from. 'You?' I say, unable to blink. My eyes begin to sting as the enormity of what I'm seeing sets in. 'No, not you. You're *not* my son.'

'Charming. That what you said when you left me outside the hospital?' His words are like venom and I can't tear my eyes away from him.

Shaking my head, I grip the papers in my hand and I want to scream. I wish my dad had warned me sooner about Barry, about the whole family. 'Getting involved with the McAdams will only come back to bite you, Lizzy. Trust me.' I *should* have trusted him.

'Marcus…' is all I can manage before I slump back onto the chair. '*You're* my son?'

'How's it goin, Ma?'

I glance up at him, my son and immediately see Barry behind the wolfish grin spread across his face.

36

LIZZY

The hairs on the back of my neck stand on end as beads of sweat trickle down the back of my shirt. This isn't real. My son is not standing in front of me, having taken away Angel Silk, the only thing I had in my life to keep the dark thoughts out. The only thing I had left that has a connection to my dad. Except that he is, because he looks just like my dad. He has Aitken blood running in his veins. As I regard his features closely, I now see myself in him. He has my nose, my chiselled chin. I can't believe I didn't see it before. Marcus has worked at the club for almost three years as head of security and I never once noticed. Was never suspicious. Now that he's standing in front of me, next to Barry, I can't believe how stupidly blind I have been. I've thought about the baby I left outside that hospital every day for thirty years. I knew he would be turning thirty this year, I'd never have forgotten that, however he'd been on my mind more so lately as I'd wondered what he'd achieved in his life. Now I know. I've been in his company every single day for the last few years, done business with him, had conversations with him. Laughed and joked around with him and Tommy.

'Why, Marcus?' is all I can manage. 'Why do this now?'

'Because it was so easy. I just used a different surname. Smith doesn't really suit me, does it?' He laughs. 'It's not hard to forge and you fell for it. I couldn't exactly use the McAdam name on the paperwork, it would have ruined the surprise.'

I shake my head and want to scream.

'Don't you want to hug me after all these years of being absent in my life?' The sarcasm rolls off Marcus's tongue effortlessly and I can't bring myself to look at him or Barry for that matter.

'You see, Lizzy. We've been watching you ever since you left our boy outside the hospital. That night you abandoned him, when I found his little body wrapped up in a blanket, I vowed that young Marcus here would always know what you did to him. Because why shouldn't he understand why his mother was never in his life when he was growing up?'

'You know as well as I do that there would've been a war between our families if I'd told you I was pregnant. If I'd kept him, we'd have lost family members. People would have died and I didn't want our baby to be a part of that.' The words hiss through my teeth in a rage. I can't believe this is happening.

'And leaving me outside in the freezing cold when I was just days old was a better fucking alternative?' Marcus says, taking a step closer to me. I move back on the chair and he stops, lifts a hand and is pointing in my face. 'You were so fucking worried about family members dying, that you didn't stop to think that leaving a baby outside in the dead of night would've resulted in the same thing?'

I think about what I did that night. I created the ultimate maternal crime and left my baby all on his own outside the hospital in the hope that a doctor or nurse would find him and he would be offered a better life. It almost killed me doing it and every second of every day for thirty years, he never left my thoughts. Not once. I'd contemplated suicide many times because I just couldn't take the guilt of what I did. But I did it for him. At the time, I liked Barry but I wasn't in love with him, so it wasn't worth the fight that our relationship would cause if our rival families found out about it.

'I'm sorry that you think I didn't care about you, Marcus. But it was never meant to turn out this way. I promise you it wasn't easy for me to do what I did. It broke my heart. It still breaks me every day that I never got to be with you when you were little. I never got to feed you, or watch you learn how to crawl, walk. I missed everything because I was trying to protect you,' I say, but I know it will fall on deaf ears. Marcus isn't going to believe a word that I say about that night because Barry would have fed him enough poison that there will be nothing I can say to make him believe my heart was in the right place. But he's right in the sense that I have missed so much. I've missed my boy growing up. I never thought for one minute that he would grow up with the McAdams. That was the last thing I would have wanted for him.

'Save the fake emotional outburst. So how was it meant to turn out then? Nah, go on tell me what you thought would happen to me. Ah, I know. You thought I'd be found by some rich couple, taken in and sent to private school. I'd get the best education, be a spoilt little bastard and you'd sit back, proud that I was being looked after by someone who could do a better job than you?' Marcus snarls at me and Barry raises a brow. I see his mouth raise at the corner, in an almost smile but he stops it from surfacing.

I don't know what else to say and now I can't stop the emotion bubbling over. It's too much to comprehend and the tears spill. I lower my head and try to cry in silence but with both Marcus and Barry standing just a few feet away from me there is no hiding it.

'You're a good actress, I'll give you that. You knew exactly what you were doing that night and you knew the fucking risks of leaving me out there.'

I look up to see Barry place a hand on Marcus's chest. 'A'right son. Calm down.' With Barry, it was all an act. He was enjoying watching this sick reunion, after all he was the co-planner of it all.

'So, you wanted to bring me here and punish me, is that what this is about?' I say through sobs.

'I told you the reason you were here. You work for us now. The club belongs to the McAdams as well as this place and you're going to run both establishments,' Barry says, lowering his hand from Marcus's chest.

'Why not just cut me out altogether?'

'When you took over the club once your old man passed away, you said that you wanted things to go legit. No more drugs, no more deals. Just you running the club and that would be it. It was the perfect way to get revenge. Your old man wanted nothing to do with us. I went to him over the years, suggested that we go into business together. There were multiple business opportunities but he always said no. He would never work with the McAdams. Well, now you've no choice,' Barry said.

I stare at Barry in disbelief. He'd been watching me ever since I gave my baby up. I hadn't given him a name. Hadn't kissed him or attempted to bond with him because it was too dangerous. My aim was to keep him away from all the violence, the threat of danger against our family. There was bad blood between the Aitkens and the McAdams, and falling pregnant by a McAdam was the single most idiotic thing I could have ever done. If only I'd known he was a McAdam at the time, I would have stayed away from Barry. But I didn't because my dad would try to keep me away from that side of things as much as he could. However, as a teenager I was good at keeping secrets and it wasn't until I was pregnant that I told my dad what was going on. I was terrified that he would disown me but I had to tell him. He was my dad. The one who brought me up on his own after my mum died when I was just two.

Even though he smiled when I told him, he wasn't happy about it. At least I thought so. Then he asked who the dad was and when I told him he exploded in rage. He was livid at the fact that his first grandchild shared blood with the McAdam clan. They weren't just gangsters. They were monsters. Traffickers and thugs. I'd been lectured, shouted at, even ignored. I felt like I'd betrayed my family. But I couldn't go through with a termination and as much as it almost killed me, I knew I had to give my baby up. I could've gone down the normal channels of adoption, but I didn't. I chose to do it in a way that kept me anonymous. Kept my child anonymous.

When I ended things with Barry, I would never have imagined that he would have had his men keep an eye on me.

'Now that you know, maybe you'll think twice about screwing the McAdams over,' Marcus says. 'I'm away, need to get back to the flat and get things moving. I'll catch up with you later.'

'Aye, see ye later son,' Barry says, patting him on the shoulder.

'Oh by the way,' Marcus turns back and glances down at his watch, 'in case you were wondering, it's after midnight. Aren't you going to wish me a happy thirtieth birthday?'

I fight back the tears and anger that are trying to burst out of me. Barry hugs Marcus and pats him on the back.

'Happy birthday son.'

'Cheers Dad,' Marcus says, his eyes never leaving me. I shiver, knowing that they were always planning this to happen on his birthday. It's a huge milestone and they clearly wanted to mark the importance of it.

Marcus leaves and when I hear the door lock for the third time, a part of me dies inside. I thought leaving him outside that hospital would have meant he would have had a life away from all this. Barry made sure that wasn't to be the case.

'You knew I was pregnant the whole time? Why didn't you just tell me?' I say.

'Because I was waiting for you to come to me. I would have looked after you. I would have looked after both of you. But you didn't give me that chance. You were going to deprive me of my own fucking son. There was no way I was going to let that happen and there is no way I can let you get away with what you did to him.'

37

AMBER

Sleep escaped me once Jade left. Once the heroin wore off and I was a little more coherent, I began to wonder if she had even come to visit me at all. Of course that's what it does to you. That poison makes you second guess yourself. I remember the conversation. I'd said too much. What if she thinks it's all lies because I was off my face? What if she goes back and tells Marcus what I said about Crystal? I'll be the next one to be killed and stuffed inside a suitcase. I could go to the police with that information but in all honesty, I'm too terrified in case they don't believe me. Where would that leave me? More vulnerable than I am now. And my family. Their lives had been threatened too many times, I couldn't put them at risk.

Pushing the thoughts out of my head, I get off the sofa I've now been lying on for almost six hours and make my way to the bathroom. I need to shower. I need to go through the daily ritual of scrubbing myself clean after a night of clients. Man after man crossing the threshold of the brothel Marcus was keeping me in to earn him money. How is this my life now? I trusted Marcus. Fell in love with him. That was his plan all along, to get me to fall for him so he could manipulate me into his sex business. I'm not a person to him, I'm a product he can sell to men. I'm in so deep now that I can't get out. My family don't want to know. Although, I haven't told them the truth about what has happened. That I'm no longer with Marcus. I don't live with him anymore and I'm now an employee rather than a girlfriend. If I tell them, they would probably take that to mean that it would be easier for me to go home because I'm no longer tied to him. But the truth is it's worse now. I have his men watching me all of the time. I did try to leave and he ended up forcing drug addiction on me. I can't get out now. I'll try, but I don't want to tell them because it would only get their hopes up and I know it would be a false promise on my end. I am determined to put an end to this horrific part of my life but I have to do it on my own. I got myself into this mess, I'll get myself out.

I climb into the shower and allow the hot water to rush over the top of my head. It trickles down my back and face and mixes with my tears. I sit down on the base of the bath and pull my knees up to my chest. I miss my family so much it physically hurts.

After thirty minutes of scrubbing myself and sobbing in the shower, I climb out and wrap myself in a towel. I go through to the bedroom and sit down on the bed before drying my hair and getting changed into a pair of jogging bottoms and a T-shirt. I go back to the living room and pick up my phone with my shrivelled fingers. Should I contact my family? Maybe I could tell them the truth and they would welcome me back home as if I'd never been away. There is one little problem with that. Marcus. He said that he would harm them if I ever betrayed him and that included my little nephew. And I believe him. He's nothing but a monster. A machine who craves money and wealth.

I stare down at the screen and convince myself that just a text to let them know that I'm okay would be enough for now. So I type. I type out a long message, telling them that I'm doing well. I'm happy. I'm healthy and that I miss them. I'll visit them soon, I say. But I know they won't believe that part. Of course they won't because they haven't seen me in so long I can't even remember. They think I've chosen Marcus over them when the fact of the matter is, I've chosen their safety over my need to be with them.

My thumb hovers over the send button for a few seconds before I decide against pressing it. This phone is only in my possession because Marcus bought it for me. If he finds out I used it to contact my family… I dread to think. Maybe I could buy a second phone, one that Marcus wouldn't know about. The only problem there is that I don't have access to cash. It's hopeless. I am well and truly stuck.

Glaring down at the table, I see the needle and the rest of my kit sitting there and I decide to clean it up to take my mind off things.

There is only one way to get the darkest of thoughts and memories out of my head and I don't have the balls to go through with it.

38

JADE

I burst through the door in a blind panic but I can't catch my breath as my phobia takes over my entire being. The fear of the attack happening again while I was out on my own was overwhelming along with the thought that Marcus was someone else, someone I didn't know and had been fooled by. This is the first time in a few days that my fear of being outside and around other people has truly gripped me. I have been so focused on the club and trying to keep Marcus happy that it hasn't managed to get to me as much. I suppose my real phobia now is Marcus. He is my physical representation of agoraphobia.

Marcus is still out and I'm thankful of that. I need time to think about what I'm going to do. On my way back from Amber's flat, I thought about not going to Marcus's at all and going straight to the police. Then I wondered what I would say. What would be my complaint? That he grabbed my wrist and my face. No real harm was caused, not in the eyes of the police anyway. I saw the state Amber was in. She's a functional junkie and a prostitute. Marcus's ex yet she's still working for him. This will happen to me if I stay with him much longer. I can't believe how stupid I've been about all this. He preyed on me at my lowest, just like Amber said he did.

I run to the bedroom and open the wardrobe, begin pulling out what little clothes I have and stuff them inside my backpack. If I have to live on the streets then I will, but I just have to get out of here and away from him as quickly as possible. Going through to the bathroom, I grab my toothbrush and put it in my pocket before throwing the rucksack over my shoulder and heading for the front door. A set of spare keys hang on a hook just to the side of the door and I lift them out of habit and shove them in my pocket.

Please, please, please don't be outside.

If he sees me with my belongings, he'll lose it with me and I'll end up like Amber. I peek around the entrance door of the building. No Marcus. Putting my hood up over my head and zipping my jacket up to my chin, I put my head down and walk around the corner on to the main road. It's busy. Busy enough for him not to notice me if he drives past.

I cross the road and make my way along Argyle Street towards the park. It's sunny and from what I can see, the park is crammed with people for mid morning. Kids playing in the swing park, dog walkers. Hiding in plain sight is probably what is going to keep me safe. I go through the gates and into the park, heading north towards the duck pond. If I can get to the other side and out onto the street, I can grab the first train that comes. I don't care where it's going.

I think of Paul now. Would he take me in if I told him the truth about why I was working at the club? Maybe I could phone him and ask. Then I remember what Marcus said, about the cameras in the club and how he could see every move I made. I would be putting Paul in danger too. Marcus has made sure I have no one to turn to without me even realising it. Bastard.

I reach the pond and turn up the path, heading along towards the exit near the train station. Turning to look behind me and making sure I'm not being followed, I'm satisfied I've not been discovered. Yet. It won't be long until Marcus is back at the flat to find my clothes gone. He'll likely have people out looking for me.

I exit the park and the train station is a few yards in front of me. I'm almost there. Almost away from the man who conned me into thinking he loved me. Of course he doesn't. He never did. What man would ask their girlfriend to become a stripper at his club? What man would make his ex-girlfriend become a prostitute? I shake my head at the thought and enter the station. I look up at the screen and see the train for home. Clydebank, where my old flat is. Not that I have keys for the place anymore. I handed them back to the council when I moved in with Marcus. That was what he wanted and I played right into his hands. Once I'd done that, it meant all I had was him.

Scanning the rest of the screen, I see information on the train for Balloch. It's arriving in four minutes and there are no changes so it's a straight run. Once I'm in Balloch, I don't know what I'll do but I have no connections there so it should be difficult for Marcus to find me. As I wait, I've never been surer of anything that I'm doing the right thing by getting on that train and never coming back.

I sit down on the bench and wait. Four minutes feels like four hours and I pray there isn't a delay. I continually scan the faces in the station, fully expecting to see him standing at the exit, watching me as I try to get away from him. My knee jerks up and down as I sit there, watching the dark tunnel from which I hope the train will emerge any second.

Thankfully, it pulls into the station bang on time and I get onto the first carriage. Sitting down by the window, I realise I only have a five-pound note in my jacket pocket and hope that it's enough to get me to where I want to be.

I'm on the train. I've done it. As it pulls out of the station, I sit back on the seat and rest my head against it.

Now, all I have to hope is that Marcus doesn't find me.

39

MARCUS

Sitting in the car outside his flat, Marcus takes a moment to process the fact that he just told Lizzy he is the baby she left outside the hospital when he was just born. His so-called mother. The rage inside was so intense Marcus thought he wasn't going to be able to control it. He had visions of lunging at her, his hands wrapped around her neck as he squeezed the life out of her. Nothing would have made him happier. The bitch had practically left him for dead that night, why should she get away with that?

Having worked alongside her for the past two years or so, the only reason Marcus managed to keep calm around her was because he knew that one day, he would be able to reveal what was coming to her. He would be able to destroy her world and take everything away from her. That's not to say it wasn't difficult, seeing her smiling face every day, pretending to be her business partner, to like her. It was all rage-inducing. Thank god for whisky.

Back at the house, his old man had prepared Marcus before going inside. Barry had told Marcus that Lizzy would do or say anything to try to make him think that she cared about him and that was why she chose to dump him. Marcus's dad was right. Her bullshit about being fucking heartbroken whenever she thought about that night oozed out of her. How she thought Marcus would believe anything that came out of her mouth was incredible.

Gripping the steering wheel, Marcus's knuckles turn white as he breathes through the rage. One, two, three. It is all he can do not to turn the car around and go back to finish her off. If she's dead, he won't have to think about her anymore.

He's wanted to kill her since his dad told him what she did. Marcus was only twelve when he asked why she wasn't around, why all his friends had mums but he didn't. Barry had told Marcus everything. Straight to the point.

'Yer ma didn't give a shit, son,' he told Marcus. 'She left you outside the hospital. Didn'y want ye. Luckily, I had my eyes on her. We were together for a while and then she ended it between us pretty suddenly, no real reason. So I had the boys keep an eye on her and that's when I discovered she was pregnant with you. I thought she would come to me and tell me what was going on, that she was having you and that she would want us to be a family. But she didn't.'

Marcus had pretended that it didn't matter to him and he'd fought hard against the crushing pain in his chest. Marcus thought things couldn't get any worse, but it wasn't until Tommy came home from football training after school that Barry delivered another blow.

'I may as well tell you both this while we're on the subject. You're not full brothers.'

Marcus knew fine well what Barry meant, but Tommy seemed a little confused. He was more naive than Marcus, a little more sheltered. He liked his football, his friends at school. Yes, as brothers they were close, but Marcus liked the darker side of life that Barry brought to the table. Tommy seemed blind to it at the age of eleven.

'After I brought Marcus home,' Barry said to Tommy as Marcus looked on at them, 'I was already seeing someone else. A woman named Sharon Smith. She had you Tommy, then decided that you'd be better off with me.'

Marcus watched as Tommy tried to hide the pain of the news from showing on his face, but he wasn't fooled by it. He knew his dad well, even as a young boy and he knew only too well that Tommy's mother didn't leave him behind by choice. She would have been forced out.

'This doesn't change anything boys, we're still a family and you're still brothers, regardless of who gave birth to you.'

It was after this that Marcus saw a change in Tommy. As much as he wouldn't admit it, even now in his adult years, Tommy was damaged by finding out he was abandoned. That was the one thing they shared and it had brought them closer together as brothers.

Ever since that day, Marcus has carried a pent-up rage about women. He doesn't trust them. They're only out there for themselves, selfish bitches who don't give a shit about anyone. Marcus learned his trade from his old man. The McAdam name was a big deal in the East End of Glasgow and he was proud to be a part of that. The family now own several nightclubs, two taxi firms and a couple of lap dancing bars, one of which is Angel Silk, and that's just the businesses that are legit. The McAdams are also gun runners, drug dealers and sex traffickers. The latter is run through Angel Silk and with its growing success, Marcus has taken the opportunity to allow it to grow even further. The money that the McAdams are bringing in now mean that they can live whatever lifestyle they want without the worry of finances drying up. The city belongs to the McAdams and that's the way Marcus wants it to stay.

Taking the only source of income from Lizzy was always the aim. Hit her where it hurts because that's the only way Marcus knew how. Killing her would be too easy, as much as he wanted to. Seeing her suffer would be a much better way to exact revenge on her.

Stepping out the car, Marcus locks up and walks up the stairs in the building. Reaching the door, he slides the key into the lock and opens the door before stepping inside. He calls out to Jade but she doesn't answer. He calls again, expecting her to appear from the bathroom or bedroom. Again, nothing.

Hanging the keys up on the hook, Marcus runs upstairs to see where she is. He checks the bathroom, the bedroom and his office. She isn't there. Pulling his mobile from his pocket, he dials her mobile but it goes straight to voicemail.

'Where the fuck is she?' Marcus says aloud, heading back to the bedroom. The wardrobe door is open slightly. He hadn't noticed that before. Marcus moves closer to it and slides it all the way along.

'The little bitch,' he hisses.

Marcus pulls his phone out and calls Tommy.

'Wits up mate?' he says, sounding chirpy.

'It's Jade. She's bolted.'

'Urgh, yer fucking kidding.'

'I'm serious. She's fucked off. Took all her clothes,' Marcus says, slamming the wardrobe door against the surround.

'Thought things were going well, that she didn't suspect anything?'

'Fuck knows, mate. But I'll sort it. I'll go see Amber, see if she knows anything.' Marcus hangs up the phone and goes through to the office. Sitting down at the desk, he notices the drawer is open.

Whatever the reason, she's gone and he's a girl down.

No female screws Marcus McAdam over and gets away with it.

40

LIZZY

I'm alone in this room and my mind is all over the place. How the hell hadn't I noticed it after all the time I spent with Marcus at the club? How had I not seen that he has McAdam and Aitken blood running in his veins? He looks exactly like Barry. He looks like my dad and me.

I shouldn't have given him up. I should have kept my son and left Glasgow. My dad should never have allowed me to go through with what I did. How could he let me, his only daughter, do what I did? My heart felt like it had been ripped from my chest because I felt like I had been let down by my dad, just as I was letting down my own child.

He saw what I became afterwards, saw what it did to me as a person. It broke me. Shattered my heart into a million pieces. Losing the one thing in life no one should ever have to lose, and he sat back and did nothing. He didn't comfort me, he didn't try to talk to me about it. All he cared about was his reputation and what my decision meant for the business.

I went off the rails after it happened. Drank myself into oblivion almost every day to block out the memory of leaving my baby wrapped in a blanket on the ground. I took drugs, partied with the wrong crowd. I even got into stripping at a local club myself. I hated it, but I was often too out my head to comprehend what I was doing. I even slept with a couple of the regular punters. They paid me sometimes which often made me feel so much worse than I already did. My choices back then put yet another strain on the relationship between me and my dad. He often had his heavies turn up to try to bring me home, back to Dad. But I wasn't having any of it. The nightmare daughter was how I thought of myself. That's how he must have viewed me too. I used to give the lads a mouthful when they turned up, saying that if they wanted to take me back to my dad they'd have to do it with me kicking and screaming. Not one of them had the guts to challenge me on that. It wasn't worth the shit they'd get if they actually tried it.

It wasn't until one of the punters tried to force himself on me that I chose to stop working as a stripper and move more into the business side of things, see how it was done. It had in some way helped me to accept the decision I'd made and get on with life. So I went home and moved into Dad's club, Angel Silk. I also ran one of the taxi firms. It was a front for his drug business, but I tried to turn a blind eye to it. Although running both businesses meant no time for myself, it was clear that was what I needed in order to keep myself sane. I ran both for ten years.

Then I took on the other two taxi firms when Dad started to wind down and ran all three plus the club for a further ten years. After a while, I was becoming tired of the dangers, the turf wars and the constant threats of the Aitken Empire being taken down by the latest family who wanted to run the show. So, I told Dad that I wanted to quit. I didn't want to be a part of this world anymore. I wanted to live a normal life, be able to earn my money and not feel guilty when I heard about the latest teenage drug death. That was when he told me he was sick. Cancer. I couldn't believe it. He died very quickly after I found out, but not before he gave me Angel Silk. I told him if I was going to run it, that I would be doing things my way. No drugs, nothing illegal. He agreed and I was relieved.

Dad and I never spoke of Marcus. My son and his grandson. I think the anger he felt towards me about bringing a McAdam into the world never truly faded even though he never said anything to me about it. Knowing he was disappointed in me when he died is something I will never be able to get over, but also knowing that he never supported me when I needed him the most is something I can't ever forgive him for.

Having sold all the businesses except for Angel Silk, it was fair to say that I was well off and in reality there was no need for me to work anymore. I could have brought in a manager to run the place for me. But where would that have left me? I had nothing and no one in my life other than work, so I carried on, putting money in the bank I wouldn't be able to take with me when I finally died. That day would come sooner than I'd realised.

The past never stays in the past, does it? Thirty years have gone by since I gave him up and I often wondered if he knew where he came from. Now that question has been answered and in the worst possible way. What would my dad say if he was here? He'd likely have his men pay Barry a visit. And Marcus. Would I allow that to happen? He is *still* my son. The unconditional love doesn't go away, even after what has just happened. I hope that was the case with my dad when he died.

I look out the window, wondering what is going to happen to me. When Marcus and Barry said that I was going to be working for them and running both establishments, they didn't tell me what *this* place actually is. It's not like the club. It's a house, for a start.

Something in my gut twists when I hear a key in the lock and I turn to face the door. I think about running at whoever is opening it, lunging at them and attempting to get away. Then I push the thought to one side because they'll be expecting it. They'll be ready.

Barry enters the room and closes the door behind him. He's not alone though. Tommy is with him. The sound of the lock turning behind him doesn't surprise me. I'm a prisoner here.

'So,' he starts as I stare at Tommy, 'we're here to go over your job description.'

'You're in on this?' I direct my words at Tommy. The corners of his mouth raise into a smirk and I shake my head. 'Of course you are. You're a McAdam too.'

He doesn't say anything, only nods in confirmation. I shake my head and turn away from him. Of course he's part of this. He came with the security firm that Marcus was running when I employed them. Tommy has been in on this from the beginning.

'I don't work for you,' I say as I look out of the window. 'I'm an Aitken and we don't take instructions from anyone. Especially not a McAdam.'

'Ha,' Barry laughs and Tommy sniggers. 'Who's we? Yer old man's dead, Lizzy. You chose to go down the straight and narrow. You're on your own and you will take instructions from me because I, along with your son, am your boss.'

He's right. I am on my own. I have no other family and I've distanced myself from Dad's contacts and colleagues so there is no one to help me. No one will be missing me. The silence weighs heavy on my chest and the knot at my breastbone tightens. There is no getting out of this.

I turn to face them and sit down on the chair next to the window. 'What's the job?'

'You'll be front of house,' he says almost triumphantly.

'What does that mean?'

'You'll take bookings from clients, deal with the payments. You'll organise the girls and make sure that everything runs smoothly,' Barry says, his eyes boring into mine.

'This place is a brothel?' I can't contain the horror in my voice. 'No way.'

'You will make sure the rooms are ready for the next client. You will organise for them to be cleaned and ensure smooth operation of the business. Do you understand?' Tommy says.

'Have these girls been forced into this the way I have?' My voice is loud, my words hissing through my teeth.

'I said do you understand, Lizzy? Come on, it shouldn't be that hard. You've been running Angel Silk for the past ten years. It shouldn't be much different,' Barry says.

'This is trafficking. It's not right and I won't be a part of it.'

'Oh, you fucking will,' Barry says. 'I'll make sure of it.'

I see the venom in his eyes, the hatred he has for me. It stops me from answering back. If I let my mouth run away with exactly what I think of him and this place I don't know what will happen to me. But I can guess.

'You'll be provided with a uniform. You must wear it at all times. Do you understand?' Tommy says. I nod, feeling defeated. He may as well hand me a white flag.

'Good. We start this evening. Get your shit together, Lizzy,' Barry says.

They leave and I am alone again. How am I going to do this? How can I be part of a trafficking organisation? My dad was right, the McAdams are dirty. My dad and his men would never have gone into this sort of business. It's wrong on so many levels.

I need to try to put a stop to this. I just don't know how.

41

AMBER

Marcus opens the door to the flat and my heart sinks. He's angry. He hasn't said anything yet but I can tell he's angry by the way he's moving towards me. I paint on my best smile as he approaches me. Then I see it in his face. Worry. A look he has never revealed before and something inside me wants to laugh at how pathetic it makes him look, but I know better than to do that.

'Is she here? Have you heard from her?' he says a little too quickly.

'Who?' I ask.

'Don't act wide, Amber. Have you *seen* her?'

I shake my head, attempting my best poker face and lie through my teeth. 'I'm assuming you mean Jade then. Why would she come here? She thinks we're still a thing remember, so she won't want to be near me.'

'Look, if you see her will you just tell her to call me? It's important.'

Recalling my visit from Jade earlier, I am one step ahead of him. I've already deleted her messages and made sure that I have wiped my call log on my phone. Helping her means helping myself. If she has any chance of getting away from him, if she can do it, then so can I.

'Yeah, of course,' I say.

He stops pacing the floor now and looks at me. 'What shit have you been feeding her?'

'Nothing.' I reach for the cigarettes on the table but he quickly snatches them out my hand.

'Funny that. We're fine then all of a sudden she pisses off with all her stuff after spending a couple nights with you? She was asking constant questions about you. Asked if there was anything still going on between us. Did you tell her something you shouldn't have?'

I don't say anything, I just watch him, wary that he's going to lash out. I need to be ready to dodge him.

He throws the cigarettes at me. I catch them in my hand and my heart leaps in my chest. 'I told her you and I were over a long time ago. You told her the same thing, didn't you?'

I pull one of the cigarettes from the pack and pick up the lighter from the table, light it and throw the lighter back down. 'Yes, that's what I told her. Nothing between us.'

A few seconds pass where nothing happens. I don't think either of us takes a breath. Everything is so still. Then, before I can comprehend what is happening, his hands are on me, wrapped around my neck and he is pushing me on to the couch. I can't get a breath, he is squeezing me too tight. I drop the cigarette and it lands somewhere I can't see.

'If I find out you've told her anything to jeopardise what I had going with her, I'll fucking kill you. Do you hear me Amber? I'll fucking kill you.' His nose is pressed against mine and spittle lands on my face. I nod rapidly and he lets go. He gets up and I lay perfectly still. I know this. It's happened before. He isn't finished yet.

'Amber, you're a fucking liability at times. Sometimes I wonder if it's worth keeping you on at all, you cause me so much fucking shit.'

I open my mouth to say sorry but before I can, he's picked up the cigarette and it's burning into my neck. I let out a scream and he moves away. His laughter echoes inside my head, vibrates in my chest.

'Make sure you're ready on time tonight. I've got a surprise for you and I won't tolerate you being fucking late.'

At that, he leaves, banging the front door behind him. Uncontrollable sobs leave my mouth and my chest heaves. The pain in my neck from the burn is unbearable but I get up and move to the bathroom to put some cold water on it as quickly as I can.

Thankfully, he didn't check my phone. Maybe he'll realise and come back to do that. Not that he'll find anything. But he could take my phone away and wait for Jade to contact him. I go to the bedroom window and look out in time to see him pull away in his car.

I hold a cold cloth against the burn on my neck, trying to control my sobs and take my phone out. I dial Jade's number and wait for her to answer. She needs to know that he's looking for her. I need to know where she has gone.

In hearing her voice, knowing that she is still alive and that she has managed to get away from Marcus without him even knowing it until it was too late, I can dream about my own escape and perhaps, begin to believe it.

As the phone rings on the other line, I wait with bated breath until she answers. It only rings three times before she answers, but she doesn't say anything right away.

'Jade? It's Amber. It's okay, he's not with me. I promise,' I say.

I hear her breathe a sigh of relief on the other end and then she says hello.

'Are you okay?' I ask.

'Well, okay in the sense that I'm away from him. Not okay in the sense that I have no money.'

I feel anger for her. Even though she has managed to put distance between her and Marcus, he's done her out of having a chance to survive without him.

'Is there anyone you can go to?'

'Well, there is one person I think could help me. The only thing is, I was in such a panic about getting as far away as my finances would allow that I jumped on the first train that turned up. So I'm in Balloch.' She gives a little laugh but I don't hear the humour in it. 'And now I have no money to get back.'

I don't know what else to say to her. We're both in an impossible position. She is stuck in Balloch with no one and no money. I am stuck here, awaiting Marcus to collect me and take me to the club for yet another shift, before the next shift of sleeping with multiple men just so I can get the fix he forced on me.

'I'm sorry Jade. I hope you can get yourself sorted,' is all I can manage without allowing her to hear the growing lump in my throat. 'And if I ever manage to get away from him and get clean, then maybe we could meet up.'

'I'll come back, Amber. I can come back and help you once I get myself sorted. I can go to the police.'

'Yeah,' I say. 'Maybe.' But the fear of going to the police sits heavy on my shoulders. What if they don't believe us? Or they do but there isn't proof? Marcus is capable of doing anything to protect himself, so I wouldn't put it past him to be able to conceal any evidence that could end his business and put him in prison.

We hang up and desperation mixed with dread grips me. Jade got away but how long will it be before Marcus or his men find her and bring her back? *If* they bring her back. She might end up in a suitcase at the bottom of the Clyde too. And if he finds out I've been in touch with her, then the same might happen to me.

42

AMBER

Marcus waits for me at the front door. He's tapping his foot impatiently and I gather my things as quickly as possible so as not to anger him before I go to the club to do a shift. If we have an altercation, it'll affect my performance tonight and that means less money, which then leads to him losing his temper with me. I feel like all I do is go round and round in my head with this.

We go to the car in silence but the tension between us is unbearable. He's still angry from earlier and the cigarette burn on my neck still hurts like hell. He unlocks the car and opens the passenger side door, making sure I get in. I put on my seatbelt as he closes the door. Out of the corner of my eye, I see him pull his phone from his pocket and he puts it to his ear. I can hear him quite clearly, but I rummage in my handbag so it doesn't look as though I'm listening to his conversation.

'Still no sign?'

He pauses, listening to the person on the other end of the line.

'We canny afford tae lose her, Tommy. Ye should get Rory onto it. He's a resourceful young lad and he's found AWOLers before.'

My heart is in my mouth as I listen. He's talking about Jade. Calling her an AWOLer makes me feel sick. We're nothing to him. I make a mental note of the name he mentioned. Rory. I don't know who this person is, so I need to be careful. This person could be watching me too.

'Aye, well should've and could've isn't going to change the fact that little bitch has done a runner, is it?' Marcus says. Another pause, longer this time. I rummage aimlessly inside my bag and keep my head down. 'Aye, just keep me updated. I'll see ye later on.'

He puts his phone back in his pocket and makes his way around the car to the driver side, opens the door and climbs in. I jump as he slams the door harder than normal.

'You're jumpy the night. Wits up with ye?'

'Nothing,' I say. Normally, I'd have come back with a cheeky or sarcastic remark. That was before he forced me on to drugs and beat the shit out of me. Now that I know what he's capable of and that he's on a rampage because Jade has disappeared, I'd rather not make him angrier.

'Aye, well you might want to tell your face that,' he says before starting the engine. 'Oh by the way,' he says as he holds out his hand. 'Phone.'

'Sorry?' I say as panic strikes me in the chest.

'Give me your phone.'

'Why?' I ask. 'It's my phone.'

'Erm, I think you'll find it's my phone, Amber. I bought it for you, remember? Hand it over.'

I take the phone out and give it to him. All I can think about is if Jade tries to contact me on that, he'll be the one to answer and then he might find her. He might have a tracker on her or be able to trace the call and where it's coming from. I wouldn't put anything past Marcus at this stage.

Pulling out on to the street, he blares his rock music all the way to the club and when we get there, my ears are ringing. I go to open the door but Marcus grabs my hand. He's not forceful though and it throws me. It's the way he used to take my hand when we were together, before I really saw him for what he was.

I turn to face him and his eyes are crystal clear. He has the same look on his face that he did the night I met him.

'If I find out you know where Jade is, you know what will happen to you, don't you?' He says it so softly I have to convince myself it's a threat. Then, he squeezes my hand to the point where I think the blood at the tips of my fingers will begin to ooze out.

I nod and he lets go, forcing my hand away. Then we both get out of the car and head upstairs to the club, all the while I'm praying that Jade doesn't try to contact me on the mobile he's just taken from me. If at least one of us can get away from him, then it's better than us both being stuck under his control.

As I climb, I can hear Marcus laughing with the man standing at the bottom as he mans the door. And while he's laughing, I am trying not to cry.

43

JADE

Wandering through the park and then onto the streets of Balloch, I'm beginning to panic. Why did I get on this train? Why couldn't I have got on the train that would have taken me straight to Paul? Now, I have no money and no way of getting to his place. Unless I walk. That would take days. He lives on the outskirts of the city and I am on the outskirts of the opposite side.

I'll have to sleep rough tonight. I don't have anything that is going to keep me warm. And what if it rains? I'll end up soaked and likely freeze to death. I'm starving and the smell of the chippy along the road is tempting. How can I get some food with no money?

I head in the direction of the smell and pray that I'll fall upon a miracle. Thinking about Paul, I decide that even though I know Marcus would get revenge on him if he found out of his involvement, he is my only option to get through this. There is no other choice. I pull out my phone and dial his number. I have it memorised from when we started going out. It rings. Rings. Rings again.

'Hello?' His voice is calm. Soft. Familiar.

'Paul? It's Jade.'

Silence hangs between us and I wonder if he's going to hang up. He doesn't.

'I didn't expect you to get in touch,' he says. 'Are you okay?'

'Not really,' I say, my voice cracking. 'I need your help.'

'Hey.' Sympathy floods his voice and I'm relieved. 'What's happened?'

'A lot. Can you come and get me please?' I am crying now and tears spill over and pour down my cheeks.

'Where are you?' he says urgently. I hear keys rattling in the background as I stop walking and sit in the bus stop next to me.

I tell him where I am and he says he'll be here in forty-five minutes. He asks if there is anywhere I can sit and wait for him.

'I'm at the bus stop across from the chippy, on Balloch Road,' I reply. 'Do you know it?'

'Yeah, I know it. My gran lived in Balloch when I was a wee boy.'

We hang up and I put the phone back in my pocket. Now, all I have to do is wait for Paul to come and get me and I might finally be safe. If Paul can help me to figure out what to do, then maybe I can help Amber get out. Maybe I could help others.

Forty-five minutes comes and goes. It's been an hour and ten since I hung up the phone to Paul and I am beginning to think that he has changed his mind and he isn't coming. Then, a car pulls up beside me and he gets out. He's smiling and I burst into tears. I'm hysterical and I can't control it.

Paul rushes around the car towards me and pulls me in, hugs me tightly against his chest. 'I'm sorry it took longer than I thought to get here. There were road works in the West End.'

'I'm sorry for dragging you out here. I just don't have anyone else to turn to.'

He leads me to the car and I get in the passenger seat.

'Is this about that nightclub? Has something happened to you in that place?'

I shake my head. 'Just take me to yours, please. I'll tell you everything once we're there.'

Paul doesn't hesitate. He does a U-turn and heads back in the direction he came from. Every so often during the journey, he glances over at me but I don't meet his gaze. I feel guilty, like I'm using him. Feel like a fraudster because other than grab my

191

wrist, Marcus hasn't actually done anything bad to me. Has he? Other than insisting I work in the club as a dancer, but can that really be counted as abusive? The confusion makes my head feel fuzzy and I push the thoughts of Marcus away.

'Almost there,' Paul says. 'The bed is already made up in the spare room, so once we get there we can get you something to eat and if you'd rather wait until tomorrow to tell me everything then that's okay.'

I smile at him in silent thanks. I feel so mentally exhausted that I don't think I could string a meaningful sentence together if I was paid. I allow all my weight to fall into the seat and rest my head against the window. Closing my eyes, I listen to the cars as a rush of wind passes us every few seconds. Then, I succumb to sleep. It's not real sleep. I'm in a vivid dream-like state where I know what I'm seeing isn't real, but it could be. Marcus is staring at me and mouthing in silence that he will find me. No matter where I go, he'll be one step behind me and if I want to survive, I'll always have to keep one eye over my shoulder.

Forcing my eyes open, his face is gone. There is only a long stretch of road ahead of me and Paul by my side.

44

JADE

The feeling of anxiety in my chest is so intense it wakes me. The smell of coffee and toast as soon as I open my eyes makes my stomach begin to growl. As I look around, I remember I'm at Paul's house. This thought alone should make me smile but I don't, because this could all be over soon. The idea that I have broken free from Marcus isn't far from being snatched away from me. The dream of Marcus telling me that he will be one step behind me wasn't *just* a dream. It was my subconscious telling me what I already know.

The door behind me opens and I roll over, pulling the duvet with me. I look up and Paul is standing just inside the bedroom with a subtle smile on his face.

'Morning. Good sleep?' He asks it the way a dad would ask his daughter and now I feel like an imposter.

'I tossed and turned most of the night. Can't get rid of the stress knot in my chest,' I reply as the pain returns. I rub at it with my fist.

'Hungry? I've made some breakfast if you fancy some?'

'Yeah, I'll be out in a minute.'

He closes the door and I sit up. The sun is shining through the window and I realise that it must be late morning. I glance at the bedside digital clock. It's eleven. I must have fallen into a proper sleep at some point then.

Swinging my legs over the side of the bed as I push the duvet off, I get up and move through to the kitchen. My stomach rolls at the thought of having to tell Paul why I asked him to come and collect me last night. Although, he's not stupid, he'll have worked it out for himself having found me at Angel Silk.

'There's toast on the table. You still like eggs, don't you?'

I nod and sit down at the table.

'There's fresh coffee and I've made a pot of tea. I remember you liked both.'

I sigh, his kindness and lack of reference to the fact that we fell apart is making me feel emotional. I swallow hard and pour some coffee into a mug which he has left on the table. I grab a piece of toast and take a bite and think about how Marcus used to make me breakfast. How he used to look after me when I first met him. He was kind, loving and generous. That person seems so far from the one I ran away from yesterday.

Paul places a plate of eggs on the table and sits down in front of me.

'So, you want to talk about it?' he asks.

'I left my boyfriend,' I say.

'Okay,' he replies, taking a sip from his mug. 'And you're still working at that club?'

'No.'

'Can I ask why?'

We're both quiet for a moment and I take longer to chew my food than necessary because I don't want to say it out loud. I feel stupid for getting involved with Marcus. For not seeing him for what he really is. But then he never actually did the things to me that Amber says he did to her. So maybe I have overreacted. There is a voice at the back of my head, screaming at me for thinking such a stupid thought. Of course I wasn't overreacting, he lied to me. Made me think I was going to be working as a barmaid when his intention all along was to have me working as a stripper and god knows what else if I'd stayed. I've done the right thing because Marcus wouldn't change his ways for me. I was always going to become another Amber or Crystal. Because the truth is I'm not as strong as Amber. Picturing her in my mind now, as a junkie and a prostitute all because he ground her down, bit by bit, I wonder how quickly I'd have become the same.

I shrug my shoulders in response to his question and he nods.

'Jade, you came to me for help. But I can't help you if you don't tell me what you need help with. So, why don't you start from the beginning? I promise I won't pass comment until you have finished.'

I glance at him and he smiles a little wider this time and I feel myself relax.

'I'll just sit here and eat in silence.'

'Oh, so you don't still chew like a pig then?' I say and laughter rises from my belly.

'Oi, it's a sign of enjoyment.'

I take a deep breath and choose my words carefully, and still now, I can't believe I am going to say it out loud.

'Jade, you've gone really white. Are you okay?' Concern is etched on his face as nausea threatens.

'I...' another breath. 'It's Marcus, my ex. He's dangerous. I know this girl, Amber. You met her at the club before I came into your booth.'

Paul lowers his head as if he's ashamed by his visit to the club. I ignore it because it's not a path I want to go down with him. It's not necessary. If he hadn't shown up that night I might not have had the courage to phone and ask him for help. 'She used to be his girlfriend, before I met him. She told me that she used to be me, in love with Marcus, would do anything to make him happy. He showered her with gifts, compliments. She moved in with him and then, she started working for him at the club. But that's not all. She's not just a lap dancer. She's a prostitute.'

Paul's eyes widen slightly but like he promised, he doesn't interrupt me. I've gone off my breakfast and push the plate away from me.

'He held a gun to her head. Forced her on to drugs. I saw it with my own eyes. Amber's a junkie because of him. The place she's living in, the building… it's like a brothel, it is one. She told me she tried to get away from him but couldn't and told me if I had half a brain I'd run while I still had the chance.'

Tears spill over but I wipe at them furiously because I don't want to cry. Not because of Marcus.

'Jesus, Jade. And that's when you called me?' Paul says in an almost whisper. I nod. 'Has he ever…' He clears his throat. 'Have you ever had to?'

'No,' I shake my head. 'But he did get violent with me and I think he was close to pushing me further at the club. And now that I've done a runner, he'll be out there looking for me. If he thinks Amber has anything to do with it, he'll hurt her. I mean really hurt her. She told me a story about how the body in the suitcase that was washed up at Luderston Bay could be one of the girls before her.'

Now that I've said it out loud, the sobs come and I can't control them.

'I said I'd go back for her once I've settled, if Marcus doesn't find me. I told her that I would help her if I could.'

Silence hangs between us like a thick black cloud. Now that I'm away from that life, I could just move on, start afresh and forget. But how could I forget about Amber? About the other girls at the club? She was decent enough to tell me to run while I could. She told me all about Crystal. I can't just keep that information locked away. I'd be letting Amber down when she has no one to turn to.

Paul rises from his seat and comes around to my place at the table. Crouching down, he hugs me. 'You're going to be okay. You're a strong person, Jade.'

'I don't think so,' I reply. 'Yesterday, when he dropped me off after my shift at the club, he hurt me.'

'What did he do?' Paul asks. His tone is calm but I can see the fire raging in his eyes.

'He asked me about you.'

'Me?'

'Yeah, he said that I should remember that he has eyes on all of the girls at the club and he could see that I was talking to you in the private booth. He asked me who you are. I told him the truth, that you were an ex. I thought honesty would be the best thing, although when he asked what you were talking to me about I just said that you asked how I was doing. But he was angry, grabbed my face and my wrist, told me that if he found out I was lying, he wouldn't be responsible for what happens.'

Paul sits back in his seat, exhales loudly.

'I didn't want to let it get any further than that. So now, I'm here.'

'And you won't be going anywhere until we've sorted this. I'll go to the police on your behalf and—'

'No,' I say loudly. Paul stops and stares at me. 'If we go to the police, he'll know it was me and it could put Amber in more danger. No, we have to get her out first.'

'How?'

I glance at Paul and I know that what I'm about to ask him could put both of us at risk. For all I know, Marcus might already know where I am and could be watching me right now. And he knows Paul's face from the club. But if it means stopping Marcus from hurting any more people then it'll be worth the risk.

45

AMBER

'Where are we going, Marcus?' I ask as the club fades from sight.

'It's a surprise. I already told you that I had a surprise for you, didn't I? he says, smiling widely at me. I smile back but I have to force it. Something is wrong. Marcus normally takes me straight back to the flat after a night at the club so I can carry on with my shift, carry on making him money. He has something bad planned for me and the fear that is coursing through my veins is making me want to open the door and jump out of the car even though we're doing almost forty miles per hour.

'I don't like surprises. Can't you just tell me?'

'Nothing's ever good enough for you, is it Amber? Look, I don't want to hurt you. Bruises aren't good for business, so do yourself a favour, just keep your mouth shut. Once you get there, you'll enjoy yourself.'

My heart sinks then because that is what he said to me when he moved me to my flat. He said that I would enjoy living there, I would enjoy the job he'd promoted me to. Job. I almost laugh out loud when I think of that word. I've been forced into this life. Forced into becoming addicted to heroin and made to sleep with strange men in order to keep the withdrawals at bay.

My stomach begins to cramp and a silky film of sweat builds on the back of my neck. Not now. Of all times, now is not a good moment to start to itch for another fix. Withdrawal is like a demonic shadow, always two steps behind me no matter what I do or where I am.

We are in the car for a further twenty-five or thirty minutes and the urban landscape is slowly becoming more rural. We're leaving the city and the streetlights behind, and I have absolutely no idea where he's taking me. It's too dark outside to be able to determine where we are. The only lights are from his car, highlighting the road ahead.

Then I wonder, perhaps he's found Jade. Maybe she's been battered to the point where she had to tell him what we talked about and he's decided he's going to finish me off. Am I being driven to my death? It would make sense to do it at night, less eyes to see what was going on.

'I feel sick,' I say. He barely hears me over the music and he turns to face me.

'Eh?'

'I said I feel sick. Pull over, Marcus.'

'D'ya think I'm fucking stupid?' he snarls. The car rounds a bend on a country road and my stomach feels like it's about to fall out.

'Marcus, unless you want me to throw up all over your precious car, then please pull over,' I almost shout.

'Urgh, fine,' he grunts and pulls into the next layby. I get out of the car and stand with my hands on my knees, hunched over.

The stomach cramps are unbelievably painful and I feel like my skin is going to crawl off me and into the long reeds of the dark field ahead of me. I breathe in deeply, cold and fresh air filling my lungs. There is something about being out here, in the middle of nowhere all consumed by the dark of the night. In a strange way, it makes me feel invisible. Like I could dive into those reeds and he wouldn't find me. He'd call my name, but his voice would be carried away in the wind and he wouldn't be able to tell the difference between the sounds of the wind rushing through the long grass and my body as it wades through the fields.

Marcus hasn't got out of the car. That surprises me. I *could* run right now and he would have to chase me. I could hide somewhere out here in the blackness and he'd struggle to see me. He wouldn't give up looking though. Losing me would be like losing a shit ton of money to him.

My thoughts are short-lived when I hear his door slam closed. He isn't stupid. I know that for sure. He knows what is going through my head and he's getting out to make sure that I don't execute an escape plan.

'Thought you said you were going to throw up?'

'I was. I think it was car sickness,' I say. 'All these winding roads in the dark.' I stand up and the cramps ease slightly. I know the pain won't go away properly until I get my next fix but if it remains at this level for the time being, I might make it through the next few hours. Unless he kills me beforehand. Is that an option that I don't fear so much anymore? Perhaps being dead would mean I'd finally be rid of his evil manipulation.

'Right, get back in the car.' Marcus stands next to me as I stare into the fields. There is a house at the top of the hill. The windows are dark, except for the warm glow of light in one. Perhaps someone in that house has heard a stationary car, has looked out the window and can see us? Maybe I could call out for help, scream and shout and make a scene. How can I make a scene out here in the dead of night? I don't know for sure if someone from that house has seen us. I might just put myself in more danger by causing a fuss.

Instead, I turn and climb back into the car. Marcus climbs in too and locks the doors. Protecting his business. That could have been my chance to run. That could have been my only chance to get away and I didn't take it.

Fear overrides the need to run and I hate that about myself. That fear has become the thing that stops me from keeping myself safe in the long run, it drives me to want to avoid immediate threat from Marcus.

'You heard anything from Jade?' he says as he pulls the car back onto the road. I put the window down slightly and the breeze against my cheek feels nice.

'No.'

'Are you sure?'

'How the hell could I have heard from her, you took my phone away?'

I hear him take a deep breath. My words have infuriated him but he doesn't react in the way I thought he might.

'Marcus, why do you think she left? I thought things were going great between you both? She seemed really happy. Happy enough to warn me off her precious boyfriend,' I say, in the hope that my voice isn't laced with the sound of lies.

'Don't push it, Amber.'

'Sorry. I just don't get why she upped and left with no explanation. Unless something has happened to her that you don't know about? I mean, you must have rivals in the city. Could someone have broken in and—'

'Nothing has happened because she took all her fucking clothes,' he says, banging his hand on the steering wheel. 'The bitch left me in the lurch.'

The words hiss through his teeth and I know I've overstepped the mark so I decide to shut my mouth. The fact that Jade has gone is really affecting him. I can hear it in his voice, see it in his face. Even his body language tells a story. He is tense, pissed off. The idea that a girl like Jade had outsmarted him like she did caused an excitement inside me because I knew that he wouldn't be able to find her, she'd left no clues as to where she was.

After a few more minutes, Marcus makes a left turn, then a sharp right and we make our way up a long driveway. The ground is lit up by solar lights which line the edges. The car stops and I'm looking up at a large house. I say large, it's more like a mansion. Bigger than any house I've ever seen. It looks beautiful, like a normal house. Like one a celebrity might stay in.

'What is this place?' I ask.

'It's your new place of work,' Marcus says as he turns off the engine.

My nerves are alight, firing inside me as I dread to think what is behind the walls of this house.

Marcus is already out of the car. I'm frozen in my seat, limbs heavy with terror. Marcus opens my door and stands back, waiting for me to get out. I step out carefully and jump as the sound of the door shuts behind me. Marcus is already getting my things from the boot.

'Right, come on.'

Staring up at the house, I don't move. I see someone in the window on the first floor, behind a netted curtain. A woman. She is looking back at me. Glaring. I turn away, knowing that she is in the same position as me. I know what this place is.

'Oi, I said move it,' Marcus says, tugging at my arm.

I follow him inside as we move through an archway which leads to the front door. It's new, I can tell by the smell. Brand new wood. Marcus unlocks the door with a key and moves to the side.

'Ladies first.'

I have to stop myself from giving him a dirty look as I walk inside the house. It's not like an ordinary hallway. Or maybe it is. I've never been in a house this big before.

It's like the reception of a hotel, or at least what I would imagine it to look like. From what I've seen in holiday brochures that my mum used to look through when I was younger, they look just like this place.

There's a desk on the right-hand side and a set of stairs in the centre, which lead up to another floor. The décor is dark and badly lit with shitty bulbs. A bit like the private booths back at the club. Marcus pulls me towards the desk and tells me to wait there.

There's a younger man, a boy I'd say, standing next to a closed door on the opposite wall to where the desk sits. He doesn't look at me, but I think I recognise him. One of Marcus's security guys, no doubt.

My heart begins to beat faster as I wait for Marcus to come back. I cannot run. Too many eyes on me, some of which I know are there but cannot see. And he locked the front door behind him so I wouldn't be able to get out.

I hear footsteps above and I turn to see Marcus coming down the stairs. He isn't alone. My stomach flips as I see who he is with.

'Amber, meet Lizzy. Your new manager. She will be organising your diary for our very new premises,' Marcus says, his wide smile matching the wideness of his eyes.

'Amber?' she says, her chin almost hitting her chest.

Lizzy and I stare at each other for a brief second and she mouths the words *I'm sorry.*

'Hang on a minute, you've been part of this the whole time?' I say in disbelief.

Lizzy shakes her head but doesn't say anything.

'You'll also be interested to hear that Lizzy here is my long-lost mother. We're keeping this a family business. Now Lizzy is going to show you to your very upmarket suite, with views of the country. The sunset from that side of the house is spectacular and you'll be glad to hear it comes with its very own master en-suite. The clients will love it because they'll feel like they're in a high end hotel with extras on the room service menu…' He smirks as his eyes dart between Lizzy and I.

I shudder at how he describes it but I can't hide the shock I feel as it creeps onto my face. Lizzy is Marcus's mum? How the fuck had that happened? I look closer at Marcus and my eyes dart between their faces. I can't see a resemblance, but then I can't believe any of this is happening at all.

Lizzy turns her back to me and begins climbing the stairs. I hesitate until Marcus shoves me hard towards the bottom of the stairs and then I follow her. As we climb, Lizzy just a few steps ahead of me, all sorts of things are going through my mind. Has she been in on this the whole time? Is she the mastermind behind the whole operation?

Then I think about the look on her face. Her expression when she saw me standing at the desk as I waited for Marcus.

She was shocked to see me. There was something else too. Sadness? Regret?

We reach the top of the stairs and Lizzy walks along the hallway and turns left. We pass two doors and she stops, pulls a bunch of keys from around her neck that I hadn't noticed before now, and unlocks the door. She opens it and steps inside the room.

'This will be your room,' she says as I enter. 'This is where you will…' She hesitates and clears her throat. 'Entertain your clients. I will arrange your bookings and you will make sure that you are ready for each one. There is a bathroom just in there.' I follow her gaze and see a door slightly ajar. A bathroom where I can clean myself up after each client.

'Marcus is your son?'

She doesn't react to my question or look at me. 'I can't believe you, Lizzy. How could you do this to me? You're a woman for a start. But of course, if he's your son like he says he is then why wouldn't you be part of it? I didn't even know you had a son for fuck's sake.' I say, my words catching in my throat as the horror of the situation overwhelms me.

'Amber, I'm not part of what Marcus has planned for this place. I promise you. I had no idea what was going on at the club. I'm ashamed to say that he was so clever, I was blind to what he and Tommy were up to. I was kidnapped and brought here against my will by his dad and…' She pauses. 'It's all a bit messed up.'

'You're telling me? You're not the one who was duped into a fucking relationship with a monster, forced into lap dancing and prostitution and…' Now it was my turn to hesitate. 'Left with a fucking addiction to heroin.'

Lizzy's eyes widen and she moves away from me, towards the door. She's going to leave. She's going to walk out of here and lock me in this room and I'm never going to be able to escape. I should have run across that field towards that house when I had the chance.

'Amber, I'm so sorry. I don't know what to say other than we'll get out of here. We will.'

'No, we won't Lizzy. You've been trapped by Marcus a lot longer than I have and you didn't even know it. We're fucked, for want of a better expression.'

I turn my back on Lizzy and breathe deeply. The sound of her leaving and locking the door behind me shocks me, because deep down I didn't think she would actually leave me in here by myself.

Lizzy, the one woman who had been at the club to protect us from the sleaze bags, has left me in a locked room as prey to the men who will travel here to this house to pay for sex.

The window on the opposite wall invites me to try to open it. I pull at the latch but as I push, the window remains firmly closed. Maybe I could throw myself at it. Maybe I could put enough weight into it that the glass would shatter and a piece of it would slice at a major artery and I would bleed out here in this very room.

I'd be free then, of what lies ahead of me. More withdrawal, more men coming and going.

I don't throw myself at the window. Instead, I collapse onto the floor and lay there in the foetal position because I don't know what else to do. Jade said she would come back for me.

Now, she won't know where to find me.

46

LIZZY

I stand outside the room in which I've had to lock Amber and the crushing feeling of guilt almost suffocates me. She thinks I knew what was going on at the club. She believes that I have been part of Marcus's organisation since it all began. I don't blame her. A woman running a club, her son is the head of security. Of course she thinks I'm part of it, why wouldn't she? I would if I were in her position. But there were no signs. No hints that there was anything untoward going on. All the personal information I had on the girls at the club seemed legit. None of the girls shared the same address, not even Amber was registered as living with Marcus. He and Tommy kept the place secure, kept a very close eye on the punters. They were just extremely good actors, playing very dangerous roles.

I take a deep breath and move towards the top of the stairs. Tonight is my first night of organising the bookings for the brothel and I don't know if I'm going to be able to do it without throwing up. How can I answer calls from men who want a list of women to choose from?

'Amber all settled in?' I hear Marcus's voice coming from the floor below and I grit my teeth.

'I wouldn't say settled in. But she's in her room.'

I glance at the doors which line the hallway. There are so many, which means there are many girls being forced to live here, or soon will be.

'It's time you had a proper tour of this place so you know who and what you're trying to sell to the customers.' Barry's voice makes me turn and I see him standing outside a room which, when I glance past him and inside, looks much like an office.

'No thanks,' I sneer. His face contorts with anger and frustration.

'It wasn't a suggestion,' he replies as he makes his way towards me. He reaches my side and I can smell him. The same aftershave he wore when we were younger. It takes me back to when I was seeing him when I was nineteen and I resist the urge to gag. If only I knew then what I know now.

'Right, there are eight rooms up here, all of which are occupied,' he starts, moving along the corridor. 'The price lists are downstairs at the desk with each girl's profile and description in a separate file. When a customer phones, you take their order and assign them a time slot.'

Nausea climbs up from my stomach. If I didn't know any better I'd say he was talking about taking a car for a test drive.

'Oi!' He starts clicking his fingers at me and I snap my head up, look him straight in the face. 'Fucking concentrate, Lizzy. You're front of house, you need to know your shit.'

As we pass each room, Barry opens every door and introduces me to some of the girls. I know them all, or at least I did at one time or another. All ex-dancers from the club. I'd had communication from them about their departure from the club. Texts, emails, written letters of resignation. Even a few phone calls. Not once did I pick up that they were being forced to do it. I had been so blind it was sick.

They look at me with disgust and I know they hate me, even if they know I've had nothing to do with how they came to be here.

Barry shows me some rooms downstairs, more girls. I don't know these ones. Marcus had them recruited out with the club apparently. I'm so deeply involved in the exploitation of these girls and there is nothing I can do to stop it.

Standing at the bottom of the stairs I'm face to face with Marcus. My son. How can this man be him? How could I have got it so wrong? I thought I was doing the right thing. I wasn't discreet enough, hadn't realised that Barry was having me watched. I'd left my son so he could have a decent life, away from the shit that Glasgow had to offer and I ended up leaving him with the one person I wanted to avoid. He was exactly like his dad, the opposite of what I'd wanted him to be. He was earning a living through exploiting these girls, lining his pockets on their misery. I shouldn't have left him. I should have held him close, left Glasgow with him strapped to my chest.

'Now the induction is done, you can get to work,' Marcus says as Barry disappears back upstairs to his office. I stand there, still and disgusted with my eyes on my son. Marcus hands me a leaflet and when I look down at it, I resist the urge to gag. The pricelist along with images of the girls stares back at me. Amber is at the top of that list, as though she were the speciality on the menu. My stomach churned at the thought. 'The phone on the desk has a digital version of the leaflet on it, when you get a call, you can send it over to the punter on the phone so he can decide who and what he wants. Got it?'

I glance up at him in disgust. All I can do is nod.

'Why are you just standing there? Get behind your desk and start taking bookings. We're going to be busy tonight,' Marcus says, rubbing his hands together.

I watch as he walks away and then the mobile phone on the desk starts to ring. My stomach churns at the thought of what is about to happen. I contemplate not answering it. I could refuse.

'Oi, you deaf?' the young lad standing by the door opposite from the desk says. 'I think Marcus told you to get answering the phone?'

He must only be around eighteen, if that. Skinhead and black suit don't really go, but he seems to want to make an impression with his boss. Exploitation is at the very heart of this place and everyone working for Marcus, regardless of whether they have chosen to or not, is being exploited. Used for financial gain.

I lift the phone and press the accept button, take a deep breath and force myself to use my best phone voice.

'Good evening,' I start. 'Angel House. Can I take a name?'

As I listen to the man on the other side of the line, I flip through our catalogue and read out the names and descriptions of the girls who are already here. There are eight of them including Amber.

I purposefully miss her out. Young skinhead doesn't seem to have noticed.

47

MARCUS

Marcus heads back out to the car. He can't stand to look at Lizzy and his dad has agreed to head up Angel House, so he can keep an eye on everything there. Tommy is running the club and Marcus finally feels like he can go home and try to work out where Jade has gone.

He sits in the car and pulls Amber's phone out of his pocket. It's off, so he switches it on and waits for it to fire up. It's a basic mobile, not a smartphone. He doesn't want any of the girls having access to the internet. It's too dangerous for business, too tempting for them to contact home if they have access to the internet. If people are out looking for them, it would be too easy for them to be found. For all the hard work he's put into the businesses to be scrubbed out by the filth that manned the streets of Glasgow. No, basic phone call and text-worthy phones are all the girls need. They can be topped up by Tommy or Marcus. Not that they do that often. There's no need for the girls to make calls, not when they should be working, but they always have just enough to call or text Marcus if they need to. Or Tommy. Of course, it's a risk by allowing them even the most basic of mobiles, but he has to have some way of contacting them.

The girls he's recruited over the time he's spent at Angel Silk are special. They have specific qualities about them, all unique. Crystal, his first. She was tall, blonde and beautiful. A clear complexion meant that she needed very little makeup to make herself look the way she did. The punters loved her at the club and she was helping Marcus and Tommy to make a lot of money. She was one of the first and gave Marcus the taste for more success from that place.

There were a few others, but none of them could compare to Amber. The fiery redhead with curls that fall to just above the waist and hips that could put a man into a trance... Marcus knew as soon as he met her that she had to be on his payroll. He almost fell for her in the beginning, but he reminded himself that he should never mix business and pleasure. Taking Amber away from the club is a risk he's willing to take. Yes, she's the highest earning dancer and one that the regulars would always come back for. But she'll be able to earn him so much more at Angel House full-time. He would be able to replace Amber at the club with two girls if it came to it. Amber feels like a prize Marcus has won.

Then there was Jade. She isn't as beautiful as Crystal or Amber, but she has the shy quality that drives some of the punters nuts. That's the one thing that was missing from the club. But he fucked up. Took his eye off the ball and now she's gone.

He looks through the messages and call logs on Amber's phone. There is nothing other than some messages between them. Jade hasn't been in touch with her, so it would seem.

Marcus sits back and thinks how he'd put in so much effort with that girl. He sought her out, watched her for months. Got to know what she liked, what she disliked. She was a nervous person, didn't like being out too much. She preferred her own space, didn't spent a lot of time with anyone. Had a boyfriend although things hadn't been going well in that department from what Marcus could understand even before he'd arrived on the scene. He assumed that was because of her need to be on her own a lot. An introvert. Someone who could easily be moulded into someone else if enough time and effort was put in.

He knew what food she liked, what she drank. He knew how she dressed, how she wore her hair. Marcus became obsessed with learning all about Jade. It wasn't until he felt like he had enough information that he knew it was the right time to make his move.

The young teams of the surrounding areas are a force to be reckoned with. The girl gangs are just as bad, if not worse than the boys. Marcus remembers it well. The young team he'd been part of was brutal. Muggings, light robbery and attacks were something that he and the lads would happily take part in if it meant a few quid went into their back pockets. No one ever reported them to the police because Marcus was always recognised. Barry McAdam's boy. You'd have to be stupid or brain dead to want to grass a McAdam.

Being part of the young team eased Marcus's need to be part of *something* for a while. He was an angry young lad. Struggled with his emotions. The day his old man told him about Lizzy and what she had chosen for him when he was just a baby had rattled Marcus. The feeling of rejection had sat heavy on his chest ever since.

Marcus's dad had let him see how business was run when he was just fifteen, let him feel part of something bigger than he could have ever imagined. Barry McAdam could see young Marcus was getting bored and quite frankly didn't want his son getting into any more trouble on the streets. Some braindead fucker on a death wish was bound to go to the police at some stage. No matter what, Marcus's old man didn't want the filth sniffing around. It would be bad for business.

Marcus moved away from the young team then. No one asked questions. They knew who he was, knew the family. There would be no messing about with Marcus or any of the McAdams.

Marcus had thought of the young teams of the East End back when he was gathering information on Jade. And that's when he realised, the best way to get close to her was to give her a reason to trust no one but him. So Marcus had gone to the YEEG, the Young East End Girls. They were hard, some of them harder than any of the lads he'd ever hung around with when he was a teenager. Some of the girls had their emblem shaved into their skulls. Even Marcus would have felt intimidated by them had he come across them in his day.

They'd surrounded him on approach, so many he couldn't count. They'd asked what he wanted, and why he was there. When he told them who he was and associated with, their hardened exteriors softened a little. One of them even said she felt like she was in the presence of royalty.

Marcus instructed them, told them who their target was. Gave them a photograph. He paid them well, a little too well but the job was done quickly. Although, when he heard that Jade was taken to hospital and of her injuries, Marcus was angry that one of the girls had gone too far, she'd had to be dragged off Jade by the others. Apparently she'd been warned beforehand by the others not to lose control but she hadn't listened.

Marcus had gone back to their usual hangout spots a few days later and had taken Tommy with him. When they saw both men approach, silence fell upon the group.

'So what the fuck went wrong? I told you what to do. So how the hell did she end up in hospital with a punctured lung and internal bleeding?' Marcus hissed through his teeth.

'Sorry Mr McAdam. It was Josane. We tried to stop her but she went into a mad frenzy. She's like that, ye know. A bit skitzo,' one of them said, twisting a finger into her temple.

'Aye,' the rest of them said in unison. Marcus and Tommy looked for her in the group but she wasn't there.

'And where is Josane now?' Tommy said.

'She's in the hoos. Properly shittin herself that you'll do her in,' another said.

Tommy had laughed at that point, told the girls to tell Josane that she'd be fine. The girl they'd attacked wasn't going to die, luckily for her. Marcus hadn't laughed. Not one bit. They could have fucked things up for him. Could have seen off another avenue in his business. Instead of losing his temper, he'd simply turned his back on the girls and said nothing. That would have been enough for them to know not to mess things up again if he ever came to them with another job, although in his head he found that doubtful.

Now, all the work Marcus had put in and all the money he'd paid the YEEG was for nothing because Jade has outsmarted him and done a runner.

'Fuck!' he shouts, banging his hands on the steering wheel. 'Jade, you little fucking bitch, if I ever find you!'

Marcus stops and takes a deep breath. He can't lose it, it won't be good for business. He promised himself the last time that he wouldn't do this again but Jade has caused such anger inside that he doesn't trust the promise he'd made to himself. Luckily, he has a good team behind him and it's not like death is a new concept to them. He's part of the biggest crime family in Glasgow, his old man has built an empire and Marcus will inherit all of it. Right now, he's running the show. Dealing with betrayal isn't something that scares him, it doesn't faze him at all. But it's a distraction. Also, the betrayal itself is something he can't get his head around.

Why do women have to have two faces? Why can't they just do what he wants, be what he needs them to be? He doesn't trust any of them and that stems from a long life of unanswered questions.

Marcus starts the car and looks up at Angel House. That's the place that's going to make him. That house is the place where things will go his way.

He can feel it in his bones.

48

LIZZY

The men who have come and gone tonight have barely been able to make eye contact with me as they've entered and exited the house. They should be ashamed of themselves. Paying for sex from vulnerable girls is disgusting, yet here I am booking them in. They appear to be wealthy men, not like some of the ones I've come across in the club over the years. Top-end cars are parked outside the house and the owners don designer clothes. These kinds of men are different, they're looking to make sure their money stretches as far as it could here and Marcus has seen a gap in the market.

Nausea overwhelmed me when I looked at the pricelist. Some of the things the girls are being paid to do are so outrageous and disgusting, I can't bear the thought of anyone who would want to put someone through that for their own pleasure. The punters for this place are just as bad as the people who own it.

Angel House is situated in the middle of nowhere, so that men of high profile and extreme wealth can drive all the way out here, away from the city and prying eyes and ears. Angel House offers privacy and anonymity. But not for the girls.

I've never understood the word helpless more than I have in the last few days. So much has happened, I feel like I have been in this house for months. I've lost and found things I didn't think were possible. The business is gone, in the hands of the McAdams. And I've discovered that my son has been conspiring against me, trying to bring me down to the bottom of his pit.

How could my sweet baby boy have turned into such a monster? One answer. Barry McAdam. The poisonous snake of a man had filled his head with the way of life I'd wanted to protect him from. Now I wish I'd just taken my baby and left. Of course that wouldn't have worked because Barry knew I was pregnant and had eyes on me from the second he found out.

Now, I've dragged so many girls into this mess. Good girls who had a life ahead of them out with the realms of the Glasgow underworld.

It's fast approaching three in the morning and the phone has stopped ringing. No more men come through the door and things are quietening down. Skinhead has left for the night and there don't seem to be any McAdam men around. So, I do what I'm supposed to do and go around to check that the girls are settling down, safe and preparing for the next night. It makes me feel sick that I'm in charge of them. It's not like at the club. Or at least not the way I thought it was. Here, I am effectively pimping these girls out whether they've chosen to be here or not. Illegal is illegal.

I climb the stairs and knock on each door, popping my head around and offering a smile. Most of them seem friendly enough. Of course they do, they don't want to upset their bosses.

I reach Amber's door and knock gently before letting myself in. As I enter, she is sitting on the bed, her eyes wide. Her hands are trembling a little and when she sees that I have noticed this, she puts them under her thighs.

'What the hell do you want?' she says, turning away from me.

'I need to talk to you. I need you to understand that I had no idea any of this was going on. I'm as much a prisoner here as you are.'

She turns to me, eyes wider than before and alight with anger. 'Are you actually kidding? You don't know the meaning of the word prisoner, Lizzy.'

I don't know how to answer her. I don't know how to explain any of this.

'So, you're mummy dearest?' Amber smiles and shakes her head. 'Are you blind? I mean, surely you *must* have seen some sort of resemblance? You're his mother for fuck's sake, you were working so closely with him for how long?'

'Two years,' I reply.

'And you had no idea? Don't talk shite.'

Silence hangs heavy in the air and I sit down on the edge of the bed. She's broken, I can see it in her. I know how it feels to think there is no way out of a situation, although our situations are very different.

'This is why you asked me to give you an advance on your wages, wasn't it? You wanted money so you could get away from him?'

'Spot on, Lizzy,' Amber whispers. Her voice cracks a little before she clears her throat. 'Shame you couldn't have figured that out then. You were supposed to be there to look after us and you had no idea what the hell was happening right under your nose, Lizzy.'

I shake my head. I regret not being more vigilant. Marcus hadn't needed to be clever about how he conducted his business. When he said he knew some girls who were willing to work in the industry, I took him at his word. I didn't question how he knew some of the girls he put through the doors, I just let him get on with it. The same way I allowed my dad to control things when he was around.

'All I can say is sorry, and please believe me when I say I'm going to try my very best to get out of here and go to the police.'

Amber explodes in a fit of laughter and it's so loud I jump, stand up and step back from the bed.

'I promise you. I do.'

'Lizzy, let's not kid on. For want of a better expression, we're all fucked here. The only way we're leaving here is in a box. Or a suitcase.'

I frown at the last comment and she sees it.

'Remember Crystal?'

I nod.

'Did she ever tell you she was leaving? Or did she just disappear like Yasmin?'

I think back to when Crystal worked at the club. She was there long before Amber. A lovely girl, full of ambition to own her own beauty business. She wanted to dance to make enough money to fund her college course in order to step onto the business ladder. After only a few weeks, she left me a letter. Dancing was no longer for her and she had a new job that would see her earn more money in a smaller time frame.

'She left me a letter,' I say.

'Aye, of course she did. Same way Yasmin sent you a text.'

I feel sick. Amber is right, how could I have been so blind to all of this?

'Luderston Bay, body in the suitcase. It was Crystal. And how do I know this? Because Yasmin told me. And what happened to Yasmin? Oh yeah, she went missing. Only this time, there is no body so we don't know for sure if she's dead. But I'll tell you one thing, if she is dead I hope it was quick. Marcus is a monster, he loves to see people suffer. Trust me, I lived with him for long enough.'

Tears prick the corners of my eyes and anger fires in my belly.

Barry McAdam had dragged our son up to treat women like property and I was in the midst of it.

'We'll get out of here,' I start to speak but Amber holds her hands up and shakes her head.

'No, Lizzy. We won't get out of here. We won't.'

I hear a stark truth in her words. And they run so deep it terrifies me.

49

MARCUS

Marcus arrives back at the Glasgow Harbour flats and gets out of the car. He knows he shouldn't have driven, but when Marcus wants something, there's nothing that will stop him. He'll deal with any fallout from driving over the limit when he's sober. From what he can tell, there doesn't seem to be any blue lights flashing nearby, so it seems he's off the hook for now.

He'd sat in the office at Angel Silk with Tommy for the majority of the night after leaving Angel House. At first, he'd caught up on some paperwork, delegated some jobs to the lower end of his staff. Debt collection, organised a drug and gun dispatch and delivery. Then, he found the bottle under the desk. Knowing that he'd taken Lizzy out of the equation, he felt incredible.

Pulling it out from underneath, he'd forgotten he'd left it there in case of emergency celebrations. It was as good a time as any to open it but before he knew it, he sank the lot. No one at the club asked questions. No one challenged him on driving the short distance back to the Harbour. They wouldn't dare. He was the boss now and would answer to no one.

The night air is cool against his skin as he heads for the main entrance. He takes the lift up to the top floor where his apartment sits on its own.

Trying to get the key into the door is a task when he is seeing two of the lock. That bottle of whisky has hit the spot, really helping him to focus on something else other than all the things that are going wrong.

Jade. The bitch is gone. But he will find her and when he does, god help the girl. If the suitcase hadn't washed up on the bay a few weeks ago, he would have liked to have disposed of Jade in the same fashion. Doing so will only bring more attention to the fact that there could be a murderer on the loose in Glasgow and he doesn't want anything to jeopardize his future. He will have to get creative, think of another way to get rid when he finds her. And he will find her, no matter what it takes.

He finally manages to get the key into the lock but he falls against the door and almost loses his balance. Regaining his stance, he twists the key and falls into his apartment. The city lights glow inside the apartment from the balcony window.

Closing the door behind him, he stumbles to the drinks cabinet and opens it. The whisky bottle that sits inside is only a quarter full. Pulling it out, he unscrews the lid and drinks straight from the bottle as he staggers towards the sofa.

Falling down on to the soft white leather, Marcus stares out at the city and smiles.

'Fucking marvellous,' he says, swigging back more of the amber coloured liquid. Fucking *Amber*. There's another bitch that causes Marcus nothing but grief. A necessary evil she is, a pain in the arse but a fantastic earner.

'Aye, I'll kill her tae,' he slurs. 'One day when she's no longer good for us.'

Marcus sits the whisky bottle down onto the floor and pulls his phone out, starts scrolling through the images in his gallery. All girls, some of whom are currently working for him, some of whom could potentially be working for him. He has many possibilities up his sleeve and he loves that fact.

Scrolling further through the images, he stops at the one that makes him the angriest. Lizzy Aitken. Dearest mother.

Staring down at her, the anger inside mixes with the whisky contents in his stomach. Swallowing hard, he tries to focus on her face. Smiling as she chats with someone in the street, unaware that he'd even been watching her. She'd looked happy. Seemed happy ever since he'd known her.

'How could you… be happy?' His words slur. 'When you left yer wee boy tae die?'

Memories drift in on a drunken haze of when he was just a boy. Every birthday, every Christmas he wondered if a card, a present or even Lizzy herself would turn up at the door. She missed everything in his life and deep down it bothers him.

He remembers the endless women Barry would bring home with him. Some lasted longer than others in terms of relationships. Some were kinder than others too. He and Tommy would get excited at the prospect of having a woman around the house, a mother figure. At the time, Marcus didn't know what to expect from a mother figure and it upset him as a child that he never got to find out. Tommy too. As they'd grown older, and the women stopped falling for Barry's charm, Marcus and Tommy had come to realise that they in fact didn't need a mother, or a permanent relationship. The clubs had come to teach them that. Women were there for one purpose only. Satisfaction. They had their pick of so many over the years, especially in their early twenties. Marcus had come to learn that the more charming he was, the likelier they were to drop their knickers for him. That was all he'd wanted and then he'd send them on their way. He never became attached. If he was honest he didn't know how to form an attachment with a female. He'd never had a role model, that was fair to say.

The alcohol begins working on his eyes, making them heavy, closing slowly as the phone slips from his hand.

Marcus's body has slid down the plush leather sofa and he's now propped up against it. Reaching for the bottle, he takes another mouthful, and another until the bottle is finished. He drops it back on to the floor and lays his head back.

Feeling around for his phone, his fingers slide around the device and he lifts it to eye level. Opening his eyes again and attempting to focus, Marcus's eyes fall upon Lizzy's face once again.

Lizzy Aitken's face is the last thing he sees as he falls into a drunken sleep.

50

JADE

I sit in Paul's house, awaiting his return. It feels strange being alone in here after everything that has happened. The last few months have been odd. I thought I was in love. I thought I'd found the one. I genuinely believed that Marcus was the guy I was going to grow old with. How could I have been so wrong about him? So blinded by him? They do say love is blind, but I'm as well not having the power of sight at all considering the red flags I missed.

The presents, the new mobile phone, the club. Not to mention the careful manipulation that again I didn't notice until I'd left. Even when Amber told me about her relationship with Marcus, or when she told me about the girl, Crystal, I still had doubts that he was a bad person. It wasn't until he was physically violent that I realised I had to get away from him. I've been gone for two days and I feel like I'm remembering someone else's life. Like I watched it on a screen. I'd have been shouting at the TV, *get out, run*. But you don't see it when you're living it. You don't feel it when you're there every single day.

When Marcus asked me to go out for walks with him, when he told me that it would do me good to get out and face my fear, I hadn't realised that he wasn't taking no for an answer. Gently pulling me to the door in order to get me to do what he wanted me to. He wanted me out the house, outside and in the open. Around people. He was doing it because he was training me into being able to withstand being away from the

223

comforts of the indoors, so I would be able to get up on that podium and dance around a pole for money. I hadn't realised that's what he was doing. Why would I? I thought he was trying to help me to overcome my fear, but it was all for his own gain.

I get up from the sofa and have a quick look out of the window in search of Paul. His car isn't in the drive to indicate he's back and I don't see him in the street. I'm fearful of what I've dragged Paul into. He probably doesn't understand the full extent of what Marcus is capable of. He threatened me when he thought I was lying about Paul, so I dread to think what Marcus would do to Paul if he ever found us together. And yet Paul is out there, doing things for me I never thought he would. He is helping me to get out of this situation and I don't think there are enough ways to thank him.

Sitting back down on the sofa, I stare blankly at the TV screen as it talks to itself.

The guilt I felt when I didn't want to go outside with Marcus overwhelmed me. I decided to put my need to please him as my first priority and do what he wanted because I loved him and didn't want him to be upset with me. His manipulation skills were on point, he got exactly what he wanted from me and very quickly. If it hadn't been for Amber, I'd probably be living in that building with her, being pimped out by my own boyfriend.

The sound of a car approaching makes me get up and look out of the window again. Still not Paul. He has been gone for almost two hours now and I'm beginning to panic. What if Marcus has him? What if Marcus hurts him to the point where Paul tells him where I am?

I shake the image from my head. The irrational thoughts that overload me are becoming too much and the pain in my chest is back. It's been annoying me since I left Marcus but only worsens when I'm on my own. I know it's stress-related but sometimes it hurts so much I can't catch my breath.

I begin to pace the floor in the living room, so many thoughts running through my brain like they're being played to me on a projector. How had I got to this point in my life? Things had been going well for me. I'd had a good job, a nice flat. Then it all fell apart.

The attack. Meeting Marcus. The club. Amber, the drug-addicted prostitute. Crystal, the dead girl in a suitcase. Closing my eyes tight doesn't help. I can still see them all.

The very idea that he would have sold me for sex with strangers twists in my gut. I take a few deep breaths, trying not to allow myself to think of what could have happened to me. When I open my eyes, I see Paul's computer in the corner. I get up and move towards it. Switch it on.

As I wait for it to fire up, my right knee shakes under the desk and my trembling hands rest on the surface in front of the keyboard. The screen comes to life and I open up the Google icon.

I type in the words that have been at the front of my mind since I heard them. 'Luderston Bay, body in suitcase.'

The screen is filled with images of the picnic spot in Greenock. Police tape, police guarding the entrance. An image of a suitcase similar to the one mentioned in the article appears. Purple leopard print. One that you wouldn't fail to notice. I feel sick as I click on the most recent article.

8th January 2020
BODY FOUND ON LUDERSTON BAY IS YET TO BE IDENTIFIED

The suitcase killer is still on the loose and may be for some time as the identity of the body is still unknown. No one has come forward with information about the girl in the suitcase and from what police are saying, there have been no missing person's reports that match the description of the female.

I click out of the article and type in the words, 'Crystal, Angel Silk, Glasgow, Dead.' I scroll through screeds of pages but nothing seems to link together. Angel Silk's website gives very little away, and certainly doesn't have names or faces of the girls working there.

The sound of a key in the front door makes me jump and I close the browser down before getting to my feet. I move out to the hallway and meet Paul at the front door.

'Hey. Sorry I took so long, the queue was massive,' Paul says as he closes the door behind him. I eye the bag in his hand and he holds it out to me. 'I got it.'

We go to the living room and sit down together. I pull the boxes out of the bag and stare down at them. Then I turn and wrap my arms around Paul.

He hugs me tight to him and I realise this is the safest I've felt in a long time.

'Thank you, Paul.'

'Hey,' he pulls away and looks at me. 'Anything I can do to help.'

I pick up the first box and open it, pull the mobile phone out and then the charger. Paul takes it from me and plugs it in to the wall and then we do the same with the second phone.

'This will work, won't it, Paul? I mean, we will get Amber away from there?' My voice trembles a little.

'I don't know, Jade. But you got away, didn't you?' He sits back down beside me and takes my hands in his.

'Yes, but she is in a lot deeper than I am. He has her hooked on drugs, Paul. He's as well chaining her to the wall in that place.'

My chest is beginning to tighten with anxiety again but I breathe through it.

Paul doesn't say anything, instead, he holds my hand as I breathe through the gripping panic and the realisation that if I fail in my bid to get Amber out of there and have Marcus and his sex business brought to justice, we could all die.

51

MARCUS

The sun beams through the large window overlooking the city and Marcus squints as he opens his eyes. The pain in his head shoots down and into the back of his neck and he groans as he attempts to sit up slowly. Nausea hits his stomach instantly and he slows down his movements to keep his stomach in one place.

His eyes come into focus and he sees the empty whisky bottles, alongside an empty bag which had contained a gram of cocaine and his phone. Turning his head to the right in the hope that his wallet would be lying next to him, he breathes a sigh of relief. Thank fuck, losing that would be a migraine rather than a headache.

'Have fun, did ye?'

'Jesus,' Marcus cries as Tommy comes into view. 'You nearly gave me a fucking heart attack, Tommy.'

Barry McAdam appeared next to Tommy and shook his head. 'Marcus, you've been on a two-day bender. What the hell are you playing at? Was this some fucked up thirtieth birthday celebration?'

Marcus sits up and runs a hand over his face, rubbing his eyes vigorously. Two days of booze and drugs. On his own. His old man was right, what the fuck *was* he thinking? Then the image of Lizzy Aitken comes into his head and he remembers. It was all a bid to forget but the reality worsened under the heavy hangover and come down.

'Aye, I was just blowing off some steam. What's the problem?' he says, getting to his feet and moving towards the

227

kitchen. He turns on the tap and sticks his mouth under, gulping in mouthfuls to take away the sand-like feeling in his throat.

'Marcus, you know what the booze does tae you. Ye canny handle it, mate. It's sends you loopy,' Tommy says, lighting a cigarette and opening the balcony door. The sound of the city floods the room and a rush of cool air flows through.

'Uck fuck off Tommy,' Marcus says with a smile. Tommy doesn't return the gesture.

Barry places a hand on Marcus's shoulder and squeezes. 'Son, I told ye in the beginning if I put ye in charge of operations you would have to be clean. You'd need a clear head. You promised that this wouldn't happen. So what's changed?'

Barry's voice is low but firm. Marcus notes the concern in his voice, but isn't sure if the concern lies with him or the business.

'Nothing's changed. I just had a blow out, that's all. We've all done it,' Marcus replies, standing up straight and turning the tap off.

'Then get yer shit together and meet us downstairs in ten minutes. We've got Angel Silk, Angel House and a couple of drug runs that need tending to and me and Tommy here canny organise the jobs and run things on our own. You wanted more responsibility, so get a fucking grip of yersel. Understood?' Barry turns his back on Marcus and walks out of the apartment.

Tommy hangs around, waiting for Marcus to get himself showered and changed. 'Hurry up, ye don't want him kicking off.'

Marcus rolls his eyes and moves to the bathroom. A cold shower would actually do him the world of good, wash the hangover off and numb his mind to the thoughts that were slowly breaking him inside.

As he stands under the cold water and it assaults every one of his senses, Jade pops into his head. That little bitch is still out there and Marcus has allowed her to remain hidden while he drank and took drugs for two days straight. His dad is right, the businesses can't be run without him.

Marcus steps out of the shower, shivering after the cold water has powered down on top of him. It has worked. He feels better now.

Picking up his phone, Marcus contacts the main girl, Josane from the YEEG. This is the same girl who took things a little too far with Jade initially, but in hindsight it worked out for Marcus. She answers after only one ring.

'Mr McAdam, wit can I dae fur ye?' she asks.

Marcus goes on to tell her about what has happened with Jade and instructs her to get the girls together to find her.

'I don't care how you do it, but just get it done. It's of high importance that this girl is back with me sooner than possible.' Marcus can't hide the urgency in his voice and it's clear that Josane can hear it.

'And what's in it fur us?' she asks with suspicion.

Marcus clears his throat. Josane and the rest of the YEEG don't know the ins and outs of Marcus's business with Jade, or any other for that matter. Keeping that quiet could be detrimental to Josane finding her. The group are nothing but thugs, but even Marcus knows there's a strong possibility that they could pull away from him if they know why he's summoning Jade back to him.

'You'll be paid double than you were last time, and if you can get her to me within the week then you get a twenty per cent bonus.'

'Fuck me,' she says. 'You really want us to find her, eh?'

Again the words float through the speaker on a wave of suspicion and Marcus finds himself trying to think of a reason why having Jade back is so important. Then he remembers who he is, and his rank in the underworld of Glasgow.

'Aye, I do. So are you interested or not?'

'Mr McAdam, have I ever let you down?' Josane replies and this time he can hear her smile. This girl is savage, he only had to look at Jade's injuries back when he first met her to know that.

'Good. Keep in touch. Oh, and Josane? When you do find her, keep her in one piece eh? I don't want a trip to A&E on my hands.'

'Right ye are, boss.'

Marcus hangs up and starts to get dressed. He knows Josane and her girls will get the job done. They did the last time so there's no reason they can't now. Jade won't have gone far. Marcus didn't give her access to cash at all in the time she was living with him, so she won't have the funds to travel.

After he gets dressed, he steps into the lounge and Tommy nods. 'Ye good?'

'Aye,' Marcus replies as he pulls out his phone. 'Just going to give young Rory a call, I need him to deliver something for me.'

'I'll meet ye downstairs then. Hurry up eh, don't want tae have tae listen as Barry moans about ye while we're waiting.'

Tommy leaves and Marcus hits the call button. Rory picks up after the second ring.

'Boss?'

'Rory, I need you to get something to Amber at Angel House. When the boys are getting ready to do their delivery later, I want you to put some by for me. I'll let you know when it's ready and then you can take it to her. Understood?'

'Aye boss,' Rory says. He likes that about the young lad. He never hesitates. A bit like Marcus in his younger days.

'Good lad.'

Marcus hangs up the phone and heads down to the ground floor, where his old man and Tommy are waiting.

'Right, I'm fresh as a daisy. Let's do this.'

Barry shakes his head but Marcus sees a very slight hint of a smile raise the corner of his mouth as they get into the car.

52

AMBER

I forget where I am for a moment, just a second, upon opening my eyes. There is nothing in my head, only blank space. Then I remember where I am, who I am and what has happened to me and the same everyday feeling of dread creeps over me and settles in my stomach. The constant nausea is hard to live with, but not as difficult as the crippling withdrawal that hits me.

I've been here for two nights now. No one has come to my room other than Lizzy. I have had no visits from any clients, thankfully, and I have a feeling that is down to her. It's the least she could do for me after letting me and the other girls down. From what I could gather, there's a pricelist floating around with all our pictures on it. Apparently that's how the punters who want to come here get to pick us. It makes my stomach turn at the thought. I thought I'd be used to this by now, I've been doing it for that long. But not like this. Stuck away in a room in a huge house in the middle of nowhere with the furniture bolted to the floor and the doors locked. The people who are running this place have already anticipated that some of us would try to get out.

Marcus hasn't been near me since he brought me here and I am beginning to wonder if this is the start of my spiral towards death. The bin in the corner is filled with my vomit and a greasy film sits heavy on my skin as the withdrawal continues to eat away at me. The room stinks and I'm at a point now where I don't really care if I die. It would release me from this hell. I shake my head at the thought. No, I can't die now. I haven't even tried to save myself. I have to give it one more shot.

Just one hit, that's all I need and I'll be able to focus on how to get out of here. I've tried banging on the door. Tried pulling the handle to open it. I've even contemplated throwing myself through the glass window but the thought of it fills me with fear. The idea of shards of glass shredding my skin on the way through it keeps my feet on the floor.

My mind has been warped with strange dreams. I'm the one in the suitcase. But I'm not sinking to the bed of the ocean, instead I'm floating on the water, desperate to move towards land. The sail is one huge purple leopard print piece of material with a rip down the centre. The wind howls through it and I'm not going anywhere. In the dream, or nightmare, I see Jade on the edge of a pier, screaming at me and holding out her hand. When I try to reach out to her, I fall into the water. It's recurring. Over and over I feel like there is a little bit of hope that I will make it through this. Then I drown.

The sound of a key in the door jolts me from going over my nightmare and I sit up on the bed, expecting to see Lizzy and her poor attempts at a smile. The face which appears before me isn't one I recognise.

'I've brought you something,' the lad says as he enters the room quickly. He doesn't lock the door.

'What?' I say, glaring at him.

He produces a small box from behind his back and sits it on the floor. I know what is inside it.

'You Amber?' he says in a thick Glasgow accent. I take in his appearance. He's slightly taller than me, slim-build, short hair styled similarly to Marcus's. He's wearing a plain black T-shirt, tailored trousers and I'll admit it, he's handsome. He has that same twinkle in his eye Marcus did too, when I first met him. Looking at him now, I'd say Marcus is trying to create a clone of himself. The thought makes me shudder. I can tell just by looking at him that he is young. Younger than me. I'd guess seventeen, eighteen at a push. But he looks physically fit and I know instantly that he would be able to restrain me if I tried to get past him.

'What's it to you?' I say, drawing my eyes away from him.

'Well, if I was a client, Marcus widnae be very happy tae hear ye talkin like that, wid he?'

I glare back at him and laughter escapes my belly before I can stop it. His expression changes then, his eyes narrowing as my laughter decreases.

'Since when did Marcus hire little boys?'

The lad rushes across the room. As sluggish as I feel because of the withdrawal, I'm quick to move out of his way. I'm on my feet and making for the door but he anticipates this and gets there before I do. His back is to the door and he holds out his arms, pushing me back. I fall down and hit the floor. The base of my back explodes in pain and he is above me now, his eyes wide with fury.

'Don't underestimate what us *little boys* are fucking capable of, ya wee fucker. You don't need tae ask why Marcus McAdam hired me, all ye need tae understand is he did and he thinks I can handle the likes of you.' His spittle covers my face and I shut my eyes, ready to take a beating. He goes quiet and when I open them, he's already up and by the door. He kicks the box towards me and smirks. 'Marcus says ye've tae sort yerself oot wae that shit and he'll be here tae pick ye up at seven.'

I scramble for the box as a wave of shame washes over me. I want to tell him to get out but I'm too focused on what is inside the box. Marcus has deprived me of this for two days. It's felt like two weeks. Getting me hooked on this stuff and then controlling how often I can have it is one of the hardest things I've had to deal with, and that's not even the worst of what he's capable of.

I glance up at Marcus's apprentice and he smirks at me.

'I don't give a shit what you think of me, at least am no fuckin junkie.'

He leaves the room and my heart sinks when I hear him lock the door.

Getting to my feet, I move towards the bed and open the box. The needle is there, like it is smiling up at me because it knows I should but won't resist. My heart tells me to flush it down the toilet. My head is telling me to let it sink deep into my vein and allow relief to take over.

As I pick up the box, I start to weep.

53

AMBER

I wish I could say that the earlier fix had sorted me out, but it hasn't. Not for long anyway. It's only been six hours since my last dose and already I am beginning to itch for more. Thankfully the feeling is easier to cope with than if I hadn't had a dose at all.

Looking up at the door, Marcus is leaning against it waiting for me to be ready to go. He has come to pick me up to do my shift at the club. I haven't been at the club in three nights. As much as I hate the place, it could be an opportunity to run.

'You girls take so fucking long to get ready,' Marcus remarks. I ignore him as I sling my bag over my shoulder.

'You're quiet,' he says as I approach the door he is standing in front of.

'What do you want me to say?'

'I want you to thank me for giving you a fucking job. I want you to be grateful for the things you have.' He leans down, his nose almost touching mine. The calmness in him chills me.

'Thank you,' I whisper. It's quite pathetic how little of myself there is left.

Marcus stands up and glares down at me for a moment longer, before opening the door and allowing me to move out of the room first. As we head downstairs and past the reception desk, Lizzy doesn't look up.

'Lizzy, things good here?'

She says yes without meeting his eye as she flicks through what looks like a diary. I suspect she is pretending to look busy.

I stop at the main entrance of the house. It's locked, of course. A prisoner at Angel House. That's what I'll call my autobiography if I ever get away from this life and get to write it.

'Right,' Marcus says as he appears next to me. 'Let's get you back in the game, shall we?'

He takes hold of my upper arm just before we step out to the drive and holds me back. Marcus doesn't say anything. It's a warning. A physical warning so that I know if I try anything stupid, he'll be on me straight away.

I don't turn to face him, I don't meet his eye. Instead I wait for his warning to end, for him to let go of me and allow me to get into the car. Yes, I need to behave like a good girl and do what he tells me then everything will be alright. Except it won't be alright because I'm a drug addict and a prostitute and I am being sold for money.

He closes the door behind me once I'm in my seat and locks the car before going back into the house. I watch him go, wondering what he's doing. He'll have forgotten his phone, or perhaps he's going inside to speak to one of his men or Lizzy. Whatever the reason, he has left me in this locked car and my mind starts to spin. Would he be stupid enough to leave a spare key somewhere in here? I glance up at the house, the windows to check that no one is watching me. When I'm sure I have a few seconds, I open the glove compartment in front of me. I shuffle my hand through bits of paper, a packet of mints. No key.

The compartment clicks closed and I reach up and pull down my sun visor. No key. I reach over and pull down his sun visor. Still no key. I blow air out of my mouth in annoyance. Of course he's not that stupid. He'll have anticipated my every move.

I sit back in the seat and wait for Marcus to return, accepting that this time, this moment right now isn't when I will make my break for freedom. If I knew how to hotwire a car, I would be out of here by now.

The front door to the house opens and I keep my eyes on him as he exits onto the drive. He's not alone. He puts his hand on her shoulder, guiding her towards the car and her eyes lock with mine.

She climbs into the car in silence and I keep my eyes ahead. Marcus closes the door and as he walks around to the driver side, I can't get my words out. I want to turn, to check that it's actually her. But I can't because now he's in the car and already reversing.

The drive to the club feels longer than it did when he brought me to Angel House for the first time three nights ago. We pass by the house at the top of the field. The field I'd contemplated running into and hiding among the long reeds, hoping that the darkness would have swallowed me up.

I look out the window at the vast countryside views as the sun begins to set, wishing I could see the beauty of the world that everyone else sees.

Then I catch her eye in the side mirror, I can just about see her reflection. She is looking at me too. I can't believe she's here, after all this time. I thought she was dead. I thought Marcus had killed Yasmin because she'd told me about Crystal. Instead he'd decided to fuck with my head, make me think she'd been punished in the worst way. Even though he never acknowledged my encounter with Yasmin, I remember the look he gave us both that night at the club when I asked to speak to her. When she'd come to my flat after our shift and told me about Crystal, I'd felt sick to the stomach.

He must have known. He has eyes on all of us.

After around a forty-five-minute drive, we pull up outside Angel Silk and Marcus walks us up the stairs and into the club. He walks us straight into the changing room and checks on the other girls. They all smile at him, chat to him. Some of them are here by choice, I know that. But that will change soon enough. Marcus is building an empire and the more product he has to sell, the more money he'll make.

'I'll be back to get you both at one. You have appointments in the diary from two-thirty. Make sure you're ready when I get here,' he says, glaring at both of us. He leaves and as I turn to face Yasmin, she is already sitting in front of a mirror in the far corner. I catch her eye and move to sit down next to her.

'Don't,' she says. 'The last time I spoke to you I ended up...' She stops talking and takes a breath before she begins applying a layer of foundation. The dark circles under her eyes tell me that I know what's happened to her because she looks the same as I do. Broken.

'I thought you were dead,' I say.

'So did I.'

'What happened? Did he find out about what you told me?'

'He's never actually said that he knows I told you about Crystal, but I'm not stupid. He's always been clear that he has eyes on his girls, no matter what we're doing or where we are.'

'So where the hell have you been? You just disappeared, Yasmin.' I have to fight back tears.

'He took me to Angel House. I was there before the place was even finished.' She holds out her arm and I see the same trademarks from my own arms. My heart sinks.

'Bastard knew what he was up to. Always has done. He's had Angel House planned for fuck knows how long, Amber. When I saw Lizzy there I was nearly sick. Did you know she was working for him?'

I watch as Yasmin applies liner to her lips. The sadness and desperation in her eyes make me even more determined to get away from here.

'Lizzy doesn't work for them. She was kidnapped, taken to Angel House like the rest of us. Apparently she's Marcus's mum and she gave him up when he was a baby.'

Yasmin smirks. 'Aye right. Good cover story. Do yourself a favour Amber, don't believe a word any of them tell you. We're here to make them money and that's it.' Yasmin's eyes fall from my gaze in the mirror's reflection. 'No offence, Amber but the last time I had a conversation with you, I ended up in a lot of trouble. So I don't think we should have any contact from now on.'

Yasmin gets up and moves towards the hangers on the back wall of the changing room. I get it, I'm not hurt by what she's said. She's just broken. That word doesn't cover it. Shattered and destroyed would fit her better. Just like me. Like Crystal. All of us.

As I turn towards the mirror and stare back at myself, I pull the makeup pouch out of my bag and begin applying my foundation to the dark circles under my own eyes. No punter in this place wants a junkie dancing over the top of them. This isn't the flat that Marcus created as my own personal brothel that I used to live in. It's not even Angel House. The punters here will pretty much take you whatever way you are. Marcus likes to pretend that they won't, that the men like their lap dancing prostitutes with a bit of class. But I've come across many who would take you if you'd just shot up and were pretty much on another planet. They're not in it for the conversation, or the personality a girl might possess. All they want is a young girl flaunting her almost naked body over the top of them.

I see Yasmin head for the door, leaving the room and heading out to the bar area. The rest of the girls do the same and for a moment, I am here on my own thinking about how I want to go home. But that place doesn't exist to me.

I have no one.

54

The club is busy tonight, then I remember it's Friday and all the sleazy men of Glasgow will be out in force. I've already done seven private dances, all lasting ten minutes each. And I know I won't see a single penny of that money in cash. It'll come in the form of drugs and a roof over my head.

I get back on to the podium and see Yasmin has gone into a private booth with a punter. She's been busy tonight too and I can't help but think about her situation and wonder where she's come from. How she's ended up here.

I dance as though I'm on my own and no one is around to watch or pay me, when a familiar face catches my eye. He's sitting at a table on his own and he motions for me to join him. I step down from my place on the pole and walk towards him. His eyes are fixed on me and I can't place where I recognise him from. It's likely I've given him a private dance before and his face is stored somewhere in my memory. Or possibly I've slept with him back at the flat. There have been so many it's impossible to remember all of them.

'Hi,' I say.

'Ten minutes?' He raises a brow.

I nod and he follows me to a private booth. The man sits down and I pull the curtain before I begin to dance. As I turn, his eyes are locked on mine and he opens his mouth to speak.

'Don't respond. Don't ask questions and make sure you don't move your mouth. If there are cameras in here like Jade said, then it's for both our safety that you remain quiet. Keep dancing as you would normally and just listen to me.'

My stomach flips when I hear him mention Jade.

'I'm a friend of Jade's. The man who owns this place hurt her and she came to me for help. She has asked me to help get you away from here. So I have stashed a mobile phone in the female toilets, in the third cubicle. It's behind the sanitary bin. It is fully charged, has plenty of credit and the charger is there too. All you have to do is get it in your bag and wait for Jade to phone you. Don't call out from it until you've heard from her.'

As he instructed, I dance as normal and then sit on his lap with my back to him. I lay my head back on his shoulder. He's right, there are cameras in these booths, on us all the time and I know where the camera is in this booth, so my head is blocking his face.

'If you understand, stand up and twirl,' he says.

I do that and then return to my position on his knee.

'Jade wanted me to tell you that she's okay and to thank you for what you told her about him. We'll get you out of here, Amber.'

I don't say a word in response. I keep my expression neutral and continue to dance. Only six minutes left. It's a long six minutes but I have to make it look genuine for the camera in case Marcus or Tommy or any of their men are watching. Which they will be.

I get to my feet at the end of the dance and Paul leaves the booth. We don't look at each other as he passes me. I take a moment to catch my breath and try to fight the tears that threaten to fall.

As my heart thumps inside my chest, I straighten myself, stand tall and walk out of the booth fully expecting Tommy or one of the other men to be waiting to interrogate me. But there is no one. The girls remain in various parts of the club, dancing, serving drinks and mingling with the punters.

None of Marcus's men seem to have noticed what has just happened. I take a moment to centre myself. It wasn't a dream, it really happened. Jade said she would come back for me and she bloody well has.

I head to the bar and ask for a glass of water. Downing it in one, I head straight to the bathroom. I can't wait for any length of time to see if the phone is there or if this is a sick joke Marcus is playing on me, which I know is an irrational thought but very possible at the same time.

I head straight for the third cubicle and close the door. Lock it. Turning, I stare down at the sanitary bin. I peer over the top of it and there, as he said it would be is a mobile phone box. I need to get it out of here and into my bag before someone else finds it. Before Marcus finds it.

I flush the toilet in case anyone else is in the bathroom. As I make my way out and across the floor of the club, I head straight for the changing room where my bag is in the hope that I am not being watched. Grabbing my bag, I turn and head out the door and back towards the bathroom. I push on the door and almost bump into Yasmin as she is coming out.

'Shit!' I say. I move back quickly and close my eyes for a moment.

'You okay?' Yasmin says, frowning at my reaction when I open them.

'Yes, I just didn't expect someone to be on the other side of the door. That's all.'

She moves out of my way and then she looks down at my bag before glancing back up at me.

'Period,' I say. 'It's a bastard in a job like this.'

I move away from the door. Inside the third cubicle, I close the door and lock it. I wait a few seconds, listening for anyone who might come in.

When I feel it's safe to do so, I open my bag and then reach down behind the bin and pick up the box. I place it in my bag and close it again. Breathing a sigh of relief that I was able to do this without being seen, I pull down the toilet lid and sit down.

This could be the most dangerous thing I've ever done since getting involved with Marcus. If I get caught, he will kill me.

He'll find Jade and do the same. I have no doubt about that. But Jade has made the effort, put herself in the firing line for me. She's involved someone else in all this shit just to help me out.

I have to take the risk to get out, otherwise what's the point of her doing what she has?

I look down at the bag in my lap. A lifeline lay inside. This could be it. The start of the rest of my life, or the end.

55

JADE

I pace the floor the entire time Paul is out. Back and forth. Up and down the stairs. I've looked out the window so many times in the hope that it will make the time pass quicker and he'll come back to me with good news.

No sooner have I reached the top of the stairs for the millionth time do I hear the key in the front door and Paul has let himself into the house. I rush back down to meet him and he's removing his jacket.

'Did you do it?'

He nods.

'And?'

'I managed to leave it in the place you told me.'

'And you saw Amber?'

He nods and the look on his face says it all. 'Jade, it was horrible. Now that I know those girls are being forced to work there against their will, it's made me look at those kinds of places differently. It made me feel sick just *pretending* I was in there for a dance.'

I nod, following him into the lounge. We sit down and Paul rubs his hand across his face.

'How did she look, Paul? Was she okay?'

'I don't know, Jade. She acted like a lap dancer, so on the surface she was fine. But I told her everything you said. I told her to put the phone in her bag and that you would be in touch.'

'And no one saw you? I mean, Marcus wasn't there or anything?'

'Do you think I'd still be standing if he had been?'

He's right, if Marcus had been there and recognised Paul… I don't even want to think about it.

'Thank you for doing this. And I'm sorry for putting you at risk like this to help me.'

I reach over to hug him and he smiles. 'I'd do anything to help you Jade. It may not have seemed like it before, after you got out of hospital. But I was in a bad place myself at the time and, well, there really is no excuse.'

'What do you mean?'

Paul is quiet for a moment. 'Well, as you know we weren't really in a good place before you got attacked.'

I nod. We weren't. Our relationship had become more like a friendship. I still liked Paul and I think he still liked me, but the excitement and fire had died out. We'd been going through the motions and both of us pretended things were fine.

'When I found out what happened to you, I felt sick. Then when I came to see you, I felt worse. If I'd been there then none of this would have happened.'

He blames himself. Paul thinks it's his fault that this has happened to me. The expression on his face makes my heart sink.

'I know that ending what we had was the right thing to do for both of us, but the guilt got too much for me and I hit the bottle. Not in a feel sorry for me way, but more like I needed to be drunk to forget about what was going on. I sent a couple of drunken texts to you but never got a reply. Then the guilt got even worse and then I got that text that I thought was from you, telling me to leave you alone.' He stops and takes a breath. 'I drank for weeks, took time off work and stopped seeing my mates. Then they came to see me, told me to get a bloody grip and that they were taking me out on a stag do. That was when I decided that the drink wasn't going to change anything. So, I stopped bingeing on my own and that was when I found you. I still blame myself a little for what has happened, Jade.'

I stare at him in disbelief. Fuck. I hadn't realised that he felt that strongly about what had happened to me. Of course, I didn't receive any of the messages Paul is talking about because Marcus gave me a new phone. I thought he was being kind at the time. Now I know he was grooming me, starting his quest to control me.

'No, Paul. It's him, Marcus is the one who did this. This is the kind of thing that would make him happy, to know that he has fucked up my life. And I'm not the only one. There's probably hundreds of girls like us under his control. I was just lucky to be able to get away and you need to remember that you are here for me now. I must be stupid choosing to put us in danger to help a girl I barely know. But she was the one who warned me and if it wasn't for her, I'd probably be living in that bloody flat with her now, being sold for sex.'

I wince at the thought.

'You're not stupid, Jade. You're a kind person. That's why you're doing it. And this is why I'm helping you. I can't change what happened to you, but I can help you to get away from this life now. As much as it terrifies me that this Marcus character will catch us, I can't abandon you again.'

I smile at Paul and remember why I fell for him in the first place, even if that feeling has gone now. I reach over and hug him tightly. There aren't many people in the world like Paul.

I pull away and look down at the second phone that Paul bought and think about how I'm going to contact Amber. I need to time the message carefully so that Marcus won't catch Amber with the phone. I'll only get one chance to get this right.

56

LIZZY

I sit the mug of coffee down on the surface in front of me and open the diary. I am going to have to come up with an explanation as to why Amber's part of the diary is empty. Because Marcus or Barry will check soon enough and if they think I've not been booking her in with clients, I dread to think what will happen.

I glance up when I hear Rory coming down the stairs. That young lad doesn't know what he's let himself in for getting involved with the McAdams. He seems to be enjoying walking around this place like he owns it. Playing at being Billy big bollocks is going to be the end of him. He must only be around eighteen, if that. Roughly the same age as Barry when I first started seeing him.

The mobile phone on the counter rings and I look down at it. I don't want to answer it and be responsible for another girl having to entertain a stranger. With Rory watching me and clearly ready to tell Barry or Marcus that I am ignoring calls, I pick up the phone and answer.

'Hello, Angel House.'

'You didn't answer quickly enough.' It was Barry.

'I do apologise,' I reply. 'But I have a lot to do here.'

I think about the job I am being held here for and it makes me sick. Before Barry had taken me and before I knew who Marcus truly was, the work I was doing at the club was honest. I would never have allowed any of it to go had I known what the McAdams were putting the girls through. I know there are girls out there, women who choose to work in the sex industry, but not like this. No female in the world would choose this kind of life. Not if there was another way.

'If the phone rings more than three times, it's likely the client will hang up.'

'Good,' I say.

'Oi, don't get lippy.'

'Oh do fuck off Barry.' I press end call and slam the phone down on the small desk.

Glancing up, Rory is staring at me in disbelief. I haven't ever seen that expression on his little face before. I like it. Maybe the old Lizzy Aitken should come out from hiding. Maybe she should never have gone into hiding in the first place. I was raised by Gordon Aitken, one of the most feared men in Glasgow, well above the McAdams. He wouldn't associate himself with them, said their lines of business were dirty and too dangerous, that the police would be crawling all over them soon enough.

Unfortunately that had never been the case. Yes, the police had their suspicions, even arrested some of them, but none of the accusations ever stuck. I've learned since coming here that Barry knew people in high places and had paid the police off to turn a blind eye to his way of conducting business.

'You're brave,' Rory says, leaning down on the desk and his cocky expression returning.

I glare up at him, wondering why he would ever think that getting involved in this line of work would ever end well.

'What's in this for you?' I ask.

'Wit d'ya mean?'

'Is this the kind of thing you imagined for yourself when you were a kid? Working in the sex industry, forcing girls to do things they don't want?'

Rory stands up, steps back. His expression has changed again. He frowns. 'That's no wit I dae.'

'Isn't it? So, what do you do then, Rory? Because right now, all I see is you checking that the girls here don't try to get out. To me that's forcing them to stay against their will.'

'Naw, that's no' my job. I'm a bouncer.'

I smile, hold in the laughter caused by his excuse.

'A bouncer? I don't think so. I'll tell you what you are. You're a dogsbody. A wee bitch the McAdams use to do the jobs they don't have time for. They've got a use for you right now, but I'll tell you that as soon as you put a foot wrong, you'll be out of here and it won't be with you on your feet.'

Rory starts to laugh but I can tell it's forced. He's listening to me, I know he is. His eyes are wider than they were before and just like a dog, his ears have pricked up.

'You're what, eighteen?'

'Aye, and wit aboot it?'

'When I was your age, I was helping to run my dad's businesses. He was the rival gang lord to the McAdams. A lot classier, mind. He did his bit for his community, made sure the wee shits on the street like you were kept in line. You see, I know all about this world. You know nothing. You only see what you want to see, the glamour, the money. I bet you've been promised a girl whenever you want. Well, just remember this, the gun you see in their back pockets? As soon as you fuck up, a bullet from that very gun will become lodged in your skull. There will be no turning back at that point, Rory. I bet you don't have one, eh? A gun?' I stop but don't let him answer. 'Because they don't think you're worthy of one. You're too young, too on edge and untrustworthy. Hence why they've left you here, unarmed. You're only good for watching over the girls imprisoned here. Maybe the odd drug run too. That's the part where you're likely to fuck up the most. You'll talk to the wrong person and you'll end up dead, regardless if it's a McAdam that pulls the trigger or a rival.'

I hold his gaze and I know my words are embedded in his brain, just like the bullet that one of the McAdams will eventually put there.

Rory goes to speak when the front door opens and Barry enters Angel House. He sees Rory standing in front of the reception desk and then frowns.

'Oi, I don't pay you to stand and fucking gossip with the house mother, I pay you to keep them fucking doors manned.'

I lock eyes with Rory and raise a brow. He knows what I would be saying if Barry couldn't hear me. *I told you so.* His expression changes back to the hard little gangster he thinks he is and he returns to his station in front of the door on the upper level.

'We need to talk,' Barry says to me. 'Once you've finished answering the phone, of course. Remember, no more than three rings.'

At that, the mobile phone rings. I pick it up after two.

57

LIZZY

I hang up after the client has made their requests and write them down in the diary in front of me, as if I'm writing down a regular doctor appointment. My stomach churns when I think of what they've asked for, so much so that I have to bite my tongue and breathe through my nose just to stem the nausea. The repulsion is overwhelming.

With there only being one diary, it's easier than I thought to hide the fact that I haven't been booking for Amber. But I'm not stupid, Barry and Marcus will find out eventually. They will only have to look through a few pages to see Amber's name missing. And I can't falsify bookings because then there would be the case of missing money. I will eventually have to give her a client or two.

I get up from my desk and walk to the bottom of the stairs. As I look up, I wonder what the content of the conversation with Barry will be. He appeared calm on the outside, but I saw the look in his eye. I understood it. It wasn't a choice I was free to make about going to see him. It was a command. The tone and his expression were enough to make me realise that there was no way it was ever going to be a choice.

I lift my right foot and place it on the first step. Raising my hand, it falls onto the wooden banister. I tighten my grip as I lift my left foot and slowly begin to climb the stairs. I glance over at Rory who is still manning the two rooms on the bottom level of the house. This grand building that is being used as an illegal brothel. An illegal establishment that I am helping to run with the police taking no notice because of the cash falling into their pockets. I take a breath to steady myself.

'Disnae matter how slow ye go, Lizzy. Ye still need tae get up there otherwise he'll just come looking fur ye,' Rory says, his teasing tone burning inside my ears. That little shit will get his karma one day, I think. I choose not to respond to him because actually, he's right. It doesn't matter how much I prolong the climb to the first floor. Barry will come and find me anyway. But I will not allow Barry to think he's got the better of me. I've still got Aitken blood running in my veins. I was part of one of the most feared families in Glasgow. Why have I allowed myself to forget that? The Aitkens were once above the McAdams. Way above.

At that, I straighten my back, make myself tall and climb the stairs. I reach the top and for the first time, I notice the detail of the décor. The coving that runs along the top of the walls must date back to when this place was first built. There are so many closed doors, all of the rooms housing girls forced into this business, whether they believe it yet or not.

As I pass by them, I focus on the door ahead of me. Barry's room. I don't want to call it an office, that's not what it is. It's just a room he spends time in when he's here. He doesn't live here. Well, not all the time. He often puts someone in here to oversee the running of things. Tonight so it would seem, he's here.

'Come in.' I hear his voice from behind the door when I approach. He knew I was here already without having to alert him. Cameras, I realise. Cameras everywhere.

I push the door open and stand there. Barry is sitting on a sofa, a coffee table in front of him. From here, it looks like a normal lounge room in a house.

'Come in, sit down,' Barry says. There's a bottle of whisky on the table. And a bottle of gin. 'Shut the door.'

I enter the room with my back still straight, pushing the door closed behind me and sit down on the edge of the sofa. I don't want to be too near him but I won't let him see that.

'Drink?'

'What do you want, Barry?' I say with a firm tone, ignoring his question.

'Come on, have a gin. That was your drink back in the day, wasn't it?' He leans forward and lifts the bottle.

'No thank you.'

Barry's expression freezes, his whole body tenses for just a moment before he says, 'Lighten up, Lizzy.'

I shift uncomfortably as I'm perched on the arm of the sofa. As I look around the room, I notice the walls are faded. A light pink wallpaper covers them. I can just about make out the outline of butterflies, birds. Jesus. This used to be a child's bedroom.

'I wanted to talk to you about something,' Barry says, resting the gin bottle back on the table. 'And the reason I brought you here to do that was because I think it's important for you.'

I turn sharply and give him a look. 'Just say whatever the hell it is you want to say to me Barry.'

'Ooft, still got some of that Aitken fire running through your veins I see,' he laughs, taking a sip from a glass.

'Never lost it.'

'Oh but you did, when you chose to go down a better path. Didn't you? You turned your back on your dad, this way of life.'

I shake my head. 'You don't know anything about my choices or my dad.'

Barry sniggers and gets to his feet. Walking around the table, he heads towards a chest of drawers under the window. Opens it.

'That's not strictly true, though.' He takes something out of the drawer he has opened and sits it on top before closing the drawer.

'And what is that supposed to mean?' I say, narrowing my eyes as I watch him. I stare at the item on the wooden surface and wonder what it is.

'You might want to make yourself more comfortable for this, Lizzy.' He turns and there is a glint in his eye. A look of pure evil.

I don't move, desperate to show him that I'm not scared, that I won't fear for my life. But that's not the truth. As he lifts the item he removed from the drawer, I watch him with caution. He moves back across the room slowly towards me.

'Take a look at that,' he says when he sits back down on the sofa. Sliding it across the leather, I glance down at it.

As I take in the image, white noise suddenly surrounds me. For a moment, I am not here in this house. I am no longer Lizzy Aitken. I am little Elizabeth, three-year-old child scooped up in her dad's arms, her mother laughing as she holds the child's hand and kisses the man on the cheek.

'Where did you find this?' I ask, staring down and into the eyes of my dad.

'It was in among my old man's things when I was clearing out his house after he died a couple years back.'

I stare down at it, unblinking. I wasn't expecting to see this photograph, here at Angel House with Barry McAdam so close.

'See that man next to your dad?' Barry says. I feel myself nodding. 'That's my old man, that's Willie McAdam. You remember him, don't you?' He pauses but I don't respond and he continues. 'He and Gordy Aitken used to be best mates back in the day apparently. Until something happened that meant they could never go back.'

My heart is thumping inside my chest. As I stare at the picture, I know who she is, the woman. She's my mother. But I don't remember her. She died when I was just little.

'No, my dad said that he would never have anything to do with the McAdams. That was why I had to give Marcus up,' I say.

Barry shoots me a glance and knocks back the whisky in the glass in his hand. He swallows hard and I hear his throat click. He's biting his bottom lip. I can tell Barry wants to say something in response, but instead he takes a deep breath and continues.

'My dad told me there was a job that needed done, a hit. Some guy who'd been causing trouble on McAdam and Aitken ground. Willie and Gordy were going in on this guy. Or at least that was the plan. Then something came up and Gordy had to go away to deal with it. Something to do with one of the other firms they had on the go. Anyway, my old man went with one of the boys. Unmarked car, a planned hit and run, burn the motor. No trace back apparently.'

I watch Barry as he speaks, picking up the bottle and pouring another whisky into his glass. I eye the gin bottle and wonder if I should've accepted the drink he offered.

'That job was the end of the McAdam and Aitken alliance.'

I open my mouth to speak but my throat has dried up. All I can do is watch Barry and hope he gets to the point.

'Turns out the guy was having an affair and the mistress was with him on the day of the hit. She died after the car hit her. It was a mistake, mind. That wasn't ever in the plan.'

I sigh and get to my feet. 'Barry, I really don't see what this has to do with me.'

'The woman was your mother. Ellen Aitken.'

'Oh do get a grip, Barry. She died in a car accident...' My voice trails off, my brain processing the connection.

'Aye, she did,' Barry says, lifting the glass to his lips. 'My dad didn't know about the affair. Neither did yours. It was just a shitty coincidence. But that's what started the feud between our families. Gordy lost it, went off his nut when he found out what happened. A fight broke out, and no' just a wee one. A brawl, fists flying. Bullets with fucking names on them. A couple of the boys died, others were seriously injured. Gordy shot my old man. Luckily, nothing serious. After that, they parted in their business.'

I stare at Barry, wide-eyed and hoping that he has conjured up this story to upset me. His eyes lock on mine and his expression remains neutral.

'You're a liar. You'll do or say anything to make me suffer more for the choice I made.' My tone is weak, no conviction to it.

'Nah,' Barry says, looking down at the photo and then back at me. 'This is real, Lizzy. When we started seeing each other, I knew who you were, that you were an Aitken and I didn't care. But then you ended our relationship. See, I couldn't get my head around why. We were going well. But it was messing with my head.' Barry stops and jabs at his head with his fingers. 'I had someone keep an eye on you. I couldn't do it myself, you'd have noticed. When I found out you were pregnant, I told Willie what was going on, he wasn't happy. Said getting involved with an Aitken was the last thing he needed to deal with.'

As he continues to talk, a wave of sickness takes over me as I try to focus. The very idea that my mother was murdered because of a job my dad was supposed to carry out sits heavy on my chest. I clench my jaw as Barry carries on.

'I was going to come and see you once you'd had the baby. I was going to tell you that I didn't care about the past and the shitstorm between Willie and Gordy. But then you left him outside the hospital and the way I felt about you turned to rage. Pure burning rage, Lizzy. And that's why we're here.'

I look away from him and grab the bottle of gin on the table. As I unscrew the cap and gulp back a mouthful, all I can see is my dad's face on the last day I saw him alive.

'How'd your dad die?' Barry suddenly asks.

'From his illness,' I say. 'In hospital.'

I think about that day when I got the phone call from the nurse. I'd been getting ready to go and visit him. I was too late. 'He was on his own.'

I sit up, take another gulp and scold myself for telling him that. Barry doesn't care. He'll use it as some kind of emotional punishment because of Marcus.

'He wasn't on his own.'

'Yes he was. He died in his sleep.'

'No, he didn't Lizzy. I went to see him in hospital.'

Glaring at Barry, his words bounce around in my head. I begin to tremble as I piece together what he has said and what may be his next sentence.

'He was on his last legs. I just put him out his misery with his own pillow.'

There it is. The words that make me throw the gin bottle across the room in his direction. He ducks and the bottle smashes off the wall, spraying gin and glass all over the floor.

Barry is laughing as he gets to his feet and grabs my shoulders. 'You dirty, murderous bastard,' I shout but before I can say or do anything else he throws me to the floor. He's on his knees and hovering above me, his fingers slip around my neck and squeeze.

'Aye, I did kill him Lizzy. The poor bastard was going to die anyway. But I couldn't let him get away with telling you to get rid of our son. I mean, I get why he would have said such a thing. But you can see my position on this. What right did he have to decide the fate of my son?'

I grab at his hands, try to release them from around my neck as I attempt to stay alive.

'I've thought about killing you too. Nothing would satisfy me more. But you're too valuable to the business.' He lets go and I roll onto my side as he stands. 'I need someone to run this place and it's thanks to your son that you're not lying there dead. Getting you here was his idea.'

Barry sits back down on the sofa and I sit up, lay my back against the leather. In a way, I wish he had killed me. Then I wouldn't have to live with the guilt of what I did, and the image of Barry killing my dad, smothering him to death.

It seems that while I thought giving Marcus up would help, it's only gone and led us both into the deepest part of the world I wanted him to be free from.

'Oh, and another thing. Stop leaving Amber's diary blank. I know you've been leaving her out of the product list when clients have been phoning. I'm warning you now, stop it. Because if you don't, it won't be you we punish for it. It'll be her.'

58

AMBER

He's waiting for me by the door. If there was any other way out of this place I would run, truly make a break for it. Instead, I walk towards him and hope that my eyes don't give away that I have something in my bag that shouldn't be there.

'Good night?' Marcus asks as we walk to the car. I see the smirk on his face and know that he doesn't care about how my night went. His only concern is how much money I've made for him. I try not to rise to it.

'Was alright,' I reply. 'Same as any other.'

We reach the car and he opens my door. I climb in and place the bag between my feet before putting on my belt. As I do this, Marcus stands by me, holding the door. His eyes bore into the side of my head. If I didn't act like things were normal, he would start to suspect something was up.

'Why you just standing there staring at me?' I turn and raise a brow.

'Just making sure you're all strapped in,' he says so quietly I almost don't hear him. He closes the door a little too hard and I jump. Then I hear the locks click. The bastard is trying to rattle me, to see if I'll snap into telling him if I've heard from Jade which in truth I haven't. Yet. But I am rattled. Truly terrified that if he finds that phone, I'm dead. I've managed to hide my fear from Marcus for long enough, a few more hours I can manage.

Marcus disappears and heads back inside and I know he's going in for Yasmin. I wonder how long she's been under

Marcus's control. A few moments later, they emerge from the club and she climbs into the back.

The journey back to the house is quiet and long. My eyes are heavy but I fight to keep them open because I realised once Paul left the club that I don't know where Angel House is located. Of course, Marcus would never give me that information and even if he did, I wouldn't trust it. So I keep my eye on the road and make a mental note of specific landmarks, turns and road signs. It means if I have a hope in hell of getting away from here, I'll be able to navigate my way back to… where? Home? I don't have a home. My family have likely forgotten about me because I chose to be with a thug. Or at least that's the way they'll see it.

We make a turn off the main road from the express way onto a long stretch. Great Western Road. I know that from when my mum used to bring me and my sister here when we were little. There was a vintage toy shop that we loved that sold old train sets and porcelain dolls. When I found out my sister was pregnant, I always said that I would buy the baby something special from there. I never really got the chance after meeting Marcus.

Heading deeper into the West End of the city, I see groups of girls standing outside pubs and clubs and try to remember what it's like to have freedom and not be a slave to the sex industry. Not be addicted to a poisonous drug that could kill me each time a needle penetrates my skin. Maybe Yasmin is thinking the same thing as I am.

The thought ignites the hunger from inside my body and the stomach cramps begin. I try to ignore them and focus on the road ahead. We remain on the straight for around eight miles before we make a right turn and on to another stretch. I make a mental note that we pass under a sign that says this lane for Aberfoyle. I've never been there. But then, maybe that's where Angel House is and I just don't know.

—

'Oi. Oi, Amber. Yasmin.' Marcus's voice makes my eyes snap open. 'Wake up. You'll have clients in the next half an hour.'

Shit, I must have fallen asleep. Damnit. I think back to the journey from the club. How far did we get before I conked out? Searching my memory, I can only think of the sign. This lane for Aberfoyle.

'Oi, I said up!' Marcus glares at me as he opens the door and steps onto the drive. He closes the door and walks around to my side.

'Amber, I can't fucking do this anymore,' Yasmin whispers behind me, her voice cracks.

I want to answer her, tell her that it's going to be okay and that someone is trying to help me and that I will be able to help her too. But I can't open my mouth because Marcus has already opened the door and I'm unclipping my belt.

As we head inside, I pass Lizzy at the front desk and she looks straight at me. She's been crying and her face is whiter than normal. Something has happened to her.

'Hope the diaries are all booked up maw,' Marcus laughs as we begin to climb the stairs. Lizzy doesn't answer him.

We get to the top and Yasmin goes straight into her room. Marcus heads to the room at the end of the hall and I watch him with his back to me. If only I had that gun he possesses, I could shoot him right in the back of the skull. But that wouldn't help me right now. I'd only start a frenzy of violence. I know Marcus isn't working alone and the others would only kill me. If that happened, what use would I be to Yasmin then?

'You forgot where you're going or what?' Marcus says, watching me in my daydream.

I don't respond as he unlocks my door and opens it. As I enter, I turn to face him but he's already closed me in and I hear the key turn in the lock. I place my hand on the wooden surface and close my eyes against the room I would trade for hell any day of the week. I spin around and move across the floor, my bag still strapped across my body. And there, sitting on the bed is another little tin. All the items I need prepared for me. It has been left there to test me. Marcus knew me before I became hooked on drugs. He'll have an idea that I want to get clean again, back to my old self. I've made it pretty clear I don't want to be around him. My face can't lie. He'll want to see what's more important to me. A fix to ease the demons, or my freedom.

I could quite easily open the toilet lid and flush the brown powder away. But I don't because I know I'll regret it later.

Taking the bag off, I place it on the bed and sit down next to it. I pull out the box containing the phone. I can't believe that Jade has done this for me. I was horrible to her in the beginning. Even when I was telling her to get out and away from Marcus I was nasty about it.

I unbox the phone and turn it on, making sure that the volume is on mute. There is no message yet. She'll be waiting for the morning when she knows that Marcus is less likely to be with me. I could just call the police on this phone. Tell them everything. The justice system in this country doesn't fill me with confidence. Even if they were to take me seriously, I don't know where I am. And if they were to find Angel House, Marcus and the rest of them would only get bail. Then where would that leave me? Yasmin? Even Lizzy.

No. What's the harm in waiting a little longer? I'll wait for her call. She will contact me. I know it.

There is a knock at my door and I know there will be a stranger on the other side, expecting me to do whatever it is he wants. It's the first visit I'll have had since I arrived here coming on four days ago now. Lizzy has kept them away from me for long enough. She couldn't keep them away forever, Marcus wouldn't allow that. Nor would the rest of his men.

I get to my feet, pull back my shoulders and take a deep breath. I've had four days of respite from men using me like a possession. I knew it wouldn't last forever, but it had been a welcome break. I had Lizzy to thank for that.

As much as it felt like a kick in the gut, it was time to get back to work.

59

MARCUS

Lifting the bottle from the table, Marcus McAdam pours himself a glass and watches as Barry hands a brush to Rory to sweep up the broken glass on the floor.

'How come I get all the shit jobs?' Rory asks, tutting as he begins sweeping.

'You pay your dues, you rise up the ranks,' Barry says. 'Look at Marcus here. He was in the same boat as you when he was your age.'

Marcus ignores them both and lifts the glass to his lips. The whisky hits the back of his throat and he grits his teeth as it burns.

'What's the update on the girl?' Barry says and Marcus turns to face his dad. 'You do have an update?'

'Nah,' Marcus replies, draining the glass and setting it back down on the table. 'I think she's long gone.'

'That's not an option, Marcus and you know it.'

'Who's the boss here?' Marcus snorts. 'It was me last time I checked. I told you, she's long gone.'

Barry eyes Marcus for a moment and then turns to Rory, asking him to leave the room and do a security check on the rooms. Rory sighs in frustration and leaves the room. Whatever it is his dad has to say, Marcus knows it's for their ears only.

'This is fucking serious, boy. Do you think she won't say anything? She could go to the filth, tell them about what we have going on here. Do you want them crawling around this place after all the work we've put in here?' Barry sneers.

'Relax, she doesn't know anything. Not really. I didn't get her that far. She was only dancing in the club before she left, that's all. There's nothing to tell. Gentlemen's clubs aren't illegal so we're good.'

The words don't pacify Barry as he starts to pace the floor. 'You'd better fucking hope you're right, Marcus.'

The men are silent for a moment as Marcus takes in the scene around him. Broken glass, the stench of gin stronger than the whisky he'd had a moment ago. He frowns.

'What happened in here tonight?'

'Your mother threw a bottle of gin at me.'

'Don't call her that.' Marcus draws his eyes away from the mess on the floor and glares at his dad. 'She's not worthy of that title.'

Barry raises a brow and then his expression softens for a moment. 'She didn't want to hear the truth.'

'You told her about Gordy and the hospital?'

'Aye,' Barry replies. 'She didn't like it.'

Marcus shakes his head, remembering the day that it happened. The argument that broke out between him and his dad was one of the worst they'd had. Marcus had insisted that he be the one to go to the hospital. He'd wanted to meet the man, the legend that was Gordon Aitken. Gordy, as his dad called him. Maybe if Marcus had had the chance to meet him, he might understand Lizzy's decision when she'd had Marcus. Barry had said that Marcus would never understand the Aitkens and he should stop trying to pick them apart. She left him because she didn't want him and that was all he needed in order to drive the organisation forward.

'I'm going home. I'll see you in a couple hours,' Marcus says, heading for the door.

'You alright to drive?' Barry asks and Marcus hears the judgement in his tone.

'What are you now? A law-abiding citizen?' Marcus says without stopping.

As he walks along the hall towards the stairs, Marcus breathes through the anger inside. He might be on his way up, but Barry will never truly let him run things without overlooking every decision.

Reaching the bottom of the stairs, a man passes by him and heads towards the main door. One of Marcus's men opens it and the man leaves quickly, without looking up. Married most likely, unsatisfied and looking for that fantasy of a younger, more exotic female. That's what this place was all about. And when the clients got what they wanted, they often had guilt written all over their faces, and their money lined Marcus's pocket.

Marcus stops and stands next to the reception desk. Lizzy is packing up for the evening and she glances up at him.

'What's up with you?' he asks.

Lizzy ignores him, pushing past him to climb the stairs. Marcus envisages that was how she walked away when she left him on his own as a baby.

The anger inside intensifies and Marcus heads for the door before he does something irreversible.

60

JADE

I hit the send button on the text message and my stomach flips. This is so dangerous and so incredibly terrifying that I almost changed my mind, but then I think how I managed to get out safely. Then I see Amber's face in my mind, remember how broken she looked. She'd helped me. I couldn't back out now.

Standing by the window, I watch as the sun appears over the hills in the distance and my eyes fill with tears.

'Hey, what's wrong?' Paul appears by my side and his hand falls upon my shoulder.

'How is this my life, Paul? How could I have been so stupid to fall for someone like Marcus? I mean, now that I know what he is, it's pretty obvious isn't it? You only have to look at him and know he's dodgy.'

Paul doesn't say anything. He doesn't pass judgement or make any kind of comment. He just listens. I turn to face him and he's staring out at the view.

'Well, I don't know what he looks like. I haven't met him. But I'll take your word for it.'

'How are we going to do this, Paul?'

Paul sighs and looks down at me. 'Let's just wait until Amber sends back a message. Once we know she's alone, we can go back to where she lives and get her. Then we'll go to the police and end this.'

I wince at the suggestion. We might not get that far.

267

61

AMBER

I wake, startled and disorientated. The first thing that comes to mind is the pain in my stomach. Then the sweats and the insane itch which creeps over my body. It's not the kind of itch that you want to scratch. It aches. All over.

As my eyes begin to fall closed again, the thing that startled me awake alerts me again. The phone under my pillow vibrates and my stomach flips. I sit up quickly and pull it out from underneath and with trembling hands, I try to open the message.

> **Unknown** 07:30
> Amber. It's me. Are you okay?

I sigh with relief as the words stare up at me. I begin to type out a reply.

> **Amber** 07:30
> Jade, I can't believe you actually took my advice.
> I thought Marcus had you under his spell.

Unknown 07:31

He did for a long time but what you said didn't sit well with me. Anyway, I wanted to know the best time to come and get you? What typical time is Marcus less likely to be at the flat with you? Are you locked in?

I stare at the last message Jade has sent and realise she doesn't know what has happened, that I'm no longer at the flat and now being kept at the house instead.

Amber 07:32

Jade, I don't live there anymore. After you left, Marcus brought me to a house somewhere around a forty-five min to an hour drive from the club. I don't know where I am.

My fingers tremble over the phone. I'm never going to get away from him, I think.

Unknown 07:33

It's okay. Don't panic. Paul set up the find my iPhone app on his iPad and linked it to your phone. We'll find you. He's doing it now. Delete all these messages and hide the phone. I'll be in touch later. It's going to be okay.

I look down at the message and almost laugh. This is too easy. It won't work. It won't. But then, maybe it will? Just maybe. My luck has been on such a bad streak these last few years, maybe things are about to change. I take a deep breath and think of Yasmin. I will get us out, with Jade's help I will put a stop to this. She looked and sounded so desperate last night.

I begin to tap out a reply when I hear a door opening in the hall outside my room. I quickly delete all the messages and turn the phone off before placing it back under the pillow. I lay down and pretend to be asleep.

Then I hear a blood-curdling scream. It's Lizzy. My eyes shoot open and I'm on my feet, across the room with my ear pressed against the door. I can barely hear anything over the sound of my heart hammering inside my chest. What the hell is going on?

She screams again, this time it's a short sound. Male voices now, a rush of feet on the floor.

'What the fuck?' A male voice I don't recognise. 'How the fuck has this happened?'

Lizzy is crying. Loud wails penetrate the closed door and I feel myself beginning to cry too. This is bad. Someone is dead. I can tell by the way Lizzy is panicking.

'Lizzy, check on the rest of the girls,' the male voice says. 'And get Marcus on the fucking phone. Now!'

I rush back to my bed and sit on it, waiting for Lizzy to unlock my door and check on me, like she was told to. I hear her fumbling with keys, opening doors. I can hear her asking if they're okay and then closing them again.

My door opens and when Lizzy's face appears in the doorway, I'm on my feet.

'Are you okay in here?' she says, trying to control her voice.

'What is it?' I say, keeping my own voice steady. 'What's wrong?'

She stops and stares at me. She is visibly shaking and tears pour down her cheeks.

'Has one of the girls been hurt?' I take a step forward, unthreateningly. I don't want her to slam the door in my face and lock me in in the fear that she'll be punished for speaking to me for longer than simply asking if I'm okay.

'Lizzy, tell me,' I press. When she doesn't answer, I break past her before she can stop me and run towards the bedroom

270

door, hoping that I am not about to see what I think I am. A man stands in the doorway, his back to the hall. As he turns, I manage to squeeze by him and into the room.

Before I can be dragged away, I see her lying there. Yasmin. She's blue, eyes open and the look of terror on her face. Bruises are visible around her neck. A needle protrudes from her arm, and she's naked from the waist down. I feel sick.

'Get her the fuck out of here, Rory,' the larger man says and soon, the young lad is dragging me by the arm out of the room. He pushes me back inside and I don't fight him. I have nothing in me.

'Keep an eye on her, eh?' the larger man shouts down the hall. Lizzy steps inside the room and locks the door.

'Lizzy, what the fuck?' I say as I begin to pace.

'I don't know,' she replies. Her chest moves heavily as she sobs quietly.

'You saw her. You know it. Someone killed her, Lizzy. Someone fucking killed her when she was shooting up. I saw the needle, the bruises on her neck.' The words are leaving my lips so fast I stumble over them a little. 'It was Marcus, wasn't it? He killed her?'

Lizzy shakes her head. 'No. Why would he kill someone who was making him money?'

I look at her in disbelief. 'Crystal?'

Lizzy runs her hand through her hair, gripping it tightly at the top of her head.

'Lizzy, your son is a fucking loose cannon. He'll kill anyone without a second thought if he thinks it will protect his business.'

'I know. But he wouldn't shit on his own doorstep.'

I think about that for a moment. Think about Crystal and Luderston Bay. Maybe Lizzy's right, perhaps Marcus wouldn't kill and leave the evidence on his own property. But then, maybe he would if he was angry or desperate enough. But why Yasmin? She was keeping quiet. Marcus doesn't know for sure

271

that Yasmin told me about Crystal, he only saw us talking. We could have been discussing anything. Yasmin had been a long serving employee of Marcus's, was making good money. So *why* would he kill her? Fear that he would be caught?

Lizzy sits down on my bed and I tense. She wouldn't tell the bosses that I have a phone even if she did find it but right now isn't the time to explain it. I've just seen a girl in the same position as me dead in her room. She was just like me. A prostitute. A junkie. That could've been me.

Lizzy is still sobbing and as I look at her, it's hard to see the woman she used to be. The house mother at Angel Silk. The woman who would have our backs if anything went wrong. I feel sorry for her right now. Her entire life has been turned upside down. Marcus is her son. How had she not known or at least suspected that? I sit down next to her and place my hand over hers.

'Lizzy, if Marcus didn't kill Yasmin, then who the hell did?'

'It could have been anyone. It *could* have been a client, Amber. You know what some of the men are like. They're sick, like to act out all sorts of sick shit. It could have been a role play incident gone wrong. It may have been an accident. We'll probably never know.'

I stare at her in desperation and disbelief. How could she think it may have been an accident? We were being kept prisoner in a fucking brothel. Deaths in these types of places are never accidental.

'Yasmin is dead. It happened right here in this house. I don't care what anyone says, I think it was Marcus. He's the only one with real motive, regardless of whether he thinks Yasmin blabbed about Crystal or not. She knew and that in itself was too dangerous,' I say.

Lizzy remains quiet. Sceptical. I have to remember that above all else, Marcus is still Lizzy's flesh and blood.

62

JADE

I've been holding the phone for over half an hour and Amber still hasn't responded to my last message. Not that I left it open for her to send a reply, but I thought she might have signed off with a response to acknowledge it. Something's wrong. I can feel it in my gut.

'You're not going to believe this,' Paul says as he enters the kitchen. I've been sitting at the breakfast bar, nursing a now lukewarm coffee and staring down at the mobile in my hands. I glance up at Paul and wait for him to continue. 'According to the app, Amber is in Ballykinross.'

'Where is that?' I ask, glaring at the phone as he holds it up.

'It's on the outskirts of Aberfoyle.'

'Why would he take them all the way out there?' I say.

'Less likely to be suspected, I would suppose. It's in the middle of nowhere. Look.' Paul waves the phone at me. 'Also means that the girls are less likely to try to escape because if they do, they'll have a long journey to get back to civilisation.'

I nod, looking at the map on the screen. I turn my attention back to the phone in my hand. 'Paul, she hasn't messaged me back. What if Marcus has found the phone? He might have already…' I trail off.

'Hey, Amber sounds like a tough girl, a smart girl. She'll be careful with it, I'm sure.'

I hope so. Because if we get there and she's already dead, I'll have just walked into a trap Marcus won't even know he's set.

'So, we go now,' I say.

'Now? Don't you want to wait for a bit, see if Amber messages you back so we can get a better idea of what's happening?'

He's probably right but I can't wait. I have to help her. As I regard Paul with the phone in his hand and the location of where Amber is, I feel it's time to tell Paul the truth about Marcus. The bare truth. He has to know what I've gotten him involved in.

'Paul, I think you need to know how dangerous Marcus is,' I start.

'I already know, Jade. You ran from him and asked me for help. What else is there to know?'

'Well, I never fully told you the story about Crystal. Remember, the body in the suitcase?'

Paul raises a brow. 'Yes, I remember. It was all over the news and Amber told you that she was one of his girls. But that body hasn't been identified yet, Jade.'

'It sounds like you're defending him,' I reply sharply.

'Am I fuck defending him, Jade. All I'm saying is don't jump to conclusions.'

I shake my head. That's the only way to survive a life with Marcus. Jumping to a worst-case scenario is the only way to understand Marcus fully. 'Paul, all I'm saying is if you wanted to get off at this stop, I wouldn't blame you. Things could get so dangerous now. This really isn't your concern, I've pulled you into my mess and I am giving you the opportunity to get out now. I can go to get Amber on my own. I feel strong enough.'

Paul sits down next to me and takes my hand. 'Jade, I am not going to allow you to do this on your own.'

I take a deep breath. I don't want to be responsible for something happening to someone as innocent as Paul. He's not weak by any means, but he has a good heart unlike Marcus and the men he's in business with. I shouldn't have pulled him into this in the first place, but I had no one else to call, no one else to turn to. If Marcus was able to get rid of someone like Crystal so easily, then what would he do to Paul if he caught us? What would that mean for his family and friends? The guilt and blame of that would fall on me.

'Maybe we could go to the police?' Paul asks.

I shake my head. 'I don't think it would be as easy as that. I've seen the state of Amber, seen how Marcus can manipulate people into doing what he wants. There is every chance that he has a backup plan in case the police come knocking. He's too clever.'

'Okay, then we go and get Amber and take it from there.'

'You're sure?' I ask, my heart beginning to thump heavily in my chest.

'Hey, you know the bastard better than I do. If you say we should go now, then we go now.'

63

MARCUS

Marcus is already in his car, speeding along the country roads to Angel House. He'd calmed down from the night before, only to be woken by a phone call from his dad. One of the girls had been murdered in her room. How the fuck had that gone unnoticed until now? There were plenty of his men securing the place. Tommy was at the club last night and Marcus has just informed him on the phone this morning about what had happened. He offered to go out to Ballykinross with Marcus however it would be better for Tommy to keep an eye on things at the club.

The sun shines strongly above and Marcus puts the window down. Blaring his music, his mind goes over what Barry had said on the phone. 'One of the girls is dead. Looks like she was done in while she was injecting. Strangled going by the state of her neck.'

Who in their right mind would go to a brothel to pay a girl for sex and then kill her? Especially when the brothel is clearly manned by security. Of course there are some of those clients who come to Angel House in order to carry out their sick fantasies and games. And Angel House is the place to do that sort of thing. It's isolated, away from the bustle of the city club. If someone wanted to take things that one step further, then being out of the way in an isolated establishment would be the place to go. Regardless of the reasoning, Marcus had lost one of his girls and that was a loss of earnings.

Pulling up outside the house, it looks normal. He steps out of the car and goes inside to be met by Barry and Rory at the door, along with a few more of the boys.

'Where is she?' Marcus asks. Barry turns and heads for the stairs, Marcus follows. They are outside one of the rooms and Barry opens the door. Marcus looks inside and sees Yasmin lying on the floor. She's the darkest shade of blue he's ever seen in a dead body.

'We won't be able to trade until she's dealt with,' Barry says.

'Then get her dealt with. What's she still doing lying there?'

'Erm, if you hadn't noticed, it's broad fucking daylight out there, Marcus. We can't just casually dispose of a body in the middle of the day even if the police are in our pockets,' Barry says, a look of disbelief crossing his face. 'If someone sees us it's still drawing attention to what is going on here.'

'Look, we're in the middle of nowhere. Plenty of land around us. I don't want this place closed for business tonight. It's the real money maker,' Marcus says, stepping out of the room and into the hall. He looks down the stairs and sees Rory and the others standing at the front door. Lizzy isn't at her desk, he notes.

'Oi, boys. Get up here, eh? You've got a job to do,' Marcus shouts. Rory and the others begin climbing the stairs.

'Are you off your fucking head? Those boys don't have the capabilities to take the fucking bins out and you want them to dispose of a body?'

Marcus glares at his dad. 'You know what? I don't like what little faith you have in me right now. I'm not stupid, so just let me get on with this.'

Rory reaches the top first with the rest behind him and stands by the door. He stands awkwardly, his eyes everywhere other than the scene behind Marcus.

'You boys know how to get rid of a body?' Marcus asks. None of them answer.

Barry shakes his head and closes the door to the room.

'Naw, boss. Never done it before,' Rory finally replies.

Marcus steps closer to him and Rory tenses again.

'Ever *seen* a dead body before?' Marcus asks.

Rory shakes his head and the rest of the younger lads don't say anything at all. Young team indeed, he thinks. All mouth, no gut.

Marcus puts his arm around Rory's shoulder and leads him back down the stairs and out to the driveway. The rest of the boys follow as does Barry.

'Rory, you and I need to have a wee chat.'

Marcus and Barry dismiss the rest of the boys. The look on Rory's face tells Marcus all he needs to know. This isn't good for Marcus's anger.

'What dae ye want me tae do, boss?' Rory asks.

Marcus begins to walk Rory away from the house towards the woodland which surrounds it.

'The truth, Rory. I want you to tell me the truth.'

'Wit d'ya mean?'

'Oh you know what I mean, wee man.'

Marcus lets his hand slip from Rory's shoulder as they enter the woodland. Gripping the back of his T-shirt, he pushes Rory on deeper into the trees. Suddenly, it's a lot darker than it was before, the sun unable to penetrate the tall conifers that surround them.

The woodland floor is uneven and if it weren't for Marcus holding him up, Rory would have lost his balance and gone down. They reach a point that Marcus thinks is deep enough, away from the house and surrounding roads.

'You know it's hunting season around here at the moment,' Marcus says as he lets go of Rory's shirt.

'Is it?'

'Aye. Lots of bangs. Gunshots, ye know. Listen?'

They're quiet for a moment and as if on cue, the sound of pheasants taking flight, wings flapping and crowing can be heard in the distance.

'Wait for it,' Marcus says, eyes to the side as he holds up a hand.

Bangbangbang

'See?' Marcus says, smiling at Rory.

Rory hesitates, then smiles back. 'Aye.'

'Like I said, hunting season.'

Silence hangs between them for a few seconds, before more gunshots can be heard in the distance. It echoes around them, the sound bouncing off the trunks towering over them. Rory eyes Marcus with suspicion.

'Anyway,' Marcus says, 'I brought you out here to give you the opportunity to tell me what happened at the house. Yasmin, she's dead. Murdered. You were on duty last night, eh?'

Rory nods, his body tense and shoulders up at his ears. It thrills Marcus to see this.

'So, what happened?'

'I dunno,' Rory shrugs.

'You didn't hear anything? See anyone acting strange?'

'Naw.'

Marcus nods, purses his lips. 'Is that right?'

'Aye, that's right.'

Marcus begins to pace slowly from left to right as the sound of shots rings out in the air around them. He likes the sound of it. Makes him feel alive. He stops and glances at Rory whose hands are now in his pockets.

'Rory, when you took this job, you asked me if freebies was a benefit as an employee, remember?'

'Aye,' Rory replies.

'And what did I say in response to that question?'

Rory hesitates before answering, as if wondering if it's a trick question. 'You said that there was no such thing as a freebie in this business.'

'That's right. You need to work for your benefits. But the girls, they'll never be part of the benefits package.' Marcus lets the words settle for a moment, allows for Rory to process them. 'You *did* do everything I asked of you last night, didn't you?'

'Aye. You said I was to deliver all the drugs to the girls after trade hours so they weren't off their faces for the clients. All except Amber. She's allowed her bag before because she doesn't perform well enough when she's in withdrawal.'

Marcus stops pacing and steps closer again. Rory instinctively steps back, but he loses his footing and falls over a root. Lands on his back.

'That's right, Rory. Well done, you recited the rules well. But here's the thing, young Yasmin was found in a position that makes me think that either she was handed those drugs before her last client arrived, or it was an inside job. Needle in the arm, no clothes from the waist down. Which is weird because if she'd been with a *client*, like her corpse perhaps suggests, then she wouldn't have a needle in her arm because I asked you *not* to give the drugs to the girls until *after* trade hours.'

Marcus stares down at Rory, whose face has gone grey. He's hit the nail on the head. Barry was right. This young lad isn't to be trusted. Marcus isn't stupid. He used to be one of the young team, one of the lads. He knows how their brains work. Minimum input, maximum payment. But that's not how things work in the real world, illegal or otherwise.

'Well,' Marcus pushes, 'what have you got to say for yourself?'

'I'm sorry, Marcus.' Rory's voice is quieter now, weak. Marcus hadn't thought he'd be able to break Rory so quickly.

'Go on, tell me what you're sorry for.'

Rory hesitates as he looks up at Marcus. A single stream of sunlight breaks through from above and shines down on the young lad. His eyes are moving across everything in sight but he doesn't meet Marcus's gaze.

'I… I dunno know what to say Marcus. I just thought that because I was working for you, keeping an eye on the girls and that, you'd no' mind if I…' Rory stops speaking again.

'I'd not mind if you what? If you take up some time for yourself? That you'd take the absolute piss out of me and then keep your mouth shut? Eh?' Marcus juts his chin out and then gives Rory a swift kick in the ribs.

Rory cries out and Marcus kicks him again, knocking the wind from his lungs. His gaping mouth gasps for breath.

'What happened between you and Yasmin, Rory? Tell me what happened that resulted in one of *my* girls ending up dead?' Marcus says. He bends down, his face close to Rory's. 'She didn't want you, did she? She told you to get to fuck and you chose to take it from her anyway? Is that what happened Rory? Are you one of *those* guys?'

Rory glances up and looks Marcus dead in the eye. 'Aren't you one of those guys? I'm the same as you Marcus. The only difference is I've not worked my way to the top yet.'

Marcus stands up straight and smiles. That was a good comeback, he'll give him that one. He'll allow it.

'So, you let her inject first?' Marcus continues. Rory nods in response and Marcus sees something in his expression that says there is more to it. 'Then what?'

Silence. He's scared to admit what happened. Marcus doesn't blame him, he has every right to be scared.

'Rory?'

'I told her that if she gave me a freebie I could get her more gear, an extra hit.'

Marcus breathes through the building rage. How dare this little shit make that kind of call, take that kind of liberty. Marcus would never have disrespected the bosses at Rory's age.

'And she declined?' Marcus suggests, even though he knows that not to be the case.

'Naw, she's a junkie. They don't say no to a bit of gear.'

'After you had your way with Yasmin, tell me what happened?'

Rory tries to get to his feet but Marcus tuts, shakes his head. 'Just answer the question, Rory.'

'Well, I gave her more, like I promised. Then she started getting lippy with me, saying I was just your rent boy, nothing more than she was. I was raging, fucking livid. I'm no one's fucking rent boy.' Rory's voice is growing in volume, in attitude as if he has forgotten who he is talking to. 'I told her that and she laughed. Ye know that laugh when they're oot their nut?' Rory pauses, as if waiting for Marcus to respond. When he doesn't, Rory continues.

'Anyway, she had this look on her face, like she'd had the last word an' that. Nobody gets tae speak tae me like that, Marcus. Well, no' the likes of her anyway. She was saying stuff about you too.'

That didn't surprise Marcus. Yasmin was never very forth-coming with him, especially after Crystal became involved with him. It was a weird scenario. He couldn't tell if Yasmin was jealous of Crystal for being with Marcus, or for the fact that Crystal was so much prettier than her. Either way, when Crystal was no longer in the picture, Yasmin became lippy. Was always saying things, throwing little digs in here and there. It wouldn't have been long before she started running her mouth about Crystal and how she'd disappeared. It wasn't until he'd seen her chatting with Amber that he'd decided he wasn't going to take the risk. So that's when he'd decided to shut Yasmin up, got her hooked on drugs and gave her a good kicking and then kept her at Angel House until the place was ready for business.

'She was saying,' Rory starts, but Marcus holds his hand up, sighs in frustration.

'What the fuck did you do to her, Rory?'

'She was in the middle of shooting up again. Had taken her eyes off me. So I gave her a slap for her cheek. Then I...' He stops.

'You got your end away again, did you?' Marcus suggests.

'Erm, aye.'

'Then you fucking strangled her?'

Rory nods, avoiding Marcus's eye.

'And did she fight?'

'Naw, she was too out of it. I don't even think she knew what was happening. Look, I'm sorry Marcus. I shouldn't have done it, I know that. But I just thought—'

'Aye, well look what thought did.'

Marcus sits his foot on Rory's right shoulder and forces him down onto the ground. Rory's eyes fill with terror as he watches Marcus's hands fall behind his back for just a moment. His hand reappears, fingers gripped around a handgun.

'Awe shit, Marcus I'm sorry. It'll no happen again, I swear. Please...'

As Marcus pulls the trigger, the sound of distant gun shots and crowing pheasants masks the sound of the gun that puts a bullet through Rory's skull.

His head bounces back on to the ground as blood spatters across the moss and branches which litter the woodland floor.

'Stupid prick,' Marcus says, turning his back and pulling his mobile out of his pocket. He brings up the number he needs and presses call.

'Aye, Tommy it's me. Can you come out to Angel House?'

–

Marcus waits at the edge of the woodland as Tommy parks the car in the drive. He gets out and approaches Marcus. 'Where is he?'

'In there,' Marcus replies, lifting his cigarette to his mouth.

'The stuff's in the boot. You sure here is the best place?'

'Aye,' Marcus replies, blowing out a cloud of smoke. 'It's private land. There's no reason for anyone to suspect a body would be buried in there.'

Tommy raises a brow. 'And what about her?'

Marcus takes a deep breath and drops his cigarette to the ground, stands on it and moves towards the house. 'Okay, there's no reason for anyone to suspect two bodies would be buried in there.'

Tommy shakes his head and heads back to the car, opening the boot. Marcus notices the look on his face and goes to him.

'What's up with your face?'

'Marcus, you know you can't just go around killing people when they do something you don't like.'

Marcus lets out a laugh he hadn't expected. 'We're not running a puppy sanctuary here, Tommy. If people do things that could jeopardize the running of the business or worse, contact the police, then I will do whatever I damn well like if I think it's in our best interests. That wee shit in there was taking the piss. Fucking strangled one of best girls, the wee bastard.'

Tommy doesn't reply. Instead he takes the supplies out of the car and closes the boot.

'Right, you go in and start preparing. I'll grab some of the younger lads in there. When they see their wee mate in there with a hole in his head, they might think twice of making the same mistakes he did.'

64

JADE

The sat nav in Paul's car has our route on screen. I glance at the time on my phone and see there is still no message from Amber. Something is wrong. I can feel it in my gut. I want to send her a message to find out what's going on but I don't, because Marcus may have found her phone. And if he has, he'll be waiting for me.

'Try not to worry too much. It's going to be okay,' Paul says, taking the turn the sat nav has instructed him to.

We're heading away from the city, out on to the country roads. If this wasn't such a shitty situation I would perhaps be able to enjoy the view. Instead, I am trying to control the building panic in my chest by taking deep breaths.

'You know, for someone with agoraphobia you're coping really well.'

I shoot him a look.

'Okay, that came out wrong. Sorry, I didn't mean that to sound as though I don't believe you have the condition. It's just that, well, you've put yourself in to this position where you feel like it's your responsibility to get Amber out of a hole. It's given you a focus and all I'm saying is you're coping really well.'

I feel my shoulders relax a little and offer a smile. 'Yeah, it's always been easier to manage when I've had something to focus on. I suppose it's like that with any condition. Concentrate on something else that has meaning and you don't have time to think about the negative stuff. Except all I'm dealing with right now is negative stuff. I feel like I'm the star in a really crap film and no one would believe the narrative.'

Paul smiles and takes my hand, squeezing it reassuringly. 'Yeah, and I'm the guy who's been brought along for the ride, eh?'

'Yeah, sorry to drag you into all this. I just couldn't live with myself if I didn't go back for her. I know I could just call the police but Marcus and his men are clever, they would be able to cover up what they're doing somehow, make it look like a legit business or something. I mean, they've got away with it at the club for so long. I'm just lucky I didn't end up further down the line.'

We follow the road for a while and I take in the scenery. How can a place so beautiful be home to such monsters? I think about Marcus and how he manipulated me into doing what he wanted without me even realising it. I truly believed he was in love with me but the worst part is I believed I was in love with him. But I was just under his control the same as Amber. The same as god knows how many more before her. And the girl Amber told me about. Crystal. How many before her?

The phone in my hand vibrates and I look down to see a message from Amber.

'Shit, Paul she's sent a message.'

> **Amber** 15:36
> Jade, are you on your way? You need to be careful. You can't let Marcus or Tommy or any of the others see you. One of the girls has been murdered. I could hear them moving her body. What are you going to do when you get here?

I relay the message to Paul and his expression turns to shock. 'What the fuck, Jade?'

'I told you this was going to be dangerous. These people aren't selling sweets to kids outside their school. They're trafficking girls, dealing drugs and they're killers, Paul. This is why I'm doing this.'

I begin to type a message to Amber in reply.

> **Jade** 15:38
> We'll be okay. Are you okay, you're not hurt?
> Where are you? Can you tell me what the place
> looks like?

> **Amber** 15:38
> It looks like a mansion. It has a huge driveway
> running up from the main road. But Marcus and
> Tommy are here. And some other guy who is
> Marcus's dad. And Lizzy too, the woman who ran
> the club before Marcus took over. He had her
> brought here too. How the fuck are we going to
> get out of here, Jade?

I take a breath and try to centre myself. The panic in my chest remains, but I am at a point now where I can keep it at bay. I begin to type out my reply and tell Amber what our plan is.

65

LIZZY

Marcus and Tommy appear in the hallway but I don't look up because I can't bear to look at them. Watching them carry Yasmin's body out of this place as if it was an old bit of rolled-up carpet made me feel sick. How could I have produced someone like him?

'Right, room cleaned up?' Tommy says, stopping and standing in front of the desk. I choose not to answer. 'Oi, I said is the room all cleaned up?'

'Yes.' I grit my teeth.

It was me who cleaned up the evidence. I'd had no other choice. It was clean it or end up body number two. No one had actually used the words but I knew that's what would happen to me if I didn't comply. And I felt like an accomplice in Yasmin's death because I was literally scrubbing away the evidence.

'Good. That phone is going to start ringing soon so I want to see that diary full tonight. You understand me?' Marcus says as Tommy heads for the stairs.

I nod and glance down at the phone, waiting for it to ring and for men to start ordering girls like they're ordering food from a menu.

'Tom, you good to stay here tonight? I've got some stuff going on at the club that I want to deal with.' Marcus glances up the stairs and Tommy nods in agreement.

'Cheers.'

Barry passes Tommy on the stairs and gives Marcus a stern look. I can't look at either of them, I feel like they would see right through me.

'I think it's important the girls stay here tonight. There's plenty others that can fill spaces at the club. I want to keep an eye on things after Yasmin,' Barry says.

Marcus is already nodding. 'Aye, good plan. Right, I'll see you tomorrow?'

Barry nods and I witness a father–son embrace for the first time. I notice an awkwardness between them, like it's a show for my benefit. I turn away when the phone starts to ring.

Barry and Marcus give me a warning look to answer it immediately and I do. 'Hello, Angel House.'

Marcus remains in his place, watching me as I hold the phone to my ear. Barry has already gone back upstairs to his office space.

Amber has told me what is going to happen. If I'm honest, I'm surprised she trusted me with the information at all, but who else could she work with if what is going to happen is to be a success? All our lives are at stake here, so I can't mess this up.

'Yes sir, we have a girl available that I think will suit your needs,' I say. I look up at Marcus and keep the disgust in my expression, because that has been the way I've regarded him the entire time I have spent at Angel House.

I start to rhyme off the pricelist and take the booking. 'Yes sir, Amber is one of our most sought-after girls. I can certainly book you in with her.'

I see a smile creep on to Marcus's face before he turns and leaves. I keep my eye on the door as he closes it behind him.

Suddenly, I feel so sick that my legs begin to tremble. The voice on the other end continues to speak and I listen carefully.

'Do you understand, Lizzy?' he says.

'Yes.'

'Good. Then I'll see you very soon.'

We hang up the phone and I get up from my seat behind the desk and run for the nearest bathroom.

66

MARCUS

Marcus climbs into the car and stares back at the house. His business. The business that is going to make him more money than he could have ever dreamed of. Yes, it was unfortunate about what happened to Yasmin. Unfortunate that Rory had decided to take for himself and lie to the boss.

Marcus knew he could count on Tommy to help him out. It took a good few hours and a lot of hard graft to get those bodies below ground. The looks on the faces of the other boys Marcus had recruited from the street along with Rory when they saw their pal with a gunshot wound to his head was priceless. Marcus had told them what happened and made sure they understood the same would happen to them if they ever did anything to put the company in danger of being exposed. He isn't sure a lot of them will stick around after being part of putting their friend in the ground. But he had to make sure that they were up to the job and what better way to test their loyalty and commitment. Of course there was the risk that they might go to the police, but that risk was low. He suspected they'd be too scared to speak out against him.

One of them was almost the same colour as Rory as he dug his spade into the ground and Marcus had wanted to taunt him about it but chose not to. He had to be professional, remain focused. Marcus wonders now if the girls from the YEEG are harder than some of these lads. But he can't have girls manning the doors and working behind them. He has to have men on the doors at the club and the house. If he had female security, there would be clients who would take the piss and Marcus wouldn't respond well to that.

The lads are just young kids, the way he and Tommy were at that age. The difference between them was that the McAdams came from a long line of men who passed down their experiences in order for the name to go on, contain its meaning in the city of Glasgow. There had been no female influence, no motherly figure to nurture him or Tommy. And that was the way he'd have it, if he could go back and change it he wouldn't.

The arrival of the Aitkens was just a blip in the market that his old man had dealt with, albeit it had taken him over thirty years to do it but good things come to those who wait.

Starting the engine, Marcus drives down to the main road and turns left to head back to his apartment. It feels strange to him to not have Amber or Yasmin in the car with him. Amber will be back to it tomorrow night, he knows that. Yasmin will be replaced. Yes, she was a good earner but there was no point in dwelling on that now.

He knows that by the time he gets back to Angel House tomorrow, a shit ton of money will have exchanged hands and that's what it's all about, the reason for the hard graft. The disposal of bodies is just part of the job. Watching his old man do it when he was a teenager had hardened him up and helped in his ability to get the job done. Yes, he'd have lost some income from the death of Yasmin, but in comparison to the amount of girls working at Angel House and Angel Silk, it would be easy to forget. Also, all girls were replaceable. He only had to think back to how quickly he'd replaced Crystal. And Amber. Now all he had to do was replace Jade. But not until he'd found the bitch.

After almost an hour due to traffic, Marcus arrives at Glasgow Harbour and heads up to his apartment for a shower. He couldn't very well appear at the club in the same clothes that he helped to dispose of two bodies in, could he?

Opening the door to his grand and luxurious Glasgow apartment, he enjoys the silence that greets him. Having the girls live with him for those periods of time had been frustrating but he knew it would be worth it in the end. Crystal, Amber and Jade. They all had their benefits when they lived there. Crystal was a good cook, from what he can remember. But she had a mouth on her and it only increased in volume once Marcus had moved her to the brothel flat. She was too aware of what was going on and she was too open with her opinion and no longer believed anything Marcus told her. In the end he didn't care that he wasn't convincing when he told her he loved her and what she was doing was digging him out of a hole. So, she had to go. Tommy and Barry agreed although they were wary. She didn't go quietly and it was a shame, Marcus did like her. She would have made him a lot of money.

Amber. Now that's a girl who knows how to work her magic on the clients. She's made him a mint and now that she's hooked and reliant on him to get her what she needs, he isn't about to let her go anywhere in a hurry. The frustrating thing about Amber is she has hints of Crystal about her personality and had he not given her that first hit, she may have ended up another body in Clyde.

Then there's Jade. The one he'd thought would be his gold-mine. Marcus grits his teeth when he thinks about her. He'd put in so much work, time and effort to get her ready for business and then she disappeared. No sign that it was going to happen unlike Crystal and Amber before her. She just upped and left even though she'd declared how in love she was with him and she'd always done everything he'd asked her. Marcus is still suspicious that Amber had something to do with Jade leaving. But then Amber is still with him at the house and making money so until that changes, he'll let things go for the time being.

He'll find Jade, he thinks. He *will* and when he does, she'll do exactly what he tells her and he'll make sure she does it with a smile on her face.

He steps out of the shower and gets dressed. Eyeing the new bottle of whisky on the drinks cabinet, he picks it up and opens it. Smelling the contents, Marcus fights the urge to have one now. Marcus decides that he will have a dram or two when he gets home. If he opens it now, he won't make it to the club. It's his weakness, that and the odd recreational snifter here and there. But business comes first. That was something his old man has drilled into him from a young age. You don't get far in this life if you don't put the work in. Working under the influence is strictly forbidden according to Barry McAdam. Marcus knows he's broken this rule on a number of occasions but when it comes to having to deal with body disposal then Marcus knows sobriety is the best way to conduct business.

Barry had been hard on him as a young lad, said that being on top of him meant he'd get the job done. He remembers the odd dig here and there about not going far in life because he'd been left scarred by the fact that his mother had abandoned him. But Marcus thought differently. Yes, he could go off the rails for that reason but what would be the point? He wanted to be successful, make a shit ton of money and enjoy the lavish lifestyle he saw his dad enjoy. So he'd worked hard, done everything he was supposed to when he was working the streets and with the young team. And it had paid off, because look at him now.

Marcus does one last check over of the apartment, makes sure the balcony door is locked and the windows are closed. He steps out into the main hallway and locks the door before heading back to the car and then onto the club.

Angel House. Angel Silk. And that's just for starters. The supply to the city is growing day by day. Tommy and Barry are seeing to that. He's running the show better than his dad ever had and it feels fucking marvellous.

67

AMBER

I'm on my feet, waiting for my client. Lizzy will show him to my room. My knees are trembling but I have to get a grip of myself. I can't be nervous or scared.

I hear Lizzy push the key into the lock and then as she opens the door, I take a step back into the room.

'Amber, this is your client. He's paid for one hour with you,' Lizzy says. Her eyes dart between us before she backs out of the room and locks the door behind us. I look at him as he stands there in silence and I don't know what to say. I go to the bed and sit down. Wait.

'Are you okay?' he asks without meeting my gaze. He's visibly uncomfortable by the way I'm dressed. Lack of material has surprised him, although I don't understand why because he's seen me in this attire twice before.

'Can I ask you a question, Paul?' I say, trying to meet his eye. He sits down on the chair next to the table in my room, dropping his rucksack at his feet. He leans forward, resting his elbows on his knees and bows his head. 'Why are you helping me? No offence but you don't even know me.'

'No, I don't. But I care a lot about Jade. And this is important to her. She wants to get you out of here and she has no one else. No family, not close by anyway. And now that I know about this place and what that guy is making all of you do, I can't stand back and do nothing.'

I regard his response. I wasn't kind to Jade when I met her. I wouldn't say that I was kind to her at all during the short time

I was around her, before Marcus brought me here. So why has she come back?

'But she could have just gone off into the sunset and lived her life. Why risk coming here and saving someone she barely knows?' I ask.

'Do you think she would ever have been able to relax? She would have been living a life in fear, constantly looking over her shoulder in the hope that Marcus wouldn't be there. Jade would never admit this but she is the type of person that suffers from guilt. If she knows she can help someone in some way and doesn't do anything about it, then it eats her up inside.' Paul clasps his hands together and glances at the door. 'Like Lizzy said, I've paid for an hour so we'll have to stay in here for that length of time so there isn't any suspicion.'

I glare at him. 'Are you expecting to sleep with me?'

The look of horror on his face tells me I've got it wrong. 'Oh god no. Sorry I didn't mean it to sound like that at all. I've paid for the time to explain what is going to happen, not the service.'

A little laughter releases from me and Paul smiles.

'So, what is the plan? And where is Jade?'

'She's in the car. Waiting.'

'Right outside? Isn't that putting her in real danger? What if Marcus sees her?'

'Marcus isn't here. He's at that club,' Paul sneers. 'I can't believe I never knew the stuff that goes on in those kinds of places. It's sick.'

I nod and then freeze when I hear a knock on the door. It's quick, forceful. I eye Paul who is now on his feet. I get up and pull the duvet back and climb under. 'Quick,' I mouth at Paul. He panics and takes off his shoes before climbing in. I pull the duvet over us when there is another knock on the door.

'Erm, I've got a client in here,' I call out.

I look out from the duvet and see that Lizzy has peered her head around the door.

'Everything okay in here?' Her eyes are wide and I wave her away. Closing the door, I shake my head.

Paul gets out from under the covers and clears his throat before putting his shoes back on.

'Look, you don't have to worry. I'm used to being so exposed to men.'

'That's not a normal thing to be used to, Amber.' He sighs then meets my eye. 'Look, this is what's going to happen.'

I listen intently, taking in every word he is saying. I don't think it's going to work. But I have to try. Jade has stuck her neck on the line for me, for all of us here and I can't let that all be for nothing. I owe it to Crystal and Yasmin to do my best to get away from here. I owe it to the rest of the girls living here and at the brothel in the city.

It's likely that someone will die tonight, or in the days that follow. I just have to hope that I can fight hard enough against the evil running this place. And I have to be strong, fight the withdrawal, the pain and the itch that blurs my thinking. If I can do that I might just win back my freedom.

68

JADE

It's a wonder no one has seen me yet as I sit in the back of the car and wait for Paul to emerge from the house. The panic that struck me on our way up the drive towards this enormous house was overwhelming. This could have been me. I could be in there right now just like Amber and being forced to… I stop myself from thinking about it. It would only bring on another attack and I was doing well to keep them away. I can't risk having one at this most crucial time.

Ensuring that the flash is switched off, I peer out from the tinted windows at the back of the car and snap and film the various men as they come and go. Some of them I recognise as punters from the club and I feel sick to my stomach at the sight, remember how belittled and worthless I felt when I had to dance topless for them. The others I haven't seen before, but I know they're clients. They've got to be. They've turning up in their expensive cars and flash suits, why else would they be here? And some of them look so guilty, looking around them as they climb out of their cars.

I watch as younger men, late teens or early twenties at a push, patrol the grounds. They're clearly Marcus's security. Luckily for me they don't approach the several cars parked on the drive. This was always going to be a risk but I couldn't just walk away. I would never be able to live with myself if another body was to be washed up and I knew that I could have done something to prevent that from happening.

I have around twenty different pictures over the space of a half-hour timeframe and a few clips of men coming and going, only being allowed to enter or leave the building by the men on the door.

I lay down in the back and wait, my heart pounding in my chest. I breathe slowly, counting to three on the inhale before letting it out. It's the only way I can control the panic, the anxiety and the level of stress the situation is causing.

The car door opens and I hold my breath. Paul climbs in and starts the car. I don't say anything. Not a word. I don't want the men on the door to see Paul's lips moving. No one can suspect him. It's far too dangerous.

The car reverses out of the space and heads back down the drive away from the house. I breathe a sigh of relief as we pull out on to the main road and start the journey back to the city.

'How did it go?' I ask. 'Did you tell her everything?'

'Yeah.'

'And she still has the phone in case she needs us?'

'Yes, Jade. I did everything as planned.'

'And the rucksack?'

'Yes she has it. Would you please sit up, you're making me nervous lying down in there.'

I sit up and put on my seatbelt. I look into the rear-view mirror and see the look in his eyes. He's stressed. Worried. That doesn't fill me with confidence.

'What's wrong, Paul?'

'There were so many of them, Jade. So many girls. I heard so many different voices, male and female. I saw men coming in and being shown into various rooms. The place is like hell on earth. How the fuck did you meet this guy? He's the fucking devil.'

My stomach rolls at the thought of there being so many girls in that house. And that's just Angel House. The club housed so many more along with the other brothel Amber was living in in the city. Paul was spot on. Marcus is the devil.

'I met him in the hospital when I was in there after the attack.'

'How the hell did that happen?'

'He was visiting someone. But that's not important. What matters is that we've given Amber what she needs. Now all we have to do is hope that she can pull it off.'

Paul shakes his head and I place my hand on his shoulder. 'I hope she does, Jade.'

I take off my seatbelt and climb into the front passenger seat. I can't be in the back, alone. I think about what might happen if Paul and Marcus ever come face to face. Paul is no match for Marcus, there's a considerable height and weight difference for a start. But I'm hoping that things will go as planned and I won't have to worry about that.

'Thank you, Paul,' I say.

He doesn't look at me. Doesn't respond. He takes my hand and pulls it across to him, kisses it and rests it over on my leg. But he doesn't let go.

69

AMBER

I could have fucked this up. I could have taken the easier route to make the pain go away but I didn't, because it wasn't just my life and freedom at stake. There are several others unknowingly depending on me to get this right and there was no way I could have the guilt of failing them on my head.

I stare down at the tin and curse as I empty the contents of the bag down the toilet. I watch as the water carries it away into the sewage system and tears stream down my face.

I get to my feet and begin to pace the room. The sweat is pouring off me now and I am in so much physical pain. This is the longest I've ever gone between doses and I know getting clean is going to be a bastard of a task.

This is it, my part of the plan is about to commence and I'm terrified I'm not going to convince anyone. The withdrawal is bad, really bad but if I'm going to make it seem that way, I'm going to have to be very vocal about it. Paul told me to do whatever I thought would work. So here I am by the door now, pulling at the handle and beating it with my fists. I'm screaming for help, for someone to come to my aid. I'm making enough of a racket that I can hear voices in the hallway. Muffled at first and then I hear Lizzy. She's outside my door. I can hear keys jangling as one finds its way into the lock on the other side. She's not alone.

I step back and fall to the floor, clutching my stomach. My entire body is trembling, a combination of fear and genuine pain.

'Amber, what's wrong?' Lizzy rushes towards me, crouches down next to me.

'The pain...' I gasp. 'My stomach. My chest.'

I keep my eyes down and see two pairs of feet in heavy black rigger type boots at the door.

I cry out again, louder this time and Lizzy winces. The tears that spill over are genuine. She turns to the men in the door. 'Tommy, we need to get her to a hospital.'

'Ha, no way. She's not going anywhere,' Tommy replies. The other man steps into the room and another wave of pain comes. It's more intense than the last one but not as bad as I'm making out. I bite down on my lip as I growl through it.

'Amber?' he asks. I look up. I see Marcus in the man's eyes. Barry, Marcus's dad. I nod as I wail in pain.

'Barry, please. She needs help. Look at the state of her.'

Barry gets to his feet and moves away from me. He stands next to Tommy and they start to converse. I can't hear them over the sound of blood rushing in my ears. I try to contain the sounds trying to escape my throat as the pain becomes almost unbearable. I almost ask for a fix because that is truly what I want and what I need but I hold it in.

Lizzy takes my hand and looks at me. Her eyes are filled with tears too.

'Right,' I hear Tommy say. 'I'll take her to the hospital.'

Lizzy lets go of my hand and stands up. She rushes across the room and pulls some clothes from the wardrobe in the corner. She hands them to me and I pull them on. Tommy hooks his hand under my arm and hauls me up. I cry out again because I can't stand up straight. Now the withdrawal is beginning to feel as bad as I'm making out. A wave of nausea is suddenly upon me and I rush to the small bathroom, then vomit violently into the toilet. My body is screaming out for a fix and I am already regretting putting myself through this. I want to come clean, tell them what I'm attempting so they'll sort me out and make the pain stop. I refuse to allow the weakness in me to take over.

I keep my mouth shut, take a quick drink from the tap and turn to see Tommy blocking the bathroom door.

'Move it. You've got money to make and you won't be very appealing to the clients in this state.'

I move towards him and he takes hold of my arm. I pass by Lizzy who is standing by Barry. Marcus's parents. Two people who couldn't be more different. How did that even happen?

Tommy pulls me towards his car and forces me into the passenger seat. He straps me in and shuts the door.

Breathe, just breathe through the pain. It'll be over once you're at the hospital.

Tommy gets into the car and starts the engine. 'Right. When we get there, I'll do the talking. If they ask, I'm your boyfriend. You say fuck all else about me. You tell them your symptoms. They give you the meds you need and then we are straight back here. If you so much as breathe the wrong way at this hospital I'll fucking kill you myself. Do you understand?'

'Yes, please just… get me there. I think I'm dying,' I say. I see a flicker of panic cross Tommy's face. He won't want me to die in his car, or even at the hospital. That would mean people would start asking questions.

'What is it that's wrong?' he asks.

'I don't know. It might be my appendix,' I gasp. 'That's where the pain is coming from.'

Tommy pulls down the drive and I'm glad it's him and not Marcus. Marcus wouldn't allow me to go to the hospital. He would allow me to die. We're all replaceable.

–

We arrive at the Queen Elizabeth University Hospital and Tommy helps me out of the car and into the A&E department. He holds me up gently, all for show of course.

By this point I can barely stand up straight, the pain in my stomach has gotten so much worse that I fear I might pass out. Maybe I am dying and this is what it feels like?

'Excuse me, can you help my girlfriend? She's in a lot of pain,' Tommy says to the medical receptionist.

I lift my chin so I can speak to her and I see the look on her face. Before I know it, I'm being helped into a wheelchair and Tommy is being told to wait for me in the waiting area. He watches me as I'm pulled through a set of doors and he doesn't have to say the words. I know the look in his eyes. He's reminding me. *Say nothing. Tell them your symptoms and get back out here so I can take you back to Angel House.*

I'm crying, wailing in pain. A nurse's hand falls upon my shoulder and she tells me I'm going to be okay. I'm in the right place.

70

LIZZY

Amber has been gone for almost three hours now. It's Friday night. The A&E department will be crammed with drunks and drug addicts. People who have gotten into fights in bars and ended up coming off the worse of the two involved. I should know. I used to run a gentlemen's club in the middle of the city. I used to witness things all the time, especially at the weekends.

I've done my rounds for the night, checked on the girls and made sure they are okay. I've told them about Amber. Told them not to worry. The last of the clients are leaving now and the security team are at skeleton level. It's just the girls, Barry, two doormen and me.

I go into Amber's room and pull the rucksack out from under the bed. I open it and check the contents. It's all there. Everything that Amber said is inside. I nod, take a breath and push it back underneath. I get to my feet and head out the door and along to the room at the end of the hall. Lifting my hand, I ball my fist and knock on it.

Barry opens the door and frowns when he sees me standing there. 'What do you want?'

'You,' I say, pushing my way into the room and closing the door behind me.

Barry doesn't reply, he looks shocked.

'Stunned you into silence, have I?' I ask, a smile lifting the corners of my mouth.

'A little,' Barry says. 'But I don't get it.'

I place my hands on his shoulders, run them down the front of his torso and push myself against him. 'Me neither. But I haven't been able to stop myself from thinking about you since I got here. We were good together back then, remember?' I reach up and my lips are close to his. I feel his breath on my skin. 'I should have been stronger. Should have gone with my heart instead of my head. I shouldn't have listened to my dad. He didn't know us, Barry. I loved you. Couldn't get enough of you.'

Barry narrows his eyes and steps back. 'What are you up to, Lizzy Queen?' His voice is low, intrigued. My stomach drops. It's what he used to call me when we first got together. It was a play on Queen Elizabeth and he used to tell me I was his queen all the time. I think back to when I first met him. I was just eighteen years old and a stupid little girl infatuated by his macho attitude. I wish I could go back and tell eighteen-year-old me to turn a blind eye to him. To think I used to like being called Lizzy Queen, now it makes me feel sick. I push on, ignoring it.

'I never thought I'd be saying this since you kidnapped me, but I can't help it. I don't think my feelings for you ever really went away. I was forced into making that decision. But I know that now. I want you. I want us.'

He looks down at me, deep into my eyes as if he's trying to work me out. Then, just like the Barry I remember, his trousers take over his thought process and he leans down and kisses me. Without holding back, I push hard against his lips and force him down onto the sofa. His hands are on my back, his eyes closed. I steal a glance to the right. The whisky bottle on the table next to us is three-quarters full. I sit up and reach for it.

'What are you doing?' he says.

'Your Lizzy Queen wants a drink? How about you?'

'Now?'

'Why not?' I say. I balance on him and open the bottle. I place it to his lips and pour a little in. He drinks it eagerly and then I gulp some of it back to.

'Thought you didn't drink the stuff?'

'I thought I hated you. Things change, just look at us now.' I smile and kiss him again. His tongue snakes its way into my mouth and I pull back a little. He starts working on the buttons of my shirt and his hands are inside it. His grip is tight and I almost pull away. Almost back out. But I have to go through with this no matter how disgusting it makes me feel.

I get to my feet and he watches me as I pull the shirt off my back and step out of my skirt. I lean down and tug at his trousers. He removes them and sits back. The urge to be sick is overwhelming, so I pick up the bottle and take another gulp of whisky for courage.

'You look just like them,' he says.

'Who?' I ask.

'The girls. Look at you standing there in your underwear and heels. You look the part. I always thought you'd look good on a pole.' His hands reach out for me and I go to him. 'Even at this age.'

'Is that right? Then maybe I should dance for you now?'

He smiles and I lead him from the sofa and push him onto the floor. He lays there under me, staring up at me. I still have the bottle in my hands and I pour a little whisky over him and start to sway in the silence of the room.

'I knew you'd come back to me eventually Lizzy Queen. I knew it.' At that, I lift my right foot and bring the heel of my shoe down on his crotch as hard as I can. And I don't miss.

Barry screams in pain and shock and I raise the bottle above me and bring it down hard on his head. Whisky sprays everywhere as I hit him a second and a third time before giving him another heel to the torso. He's on his side. There's blood coming from his head. The bottle is still intact.

Barry groans as I step away from him and grab my shirt and skirt from the floor, still holding the bottle. He's barely moving and I rush towards the door and out of the room but not before I grab the keys from the lock on the back of the door. Turning the key and securing the door with Barry still inside, I turn and rush along to Amber's room and close the door.

I lean against it and take a few steadying breaths. I can't believe I just did that. I place the bottle on the floor and put my clothes back on. I step out of my shoes and into the trainers that are next to Amber's bed. They're a little too big for me but they'll have to do for now.

Pulling the bag out from under the bed, I pull the small petrol canister out and begin pouring. Then I head out to the hall and pour some on Barry's door. I can hear him moving around a little inside, urging me to move faster. I unlock the doors all along the hall and push them open. The girls inside stare at me in wonderment. They'll know what to do in a moment. They'll know to run.

I go back to Amber's room and lift the matches out of the bag, my heart hammering against my chest. I step back into the hallway and stand at the top of the stairs. I strike the match against the box and watch as the flame dances in front of me. I hear Barry, he's pulling on the handle of the door and shouting. His voice is muffled as I drop the match. Flames trail along the floor and up around the woodwork of the door. And the door itself is ablaze in seconds. He won't be coming out of there unscathed.

The fire takes hold quickly and I turn to see the girls coming out of their rooms. They're doing what I'd hoped for. They're taking the opportunity to grasp at their freedom.

Turning, I rush down the stairs and the girls are not far behind me. I start banging on the door to the boys outside.

'Fire, fire! Help.'

The door opens quickly and when they see the fire, they step back in shock. I push past them and the rest of the girls rush out behind me and scarper in various directions. Some of them together. Some of them on their own. But most of them head for the woodland. The boys on the door watch as we disperse, they don't know what to do.

I turn and run, faster than I thought my legs could carry me. I head down the drive in the hope that I will make it to the main road and a passing car will stop and help me.

I reach the bottom of the drive and keep running. I turn for a split-second to see flames rising into the air. I don't stop. I don't allow complacency to take over my thinking. Barry wasn't dead when I left him in that room. Unless I see his dead corpse, I'll never believe it.

71

AMBER

I've been here for hours and the pain has eased along with the panic. The hospital is busy with various members of the public. Drunks who have been brought in after fighting in a bar or the street. Junkies who have overdosed. A drunk driver lies in the cubicle across from me lucky to be alive. I heard him tell the nurse that he was sleepy due to his medication. His blood results proved otherwise.

'Amber?' I hear a nurse say.

'Yes,' I nod. I pray she isn't going to tell me I'm fine to leave and go home. I pray I get to stay here for the night. This is the first time I've been away from Marcus and Tommy in such a long time, even in the confines of this hospital, I feel semi-free. But Tommy is out there, waiting on me. He'll be anxious right now, desperate to know what I've told the medical staff here. I've been warned to say nothing and the terror of what could happen to me if I do is the reason I've kept quiet.

'How are you feeling?' the nurse asks, pulling the curtain only halfway around. I can still see the drunk driver across from me.

'Your test results show that you're in withdrawal.' She pauses. I don't give her time to explain to me what my body is crying out for because I already know. I'm not stupid.

'I'm a heroin addict.' Her eyes lock with mine, her expression soft and full of empathy. It makes me want to cry. 'I was trying to get clean, stay off it.'

'I see,' she replies. 'And you've seen your GP about this?'

I know that's more a suggestion than a question. She'll have seen my medical records. I haven't seen my GP since I got together with Marcus.

'No. I was kind of going it alone. Cold turkey, you know?' I run my hand through my hair, pull my eyes down and away from her gaze.

'Do you feel like you'd benefit from help? There's plenty support out there for people in your position.'

'I doubt that,' I sneer. It isn't directed at her though, I think she knows that by the look on her face when I lift my head again to meet her.

'You'd be surprised how many people we treat with your symptoms.'

I start to cry and scold myself for doing it in front of her. I never cry. Not in front of anyone. I learned it's best to keep my emotions locked away at the very beginning of this job.

'Amber...' Her voice is softer now. 'Is there something else?'

I can't say it. This is my chance to get out and I can't even form the words. My body trembles as I sob quietly. I feel pathetic.

'Is there someone here with you that we could fetch for some support?'

'No!' I shoot her a look. She doesn't jump at my sudden outburst. 'No, don't bring him in here.'

'But he might be able to support you.' She says it without conviction. She knows I don't want him in here for a specific reason.

'No, he won't.'

'Why not, Amber?'

Can I tell her? Can I trust that she'll believe me if I do? If I tell her who Tommy is and what I've been forced into, he'll kill me. But if I do nothing, just sit here with the nurse and pretend that everything is fine, I'll have to go back to Marcus. That could result in my death too. I could only carry on as a prostitute with a heroin problem for so long before either Marcus or the drugs would kill me.

What about Crystal and Yasmin? They didn't have the chance to make a change, to rid the world of people like Marcus and Tommy. But I do. Jade has put herself in the most dangerous position for not just me but all of us at Angel House. And here I am, with the opportunity to put a stop to all of it and I'm already getting cold feet. Lizzy would have already started her part in ending this. I can't fuck that up.

'Amber?' The nurse presses.

'He won't support me because he's my boss, sort of. Well, supervisor.' I shake my head in disgust that I'm honouring him with that title, but in truth that's what he is.

'And you were at work when the withdrawal pain began?'

I nod, tears falling from my eyes and onto my top. The nurse is quiet for a moment before she asks me her next question. The space between us is heavy and the weight of my situation bears down on my chest. I have to take a deep breath to stop myself from panicking and flaring up the pain again.

'Amber, what do you do for a living?'

'I'm… I'm a dancer.' The last word whispers off my lips as I gasp at the sheer reality of my life. 'I'm a prostitute.'

'Through choice?' She moves from around the bottom of the bed and is now standing next to me. Her hand falls on mine and it's the first time in three years I feel like I may finally get the freedom I've been craving.

'No.' My voice is high now, it cracks and that's when I sob uncontrollably.

'And the man in the waiting area, your supervisor you said?'

'He's… the one that is… keeping an eye on me for…' I have to stop and take a few deep breaths before I can continue. My words are caught up in the emotion and terror that is trying to burst out of me and I need to make sure I am clear.

'It's okay. Take your time.' She squeezes my hand reassuringly.

'The man in the waiting area is called Tommy McAdam. He's keeping an eye on me for the real boss. I've been forced into prostitution to fund my heroin addiction, which was also forced on me. I flushed my last stash down the toilet and the withdrawal pain got so bad I couldn't take it anymore. I begged him to bring me here.'

The expression on the nurse's face falls but only for a second. She straightens herself and smiles. 'Thank you for telling me that, Amber.'

'Please,' I say. 'Please help me.' Now I'm sobbing.

'I will, Amber.' But she doesn't leave me. Instead, she slides an arm around my shoulder and stands with me as I sob silently.

Once I've managed to compose myself, she excuses herself and steps out of the cubicle. I shift in the bed. Tommy could burst through here at any moment, demanding that I go back with him. If I refuse, what would happen? Would he make a scene? I don't know, people do strange things during times of desperation and now may be one of those moments for Tommy because the house just lost Yasmin. They won't want to lose me too.

I wait, somewhat impatiently as the nurse is gone. I don't even know her name. I've been so involved in my own shit that I don't even know the name of the woman who could potentially save my life.

I look up and see my nurse standing in the space where the cubicle curtain is open. Behind her are two police officers. One male, one female.

'Is it okay for us to come in and have a chat, Amber?' the female officer asks.

A wave of nausea washes over me and the nurse recognises it. In a second, she is by my side, holding a sick bowl under my chin. Nothing comes as I retch other than some mild stomach cramps and a new layer of sweat on my brow.

'Yes,' I reply. 'Yes it's fine.'

The female officer approaches me and the male officer stands back, takes out a notepad and pen. He looks on expectantly at the female officer, awaiting the words he should write down.

'Amber, I'm PC Fletcher, and this is my colleague PC Munn. Can you tell me what you told Sarah here?' PC Fletcher glances to the nurse and I smile at her. Sarah, I think. I'll remember her.

I repeat what I told Sarah. I tell the police in great detail everything. From beginning to end.

By now, Angel House should be up in flames. I hope it is.

72

LIZZY

Pushing through the overgrowth, I move as fast as I can. Wild brambles, thorns and branches scratch at my skin as I run through the woodland. I raise my arms to protect my face. Having reached the main road, I chose to head back into the cover of the trees on the very small chance that Barry somehow managed to get out of that fire alive and come after me.

The rain starts to pour heavily and my shirt clings to my body. Heavy droplets fall onto the leaves creating a rushing river like sound above me. I look up, water rushing over my face and feet sinking into the saturated woodland floor. I wonder if the ground will swallow me. That would be better than Barry finding me.

I continue on, dodging half fallen branches. My feet and my back ache but I don't stop. The tops of the branches glower over me intimidatingly like a dark audience. Then I stop, a sharp and menacing sound creeps over me. A voice. Barry's voice. He calls out to me, ominously. He's close. He's alone. The boys must have let him out, extinguished the fire somehow before going off to try to round up the rest of the girls. Or maybe he got out via the window. I hope the girls get away or can hide until I can get help. As much as Barry told me the police were in his pocket, I still have to try.

I don't shout back even though I want to tell him to fuck off away from me, leave me alone. I can't allow him to hear me and track where I am. I can't go back to that place, that house. Evil resides there, the men who man the doors, recruit the girls and keep them there make me sick. The house itself was beautiful and was clearly a home long ago before the McAdams got their hands on it. Now, the place is like a prison run by parasites that feed off the misery of the people being held against their will.

I think about Amber and Yasmin. One dead and one attempting to get away from this life. And Crystal… the poor girl who Marcus, my son, had killed. Amber was certain of that. I'd wanted to ask Yasmin about it, they'd been friends, but I just couldn't get a moment alone with her. She was either with a client or off her face.

Death is clearly the McAdam way of protecting their business. Whether that means against people like young Rory who'd taken advantage, or the girls themselves including me. I can't die tonight. Not because I don't want to or because I'm scared of what death means, but because I owe it to the rest of the girls to get help.

The cold air catches in my throat as I duck through the trees. Barry is closing in, I can hear him calling out. He's angry, calling my name. 'I'll fucking kill you, I swear I'll kill you Lizzy.'

He sounds like an injured animal and I know I've done some damage with those heels. Good. I want him to suffer, it's my only hope.

I stop at the edge of the forest and look out onto the road. The moon shines down on the soaked concrete. It looks pretty, almost peaceful out here. The sound of the rain falling on a river somewhere helps to centre me. The rain lashes down and I look up at the sky, imagining how the rain is washing away all of the bad things that have happened in my life. Giving birth to a baby I didn't want to have, leaving him outside the hospital in the hope that he would have a better life than I could offer. In reality, I'd left him in the firing line and now that I know what happened to him, who had brought him up, I've never regretted a decision more in my life than that one. Marcus is the person he is because of Barry. If I'd just kept him, moved away, none of this might have happened.

My name echoes out again, Barry's voice a deep growl. He's more than angry. Without turning to see if he's approaching, I climb carefully across the barbed fence and onto the road. If Barry emerged from the forest now, he would see me. So I keep to the edge line of the trees in the hope that he won't be able to see me.

Headlights ahead, fast approaching. I step into the middle of the road and wave my arms frantically at the car. It manoeuvres around me and comes to a stop a few yards ahead of me. I run to the car and pull on the passenger door. It's locked. I peer through the glass at the woman in the driver seat, her eyes wide. The window lowers a little. She is cautious. I understand.

'Please,' I cry. 'Please open the door, he's going to kill me.'

The driver looks out at the road, her eyes darting back and forth along the edging of the trees. Her eyes fall upon me again.

'Please let me in, I'm not going to hurt you I promise.' I'm still pulling at the handle unsuccessfully.

The woman in the car hesitates, of course she does. If I was in her position I would be scared too.

The rain hammers down on the car and the windscreen wipers move quickly over the glass. 'Please, open the door. I need help. He's going to fucking kill me. There are others, I need to get them help.'

My voice is shaking inside my throat. The woman's expression changes, her eyes dart down to the unlock button on the inside of the door. Yes, I think. Thank god. But then she looks up and past me out to the darkness.

I turn, see his shadow standing on the edge of the forest. He is unmoving. Menacing. I turn to the driver again, tapping on the window and pulling frantically at the door.

'Please, don't leave me out here. Open the door.' I pull hard to the point I think the handle might come away in my hand. Then the car begins to pull away, slowly at first and then it speeds off into the night.

'No, no please,' I call but the car is already gone, red lights in the distance. I can't believe that my chance for survival has just slipped away from me.

I don't have time to mourn that loss, I need to move. I cross the road, my legs heavy. But I run into the other side of the forest, deeper and deeper into the conifers and thorn bushes. He's not far behind me, I can feel his presence. He isn't calling my name now. He doesn't want me to know where he is.

I push through the pain of the branches and thorns as they scratch my skin and rip my shirt. Water drips from every inch of my body and even though I'm hot from running, my skin is cold.

I come to a clearing and I find myself on the edge of concrete overlooking the river I could hear before. My surroundings are familiar, like I've been here before. There's a slope to my left and I move down carefully, closer to the water rushing along the river channel. The drop isn't high but at the bottom there is a cavity and I climb over loose rocks and boulders to get inside.

A memory comes to me now, it's slight but it's real. I used to come here as a child. Pretended to fish for salmon while my dad did it for real. I used to play in this small space which I thought was the cave from the story of Peter Pan. Why haven't I recalled this before? How did I know this was here?

I sit against the concrete, my skin sore and cold from the saturated clothes that cling to me now. The adrenaline pumping through me alerts me to the sound of footsteps overhead. He's here. Barry has found me.

I move back as far and as carefully into the darkness of the cavern as I can, stepping over more rocks and boulders. The keys in my pocket are heavy and cold against my skin and I pull them out slowly, bunching them together in my hand so they don't make a sound. I'll need something to hit him with if I have any hope of getting out of here alive. Maybe he's not alone, the boys could be with him. I could be surrounded, about to be taken out.

I hold my breath as the footsteps inch closer, he's climbing down the slope which leads to me and I squeeze the metal in my hands. The approaching sound halts. The rain hammers down above me on to the cavern's roof and I look at the opening, expecting him to appear at any moment. The gushing river in front of the opening is rising, and I know this space will flood soon enough. I'm shivering so much I can't control the chatter of my teeth.

'Ah, there you are.' His voice echoes around me and somehow booms over the sounds of the raging river and the hammering rain. His head is bleeding and he is hunched over. He's in pain and I could use that to my advantage.

'Don't come any closer, Barry. I mean it.'

'Or you'll do what? It's not like there's anyone else here, Lizzy. It's just us.' He raises his hand to his head and dabs his fingers at the blood as it seeps down. 'That was some blow back there. You're a feisty fucker, aren't you? Trying to lure me into shagging you so you could kill me? Setting fire to the house, I mean you're not that clever. Who helped you out with that one?'

He inches closer again and I pin myself to the wall as the water level rises and begins to flow into the dark cavity I am now trapped in. Maybe this is the gateway to hell?

'I didn't do a very good job so it seems, you're still fucking breathing,' I hiss at him. He slips a little, almost loses his footing on the wet rocks below. As he regains his balance, I grip the keys harder in my hand. It's not much but could cause enough damage to buy me some time.

'The water is getting deeper, Lizzy. It's cold too. I could hold you under and no one would be able to stop me, not even you.'

He's close and shoots an arm out, makes a grab for me. I launch my fist at him, allowing the keys to fall loose from my hand and dangle before swiping them against his face. I aim for the eyes and as he jumps back, he slips and falls back into the water. I move carefully and lift one of the rocks at my feet, pick it up with my hands. Barry squirms, slips and slides in the water against the algae-covered depths. The moonlight shines a little inside the cavity and I can almost see his blood mixing with the river.

I balance myself over him as he tries to get up and bring the rock down on his head, just like I did with the bottle. He wrestles for my ankle but I hit him again, and again. Harder and harder with each blow, I start to scream. The water splashes up and around me, the rain hammers down and the river swirls in between and around us.

Barry isn't moving now, isn't fighting. And I continue to power down on him with the rock. Harder and harder, faster with each blow. I can't allow him to get up this time.

'Please,' I cry out, screaming in torment. 'Please, Barry just fucking die!'

As I stare down at his face, I don't see any burns from the fire. In fact, I barely see a face having smashed down on him so much. My eyes dart between his head and my hands as I try to process the blood. So much blood.

73

LIZZY

I step out from the forest and onto the road, dripping wet and shivering. My body is numb as I struggle along the road. It's dark, the wind is howling and the rain is now coming in sheets. Barry is dead, there is no doubt about that. I'd made sure of it. Brain matter and blood flowed into the river as I'd smashed the rock into his head. I'd cried, howled like an animal as I did it. That isn't me. I'm not like them, the McAdams. Killing would be like second nature to them. Not me. I'd piled rocks on top of his body in the hope that the river wouldn't carry him away. I couldn't let him out of there. Not yet.

Headlights from behind me illuminate the road ahead and the car stops beside me. The window rolls down and when I look inside, I notice a woman. Shock and horror etched in her expression, she leans over and opens the door.

'Oh my good god, are you okay?' she says as I climb into the car. 'What are you doing out here at this time by yourself? You'll catch your death.'

The woman is around my age and I try to offer a smile. My muscles won't work to form that expression.

I look down at my trembling hands and thank Mother Nature that the river washed the blood away. 'I need to go to the hospital. Can you take me?'

'Oh yes of course I can. Here. I have a blanket in the back. Get out of those clothes.'

I do what she says, leaving my soaked clothes in the footwell and climb into the back of the car. I lay down as she drives.

I can't close my eyes. All I'll see is Barry's dead, drowned and bashed in face staring back at me.

–

We reach the hospital and the woman helps me in, ensuring that the blanket is firmly wrapped around me. Her kindness has reduced me to tears as I attempt to walk from her car into the hospital. I note the police car outside and pray that they don't question me about what's happened.

'Right, come on love. Almost there,' the woman says as she helps me inside. As we enter the A&E waiting area, I stop dead at what I'm seeing.

Police officers are holding a man down, he's shouting obscenities, claiming to be innocent and they've got the wrong man.

'Oh for god's sake, hospitals on a Friday night these days, eh?' the woman says as we take the long way to reception to avoid the chaos unfolding.

They get the man to his feet and we lock eyes. It's Tommy. They're arresting Tommy McAdam. She did it, Amber fulfilled her part of the plan. A lump forms in my throat at the thought, pride and relief rush through me.

'Look, she'll tell you. Lizzy,' he shouts out and the woman beside me stops. I can feel her eyes burning into the side of my face. 'Lizzy, tell them. You know me. Come on.'

I watch as he struggles under the grip of the officers. 'Come on, mate, you're not making this any easier on yourself,' one of the officers says.

'You know him?' the woman asks.

'No,' I say. 'I've never seen him before in my life.'

I give reception my details and soon I am being led through a set of double doors by a nurse. I am told to wait in a cubicle where a nurse will come and do a blood test and other things. I'm not listening to the specifics. I'm too distracted.

'Lizzy?' Amber's voice trails across the room. 'Oh my god.'

She wraps her arms around me and sobs into my shoulder. 'Did you see him? Did you see Tommy?'

'I did,' I reply, my voice barely a whisper.

'And you got out? You're here,' she swallows. 'What about Barry?'

I don't answer when she pulls away and stares into my eyes. I can't say it out loud. But she understands. I can see it. She knows Barry is dead.

'We're free?' she asks. But I can't answer. I'm already consumed by uncontrollable sobs. The enormity of what has happened to us, to the girls, hits me like a freight train. Faces flash in my mind, the girls staring at me as I opened the doors at Angel House. Amber. Yasmin. Crystal. All who suffered at the hands of the McAdams plague my vision.

Amber pulls me to her and hugs me tighter than I thought possible. My tears come in waves now as well as Amber's and I don't know if we'll ever stop.

74

JADE

Standing outside the apartments, I look up to the place that was home for a while. Now when I think about it, it was never home. It was a prison cell that I was able to come and go from under Marcus's instruction. Not that I realised that at the time, I was too under his spell then. And if it hadn't been for Amber putting her life at risk to tell me the truth, I still would be.

The rain pours down on me and I huddle under the hood of my coat. The keys weigh heavy in my hand as I look up at Marcus's apartment. The lights are out. It's only gone eleven. The dancers don't normally stop until two and the club doesn't officially shut to the public until three. If I'm lucky, if he stays there until closing then this might just work because he won't get home until about four.

I move towards the entrance door and wave the fob over the black plate. The lock releases and I push the door open and head for the lift. As I stand in the small and confined space and the suspension cables lift me to the top of the building, I begin to feel sick at the thought of what I'm doing. But there is no other choice. No other way.

The lift stops and there is a low chime as the doors open. I step out and press my ear against the door. Listen. It's quiet. Too quiet. If he was here, I'd hear him. His music would be loud or the television would be talking to itself. He's at the club.

Letting myself into the apartment, I stand in the lounge and look out at the city. There must be so many others like me. So many girls being kept against their will, being force fed drugs and made to have sex with countless men, some of whom have strange and quite frankly terrifying fetishes. These girls' lives are at risk every single day, not just by the men holding them or the clients paying for them, but by the poison they are forced to put into their body. Like caged animals who are only fed and let out at the discretion of the keeper, I can only imagine what it must feel like. Because I was the lucky one who managed to get out before I was plunged into the deep end.

I move through to the bedroom I once shared with Marcus. I think about all the times we'd slept together, and how towards the end he'd started to come up with excuses as to why he couldn't. He was tired. He was too busy. I didn't realise it then, but he had no interest in me in that way. Marcus used sex and intimacy as a way to lure me deeper into his world. He wanted me to fall so hard for him that I wouldn't be able to climb back out.

I step back into the hall and move through to the lounge again. The place is spotless. Immaculate. It was always like that. Marcus likes things done a specific way and I was never allowed to clean or tidy. He told me the cleaner would do their job the way he'd instructed. I'd never met the cleaner. But I knew their prints would likely be all over this place. The same as Amber's would and Crystal's and god knows how many other girls.

That's what scared me the most about Marcus. Not knowing how many times he'd done this, made girls fall for him and then dragged them into his world without so much as blinking. He was very good at manipulation and control. Coercing girls into doing what he wanted was a skill he'd perfected.

I look around the apartment and decide his office is the best place I'll find any sort of evidence of what he has been doing. If he's to be brought to justice then I have to keep digging. I push the door open and move towards his desk. The computer sits proudly on the centre of the desk, but that's not what I'm looking at. I'm eyeing the folder sitting next to it. It's thick with papers inside and I lift it open. What I see is astounding. Screeds and screeds of pages that are typed out in the style of a CV. Girl after girl after girl, some of whom I recognise. Some from the club.

I find Amber's page. Her picture at the top, a photograph that has been taken without her knowledge. Lines of text with dates of when she'd come into contact with Marcus for the first time, the second time and so on.

- *Have been keeping watch of a girl with fiery red hair and a clear complexion. Perfect for the club.*

- *Met Amber after three weeks of watching her.*

- *Fell for Marcus almost immediately. Easily charmed. Easily fooled.*

- *Close family with opinions. Note* if things don't improve with their attitude, they'll need to be dealt with.*

- *After a few dates, Amber opens up about how the family aren't keen on Marcus. Managed to manipulate her into moving away from them. Easily done. Provided new phone. Easily isolated.*

- *Appeared happy to become a dancer at the club.*

- *Appeared happy to move into sex work with clients.*

- *After a few months, Amber decided to leave.*

- *Marcus moved to next phase of holding on to Amber. Injected heroin.*

- *Amber will become part of Angel House once all plans are finalised.*

There are pictures of her posing in underwear, naked images in compromising positions. I turn the pages quickly, trying to keep her dignity from being damaged anymore.

I find a page named Crystal. At the top in red letters is the word 'deceased'. He's been logging when they die and I feel sick.

I read through Crystal's file. She was English. Beautiful from the picture at the top of the page. Blonde, clear complexion and perfect eyebrows. She'd come to Scotland to go to university from what Marcus has recorded. He met her in a pub in Glasgow and bought her a drink, spiked it. He took her home to his apartment, laid her on his bed. Although, he kept his hands to himself – from what I read, he didn't touch her. The way he's recorded his meetings with Crystal is like a report, cold language and short sentences. I read:

- *Met Crystal. Appears to be exact profile that would fit the club.*

- *Easily charmed. Able to spike her drink without her noticing.*

- *Easily led and gullible. Believed she drank too much thanked Marcus for looking after her.*

- *Marcus starts dating Crystal – again easy to lure her in. She fell for Marcus quickly. Said she was in love after just a few weeks.*

- *Didn't protest at suggestion of working at the club.*

- *Picked up the trade quickly and appeared to want to please.*

- *Refused to move into sex work once it was suggested – tried to leave. Caused trouble.*

- *Threatened to go to police and tell as many as she could about what she'd seen at the club.*

- *Marcus killed Crystal. Death by strangulation.*

- *Body disposed of in suitcase and weighted to the bottom of the Clyde.*

Amber was right, Crystal *was* the girl in the suitcase at Luderston Bay. It says it in black and white in the file. As I glance over the bullet points, I think about Crystal and what she could have become if she'd never met Marcus. My heart breaks at the thought of what he's done to so many girls. I've been the lucky one.

75

CRYSTAL

Crystal lies slumped on the floor, her back arched at an angle and her head against the sofa. The pain in her cheek and the side of her head had felt like an explosion. He'd hit her so hard it completely knocked her out. Raising her hand instinctively, she realises he's broken the skin. A trickle of blood runs down like a teardrop and she glances down at her finger to see it. A little higher and he could have killed her.

Attempting to sit up straight, Crystal glances around the room. Marcus isn't in there with her, but she knows he won't be far. After how he'd reacted to her attempts to leave, she wouldn't be surprised if he were barricading the door shut. She'll have to arm herself for when he comes back because she knows he won't stop at one punch next time.

Getting to her feet, she looks out of the window at the city. So many people out there, so much space and so many opportunities. And she was here, stuck in this apartment with a man who wanted her to sell her body for sex so he could earn fuck knows how much money. There's no way she's going to let that happen and Marcus knows she's going to fight for herself, hence why he knocked her about.

Looking out from the penthouse apartment, Crystal knows there's no way out of there except the main door. She's too high up to climb out the window. She goes to the kitchen drawer and lifts out the smallest knife that will fit into her jacket pocket. Sliding it in carefully, she hopes she won't have to use it.

Making her way through to the bathroom, she checks the other rooms for Marcus on the way. He's not here, thankfully. However she has noticed the half empty bottle of whisky. If he's on it like she has seen him before, then Crystal knows she's in the shit. Things are bad as it is without whisky twisting things to make it worse.

Pulling on the front door, she isn't surprised to see that it's locked. Her suitcase is still in the hall, packed with her things and ready to leave. The question is, how is she going to get out if Marcus isn't here and the door is locked? Even when he comes back, he won't let her leave, will he?

Looking at her reflection in the mirror, she sees the state Marcus has left her face in. She winces at the sight of it.

'What an absolute bastard,' she hisses. Running the tap, she starts to clean herself up, all the while ignoring the dread that runs through her veins, carried in her blood.

Crystal isn't blind, she knows the kind of businessman Marcus is. She's seen it with her own eyes. But because she was so in love with him in the beginning she'd chosen to turn a blind eye. Dancing at the club for a few quid wasn't an issue. She didn't mind it at all and Marcus seemed to be happy with how she was performing. In a way, it had made their relationship better.

Crystal thinks of Yasmin, her best friend. She'd warned Crystal about the kind of man Marcus could turn out to be and she hadn't listened. That was typical Crystal, head easily turned by a handsome man with money. But she didn't deserve this, did she? Who in their right mind would want their girlfriend to sell themselves for sex?

Crystal finishes cleaning up her face and reapplies a little more makeup. If she's going to try to charm Marcus, then she has to look good doing it. Crystal is good at turning on the charm, she learned from the best at the club.

She steps out of the bathroom and into the hall just as she hears the key in the door. Her face still aches from the knock she'd taken from him, but the pain disperses when she hears him coming through the door. Her whole body goes numb with fear, but she makes sure not to show it.

Turning, Crystal watches as Marcus comes in and locks the door behind him.

'Hi,' she says. He pushes past her, clearly intoxicated. How long had she been out?

'Don't fucking hi me. A couple hours ago you wanted to fucking leave,' Marcus spits. He stops in front of her, his face so close she can almost taste the whisky herself. He's had a skin full, that's abundantly obvious.

'I know, but I didn't mean it.'

'Don't stand there and fucking lie to me, Crystal.'

'I'm not lying,' she says as she straightens her back. 'I've thought about your offer and—'

Marcus holds his hand up and his bloodshot eyes bore into hers. 'It wasn't an offer, let's just get that straight. You *work* for the McAdams and I am telling you that you're being promoted. End of fucking discussion. So...' He turns and knocks the purple leopard print suitcase over with his hand. 'You can unpack your shit and get ready for your shift tonight.'

He stumbles past her and her stomach lurches as he pulls a bag of coke from his pocket. He dips his finger in and balances a small amount on the nail before snorting it up through his nostril. The sound makes Crystal shiver in anger and disgust that she could have ever fallen for someone like him.

'No, Marcus.'

'Eh?' He turns back.

'I said no. I am not going to unpack my shit and I will not do what the fuck you tell me. You're supposed to be my boyfriend, not my fucking boss. I swear Marcus, if you don't let me out of this fucking apartment I will fucking scream the place down until someone hears me and phones the police.'

Crystal leans down and picks up the suitcase so it's sitting on its wheels. The whole time, Marcus is staring at her, his brow furrowed but eyes wide with fury.

'Are you fucking delusional, Crystal? You do realise I am not going to let you out of here? I fucking own you.' He sneers and takes a step forward. 'How fucking hard do I need to hit you to get it into that thick skull of yours?'

Ignoring his attempts to manipulate her into doing what he says, Crystal reaches into her pocket and pulls out the knife. It would do enough damage if she had to use it and it might make him think twice about lifting a hand to her a second time.

'Ha,' Marcus says, looking down at it. 'What the fuck you going to do with that pissy little thing?'

'Nothing if you just let me the fuck out.' Crystal makes her voice loud and her stance tall, all the while absolutely terrified that he's going to call her bluff.

Silence hangs between them for a few slow seconds, before Marcus raises his hands quickly and makes a move towards her. She is too quick for him and raises the knife, bringing it down on his hand. He cries out in pain loudly as blood appears on the surface of his skin. The sound causes such a fright in her that she drops the knife but before she can reach it, Marcus kicks it out from her reach.

His hands are on her now, his fingers snaking around her neck. He raises her so her feet are off the floor and all she can do is wrap her hands around his wrists and fight.

Dragging her along the hallway, Marcus pushes Crystal against the closed bedroom door and holds her against it.

She fights, scratches and tries to find the wound on his hand to dig her fingers in. But her vision soon becomes hazy, her eyes feel like they're about to pop out from their sockets. She can't get a breath in or out. She tries to kick but she can't find the energy. Instead, her body begins to slump and Marcus keeps his grip and falls with her.

She's on the floor. Marcus is over her and she is staring into the depths of hell. *Please, please let go. I don't want to die. Not here like this.*

'I fucking warned you this would happen, Crystal. If you disobeyed or betrayed me, I told you I'd kill you. You should have listened.'

Her empty lungs burn, like a raging fire inside her body. A sudden coldness creeps over her, just cool at first then quickly, it turns to ice.

Please, let go. Please.

76

JADE

Looking down at the folder on the desk which was a recruitment file as well as a personal diary to Marcus, which he'd oddly
written in the third person, makes me feel sick. It's like he gets
off on recording every detail of what he's done to every girl
he's ever come across. And the way he's written it reads like a
business plan, rather than an account of people's lives.

Poor Crystal. What must have been going through her head
in those last moments?

Then as I continue to search, I find my own file. A wave of
nausea washes over me as I glance over the page. My story is
the worst of them all without death as the outcome.

- *Found a girl. Different from the others. Not as fiery but beautiful
  in her own way.*

- *Appears less confident than the others.*

- *Works in insurance in Clydebank.*

- *Lives in a flat on her own in same area.*

- *Has a boyfriend. Things seem to be going sour there. May be
  able to manipulate the ending of that.*

- *Has the usual social media pages. Privacy setting left open. Has
  few friends from what can see.*

- *Has liked pages related to phobias, in particular agoraphobia.*

- *Is attending support meetings. Seems to be working as she is going outside a lot more.*

- *Approached the YEEG (the Young East End Girls) arranged payment for attack.*

- *Kept an eye on Jade in hospital.*

- *Made move in hospital shop.*

- *Fell easily for Marcus.*

- *Moved in quickly and accepted new phone.*

- *Ex-boyfriend becoming a bit of an issue. Text him from Jade's phone. Told him to leave her alone. No more contact.*

- *Setting her up as dancer might be trickier than the others.*

- *Moved Jade into club.*

I feel sick as I scan the bullet points, like I'm some sort of business plan. I didn't think Marcus could get any worse until I read that my attack was orchestrated by him. He'd planned the whole thing.

I think back to that night after work when I was jumped on. There were too many of them and I had no chance. He'd instructed them to do enough damage that would set me back. I'd lost my job, my flat. He knew about Paul. We were so lucky that Marcus didn't see or recognise him in the club the second time. So lucky.

He swooped in at the hospital like the handsome stranger and swept me off my feet. And I fell for it like a stupid, naïve and gullible teenager. I didn't think people like Marcus existed, men who would use women for their financial gain. I was so wrong.

I take the phone out of my pocket and start taking photos of the pages. Each and every one. Then I close the folder and use my sleeve to wipe it clean of my prints.

Marcus can't get away with this. None of them can.

I head back to the lounge and straight for the kitchen sink. I bend down and open it, peer inside. I knew I'd seen it in here when I was living with Marcus. I take the bottle out and sit it on the worktop before going to the drinks cabinet and lifting the bottle of whisky.

I pour half the whisky down the drain and then fill it up with the solution before placing the whisky bottle back on the drinks cabinet. I take the rest of the solution and pour it down the sink too and wash the remnants away with water. I slide the empty bottle into my coat pocket before giving the flat the once over. Still perfect, the way it was when I arrived.

That bastard has what's coming to him, death is the only way to stop him from what he's doing. If he's gone, the girls will be able to get on with their lives. I don't even care if the police discover it was me. I really don't. That doesn't mean I want them to catch me. Or that they will.

I step out of the apartment and into the hall, ensuring the door is locked. As the doors close on the lift, I can't help but smile, knowing that Marcus's tipple will kill him, slowly and painfully.

77

MARCUS

Marcus smiles as he counts the takings for the night before placing them in the safe. Angel Silk is making more money than ever before and pleased was an understatement.

The girls were escorted back to the accommodation Marcus had provided and he knows that more money will be coming his way because he's put the prices up. The girls are worth more and that means more cash in his pocket.

He locks up the club and is a little relieved that he doesn't have to drive back to Angel House for the night. He can go home, put his feet up and have a whisky, or two. Maybe even the whole bottle if he feels like it. Marcus pats the pocket in his jacket and feels the small bag inside. A gram of coke and maybe a girl or two of his choice. His dad always warned him not to mess with his own merchandise but it's his company and he can do what he wants with it.

Marcus climbs into the car and heads back to his apartment at the Harbour, makes a call and orders two of the girls to meet him at the door. He wants to celebrate his success and he'll do it the way he wants.

Arriving at the apartment, he notes that the girls are not waiting for him. Normally this would annoy him but he's in a good mood tonight and good things come to those who wait, don't they? He gets out of the car and heads up to his apartment. Opening the door, he switches on the lights, puts on his Motley Crue playlist and pours himself a large whisky before laying out a couple lines on the table.

An hour or so passes and Marcus slumps on the sofa. He feels pretty shitty. The room is spinning, growing duller by the second.

The doorbell rings out and it echoes in his ears. He tries to get up but his limbs aren't working, not doing what he wants them too. Darkness creeps in from the corners of his eyes as foam seeps from his mouth. Then there is nothing. No sound, no colour, no light. Nothing.

78

AMBER

(Three months later)

The sun shines on my face and I close my eyes, enjoying the heat as it warms my skin. The sound of splashing water and toddler giggles makes me smile and I open my eyes to watch my nephew as he plays in the paddling pool.

'You okay over there?' my sister, Kirsty, asks.

'Yeah, I'm okay.'

The trial date has been set for Tommy. He will stand alone, accused of human and drug trafficking among other things. Marcus is unable to take the stand and Barry is dead. Tommy will have to take the fall all on his own and that in itself seems justice enough. He has no one to back him up other than his lawyer. But there is no way he will get off. There's too much evidence against him. And the younger lads are behind bars too, awaiting their part in the trial. They're too young and inexperienced to know how to defend themselves let alone someone else.

I don't have to see him face to face. I am allowed to present myself via video link for my own protection, along with the rest of the girls.

'Auntie Amber, you want to play splash splash?' My nephew is at my feet holding a water balloon with a cheeky wee grin on his face. I hear my sister laugh in the background as he throws it at me and misses spectacularly.

'Oh you wee monkey,' I say.

I glance down at the time and get to my feet. Kirsty looks at me and smiles. 'Chemist?'

'Yep. Dad's going to pick me up,' I reply.

'That's good. You feel you're getting better every day?'

I think about her question and wonder if I am. I still suffer each day with the need for a fix. But I fight it because it's not real. It's not what I would have chosen for myself and I know I can beat this. The methadone programme is helping me along with the counselling my parents are paying for. They're intense sessions but I'll do anything I can to recover from my ordeal.

'Yeah, I feel better.'

I head out to the street and get into dad's car. He smiles over at me and then gives me a hug and I have to fight the urge to cry. I never thought I would ever see any of my family again, I genuinely believed that I would die at Angel House.

I'm so grateful for what Jade did for me. For what she did for all of us.

79

JADE

I lay the flowers down on the edge of the grass where it meets the sand and stand back next to Paul. It had been reported on the news that Crystal's body had been identified by DNA and her parents had been informed.

They are now temporarily living in Glasgow awaiting the trial and I can only imagine the pain of what they're going through. I am quiet and bow my head as a mark of respect during Crystal's memorial service.

The heat from the sun beats down on us but I still grip Paul's hand as he stands next to me. I hear Crystal's mum sob and I look up to see her dad barely holding it together.

The McAdams have been dealt with in various ways and I don't care how much they suffered. It doesn't compare to what they put me, Amber, Crystal and the others through.

Yasmin's memorial service is tomorrow and Amber has agreed to meet me there. She isn't here today and I understand why. Getting clean and staying clean is what's needed for her right now, so attending every appointment and every session is important.

Paul puts an arm around me as we head down to the shore and watch as Crystal's parents throw rose petals into the water, followed by her close friends and the rest of her family.

'Hey, this is all because of you, you know that? This woman wouldn't know what happened to her daughter if you hadn't risked your life and gone back to that place.'

I smile up at Paul and he kisses me on the forehead.

'I couldn't have done it without you,' I say.

Just a few weeks after that night, I'd decided to start applying for jobs in the sector I used to work in before Marcus tried to tear my life to pieces. I ended up bumping into someone from my old office and they told me that there was a job going in the Glasgow office. I'd already lost everything so I applied for it and got the job. I'd started a few days later and since, I've moved into a new flat in the west end of the city. Paul and I are still friends, but that's all we'll be. The problems we were having as a couple would never change. We work better this way, and we both agree we don't want to ruin that.

I'm doing okay, but every time I close my eyes, I see Crystal in Marcus's hands, gasping for her life. I'm seeing my old support group which seems to be helping.

I'm just thankful that no one seems to know what I did to truly put an end to this. One day, I might be found out but I can only hope that I can move on with my life and continue to rebuild it. I think I've suffered enough. We all have.

I did what was necessary, what was right. Sometimes the justice system itself just isn't enough.

80

LIZZY

I remembered the cave from when I was little for a reason. It was a local play spot for us when I was just a child. Me, Mum and Dad. When my world was innocent and light, when there was nothing bad and my parents were just that, parents. Not adulterers, not criminals and killers.

After everything that happened that night, the memories of my early childhood had continued to creep in and I knew there was nothing I could do to stop them. My subconscious wanted me to remember, wanted me to know.

Angel House hadn't always been a brothel. It had been a home. My home. The night I'd gone in to see Barry, noticed the butterfly wallpaper and realised it had once been a child's bedroom, I hadn't thought for a moment it had been my bedroom as a child. It had been our home for a short time.

After Mum was killed, Dad and I stayed there for a while but then we moved closer to the city. In my time at Angel House, I hadn't remembered because I was too busy trying to work out how to get out of there. Trying to get the girls out of there. It wasn't until a few weeks after the fire that I remembered. All because of that photograph Barry showed me. I'd dug out more of my memories, more pictures and I was able to match them to the house.

Barry McAdam had had this planned for years. He'd somehow managed to purchase Angel House and brought me to it. He wanted to torment me and punish me for what I'd done to Marcus. And it worked.

343

When I set that fire and opened the doors for the rest of the girls, they'd all fled in different directions. To my surprise, I discovered later that they'd all managed to get away from the younger lads chasing them through the woods.

Barry had paid off some of the higher-ranking officers within the police. It had become a huge scandal and the press are reporting on the developments regularly in line with the trial. My head is so full from it all I can barely hear myself think. From what I know, the girls are all rebuilding their lives at their own pace. Each one of them will stand and give evidence against the McAdams and their business ventures, as will I.

For now, I sit on the chair next to the hospital bed and stare out of the window. There are only so many magazines I can read, so many crossword puzzles I can get through before the trauma and enormity of what happened creeps its way back to the front of my mind.

The sun shines through the window and on to his face. His eyes are open, unblinking. A trail of spittle drips down and I lift a tissue from the box and wipe it away. His eyes flicker and meet mine and I smile at him.

'Morning. Did you sleep well?' I ask. Of course he doesn't answer. He can't talk. Can't move. The high level of anti-freeze in his blood and in his system mean his organs are severely damaged, with no hope of recovery. The doctors have said he doesn't have long to live. In some ways, it would have been better for all of us including him if he'd died that day. But the doctors had managed to save him. That's their job, isn't it? To preserve life. Even for someone like Marcus.

The brain damage caused by the toxins in the chemical he'd ingested has left Marcus disabled from the neck down. He can't do anything for himself now. I have to do it all. Feed him, wash him. I have to do it because I am his mother and this is all my fault. If I hadn't left him with Barry then he wouldn't have lived the life he did, he wouldn't have ended up like this.

Marcus is my responsibility now. The police had been instructed by the doctors that Marcus would not be able to stand trial for any of the crimes he'd committed because he would never recover to more than what he is now. To me, that's a sentence worse than life in prison, which is what he would have deserved had he come out of this poisoning relatively unscathed.

But he didn't. And when the doctors deem him fit for discharge, he will come home with me and I will look after him for the rest of my life because that's what mothers do. Even if they do hate their son with every ounce of energy and every breath in their body. But I love him in equal measures.

I get to my feet and lift the plastic cup of water from the table and place the straw in Marcus's mouth. He attempts to suck up some water and some of it spills out of his mouth and runs down his face.

I lift the tissue and dab at it. This is my life now.

I take Marcus's hand in mine and hold on to it, like I should have done when he was a baby. Tears spill over and I know there will never be enough to wash away the guilt of what I've done.

I abandoned my child at the beginning of his life. I'm not going to do the same at the end.

A letter from Alex

As I sit to write this letter to you, the reader, I can't quite believe this is my fourth book. What a year it has been, with all the craziness of Covid and lockdown. I truly hope that you are all safe and well.

Firstly, thank you so much for choosing to read *The Angels*. If this is your first Alex Kane, then I am so happy that you've discovered my work and I hope you enjoyed it. If you're returning having read my previous titles, then thank you for coming back. I can't stress enough how thankful and grateful I am to be in a position where I can get my words out to you all.

This is a slight genre change for me, with the last two books being psychological thrillers. I have to be honest and say writing this book has been my very favourite, as dark as it is. I have loved creating the characters, the girls and the world around them.

Amber, Jade, Lizzy, along with Yasmin and Crystal are what I would deem as angels in a hellish underworld. I loved writing about their lives and how each of their circumstances came together in order to bring down the McAdams. However I also loved writing the McAdams, especially Marcus. He had such a dark mind, so damaged by his mother's abandonment even though he'd never admit it.

I wrote this book during lockdown and that is something I never thought would happen. But I used the time to block out the negativity of what was going on in the world and focused on my characters. I used the anxiety of what was happening around us in real life to drive the story.

I hope that you enjoyed the book and would love to hear your thoughts in a review. If you would like to discuss the book with me directly, you can contact me via:

www.facebook.com/alexkanewriter
www.twitter.com/AlexKaneWriter
www.instagram.com/alexkanewriter
alexkaneauthor@gmail.com

Again, thank you so much for your support, your dedication to reading and for reading *The Angels*.

Best wishes

Alex Kane

Acknowledgments

Firstly, I would like to thank Keshini and Lindsey at Hera for once again making all of this possible. They never disappoint, are always honest and professional and strive to push their authors on to bigger and better. I cannot stress how lucky I feel to be working with them.

Thank you to my copy editor, Dushi Horti, for picking out the little things I missed.

Thank you to my proof reader, Vicki McKay.

A massive thank you to everyone who has supported me in my writing career to date, including my family and my friends who have listened to me waffle on about my dream. I really appreciate it. In particular, I want to thank my husband, Chris, for his constant encouragement and understanding for my need to be in my office to put the words down.

But my biggest thanks go to the readers. Without your support, downloads and reviews, I wouldn't be where I am now.